LAST CHANCE
FOR GLORY

OTHER NOVELS BY STEPHEN SOLOMITA

A Good Day to Die
A Piece of the Action
A Twist of the Knife
Force of Nature
Forced Entry
Bad to the Bone

LAST CHANCE
FOR GLORY

STEPHEN SOLOMITA

**OTTO
PENZLER
BOOKS**

NEW YORK

Otto Penzler Books
129 West 56th Street
New York, NY 10019
(Editorial Offices only)

Macmillan Publishing Company
866 Third Avenue
New York, NY 10022

Maxwell Macmillan Canada, Inc.
1200 Eglinton Avenue East,
Suite 200
Don Mills, Ontario M3C 3N1

Macmillan Publishing Company is part of the Maxwell Communication Group of Companies

Library of Congress Cataloging-in-Publication Data
Solomita, Stephen.
Last chance for glory/by Stephen Solomita.
p. cm.
ISBN 1-883402-27-1
I. Title.
PS3569.O587L37   1994
813'.54—dc20   93-38616
CIP

Otto Penzler Books are available at special discounts for bulk purchases for sales promotions, premiums, fund-raising, or educational use. For details, contact:

Special Sales Director
Macmillan Publishing Company
866 Third Avenue
New York, NY 10022

10 9 8 7 6 5 4 3 2 1

Printed in the United States of America

I need to thank an old friend of mine here, Dr. Alan Bindiger. Thinking back, I can't recall finishing a single book without consulting him at some point. I inevitably found him patient, knowledgeable, and curious. From my point of view, that's an unbeatable combination.

PART ONE

PROLOGUE

November 27: 2:48 AM

The howl begins as a single note in the upper range of a polished contralto. It holds steady for a moment, then slowly rises through the octaves, finally disappearing somewhere beyond the range of the human ear. Melody Mitchell, asleep in her bed, tries to incorporate the howl into her dream, hears it as a distant siren on a deserted city street. She visualizes the headlights of an ambulance rushing to an emergency, sees wet roads, red and blue reflections on rain slick asphalt.

It doesn't help, though. It never does. The howl begins again, proceeding from the same note to the same emptiness, then drops to a soft moan as the covers begin to slide across her back.

Even half-asleep, still pulled by the fading edges of her dream, Melody Mitchell is not shocked by the liquid brown eyes that meet hers when she lifts her head from the pillow.

"You're gonna be the death of me, Roscoe. The absolute death," she mutters.

Roscoe, undaunted, does a little dance, the moan now transformed into a series of sharp barks.

My fate, Melody thinks. Other middle-aged women have husbands and children; I have a geriatric Doberman with a weak bladder.

She shrugs into a long, goose-down coat, jams her feet into fleece-lined boots, snaps the leash onto Roscoe's collar.

"Roscoe," she repeats, "you're gonna be the death of me. No doubt about it. And don't give me that look. What I should do is swap you for a girl dog. At least they pee all at one time. They don't have to wet every hubcap on the block."

She steps out of the elevator to find Petya already holding the door. The rumor, among the residents of 551 Gramercy Park North, is that Petya, instead of protecting the shareholders from New York predators, sleeps the night away. If that's the case, Melody has yet to catch him at it.

"Is late, Miss Mitchell. I am thinking for once dog waits till morning."

"No such luck, Petya. What's it like out there?"

"Is cold. Winter begins."

Petya arranges the crags and crevices of his battered, Russian face into what Melody can only see as a look of resigned martyrdom. The saint tied to the stake, already smelling the acrid stink of smoldering pine.

"Great."

Urged along by a now-desperate Roscoe, Melody heads directly for the curb. A stiff wind brings tears to her eyes.

"Please, Roscoe, don't take all night with this. It's awful cold out here."

Roscoe lifts his leg obligingly, then freezes in place. A low growl rumbles deep in his chest. Melody looks down for a moment, then follows the dog's eyes to the middle of the block. She sees a man in a dark overcoat standing next to a polished Mercedes. The man turns and looks at her for a moment, then walks away.

"Hush, Roscoe. It's nothing. A man parking the car."

Roscoe, in apparent agreement, lets go, drenching the bumper of a rusting Toyota.

They make their way along the row of parked cars, Roscoe pausing every few yards to sniff the pavement. Melody, now thoroughly awake, grows more and more impatient. Her feet are freezing.

"One more chance," she warns as they come abreast of the Mercedes, "and back you go." She looks through the window, wondering, as New Yorkers will, if the man she saw was a thief.

Not likely, she thinks. He was too well dressed to be after a radio. Or even the whole car.

The street lamps throw a light somewhere between amber and beige. The tone efficiently filters the sharp urban edges, blending light and shadow into a smooth continuum. Nevertheless, even without looking twice, Melody is certain that what she sees lying on the backseat is the blood-soaked body of a naked woman.

4:53 AM

Melody Mitchell is sitting in front of the TV, her eyes propped open. A mug of useless coffee rests on the end table. She is watching a C-Span re-telecast of the prior day's proceedings at the House Ways and Means Committee. She doesn't comprehend a word, wishes only for her bed.

When the buzzer finally sounds in her apartment, she is angry enough to say, "It's about time." That's not her style. It's not *the* style for a forty-eight-year-old, Barnard-educated WASP. On the other hand, it isn't every day that a bull-necked cop in a cheap suit orders you to remain awake.

"I got a few more questions, but I wanna get a look at the body before the ME takes it away."

That from a flat-faced detective with a huge nose and hair so fine that even cut within an inch of his broad, square skull, it lies flat against his scalp. Detective Kosinski.

"I've already spoken to Detective Brannigan. I don't believe I have anything to add," she'd quite properly responded.

"Let me be the judge of that, Ms. . . ." He'd looked down at his notebook. "Mitchell. This here is a homicide. You know? Like a person dead from murder. You do wanna help, right?"

Melody opens the door to find Detective Kosinski's small, blue eyes staring through the back of her head. Brannigan is right behind him.

"Thanks for waitin'."

Kosinski strides into the living room and plops himself down on the sofa. Brannigan shrugs, half-smiles, and follows.

"Don't bother with coffee," Kosinski says. "This shouldn't take long." He looks at his partner, manages a tight grin. "Cut to the chase, right?"

"Right, Sarge." A thick mop of curly hair dominates Brannigan's blue eyes and small, inoffensive nose. Two nearly vertical lines run from the top of either nostril to a wide, mobile mouth. Quick to smile, Brannigan's mouth animates an otherwise expressionless face.

"Start at the beginning," Kosinski demands. "What you were doing on the street at two-thirty in the morning. What you saw. How you saw it. Like that."

Melody Mitchell clears her throat, tries to swallow her mounting anger. They're treating me like a criminal, she thinks.

"I've already given that information to Detective Brannigan."

"Yeah, well, maybe you forgot somethin'. I gotta hear it for myself."

"For yourself?"

"Right."

Melody doesn't know whether her sarcasm flew over Kosinski's head or merely bounced off his thick skull, but there being no sign that it penetrated, she decides to give him what he wants. It's that or refuse all cooperation, which she cannot do. A crime has been committed, a woman murdered and probably raped. Melody can trace her ancestry back to a time when the Dutch ran New York City, an inheritance that includes responsibility and obligation along with its many perks.

She goes through it once again—the aging dog, Petya in the lobby, the growl, the man by the Mercedes, the blood, and the body.

"The man was of average height or maybe a little above. Average build, too. His hair was thick and dark, as were his brows. Something like Detective Brannigan's. He was wearing a dark, expensive-looking overcoat. It might have been blue or black or brown. How can you tell with those orangey streetlights? Dark is all I can say about it."

"What color was *he*? White, black, brown?"

"White."

"What was he doing next to the car?"

"Nothing I could see. He was just standing there. Then he looked at me."

"He didn't have a set of keys in his hand?"

"Not that I remember."

"Or a knife?"

"I don't remember a knife."

"And the door wasn't open?"

"No. I'm sure about that. He looked at me for a moment, then walked away. If he'd closed the door, I would have heard it. I'd remember."

"How long did he look at you?"

"A moment. I don't know."

"Make a guess."

"Five seconds? I'm not sure."

"So it could have been ten or fifteen seconds."

"I suppose so."

"And he could have had a set of keys in his hand."

"It's possible. I wasn't looking at his hands."

"Could you identify him if you saw him again."

"I don't think so."

"C'mon, Ms. Mitchell. You stared at him for fifteen seconds. Try to remember."

"I *am* trying, Sergeant Kosinski. And I resent your suggesting that I'm not."

Melody watches Kosinski and Brannigan exchange a knowing look. Male bullying, she thinks, in the guise of male bonding.

"No offense," Kosinski says, turning back to her. His mild voice proclaims the fact that *he*, at least, is not offended. "See, it's like this here: Witnesses remember much more than they think they remember. It's just how you can get to it. What'd be best is that you come into the precinct tomorrow and look at some mug shots. We'll get a police artist, work up a sketch. Meantime, try to fix this guy in your head. Remember whatever you remember, then add to it. You don't know what you might come up with if you put your mind to it. Believe me, I got a lot of experience in this matter."

November 30: 11:15 PM

"I don't like nothin' about this, Tommy," Bela Kosinski informs his partner. "Not a fuckin' thing. I don't like fuckin' Queens. I don't like fuckin' parking lots in Queens. And I don't like bein' ordered out to a parkin' lot in Queens by a fuckin' slimeball captain. Look around yourself; there ain't a white face within five miles. So what are we doin' parked here with the lights off?" He pauses, then answers his own question. "What it feels like to me—and I got experience with this— is a setup. Maybe Internal Affairs. Maybe the headhunters." He runs his fingers through his short hair. "I'm two years away from the magic pension. I don't need this."

What Tommy Brannigan wants to say is stop being an asshole. Somebody offers to hand you the key to an unsolved homicide—the actual name of the perp, for Christ sake—what you do is kiss their ass. When that somebody is also a captain who can help you in a hundred ways, you keep on kissing until your lips fall off. And you don't complain, either. No, what you do is remember to thank the Lord Almighty when you say your beddy-bye prayers.

But, then again, Tommy Brannigan, son of a son of a son of a cop, has seen the NYPD as the Land of Opportunity right from the beginning. Take what you can, always make the man happy (the man being whoever sits above you on the ladder), and keep your business to yourself. In this case, Tommy Brannigan's business is getting his dumb ass transferred out of Homicide. That's because there's no money in

Homicide. While ordinary men close their eyes and see aroused star-
lets in the act of disrobing, Brannigan dreams of Narcotics or Vice, of
stumbling onto fistfuls of dead presidents hidden beneath threadbare
mattresses.

So, what Tommy Brannigan actually does is grunt and continue to
stare out the window. Remembering that not only does Bela Kosinski
outrank him, Bela Kosinski is the ultimate burnout hairbag, a dedicated drunk who cannot be insulted or threatened, only contained until
such time as Tommy Brannigan can locate a new partner.

Ten minutes later, a battered Chevy sedan pulls into the lot and
stops next to Brannigan's window. The bald, middle-aged man sitting
behind the wheel flashes a captain's shield, then states his name.

"Grogan, Aloysius."

Brannigan notes the black man sitting next to the captain. The
tattered watch cap perched on the man's head is beginning to unravel.
Strings of wool hang over his small ears.

"You got our attention, Captain. What's up?"

"Get in the back. We're gonna make this short and sweet."

The partners do as they're told. Ducking out into the cold, trying
to get a look at the black man's face as they climb into the backseat
and close the doors.

"Awright," Grogan begins, "this here is Mack. Mack's here to give
you information. He will not be a witness. He will not testify. He will
not be available to you after tonight. He is my snitch and we are working on a major case. Understand?"

"Yeah, sure." Kosinski's voice holds equal measures of boredom and
contempt.

"I'm handing you the ball. It's up to you to run with it. If this
wasn't a homicide, we wouldn't be talking at all. Understand?"

Brannigan speaks up quickly. "Understood, Captain. And don't
think we don't appreciate what you're doing. This case was going
nowhere in a hurry." That, Brannigan knows, isn't entirely true. While
they aren't about to arrest Sondra Tillson's killer, the case is moving
right along with most of his and Kosinski's attention focused on the
husband, Johan. Though Johan Tillson's alibi is ironclad, he's been
less than honest about his wife and her day-to-day activities.
Brannigan is convinced that a boyfriend lurks somewhere in the
darkness.

"Good, now we're clear. Mack, tell 'em what you told me."

Mack keeps the back of his head to the two detectives as he speaks. He's dressed in a ragged wool jacket that matches his watch cap nicely. Brannigan can smell him from the backseat.

"See, here, like what ah'm sayin' is what Billy Sowell actually *tole* me. Ah didn' hear it from nobody else. It come out his own mouth. We was drinkin' by the river like we usually does. Thunderbird out the bottle. Talkin' 'bout nothin' and evvythin'. That's also how we usually does. I was going on 'bout this friend we had who got found in the river. Sayin' how I figgered the boy was kilt and tossed in the water. Then Billy say how he kilt this bitch over by Gramercy Park. That's the park got the locked gates on it. I say, 'Man, you bullshittin' me,' but he say, 'No man, I done it. I kilt the bitch. She wouldn' let me fuck her, so I kilt her.' I still say how I don't believe it, so Billy show me this long knife. Man, it was about a big mother-fucker. Look like a gottdamn sword. He say, 'I kilt her with this here knife and now I got to be rid of it.'"

Brannigan looks over to find his partner staring out the window. "Billy Sowell have an address?"

"He live by the river, 'round Twenty-third Street on the East Side. In a box."

"A box?"

"We homeless, officer."

"Did he tell you anything else."

"Nawssir. See, at the time I jus' figger it was the booze talkin'. Billy ain' fas' or nothin'—like, the boy's retarded, really—so, I didn' think much of it till I asks around and hears 'bout this bitch what got kilt near Gramercy Park. Stabbed to death, jus' like Billy tole me. So then I figger maybe he really done it and I tells the officer."

Back in his own car, Brannigan starts the engine and turns on the heater while his partner fumbles with a small flask.

"What it is," Kosinski announces, "is nothin'. *Nada.* As in, nada fuckin' thing."

Brannigan feels his blood start to rise. "You don't wanna check this out?"

"No, Tommy, I don't wanna check out what some drunken derelict who smells like he slept in his own piss says about another drunk. Major case? The Captain says the derelict and him are workin' a major case? That's bullshit, Tommy. For that bum, major means some bleeding-heart citizen tossin' him fifty cents instead of a dime."

"We have a witness, Bela. Why don't we run Billy Sowell's photo by her?"

"Why? How 'bout 'cause Melody Mitchell can't identify the perp? That's if she ever got a good look at him, which I doubt. How 'bout 'cause Melody Mitchell said the perp was wearin' an expensive over-coat? Which don't exactly make him homeless. How 'bout 'cause puttin' this Billy Sowell at the scene don't make him the perp. How 'bout 'cause I got six days off and I'm plannin' to enjoy every minute? You wanna play detective on your own, be my guest."

December 11: 10:15 AM

Billy Sowell, emerging from his packing-crate home, sees the tall cop and smiles. Just like he always does when he's confused or threatened, which is really the same thing to him.

"Hi, Billy."

The tall cop squats down. He is smiling, too.

"Hi."

"How ya doin'?"

"I'm doin' okay."

"My name is Detective Brannigan. Do you wanna see my badge?"

"No. I believe you."

"I need to talk to you, Billy. About something that happened two weeks ago."

"A few weeks?" That's bad. Billy has problems remembering. He wants to make the cop happy so the cop will go away, but now he doesn't think he can do it. "I can't remember two weeks."

"No, Billy, this is something very important. This is something you can remember."

Billy shuts his eyes, attempts to remember two weeks ago. He sees a blur, a smudge. When he tries to concentrate, the smudge begins to spin.

"Billy? Open your eyes, Billy." The cop waits until Billy smiles, before continuing. "This is about a woman who was murdered near Gramercy Park? Do you know where that is?"

Billy nods.

"Someone told me that you killed the woman, Billy. He told me that you stabbed her with a knife. That would be very serious. Did you kill that woman, Billy?"

Billy shakes his head. The smile fades. He's not good at this, at explaining things.

"I wouldn't do anything like that," he finally says.

"I believe you, Billy, but when someone makes an accusation, I have to check it out. That's my job. But it won't take long. I promise. We'll just go down to my office and straighten it out. I've got coffee and sandwiches there. We can have lunch. Do you wanna go with me?"

Billy doesn't know what "accusation" means, but he's been on the street long enough to know that cops mean trouble. And that going someplace with a cop means *bad* trouble.

"I wanna stay here," he says. The smile is now frozen to his face. His lips feel numb.

"Don't you want to clear this up?"

The cop seems unhappy, which Billy doesn't understand. But the cop's not mad, which is good.

"Sure I'd like to," Billy says, "but I didn't do it."

"That's the whole point, Billy. If we can just clear it up, you won't be a suspect any more. But you have to tell me what you were doing when the murder happened."

"Two weeks ago?"

"That's right. On November twenth-seventh."

"What if I can't remember?"

"Don't worry, Billy. I'll *help* you remember. Between the two of us, we can work it out."

1:35 PM

"Jesus, Billy, you're not doin' too well. You don't seem to remember a damn thing."

"But I'm trying, Detective Brannigan. I'm trying as hard as I can."

"You drink a lot don't you, Billy? An awful lot. You drink a lot of booze."

Billy hangs his head, nods yes.

"Do you drink every day?"

Another nod.

"You know what that means, Billy? It means we can't establish an alibi for you."

Billy Sowell looks up. "What's an alibi?"

"It means we can't prove you were somewhere else when the murder was committed. By the way, did you know Sondra Tillson?"

"No."

"Are you sure, Billy? She was the lady who got murdered."

"I don't know any ladies except for Batbrain Mary and Lisa MacCready. They live down by the bridge. The Williamsburg Bridge."

"I believe you, Billy, but we're going to have to prove that."

Billy, perched on a stool in an otherwise empty room, a room with barred windows, watches Brannigan pace back and forth, back and forth. Billy wishes he'd never come to the station house with Detective Brannigan. He hasn't had the sandwiches Detective Brannigan promised. He hasn't even had a glass of water.

"I got it." Detective Brannigan stops pacing. He holds one finger in the air, a huge smile lighting his face. "We could check the evidence. All we need is a little bit of your hair and some of the hairs from your overcoat. And we need to take your picture to show to a witness. And we need a little bit of your blood, too."

"My blood?"

"A little."

"With a needle?"

"It won't hurt, Billy. Just a teeny pinch."

"I don't want a needle, Detective Brannigan. Can't we find some other way to prove I wasn't there? I'm getting very tired."

"You know, Billy, you don't have to stay here if you don't want to. You can leave. But I think you should try to clear this up before it goes any further. I mean, *if* you didn't do it."

"But I didn't do it. You said you believed me."

"I do believe you, Billy. I believe you because you're helping me do my job. But if you go home before we can prove that you're innocent, I might have to think something else."

7:20 PM

Tommy Brannigan rubs his weary eyes. He is sitting at his desk in the detectives' squad room, trying to ignore the chaos around him while he works on the photo array spread across the desk. The problem is that he can't make Billy Sowell's Polaroid photos look anything like the eight mug shots surrounding them. For one thing, the Polaroid film stock is a good deal thicker than the mug shots and he has no effective way to flatten it. For another, the mug shots were printed on a single sheet of paper, full-on and profile. Billy's two Polaroids, even cut down to the size of the others, stand out like a sore thumb. That alone will keep it out of court, even if Melody Mitchell can make a positive ID, which she probably can't, not without some help.

But how *much* help? That's the real question. Tommy Brannigan isn't a lawyer, but he's been in the system long enough to know that some judges are much more likely to throw out evidence than others. He also knows that some judges admit virtually anything, because they figure that while the average voter cannot define the word appeal, he or she knows all about technicalities. Especially if the perp goes right back out and does it again.

"Hey, Lieutenant." Brannigan tugs at a passing sleeve. "You got a minute to look at this? I don't wanna screw it up."

Lieutenant Corelli turns on his heel with the grace of a ferret. "Whatta you want, Brannigan? I'm busy."

"I have a suspect in the Tillson case. And a witness. What I wanna do is work up a good sheet, but I don't think we can get this in."

Corelli glances at the photo array. "This the suspect?" He points a long, bony finger at a smiling Billy Sowell.

"That's him."

"The profile shot's fucked up, Tommy. You got the perp facing the camera with only his head to the side. You were supposed to have him turn his shoulder into the camera. The array's biased."

"You think it's hopeless?" Brannigan's usually smiling mouth drops into a disappointed frown. "See, I'm working with the mutt's cooperation."

"You read him his rights?"

"He's not a suspect, yet. I got him to sign a release for the photos, some hair, some blood, and a few fibers from his coat, but he can walk out the door any time he wants to."

"So, why's he stayin' around? This is a homicide we're talkin' about."

"He's slow. Retarded. I mean he can talk and write his name, but the kid's definitely retarded. Plus, he drinks every day and that adds to it. I told him I was gonna try to clear him—which I am, in a way—and he bought it. At least, for *now* he bought it."

Tommy Brannigan, smiling again, watches Lieutenant Corelli study the photos. Involving the whip helps in two ways. Not only will it result in a photo lineup more likely to be admitted into evidence, it commits Corelli to the case. Without Corelli's approval, Brannigan has no way to get to the prosecutors. And there's no guarantee that Corelli will go ahead with a flawed case. Department policy is to not further burden already overwhelmed Assistant DAs with bullshit.

"Did the witness mention an overcoat when she gave her description?"

"Yeah."

"Your suspect's the only one wearing an overcoat. The rest of them are wearing jackets. That's a little obvious, Tommy. In fact, that's a *lot* obvious. Did the witness happen to mention a scar on the perp's left cheek?"

"No, Lou. No scar."

Corelli looks up in surprise. "Your suspect has a scar. How are you gonna get an ID with that?"

"It's not my fault, Lou. That's just the way it came up. Look, all I wanna do is take it one more step. I wanna get the witness to look at the perp's photo. See what she says and go on from there."

Corelli shakes his head. "I'm probably crazy, but here's what I want you to do. First, get a felt pen and put a scar on every photo. Under the eye, like the perp's scar. Then glue the photos to a piece of poster board—flatten 'em real good—and photocopy the whole thing. That'll take care of the problem with the film. Remember, no matter what, don't let the witness see the original. If she can't make an ID off the copy, you let the suspect go. Maybe you'll get lucky in the lab."

"You want me to bury the original, Lou? Like it doesn't exist?"

"Are you kidding me? We're tryin' to show good faith here. We're tryin' to show that we're tryin' to respect this scumbag's civil rights. Tag it and turn it in."

9:15 PM

Melody Mitchell, upon opening the door, is relieved to find a smiling Tommy Brannigan standing in the hallway. She is relieved to find him alone. Detective Kosinski reminded her of those construction workers who once upon a time (and not *that* long ago) verbalized their most obscene fantasies as she walked down the street. By contrast,

Detective Brannigan, with his quick broad smile and mop of unruly hair, looks almost boyish. He looks like an overgrown elf.

"Come in, Detective. Please."

"Thanks. I'm not keeping you up, am I?" Brannigan stops to scratch behind the dog's ears. "So, this is the famous Roscoe. Without Roscoe's bladder, where would the criminal justice system be?"

Melody finds herself returning the detective's smile. How can she do otherwise? His good humor is infectious, even though he's only trying to put her mind at ease.

"Would you like a cup of coffee, Detective?"

"As a matter of fact, I would. And if you don't mind, we can use the kitchen table to set up the photo array."

"Is that what it's called? A photo array?"

"That's how the lawyers say it."

Melody sits Brannigan down and turns to the cabinet above her sink for cups and saucers. "How does it work? This photo array?"

"What I've done, Ms. Mitchell, is arrange eighteen photos of nine individuals on a single sheet of paper. All you have to do is look them over and tell me if you see the man you saw on the night of the murder. Believe me, it's a lot easier than going through hundreds and hundreds of mug shots."

"Does that mean you know who the killer is?" Melody comes back to the table, her hands filled with cups and saucers, spoons and napkins. She notes Detective Brannigan's concentration. Whatever he's thinking, she decides, he wants to make sure he gets it right.

"I guess that's obvious enough, but I have to inform you that the man in question is only a suspect. He hasn't been arrested yet. A lot depends on your identification. If you can *make* an identification. I don't want to prejudice you."

Melody pours the coffee, sets sugar and milk on the table, sits down. "You seem to be treading on water, Detective."

"It's the courts, Ms. Mitchell." Brannigan shrugs his shoulders, sighs. "If the judge throws out the photo array, he'll most likely throw out any further identification you make. In fact, he'll probably throw you out altogether. Believe me, the suspect's attorney will question you closely on what we do here tonight."

"I understand." The thought of being cross-examined in an open courtroom sobers Melody up. What, she thinks, will I do if there are reporters present? Or if it's *televised*?

"Would you explain the procedure, please?"

"I'm going to set the photo array down in front of you. I want you to look at it for a full minute before you say anything. Take as long as you want, but even if you can make an identification the instant you glance at the sheet, keep looking for a full moment. Look at every single face."

Melody, peering down at the nine faces, the eighteen poses, thinks that Detective Brannigan needn't have bothered with that last instruction. The men seem no more distinct than the faces she's already seen. Still, she goes over them, one by one, trying to view each man as an individual, reminding herself that there's an actual suspect on the page. A minute goes by, then another, then a third before she finally raises her head.

"I don't know," she explains. "Nothing jumps out at me. I'd have to say that number three and number nine come the closest. But I don't remember the scar."

"If the scar wasn't there, would you identify number three as the man you saw that night? Take another look. Please. Give your memory a chance."

Melody stares at the young man in the black overcoat, trying to excise the scar beneath his eye. He does, she admits to herself, look familiar. Something about the dark eyes and the coarse dark hair.

"If I'd only known the man I saw was a killer when I first saw him," she says, "I'd be able to remember. He looked right at me, but I didn't think anything of it at the time."

"Even though it was almost three o'clock in the morning?"

"It was Saturday night, Detective Brannigan. In New York City. But I will say there was nothing about the man that alarmed me."

Brannigan drains the cup, sets it back on the saucer. "Let me see if I've got this right. You said numbers three and nine look most like the man you saw. Is that right?"

"Number three is closer. Except for the scar."

"But you wouldn't be able to identify him in court."

"No, I'm not that sure."

Brannigan straightens up. He leans over the table, his features composed and serious, his eyes intense. "Ms. Mitchell, do you know what hypnotic regression is?"

"Yes, of course. I hope you don't intend to hypnotize me."

"Not me," Brannigan manages a laugh. "See, I don't know how far you're willing to take this. Hypnosis has worked for us in the past, but not if the subject feels coerced." He taps the tabletop with a finger, turns his head away for a moment. "What I'd like to do is identify or eliminate this particular suspect. To be honest, I don't really care which way it goes. I mean I don't want to spend a lot of time pursuing a dead end, but if the suspect is actually the perpetrator, I don't want to see him walk away, either. I don't want to put a killer back on the street."

The implication, as Melody understands it, is that if she refuses to be hypnotized, *she* will be the one putting a killer back on the street. Her first reaction is resentment. She doesn't appreciate being pressured, but she can't deny the truth of what Detective Brannigan says, either. After all, she saw the body for herself.

"When would you want to do this, Detective? The hypnosis."

"I can set it up for tomorrow morning. We'll be using a clinical psychologist, Doctor Elizabeth Kenton. We've used her before."

"Well, I guess I can spare a few hours in the interest of justice." She grimaces. "Being as I have nothing else to do, anyway."

Brannigan's grin spreads from ear to ear. "Great, that's just great. Listen, you think I could use the phone for a couple of minutes?"

"Certainly. Take the one in the living room. I'll tidy up the kitchen."

December 12: 4:40 AM

Tommy Brannigan enters the Thirteenth Precinct, nods to the sergeant, then charges into the toilet. Three containers of coffee after four hours of sleep have strained his bladder to the breaking point. He thinks of Roscoe, Melody Mitchell's dog, as he stands in front of the urinal.

"Roscoe," he says out loud, "I know just how you fucking feel."

"How's that?"

Brannigan turns his head (while, fortunately enough, keeping the rest of his body pointed in the right direction) to find Sergeant Adolphus Cobb standing right behind him.

"Jeez, Sarge, don't walk so soft. I didn't hear you."

"Jeez, Tommy, don't piss so loud. You wouldn't have heard an elephant if he blew a kiss in your ear."

Cobb stands with his legs apart, hands jammed on his hips. He is every inch the spit-and-polish professional, the veteran sergeant with a hard-on for every cop above or below his rank. Brannigan, however, is not intimidated. He knows that Adolphus Cobb entered the job at a time when a black cop's fellow officers left King Kong posters in his locker. Bunches of bananas. Watermelons. Now Cobb has to order these same cops around.

"I took care of business for you, Tommy. Just like you asked. I gave the perp a sandwich right after you called. Took it out of my own lunch pail. Around one, I brought in a cot and told him to go to sleep."

"He give you any trouble?"

"He made noises like he wanted to go home, but I reminded him that it's nice and warm in here. 'Son, it's twenty degrees outside,' I said. 'And the wind is blowin' up a storm. Plus, you got to walk all the way back to the river and sleep in a box. And it ain't gonna do you no good, neither, 'cause we're just gonna come lookin' for your sorry ass tomorrow.'"

"Did he get the message?"

"Yeah, he's dumb, but he ain't crazy. Fact, he's a nice kid. Don't seem like the type to go out and kill nobody."

"Shit, Sarge, most of the time Billy Sowell's so drunk he doesn't know what he's doing or when he's doing it. He couldn't even tell me where he was the day before yesterday. Look, I owe you for this. You need a favor and I can do it, it's yours."

"Understood."

"By the way, you want a piece of this collar? Being as my partner's off and I could use a little help."

"What kind of help?"

"I'm gonna start turning this perp around and I could use someone to play the bad cop. I don't know why, but I got this feeling you'll do just fine."

5:15 AM

Billy Sowell wakes from a deep, almost drugged sleep to find a very somber Detective Brannigan leaning over him. For once, Detective Brannigan isn't smiling. In fact, he seems puzzled and worried and sad all at the same time. Billy rubs his eyes, attempts to pull it together.

He needs a drink and he knows it. His hands are shaking and he can't seem to focus very well. Nevertheless, he has no problem seeing the face that suddenly appears behind Detective Brannigan's shoulder.

"Drag the boy off that cot," the face says. "He's fakin'."

Faking what? Billy thinks. I just woke up.

"Billy," Detective Brannigan says, "this is Sergeant Cobb. He's gonna be working with us this morning."

"Hello," Billy says. He notes Cobb's black skin, but that doesn't bother him. He's been living on the streets too long to be automatically afraid of a black face, although it wasn't always like that. No, when his mother died and he had to go to the shelter, the only thing he knew about black people was what he'd seen on television. For the first two weeks, he thought every black man in the shelter was out to kill him.

"Billy, we have a big problem here," Detective Brannigan says calmly. "Try to wake up and pay attention."

"I need a drink." Billy smiles when he says it, smiles apologetically. He knows his problem is getting worse, but he doesn't know what to do about it.

"I understand, Billy." Detective Brannigan lays a hand on Billy's shoulder. "But we've got to clear this up first. You can have some coffee, if you like."

"Don't give him no damn coffee," Sergeant Cobb barks. "Don't give him nothin'."

Detective Brannigan turns to face Sergeant Cobb. "Take it easy, Sarge. We could *all* use some coffee."

Sergeant Cobb fixes Billy with a threatening stare, one Billy has seen many times. In the past, the stare always meant that somebody wanted something—his alcohol, his shoes, his toothbrush, even his body. Most of the time, Billy gave up what they wanted, because he didn't know how to fight. He hadn't grown up that way. Living with his mom, there hadn't been anyone to fight with.

Billy watches Sergeant Cobb walk out of the room, wishing, as he has so many times, that his mother was still alive, that he was back in their little apartment. He imagines them sitting down to dinner, watching television, doing a puzzle. They had lived as if they were the only two people in the world.

"Are you with me, Billy?" Detective Brannigan is smiling again.

"Yes."

"We showed your picture to a witness, Billy, and she thinks you were there when Sondra Tillson was murdered."

"But I wasn't. I wasn't there."

"How do you know, Billy? How do you know that you weren't there?"

"Because I didn't do it."

"That's what I used to believe, Billy. But I'm not so sure, now. Maybe you did do it."

"No, I . . ."

"Hush, Billy. Just listen for a minute. Maybe you killed that woman and forgot about it. Maybe you were very drunk that night. Do you know what a blackout is?"

"No."

"When people drink, sometimes they can't remember. Sometimes they lose whole days and nights of their lives. It's very common, Billy. People who drink forget what they've done."

"I wouldn't forget that. I couldn't forget something like that."

"How do you know? See, if you could just tell me where you were on the night Sondra Tillson was murdered, I could check it out, but you can't tell me anything. So, what am I supposed to do? I have to go by the evidence and right now it's all against you."

Billy doesn't know what to say. Detective Brannigan must be right about the blackouts, because he, Billy, definitely doesn't remember Sondra Tillson or what he's come to think of as "that night."

"Look, Billy," Detective Brannigan says, "if you're really innocent, I still want to clear you. Maybe, if I go to your place by the river and look through your things, I can find something to help you."

"I don't think there's anything to find."

"We won't know unless we look, will we?"

"I guess not."

"Now, I'm going to need your permission. I can't do it unless you let me. Please, Billy, it's for your own good."

"Have you lost your goddamn mind, Brannigan?"

Billy looks up to find Sergeant Cobb standing in the doorway. The Sergeant is angrier than ever.

"What we oughta do," he says, pointing a finger at Billy, "is lock him up in a cell. Let the boys fuck his killer ass for a few days. Loosen the little prick up."

6:15 AM

"I just know there's fleas in these fucking blankets." Adolphus Cobb shines his six-cell flashlight around the interior of Billy Sowell's packing-crate home.

"Don't worry about it. We're not gonna be here long. I'm not lookin' for a written confession."

"Just what *are* we lookin' for, Tommy? What are we doing here at six o'clock in the goddamned morning?"

"We're lookin' for this, Sarge. This murder weapon right here." The knife Brannigan holds between his thumb and forefinger sports a six-inch blade.

"Oh, man," Cobb complains, "that don't prove shit. A man sleeps on the street, he's gotta keep somethin' with him. You see blood on it?"

"Hard to say. But it could have been the murder weapon. The ME says she was killed with a blade at least five inches long. The perp cut her three times. Twice on the arm where she tried to defend herself, once in the throat. She bled out."

"Any blood on Sowell's clothes? There'd have to be blood on his clothes."

Brannigan, having put the knife into an evidence bag, is examining Billy Sowell's clothing, one item at a time. "Not that I could see, but he had two weeks to get rid of the clothes."

"Yeah?" Adolphus Cobb shines his flashlight directly into Brannigan's face. His unexpected laughter is deep and rich. "Well, it's your case, Tommy, but if he got rid of the clothes, how come he kept the knife?"

11:45 AM

Q: I want you to imagine that you're standing at the top of a flight of stairs. The flight has fifteen steps and as you descend, you will find yourself drifting back in time. Drifting back one day with each step. When you get to the landing you will be all the way back to the night of November twenty-seventh. You'll awaken in your bed, relaxed and comfortable. Now, begin your descent, Melody. One step, then another and another. Perfectly relaxed. (*pause*) Melody?

A: Yes.

Q: Can you tell me where you are?

A: I'm in my bed.

Q: Does something wake you up?

A: Yes, it's Roscoe. My dog. He's whining and barking. He wants to go out.

Q: And how do you respond?

A: I know I have to take him. If I don't, he'll urinate in the apartment. Roscoe hates that. He feels humiliated. He doesn't like being an old dog.

Q: Do you get dressed?

A: No, I put on my coat over my nightgown. Then my warm boots.

Q: Is it cold?

A: It's cold outside. It was cold when I took Roscoe out after the news.

Q: What do you do next, Melody?

A: We take the elevator down to the lobby. Petya is standing by the door.

Q: Who is Petya?

A: Petya is the doorman.

Q: Can you see him?

A: Yes. He's complaining about the cold.

Q: Look carefully. Can you tell me what Petya's wearing?

A: He's wearing his uniform.

Q: Can you describe this uniform?

A: Petya's wearing a white shirt and a black bow tie. His jacket is tan. It has four buttons, but the last button is open. His trousers match his jacket.

Q: Does he always wear the same uniform?

A: No, he has a gray uniform as well. (*laughter*) But he always leaves the last button unbuttoned. That's because of his potbelly.

Q: What happens next, Melody? What do you do?

A: I take Roscoe to the curb. I guess I'm still half asleep, because I don't notice anything until Roscoe growls. I look down the street and I see a man standing by a car halfway down the block.

Q: I want you to slow down, now. I want you to go very, very slowly. Begin with his shoes. Can you tell me what color his shoes are?

A: No, I don't remember the shoes. I didn't look at his shoes.

Q: That's all right, Melody. Just relax. Do you remember what we discussed earlier? About this not being a test?

A: Yes.

Q: And do you remember what I told you about not trying to see anything that's not there? That you're just a reporter, a camera?

A: Yes.

Q: Now I want you to let your eyes move up along his body. Can you see his hands?

A: Yes. He's holding something in his right hand. Now he's turning away, moving his hand behind his body. I, I . . .

Q: Easy, Melody. Take your time. Look at his hands again. Remember, it's just like watching a videotape. You can stop it, reverse it, anything you like. Now, he's holding something in his right hand. Is there a gleam? Does it reflect light? Is it metal?

A: Yes. I think he's holding a set of keys.

Q: How is he holding them? Are they in his fist?

A: He's holding them between his thumb and forefinger.

Q: How many keys can you see?

A: I can't tell. I see a bunch of keys on a key ring. All dangling down.

Q: Fine, Melody. You're doing just fine. Now, let your focus drift upward, up to his neck. Tell me when you can see his chest and his neck.

A: I can see his chest and his neck.

Q: What is he wearing?

A: He's wearing an overcoat.

Q: Can you describe it?

A: I would say it's expensive, but I'm pretty far away and it's night. (*pause*) It doesn't seem to be dirty or torn.

Q: Is he wearing a tie?

A: His overcoat is buttoned to the top. I can't tell.

Q: Can you see his throat above the collar?

A: Yes.

Q: Do you see anything unusual? Any marks? Any scars?

A: No.

Q: All right. Take another deep breath. Good. Let it out. Your focus is moving upward again. Up and up until you're looking directly at his face. Are you looking at his face, Melody?

A: Yes.

Q: Will you describe his face for me?

A: He has dark curly hair. It's standing off his scalp, spilling onto his forehead. The streetlight is behind him and his hair is casting a shadow over the upper part of his face. His eyebrows are bushy. I can see that much. His nose is straight and his lips are full. He has a broad, square skull, a strong chin.

Q: Can you tell me the color of his eyes?

A: No, his eyes are in the shadow.

Q: Does he have a round chin or is there a cleft?

A: I can't be sure.

Q: Are his ears flat against his skull or do they stick out?

A: Flat.

Q: Is he wearing an earring?

A: No.

Q: All right, now go back to his face. Focus on his face.

A: His eyes are in shadow. I can see a line. No. . . . It's very hazy. It might be there and it might not. I just can't be sure.

Q: Can't be sure about what? What are you seeing?

A: No, no. I can see something, but I don't know what it is.

Q: Shhhhhh. Just relax, Melody. Stop the video and take your time. Remember what I told you before we started? I only want you to tell me what you see. Don't try to tell me what you don't see. All right?

A: Yes.

Q: Good. You can go ahead, now.

"How are you feeling?"

Detective Brannigan is wearing his serious, sincere look. Melody wishes he'd smile.

"I feel fine," she replies. "But I guess I wasn't much help."

"You remembered the keys, Ms. Mitchell. That puts whoever you saw *in* the car. He wasn't just a passerby who didn't want to get involved. The man you saw must've been the killer."

Melody feels her chest tighten. It's funny, she thinks, you hear, see, and read about crime every single day, but you don't have any idea what it feels like until it happens to you. Or, at least, until you get close to it.

"Well, Detective, if there's anything else I can do for you . . ."

"There is one thing, Ms. Mitchell. Before you go, would you mind taking another look at those photographs?"

1:15 PM

Billy Sowell has been asleep for all of two hours when Sergeant Cobb enters the interview room. Billy is dreaming about his mother. She is telling him that he won't have to go to school any more, that she is perfectly capable of teaching him every single thing he needs to know. Hasn't she taught him the alphabet? Hasn't she taught him to print his name? The other children are too fast for him. Too fast and too cruel.

Billy hears Sergeant Cobb shout his name, but in his dream, the sergeant's voice becomes the voice of his mother calling him down to breakfast.

"Get up, Billy. Get up."

Billy responds by rolling over on the cot, muttering, "In a minute, Mom."

The next thing he knows, he's crashing onto the floor of the interview room and his eyes are opening fast. Opening on Sergeant Cobb's enraged face.

"When I tell you to do somethin', you do it, boy. And you do it fast."

Billy smiles. He looks for Detective Brannigan's face. Looks for protection. Looks for his mother.

"You lookin' for your girlfriend? Huh, sissy? You lookin' for Dee-tec-tive Bran-ni-gan? Is he your sweetheart? Answer me, bitch."

"I don't understand . . ."

"Stand up. Right the fuck now."

Billy starts to obey, but Sergeant Cobb's hands are in his shirt before he can move. He feels himself propelled upward, finds his face within inches of Sergeant Cobb's. Sergeant Cobb's eyes are huge, and round, and red with anger.

"You killed that woman, Billy. We found your knife in that box you live in. We know you killed her."

"No, I . . ."

"Yeah, you did. And here's how it went down. First, you watched her park the car. Nice pretty blond like that. You watched her and you wondered just what her pussy would feel like. You wondered until you were so crazy, you didn't know what you're doing. Then she opened the door and you went up to her. You went up to her and told her exactly what you wanted to do."

"Please, I don't remember. I don't . . ."

"She looked at you like you were a bug. Something she wanted to step on. A retarded, smelly, homeless bug. That made you angry, didn't it, Billy? It made you so angry that you forgot all about your dick and how hot you were. You hit her. You hit her in the face and pushed her back into the car."

"No."

"Then you got in after her. You closed the door and looked at her. She wasn't disgusted then, was she? No, she was afraid and you liked that. You took out your knife and stabbed at her. Once, twice, until the pain made her yank her arm down. Then, Billy, then you could see her throat, her soft white throat, and that's exactly where the knife went. Into her soft, white throat."

"Oh, God. Mama, help me. Mama, Mama, Mama . . ."

"You watched her choke on her own blood. There was lots of blood, wasn't there? Lots and lots and lots of blood. Blood on the seat, blood on the windows, blood on the floor, blood on *you*. You knew you had to leave before somebody saw what you did, so you pushed her into the backseat, got out of the car, and locked the door. Then you heard a dog growl and you looked up. There was a woman staring at you. She *saw* you with the keys. You wanted to kill her, too, but you were afraid of the dog."

"No . . ."

"She says you were there, Billy. You had the car keys in your fuckin' hand."

"I wasn't there. Please, God, what are you doing to me? I want to go home."

"Home? The only place you're going to is hell. You understand that, bitch?"

Billy isn't prepared for the punch that catches him in the stomach. He doesn't realize what happened until he's on the floor, trying to regain his breath.

"Now, you listen to me, you little fag. De-tec-tive Bran-ni-gan might be willin' to take your shit, but I ain't cut from that cloth. You sass me one more time, I'm gonna rip your heart out and make you eat it. Understand what I'm sayin'?"

"Yes."

"Get up."

Billy struggles to his feet, is spun around, cuffed, then spun again to face Sergeant Cobb. He looks into Cobb's eyes and thinks that this is a man who likes to hurt people. Billy's seen that look before. Seen it on the faces of men he learned to avoid. They were the reason he left the shelter and took to the streets.

"Now, you're gonna do the right thing, ain't you, Billy?"

"Yes."

"I want you to repeat what I say. Exactly the way I say it, under-stand?"

"Yes."

"And no bullshit, neither. *Exactly* what I say."

"All right."

"I was out beggin' for spare change."

"I was out begging for spare change."

"And I saw this blond woman."

"I saw this blond woman."

December 14: 10:00 AM

"Now, don't worry, Ms. Mitchell, this is a one-way window. You can see in, but the suspect can't see out."

Melody Mitchell barely hears Detective Brannigan's words. She's seen too many television cop shows to be surprised by any of this. Besides, *she* wasn't the victim; *she* has no horrible experience to relive. Nevertheless, she waits patiently (and politely) for Detective Brannigan to finish.

"The platform is empty, now, but in a minute or two, nine individ-uals will come out and take their places. I don't want you to rush this. Look at every single face before you make a decision. If you want to see their profiles or hear them speak, all you have to do is ask."

"Fine, Detective. I guess I'm as ready as I'll ever be." When the men begin to file onto the platform, Melody is not surprised to find them equally seedy, equally nondescript. (That, she thinks, is what a fair lineup is all about.) No, what shocks her is a sudden burst of recognition that flows through her body, from her toes to the rising hairs on the back of her neck.

"My God," she says, pointing to Billy Sowell, "that's *him.*" She puts her hand over her mouth and steps backward onto Brannigan's toes. "That's the killer. That's him."

"Which one, Ms. Mitchell?"

"Number five. On the right."

"Are you sure?"

"As sure as I'm standing here. He's a lot different in person. Different from his photo, that is. But now that I see him, I'm a hun-dred percent positive. That man, the one with the scar, is the man I saw by the automobile."

"Will you testify to that in a courtroom? Think twice, Ms. Mitchell. Criminal trials have a way of getting rough in a hurry."

Melody Mitchell turns to face the tall detective. She jams her hands into her hips. "It may surprise you to learn," she declares, "that there are people in New York City committed to the idea of justice. *Ordinary* people, not policemen. I not only positively identify this man here and now, but I will do it as many times as necessary. And I will do it in front of anyone and everyone with a need to know. Is that enough for you?"

"Yes, Ms. Mitchell." Detective Brannigan's composed features suddenly jump into a huge grin. "That is definitely, absolutely, positively enough."

1:00 PM

"I think it's time, Billy. I think it's time we got it over with."

Billy Sowell looks up through tear-stained eyes, nods slowly.

"Don't cry, Billy. It's gonna be okay." Tommy Brannigan lays his palms on either side of Billy's face. His own eyes are brimming. "We tried to clear you, but we just couldn't. It's nobody's fault."

"I'm so tired, now." Billy lets his head drop. "When it's over, can I sleep?"

"Sure, Billy. You can sleep as long as you want." Brannigan steps back, pulls a tape recorder from his jacket pocket, holds it up for Billy's inspection. "Do you know what this is, Billy?"

"Yes. Mom had one."

"After I turn it on, I'm gonna ask you a series of questions. Do you know what you're going to say?"

"I think so."

"If you lose your way, I'll help you. Understand?"

"Yes."

"Good, Billy. Very good. Now, here we go."

Q: Would you please state your name.
A: William Sowell.
Q: Also called Billy Sowell?
A: Yes.
Q: Now, Billy, you know you don't have to speak to me, right? I've already told you that?
A: Yes.
Q: And you know that anything you say to me can be used in court against you? I've already told you that, too?

A: Yes.

Q: And you know that you can have a lawyer if you want one? And the lawyer won't cost you anything?

A: Yes.

Q: So, you're making this statement of your own free will.

A: Yes. I want to get it over with.

Q: Billy, can you tell me where you were in the early-morning hours on November twenty-seventh?

A: Is that the day it happened?

Q: Yes, Billy.

A: I was begging.

Q: Do you mean panhandling? Asking strangers for money?

A: Yes.

Q: While you were panhandling, did you happen to go over to Gramercy Park?

A: Is that the one with the locked gates?

Q: That's the one. Did you go over there?

A: Yes.

Q: All right, Billy. Now, I want you to tell me what happened when you went over to Gramercy Park. Tell it in your own words.

A: I saw a woman.

Q: And what was she doing?

A: What was she doing?

Q: Yes, when you first saw her.

A: She was parking her car.

Q: Can you describe the car?

A: I . . . I don't . . .

Q: If you don't remember, just say, "I don't remember."

A: I don't remember the car.

Q: You don't have a driver's license, do you, Billy? You've never driven a car?

A: No, I never learned how.

Q: Can you describe the woman driving the car?

A: No, I don't remember.

Q: C'mon, Billy. You described her before. Was she blond?

A: Yes, she was blond. Now, I remember. She was very pretty and I wanted to fuck her. I went up to her, but she said, "No." Then, I pushed her back in the car . . .

Q: She was out of the car?

A: Huh?

Q: You said that she was parking the car when you first saw her. Did she get out of the car before you went over to her?

A: Yes, she got out of the car.

Q: Then what happened?

A: She was very pretty and I wanted to fuck her. I went up to her, but she said, "No." Then I pushed her back in the car. I was very angry. I took out my knife and I stabbed her. Once. Twice. Three times. I stabbed her in her arm and in her neck. Then I pushed her into the backseat. I got out of the car and locked the door. There was a woman in the street with a dog. I wanted to kill her, too, but I was afraid of the dog, so I went home.

Q: Billy, is this your knife?

A: I . . . I'm not sure. It looks like my knife. Yes, it's probably my knife.

Q: Is this the knife you stabbed the woman with?

A: Yes.

Q: Did the woman say anything to you before you stabbed her?

A: She said she wouldn't fuck me.

Q: What were her exact words?

A: I don't remember.

Q: Is that because you were so angry?

A: It must be.

Q: You were so angry that you didn't listen to her words?

A: Yes.

Q: Did she say anything when you pulled out the knife?

A: No.

Q: Was she frightened?

A: I think so. Yes, she was frightened.

Q: When you stabbed her, did you get any blood on your coat? Think carefully.

A: I can't, Detective Brannigan. I'm so tired I can't think carefully.

Q: Would you like some coffee? You can have some coffee.

A: Yes.

Q: All right, Billy. I've turned the tape recorder back on. Are you ready to start again?

A: Yes.

Q: Do you feel a little better? Are you more awake, now?

A: Yes.

Q: Okay, let's back up a little bit. Did you touch the woman after you pushed her back into the car?

A: I touched her breasts.

Q: And what did she say?

A: She said, "No, no, no."

Q: And when you took out the knife, did the woman say anything to you?

A: She started crying. She said, "Please don't hurt me."

Q: And then what happened?

A: Then I stabbed her. Once. Twice. Three times.

Q: Did you get any of her blood on your coat?

A: Yes. After I went home, I threw the coat away. Then I went to the mission and got another coat.

Q: Which mission was that, Billy?

A: I don't know the name. It's on Twenty-eighth Street.

Q: And what did you do with the knife?

A: I washed it off.

Q: And did you keep it?

A: Yes.

Q: Where?

A: Huh?

Q: Where did you keep the knife?

A: I kept it in my home.

Q: And where is your home, Billy?

A: By the river.

Q: Is that the East River just below Twenty-third Street?

A: I think so.

Q: And is your home a packing crate?

A: It's a box. Yes. I live in a box. I'm homeless.

Q: And is everything you've told me here true and honest to the best of your recollection?

A: Yes.

Q: And did you give this statement of your own free will?

A: Yes.

Q: Thank you, Billy. It's all over now.

ONE

When the fight started, Marty Blake stepped from the blazing interior of his yellow cab onto the blazing pavement of West Forty-seventh Street to get a better view. He felt no impatience, no anxiety, despite the painfully obvious fact that when the wheels of a cab don't turn, the driver doesn't make any money. Despite knowing that by the time he paid off the 5 AM–5 PM lease and filled the tank, he'd be lucky to have enough for dinner and a beer.

Marty Blake was not a bloodthirsty man. He would've liked nothing better than to leave without a backward glance for the two lunatics about to do the urban shuffle. Unfortunately, the combatants' cars were between his cab and the corner. The only way around was the sidewalk and even if he had the courage to face the pedestrians gathering to watch the fight (which he didn't), his route to the curb was blocked by an illegally parked van with enough tickets stuffed beneath its wiper blades to fill the street's gaping potholes.

"Please, Mister Cabbie, I'm not feeling well. I can't stop here. I'm a *passenger*."

The woman's face, caught in the intense glare of the midday sun, seemed almost featureless. The sweat-moistened powder on her forehead gleamed with pinpoints of light, as it did along the bony length of her nose. Blake could see a tiny sun in each lens of her cats-eye glasses.

"There not a lot I can do about it, ma'am." Blake managed a shrug. "It's in God's hands, now."

He was hoping the pious reference would shut her up. Fat chance.

"I can't take the heat. It's too much for me. You should have chosen a different route."

Blake had picked up the old lady and her bundle of packages on Sixth Avenue near Macy's in Herald Square. She was headed for West End Avenue and he'd dutifully plowed uptown, fighting the traffic while he looked for a way out of the Midtown mess. Forty-seventh

Street had been clear to Seventh Avenue, which was as far as he could see. Now, he was a hundred yards short of Tenth Avenue and immobilized for the duration.

"You're right," Blake admitted. The woman's face was contorted by running mascara, as if she'd been weeping tears of black blood. "I should have taken a different street, but I didn't. Now we're screwed."

He managed a quick smile before turning back to watch the fight. The tall fat guy was still leaning over the Ford, screaming at the black man trapped inside.

"Black-assssss. You are black-assssss. We should send all black-ass back to Africa."

The man in the car seemed more confused than afraid. Blake had had any number of conversations with the Russian cabbies who hustled the hotels. They used the term "black ass" the way others used the word "nigger."

"Mister Driver, please."

Blake turned back to the woman. On average, he carried sixty passengers a day. He liked to think of them as packages.

"What do you want me to do, ma'am? There's nowhere to go."

"Why did you take this street? I demand an answer."

"Just lucky, I guess."

"Ha, with your big mouth. I'm an old lady."

"I sympathize, but it's not my fault."

"And I'm dying from the heat. It's a hundred degrees in this taxi."

"A hundred and ten, actually. I've got a thermometer in the front. It was a hundred and ten when I got out."

The black man trapped in his car was making noises like he wanted to mix it up. His problem, as Blake saw it, was how to get out without being sucker-punched.

"Please. Don't ignore me. I'm a passenger and I have rights."

"Lady, all you have to do is walk up to Tenth Avenue and find another cab. There's no trick to it."

"If I have to walk, I'm not paying."

Blake reached into the cab and shut off the meter. There was no way, short of physical violence, that he was going to collect this fare. At another time, a few months ago, he would have argued, demanded, threatened to call a cop. Not today. After 364 days of exile, he was going home. Home being, in this case, Manhattan Executive Security, Inc.

"That's okay, ma'am. You must need the money more than I do." He opened the door and stepped back. "Don't forget your packages."

The woman (seemingly refreshed by the prospect of saving a big three dollars and fifty cents) slid from the back of the cab, cradled her bundles against her bony chest, and skittered off down the block. Blake watched her for a moment, thinking that she reminded him of his Granny Emma who'd told stories of the Great Depression the way his other grandmother, Granny Agatha, recited Mother Goose. Granny Emma, his mother's mother, had spent the final decades of her life meditating on the nickels and dimes she'd saved at the supermarket. Or the sweater she'd plucked from the clearance rack of a hospital thrift store. Her considerable estate was now supporting her daughter.

Blake turned back to the fight just in time to see the initial escalation from words to deeds. The fat Russian suddenly reached into the interior of the black man's car only to find his knuckles between the black man's teeth. The Russian leaped back, screaming, while his opponent took the opportunity to escape through the far door.

No weapons, Blake thought. Please no weapons here. If they really fuck each other up, the cops'll have me giving statements for the next six hours.

His plea went unheard. The black man came around the back of his car waving a three-foot length of iron pipe. Which, Blake had to admit, wasn't such a bad idea. Not only was he six inches shorter and a good hundred pounds lighter than his adversary, he couldn't turn tail and run. His car was trapped behind the Russian's.

As the two men began to circle, Blake let his eyes drift over the crowd. Mostly male, their eyes glittered with anticipation, like men at a stag party watching the whore move from lap to lap. Jaws rigid, skin glistening, fists clenched—their clothing was already soaked with sweat. Later, the executives would shower and change; the alkies and the crack junkies would itch and stink.

"Yeah, get him, get him. Smash his fuckin' face in. Kick his fuckin' ass."

What it is, Blake decided, is street-ecumenical. The homeless meet the CEOs. Democracy in action. The vision of Thomas Jefferson sucked out of the Bill of Rights and dumped onto the pavement.

Blake turned back to the combatants. The black man clearly didn't want to fight. He was waving the pipe around, but making no effort to close the six feet of ground between himself and the Russian. The

Russian, for his part, continued to circle, continued to chant the same curse in the same intense monotone.

"Black-assssss; black-assssss; black-assssss."

In the end, the black man's indecision decided the fight. When he finally struck, the blow, though it contacted the Russian's scalp with an audible thump, was neither killing nor disabling. The Russian, laughing, now, ignored the blood streaming over his left eye; he grabbed the smaller man, forced him to the ground, slammed his face into the pavement.

"Black-assssss."

Slowly, as if trying to assert his dignity, the Russian heaved his bulk erect. He began to kick his stunned opponent, taking his time about it, grunting with the effort. Again and again and again.

Blake waited until he was sure the Russian wasn't going to stop. Until the small figure on the pavement lay motionless. Then he stepped forward.

"That's it," he said, trying to put enough command into his voice to get the Russian's attention, a necessary first step. "You won. The fight's over. C'mon, enough."

The Russian turned his head slightly. "I kill you, too," he grunted. His eyes, Blake noted, were still in lunatic heaven.

"You don't wanna talk about killing, pal." Blake held up his hands, palms out. "They do horrible things to you for killing people. Twenty-five years to life kind of things. In Attica."

He'd intended his counsel to be calming, but the Russian wasn't ready to listen. He did, however, move away from his fallen adversary, which Blake saw as a victory of sorts. Or it would have been a victory if the Russian hadn't been coming straight for *him*.

Blake wasn't afraid. Four years on the varsity wrestling squad at City College (good enough to get invited to the Olympic trials; not good enough to win a single bout) had taught him to keep his head. Ten years of post-college workouts in a sweaty YMHA in Forest Hills had only added to his confidence. At present, he was benching three-twenty-five, a hundred and forty pounds more than his body weight. He may not have been a candidate for power lifter of the year, but he was certain he could tie a lumbering, blubbery Russian into enough knots to fill a Boy Scout manual.

"Look, you're makin' a big mistake here." Blake continued to back away. "What happened before? You could claim self-defense. After all, the man hit you with a pipe and you've got the wound to prove it. But me, I'm unarmed." He raised his hands again. "And I'm running away. You hear the sirens? The cops'll arrive any minute. Don't you have enough problems without having to explain a second assault? Think about it."

Blake saw a flicker of awareness float through the Russian's eyes. He decided that while it wasn't exactly intelligence, it did indicate a certain shrewdness. A memory, perhaps, of his own native land and what the authorities in that native land could do to you.

"Why you no mind own business?"

"I should have. I admit it. But there's no sense in going any further. What we oughta do is let it drop and wait for the police."

"You are dirty coward."

"Okay, I can accept that."

"You are dirty *American* coward."

The Russian turned to face the oncoming police, and Blake, acting entirely on impulse, stepped forward to drive his fist into the fat man's lower back. While his blow (like that of the little man with the pipe) was not a killing blow, it was entirely disabling. The Russian fell to the ground and howled like a castrated pig.

Blake shook his head in disgust. "Check it out, *putz*. The first rule of American street life is never turn your back on a man you've just humiliated."

"Sarge, my whole family was on the job," Blake explained. "Two uncles, my old man, a bunch of cousins. Since 1883 when my great-great-grandfather was appointed to the cops by a Tammany boss named Kilpatrick."

"So what happened to *you*?"

They were sitting, Blake and Detective-Sergeant Paul O'Dowd, in a mercifully air-conditioned blue-and-white on Tenth Avenue, happily blocking the already snarled evening traffic while they chatted away.

"What happened, Sarge, was that my Irish father married a nice Jewish girl from Forest Hills. And what I did was become a computer freak with a bad attitude."

It was true, as far as it went. Blake had come out of CCNY in 1983 with a BS in computer science and a job worth thirty-five grand a year. Not bad, for a twenty-one-year-old kid. The only problem was that he'd hated his work. Customizing software for investment bankers had seemed interesting enough, especially from the prospective of an undergraduate with no money to attempt a master's degree. In fact, it'd turned deadly dull in a hurry.

"So, how come you're drivin' a cab?"

"It's a long story. You sure you wanna hear it?"

"That coon's in a bad way, Blake. If he should happen to expire, it'll go down as a homicide. You're a witness. Good or bad is what I'm trying to find out. So, how come you're drivin' a cab?"

"You ever have a job you hated, Sergeant?"

"I hate the one I'm doing now."

"Well, pretend that somebody you just happened to meet at a party offered you a job that was a thousand times more interesting and paid better than being a cop. Would you think you stepped in shit?"

"Keep goin', Blake. There's gotta be a punch line here; I can feel it coming."

"The someone I met is named Joanna Bardo, president and sole shareholder of Manhattan Executive Investigations, Incorporated. When I told her I was a computer programmer, she offered me a job on the spot."

"Doing exactly what?"

Blake smiled. "Sarge, you know about knocking on doors? Burning shoe leather? Well, at Manhattan Executive, we don't knock on doors until after we knock on the computer. Motor-vehicle records, accident reports, criminal records, insurance records, property sales, births, deaths, marriages—it's all there, all legal. All just a phone call away."

"I take it the computer makes the phone call."

"That's right. Give the computer a social security number and it'll find you anywhere. Manhattan Executive was one of the first companies to use the computer for skip-tracing. There was a time, about five years ago, when every bail bondsman in the city was sending us business. There's a lot more competition, now, but we still get to pick and choose."

"It sounds okay, Blake. Probably good money in it, too."

"It would have been better if I'd stayed with the computer, but I wanted to do field work, so I got my license. I'm a full-fledged private eye. Or, I will be in about six hours. Right now, I'm on suspension. What happened was I set up an illegal surveillance and *almost* got caught. The case against me was pretty weak, but I didn't have the heart to take a chance at trial, so what I did was plead nolo contendere before the board and accept a year's unpaid vacation. Today's my last day off."

TWO

It was way too early, just a little before six, but Marty Blake was already in the bathroom, soaping his dark, heavy beard. Though he'd been hoping against hope for another hour and a half's sleep, he hadn't even bothered to set the clock. What was the point? On an ordinary day, he'd already be cruising Manhattan, timing the lights as he methodically worked the avenues, from Ninety-sixth Street down to Houston Street. Looking for the last of the night people, the first of the office workers.

That nightmare was now officially over (though the memory lingered on). He'd done his time, served his sentence; he was going home. Maybe.

When he'd called Joanna Bardo, he'd expected a lot more enthusiasm. In fact, he'd expected a hero's welcome, because he *was* a hero. Even during the worst of it, when the prosecutors were talking fifteen years, when his own lawyer wouldn't meet his eyes, when the prosecutors were offering to let him walk away with his license if he gave up Joanna Bardo, he'd stood fast. He'd taken the heat like a good soldier.

The case had been simple enough. A small brokerage firm, Hattmann Brothers, suspected one of their executives, an accountant named Porcek, of insider trading. Namely, Porcek was feeding information on new issues to his brother-in-law who was passing it on to a cousin who was buying shares in his wife's name. The firm wanted to dump the accountant before the feds caught on, but they needed more than a paper trail. They needed enough hard evidence to convince Porcek to leave without a fuss. Or a scandal.

Hattmann Brothers had given the job to Joanna Bardo who'd given it to Marty Blake, her number-one investigator. Especially when it came to black-bag operations.

"They don't want to know what we're going to do, Marty," she'd said matter-of-factly. "They just want it done."

He'd taken the hint, entered Porcek's apartment while he was at work, bugged the rooms, and tapped the phones. It wasn't supposed to be a big deal. Despite the high-tech image cultivated by modern private investigators, the business was still as corrupt as it had been when private investigation meant catching errant spouses with their pants down. Clients expected results, but they weren't prepared to pay for six months of by-the-book investigation. If you wouldn't cut through the red tape, your competition would. It was that simple.

By the time Blake had realized that Porcek's extra-legal pursuits involved more than insider trading, the IRS had busted into Porcek's apartment, seized two million dollars in counterfeit currency, and discovered the various taps and bugs. The feds had kept the bogus fifties, but passed on the hardware to the New York State Attorney General. The AG had gone to Hattmann Brother's who'd implicated Manhattan Executive and Joanna Bardo. Joanna (with no real choice in the matter) had named Marty Blake.

In the end, it was the AG who'd blinked. Despite their blustering, the prosecutors hadn't had enough to go to trial. They'd offered Blake a dismissal of the criminal charges in exchange for a year's unpaid vacation. He'd taken it because he didn't have the courage to put a decade of his life in the hands of a jury.

Marty Blake rinsed off the last of the shaving cream, toweled dry, then took a moment to appraise the face in the mirror. He would have preferred something a little more dignified. Something just a bit aristocratic. The clients with the big bucks were mostly corporations, now, and they expected the investigators who served them to maintain a certain corporate image. Cigars, rumpled suits, and hip flasks were definitely out.

But Marty Blake's face would never be dignified, and he knew it. His hair was too curly, his nose too long, his lips a bit too full. The dark blue eyes would have been all right but they were slightly off-line, as was his nose. Ten years ago, an overeager sophomore had slammed the left side of Marty Blake's face into the floor of a CCNY gym. There'd been no malice in it. The sophomore had been trying to take him down and he'd been trying to get off the mat. Both had succeeded and the end result, after the fractures had healed, was a somewhat goofy expression, especially when he smiled.

The goofiness didn't bother Marty Blake. In fact, he considered it an asset, reasoning that when you're five-nine and weigh a hundred and eighty-five pounds, when you sport an eighteen-inch neck and a forty-six-inch chest, it's real easy to look like a refrigerator with arms. It's real easy to look like you spend your weekends collecting for a loan shark.

It was the smile that changed that inevitable first impression. When Marty Blake smiled, when he opened those dimples and crinkled those lopsided blue eyes, corporate clients forgot to be intimidated. He seemed eager, boyish, and (best of all) subservient. When he began to speak about computer searches and surveillance techniques, he added quiet competence to the equation. The end result (the result he strived for) was, *I can do your shitwork without challenging your macho self-image.*

"Hey, baby, what are you doing up so early? Your appointment isn't until ten o'clock."

Blake, as was his habit when dealing with Rebecca Webber, responded to the tone of her voice, rather than to what she actually said. That husky, sleepy quality didn't mean she wanted to go back to bed. It meant she was horny. Which was exactly why she'd come to him in the first place.

"What I'm doing is preparing my cheeks so they won't scratch *your* cheeks."

"How considerate."

Blake put the razor back in the medicine chest, then turned around. Rebecca Webber, sleep-rumpled, devoid of makeup, was still in-your-face beautiful. Her eyes were huge and dark, knowledgeable and arrogant. They dominated her face, proclaiming the fact that she knew exactly what she was doing, asking a simple question: *Do you?*

Her body asked the same question. In an hour, she'd be at the Sutton Athletic Club. Her personal trainer, Carolyn Tannowitz, would be in attendance. Together, they'd evaluate Rebecca's body the way judges evaluate a show dog. Face, neck, shoulders and arms, breasts, upper and lower abdomen, waist, butt, hips, thighs, and calves. The results never seemed to satisfy Rebecca Webber, but they were perfectly acceptable to Marty Blake.

"Lift that up."

She was wearing a gold camisole over nothing.

"Untie that." She flicked a long elegant finger at the towel around his waist.

Blake tugged at the knot that held the towel, watched Rebecca lift the camisole. She did it slowly, the hint of a smile tugging at the corners of her mouth. Blake stared at the dark patch of hair, the soft, pink flesh, the carefully toned and tanned belly. The camisole caught on the tips of her breasts, pulled them up, let them drop to bounce softly.

"Amazing, just amazing," he admitted.

He took her into his arms, felt her nipples against the wiry hairs on his chest, her thighs encircling his right leg, the impossibly hot, wet flesh against his skin.

"Come into the shower," she said.

Her voice was little more than a hiss, but Marty Blake understood. He allowed himself to be pulled into the shower stall without protest, having long ago realized that Rebecca's powers had their roots in her own desire. When she wanted him this badly, he followed her like a puppy following its master.

In the shower, with the hot water flowing down between their joined bodies, Blake lost all concern for his economic future. When the bar of soap in Rebecca's hand bumped along the ridges of his spine, when it plunged between his buttocks, his conscious mind shattered. It left his brain to imbed itself in the outermost nerves of his flesh. He dropped to his knees, forced his head between her thighs, accepted her grudging orgasm as his own peculiar triumph.

He wanted this emptiness, yearned for it when he heard her voice on the telephone, when she rang his bell. It helped him forget that he wouldn't be seeing her for another week, that she'd go home, if not exactly to her husband, then to her husband's life, the life of a man born to such wealth that his profession was no more than a hobby.

Blake knew that even if William Webber should somehow disappear, he, Marty Blake, son of a cop, could never be part of that life. He also knew that Rebecca would never leave it. That this was all it would ever be about—the feel of his cock inside her, the round balls of her ass beneath his fingers, the smell of her flesh driving him toward oblivion.

THREE

Manhattan Executive Security, Inc. hadn't changed much in a year. The same gray, top-of-the-line, Karastan carpeting covered the floor. Cynthia Barret still sat behind her free-form, glass-topped desk, answering phones, greeting clients. Black-and-white photographs, all cityscapes, all signed, hung in their accustomed places on the wall. Only the stiff, leather couch was new. The old one, as Blake understood it, had been cut to pieces by what cops like to call a "disgruntled" employee.

The employee's name was Vincent Cappolino and his very existence demonstrated the dual nature of Manhattan Executive. On one level, there was Cynthia Barret with her smooth smile, discount designer dresses, cinnamon skin, flashing white teeth. The offices directly behind her desk housed investigators, computer technicians, electronics experts, a forensic accountant, a part-time attorney. Joanna Bardo's office was at the end of the hallway. Furnished with nineteenth-century American antiques, it was, as she liked to say, fit for a CEO.

As far as Manhattan Executive's clientele was concerned (the ones who used the front door, anyway), Joanna was the end of the line. They knew nothing of the back offices. Or of the investigators who hunted bail jumpers for a percentage of the bond. The industry liked to call these detectives *skip tracers*, but Marty Blake preferred the traditional term, "bounty hunter."

Blake had worked with these men when he'd first come into Manhattan Executive as a computer technician. Some, he knew, like Vinnie Cappolino, were as crazy as the criminals they hunted.

"Martin? You can go in now." Cynthia's smile was dazzling, as always. "It's nice to have you back."

"Is that a prophecy, Cyn? Or do you know something I don't?"

Rumor had it that Cynthia Barret and Joanna Bardo were on-again, off-again lovers. Blake knew both well enough to be sure it wasn't true. They *were* good friends, though. Good enough for a notoriously cheap Joanna to pay Cynthia a living wage, roughly twice the going rate for New York receptionists. What Joanna got in return was doglike devotion.

"You better go in, Marty." The smile had disappeared, replaced by a slight widening of already large eyes, a quick downturn at the corners of the mouth.

I'm in trouble, Blake thought, as he made his way down the hall. I'm in trouble, and I don't know why.

But he did know that Joanna liked to think of her business as a family, had actually made the comparison on several occasions. She, of course, was the mother, and she loved all her children, even the roughest, even Vinnie Cappolino who was still employed by Manhattan Executive, despite having destroyed Joanna's two-thousand-dollar couch.

Blake, on the other hand, thought of Manhattan Executive as a medieval court with Joanna Bardo seated firmly on the throne. The despot, not the matriarch, arbitrary, capricious, occasionally ruthless.

"Marty, it's good to see you again."

The smile seemed genuine enough, but then, everything about Joanna Bardo seemed genuine, from the gathered drapes framing the windows, to the Chippendale chairs in front of her desk, to her double-breasted Karl Lagerfeld business suit, to the pearl choker encircling her throat. Everything *seemed* genuine, but Blake knew that half the "antiques" were actually stressed reproductions. That Joanna's suit, shoes, and jewelry came from a garment-center loan shark whose corporate offices were regularly swept for bugs and taps by Manhattan Executive technicians.

"It's nice to be home." If Joanna wanted to be rid of him, Blake was determined to make it as hard as possible.

"Sit down, Marty. Have a cup of coffee."

As if by magic, Cynthia Barret, bearing Manhattan Exec's top-of-the-line coffee service, appeared in the doorway.

"That's bad," Blake said, as soon as they were alone. He pointed to the tray, then sat down.

"Why do you say that?"

"Because I'm not a CEO. Because I'm not even a senior vice president. Because you didn't offer me a mug and let me fill it myself."

Blake watched Joanna compose her features. She hadn't changed much. The same slightly protruding Mediterranean eyes, with their dark, arching brows, dominated a straight nose, cupid's-bow mouth, and small, sharp chin. Set in a narrow frame, her doe-eyed, vulnerable face appeared soft and weak. Which was a big joke to Blake, who knew that carefully maintained expression masked a sharp, straight-for-the-jugular intelligence. He'd seen Joanna in defense of her realm, her queendom, her subjects. Seen times when she showed all the vulnerability of a cornered wolverine.

"When you haven't been somewhere for more than a year, you become a special visitor."

Blake shrugged, stalled for time. Wondering if she'd been hurt by his neglect. If he was dealing with nothing worse than a bruised ego.

"The thing of it is, Joanna, I came within a yard of going to jail for ten years, within an inch of losing my license forever. So, I decided to do a Caesar's wife bit. You know—above suspicion." He gave her the crooked smile, but she didn't buy it. Her expression remained neutral, remote.

"And that's why you decided to drive a . . . a taxicab?"

"I had to eat."

"With your background, you could have found something in the computer field. Even if it was just data processing. You could have found something." She shook her head decisively. "Hell, Marty, you could have worked here. With *our* computers. I needed you."

"You're accusing me of disloyalty?" It was like being told the sky was green. "In case you've forgotten, Joanna, I was the one who kept your ass out of jail."

"I know that, Marty, but . . ."

"Then act like it."

". . . but it's not that simple."

"The Attorney General thought it was *that* simple. He was ready to cut me loose altogether." Blake was near to losing it. He sat back in the chair, crossed his legs, took a deep breath. "I know you would have given me some kind of a job, if I'd asked for it, but they play a lot of funny games back in that computer room. You bill your clients for those games, remember? As for me, with the AG looking over my shoulder, I figured it was best to stay away. Give the powers-that-be a chance to forget Marty Blake."

"But, a *taxicab*?" Her fingers went to the pearls around her throat, caressed them for a moment. "You could have done better."

"Did it offend you?" Maybe she was pissed because he hadn't maintained the corporate image demanded of Manhattan Executive investigators. Maybe she was just running from the fact that her father had spent all forty years of his working life in the Fulton Fish Market.

"You could have done better," she repeated.

"Hey, we're in the middle of a recession. I paid the rent and bought the groceries while I killed time. It's not like I didn't know what I was doing; I drove a cab every summer all through college. Let me tell you something, Joanna. In fact, let me tell you two somethings: first, I can't punch a clock any more. It's too depressing. Second, I can't have a boss hanging on my shoulder. I have to be out in the field. Driving kept me on the street, which, under the circumstances, was the best I could do. You understand?"

Suddenly, Blake realized that she'd won. Without his knowing quite how, she'd put him on the defensive when logic demanded the reverse. Once again, as he had many times before, he found himself envying her premeditation. Blake liked to think of himself as an analytical type, but compared to Joanna Bardo, he was more like an ape trying to be human.

"I'm sorry to hear that. Because if your plan included stepping back into your old shoes, it's not going to be that simple."

She lifted the cup, brought it to her lips, a gesture at once utterly precise and utterly feminine. Her eyes gave nothing away, not a single thing. Blake, fumbling for his own cup, remembered that Joanna had once been a role model for a twenty-one-year-old computer technician just out of City College.

Maybe, he thought, that's why this game we're playing is so bitter.

"Keep goin', Joanna. I don't have anything to say. Yet."

"When the accusations against you became public, we lost fifty-five percent of our corporate clientele." She flashed a bitter smile. "I suppose you could say they asserted their own Caesar's-wife defense. 'So sorry, Joanna, but we can't afford to have our glorious corporate image associated with your degraded criminal enterprise.'"

"Or words to that effect?"

"Well, we survived, Marty. Without laying off personnel."

"Got the boys in the back office to work overtime, did you?" As far as Blake could see, there was no other way Manhattan Executive *could* have survived. The only thing bail bondsmen have to protect is money and money doesn't worry about its corporate image.

"It was a group effort. Everybody pulled." She looked down at the polished surface of her desk, shook her head. "We had to send Paul Rosenbaum to Pittsburgh after a rapist. It would have been funny, if we weren't so desperate."

Paul Rosenbaum was Manhattan Exec's forensic accountant. When enterprising executives cooked the books, he was the chef who unraveled the recipe. Blake tried to imagine him slinking through the mean streets of Pittsburgh, pushing his way into crowded biker bars, confronting wired speed freaks with tattooed eyelids.

"Things are better, now." Joanna raised her eyes to meet Blake's. "Partly because you didn't go to trial and partly because people forget. But that doesn't mean we're not treading water. It doesn't mean I can put you back in a front office."

The bottom line. Blake couldn't repress a bitter frown. Joanna's corporate clients had betrayed her and now she was going to betray him.

"So, where do you want to put me, Joanna. In the computer room? Or, maybe in the back with the bounty hunters?"

"The skip tracers," she automatically corrected. At one time, it'd been a standing joke between them. "Understand something, Marty. Your call last week caught me off guard. After a year without a word, I'd just assumed that you'd made other arrangements, maybe gone into business on your own."

"Cut the crap, Joanna. You've never been 'off guard' in your life."

She rose, crossed to the window behind her desk, pulled the curtain aside. The view of Midtown from her eighth-floor Greene Street loft was spectacular. Blake had often wondered why she'd chosen to cover the windows with curtains and the curtains with drapes.

"True or not, it doesn't change the facts. I *can't* put you in a front office."

Blake wanted to get up and smack her. He wanted to show her what would have happened if he'd given in to the AG. If he'd sent Joanna Bardo to prison. He, himself, had spent the worst forty-eight hours of his life in the holding pens at Central Booking. Discovering that his kind of tough didn't amount to shit in a world where men kill other men for a pair of sneakers. Kill them in their sleep.

"You wanna talk about severance pay? As long as you're firing me."

"It doesn't have to come to that." She let the curtain drop, turned to face him. "We might be able to work something out."

Perfect, Blake thought. In the court of a ruling monarch, nothing is ever straightforward. Rituals must be observed, psyches maneuvered. He felt like bowing.

"Something?"

"Take a walk with me."

Blake (following, naturally) noted the rise and fall of Joanna's buttocks with some satisfaction. For all her aristocratic pretensions, she had a peasant's fleshy ass, wide hips, and heavy, rippling thighs.

She led him out of the office and down a short hallway to a door. A door, as Blake well knew, that led to the infamous back offices.

"Look here, Joanna, in case I haven't made it clear, I have no desire to become a bounty hunter."

"Skip tracer."

"Whatever you want to call it. It's too dangerous, too crazy." The sinking feeling in the pit of his stomach announced (to him, at least) the fact that he *would* take it. That he had no real choice in the matter. If Joanna wouldn't accept him, neither would any of the four or five other firms working the elite end of the business. What it boiled down to was the sleaze or another line of work.

"Actually, that's not what I had in mind."

Joanna pushed the door open to reveal a large, very dusty, very empty room. A year ago, it would have been crowded with Joanna's cowboys.

Blake stepped inside, looked around. The smaller offices were empty as well. "I guess it's been longer than I thought."

"I incorporated their function under the name Woodside Investigations and moved the operation out to Queens. Manhattan Executive does their computer work, and bills them for it. That's the only connection."

"It must have been pretty expensive. Didn't you say you were in trouble financially?"

"Vinnie Cappolino and Walter Francis put up most of the money. They own one hundred percent of the stock."

"Sounds like the partnership from hell. Walter's less reliable than Vinnie. How long before one of them self-destructs? Six months? A year?"

"By that time, I won't need them."

Blake took a step back, thinking that it should have been obvious. "Why didn't you just close the operation down? Why the charade?"

"Vinnie, Walter, and all the rest of them have been with me for a long time." She hesitated, reached into her jacket pocket for the cigarettes she'd given up years before. Her hand came out empty, and she looked at it for a moment before turning back to Marty Blake. "Over the last few months, we've begun to do some political consulting. Nothing big; not yet, but the potential is enormous. I don't have to tell you that politicians and political parties are even more image-conscious than our corporate clientele. 'Discreet' is the word they like to use."

"I get the point, Joanna, but, still, why the charade?"

"Because they deserve a chance. Vinnie and Walter. They deserve a chance to make their own mistakes. I owe that to them, and I always pay my debts."

Blake nodded wisely. She was finally getting down to it.

"No markers, Joanna?"

"Debts cloud the future, Marty. Especially if you can't control when, where, and how they're to be repaid."

Blake turned and walked back to Joanna's office, leaving her to trail behind. When they were inside, when he was comfortably seated, he got to the point.

"Repay me, Joanna," he said calmly.

"I don't know that I can ever properly . . ."

"Cut the crap. You're not the queen of fucking England. Just tell me what you have in mind."

She flinched at the obscenity, took a second to gather herself.

"I want you to open your own firm."

"Like good old Vinnie and good old Walter?"

"You're different, Marty. You're stable, educated." She leaned forward, all business. "Let me give you a scenario, then tell me what you'd do. A client calls, a very important client who holds the key to a very important account. He tells you that his sister's husband took off with the kids. 'Nasty divorce; bad situation; Sis can't stop crying; Mom can't live without her grandchildren.' He wants—no, *expects*—you to find the children. What do you do?"

Blake shrugged. You couldn't refuse and you couldn't accept. The matrimonial end of the business was held in even lower repute than bounty hunting.

"Scenario number two." Joanna paused to refill their cups. Without asking, she added a lump of sugar and a small dollop of cream to Blake's, then passed it over. "Councilman Smith calls. His brother, Joe, has been arrested for armed robbery. Joe's lawyer wants to hire a private detective to scare up witnesses, establish an alibi. All very discreet, of course, because Councilman Smith runs on a law-and-order platform. He can't be seen to favor common criminals, related or not. In fact, he's already released a statement declaring his faith in the system."

Blake was tempted to crush Joanna's Limoges cup, just to see her reaction. He could feel his sense of helplessness slowly begin to dissolve, feel the pure elation as it trickled into the vacuum.

Don't show her a fucking thing, he told himself. Not a fucking thing.

"Let me see if I've got this right. You want to feed me your shit-work cases. The ones that are too sordid for Manhattan Executive Security. I'm to become a corporate toilet bowl. That about it?"

Joanna Bardo's small mouth tightened down. Her nostrils flared and her eyes narrowed. She'd had enough and Blake knew it.

"Just spell it out, Joanna," he said quickly.

"I won't ask you to do anything that would jeopardize your license."

"How considerate."

"Naturally, both our computers and our techs will be open to you. At a thirty-percent discount. You repay us when you collect from your client."

"Fifty percent, Joanna. And if I can't collect, you write it off."

"At fifty percent, I'll lose money."

"You can always make it up by adding a few hours to somebody else's bill." Blake didn't bother to mention that Joanna was *already* padding the bills. "And I want access to any surveillance equipment I need. Unless you plan to give me ten thousand dollars to buy my own."

"You can have anything not in use."

Blake put his cup down, leaned forward. He'd been daydreaming about life on his own for a long time (and, of course, Joanna had to know that, had taken it into her calculations), but had never quite found the courage to face the years of struggle. Now, with Manhattan Executive feeding him business while he established his own client base, there didn't seem to be any risk.

"I'll be working out of my apartment at first. You might want to warn your clients not to expect antiques." Blake waited for her to nod agreement before continuing. "And I'll need some sort of a guarantee. In case you can't throw me enough work to keep me in groceries."

"I'll see that you get the work. In fact, I have something for you right now."

"Why am I not surprised?"

This time, Joanna's smile was genuine. Blake could tell by the way she wrinkled her nose. It was the smile of a little girl bringing home a good report card.

"Believe me, Marty. I've been thinking about this for a long time. I feel responsible for you . . . and damned grateful. This is going to work out, I just know it. You've got the independence, the intelligence, the persistence. *And* you can run a spreadsheet. It's perfect."

FOUR

The exterior of the Foley Grill on Spruce Street, shadowed by the stone pillars and spider-web cables of the Brooklyn Bridge, was as unpretentious and nondescript as any neighborhood bar in the outer boroughs of New York. In fact, Marty Blake, looking for the kind of midday watering hole likely to attract a legal superstar like Maxwell Steinberg, walked right past it—twice. Maybe it was the missing *l* in Foley. Or the missing *r* and *i* in Grill. Or the sooty windows, the faded green paint on the narrow door, the beggar panhandling in the entranceway. Whatever, the last thing Blake expected, as he pushed through the door, was a determined maitre d' with an attitude about neckties.

"Sorry, sir, but neckties are required in the Foley Grill." He shook his head (slowly, of course, so as not to disturb his blow-dried hair), and lowered his eyes. "House rule. So sorry."

"What about *him*?" Blake jerked his chin at a tieless man at the bar. "And *him*? And *him*?"

The maitre d' managed a double take worthy of Ralph Kramden reacting to a fat joke. "I'll have to speak to those gentlemen."

Blake smiled politely. "Give me a tie and I'll put it on."

"We have no ties, sir. Did you have a reservation?"

"No reservation." Blake took a minute to count the number of fifteen-hundred-dollar suits scattered about the restaurant. He stopped at twenty, bemused by the reverse snobbery that brought Manhattan's legal elite to a dive like the Foley Grill. The cluster of federal, state, and local courthouses in Manhattan's civic center may have been responsible for the sheer numbers, but these were men (and a few women) who could afford the Four Seasons. And the limousine to get them back and forth.

"Perhaps another restaurant. We have no tables, in any event."

Blake nodded thoughtfully. In Hollywood, the extras would have been movie stars; in Manhattan they were attorneys. Either way, it was about status, about who deserved to bathe in the reflected glory of the gathered celebrities and who did not.

"Oh, I'm not looking for a table." Blake flashed an affable, goofy smile. "And if I go to another restaurant, the fat guy over there, the one with the cheap wig, is gonna be very disappointed. He's expecting me."

The maitre d's mouth squeezed itself into a disapproving pout. "Why didn't you say so?" He sounded like an eight-year-old who'd just been kicked in the ass by the neighborhood bully.

Blake slid a ten-dollar bill into the man's hand, watched his eyes flick downward.

"That's because I don't want to join him right away. I'd like to have a drink at the bar first."

The maitre d', his dignity restored, nodded solemnly. "Go right ahead, sir. And please enjoy your meal."

Meal? Blake knew he'd be lucky to get a beer's worth of time from Maxwell Steinberg. He ordered a cup of coffee, weathered the bartender's sour, disapproving frown, then settled back to study his prospective client. Blake consciously thought of himself as "all things to all people." He'd once described himself (to Joanna Bardo, as it happened) as "shallow, you scratch the surface, all you find is curiosity." It was that lack of a central, rock-ribbed Marty Blake that allowed him to present whatever surface his companion-of-the-moment wanted to see.

So, what did Maxwell Steinberg want to see? Blake watched as the table-hoppers paid court, stopping at Steinberg's table, muttering a few words. Steinberg, forking lobster into his mouth, didn't miss a beat. He didn't ask anyone to sit down, either. The only way to mea-sure the relative importance of the various courtiers was loosely affixed to Max Steinberg's head. The famous dancing wig. It was as if some modern-day alchemist with a poor understanding of economics had deliberately transformed hair into polyester. The wig's soft, straight texture contrasted strongly with the coarse hair curling over Steinberg's ears. The color was off, as well, a faint, graying orange laid over a yellow-white fringe.

But the wig, itself, the *physical* wig, was the least of it. If it had stayed in one place (if he'd bothered to fasten it down) Steinberg would have been just another vain, aging fool. But it didn't sit still, not for a second. It jiggled to the right, then to the left, dropped far back, then slid forward to drape his forehead. Chewing made it shuffle from side to side. Consternation (such as might be reserved for the testimony of an especially damaging prosecution witness) set it to bouncing like spit on a hot grill.

"Hey, guy."

Blake turned to find a cup of coffee sitting on the bar. "Four bucks."

"Thank you for sharing that with me." He handed over a five, left the cup where it was, turned back to watch a young man with a toothy smile and a suit good enough to make his soft, fat body presentable approach the great man. The kid spoke rapidly, but Steinberg didn't look up. The wig was draped over the attorney's forehead, a sure sign of dismissal.

What Steinberg wants, Blake thought, is a tough guy he can push around. No, not push around—manipulate. He has to be on top. Even if being on top ruins him.

After his meeting with Joanna Bardo, Blake had gone directly to Manhattan Exec's computer room, where he'd entered Maxwell Steinberg's name into a data base called NEWSSEARCH. Ten minutes later, he had three articles in his hand, two from newspapers, *The New York Times* and *The Daily News*, and one from *The New York Trial Lawyers' Journal*. The newspaper profiles had dealt with the flamboyant Steinberg, noting that he'd been thrice divorced, twice filed for bankruptcy, once disciplined by the New York Bar Association. The wig had played prominently, of course, but both articles had noted that when the occasion demanded it (when Steinberg, for instance, was eye-to-eye with a jury), the buffoonery dropped away and the real Steinberg emerged, a radiant prince out of a frog's body. The *News* had compared him to Svengali; the more sedate *Times* to Clarence Darrow.

The *Trial Lawyers' Journal*, on the other hand, had paid lip service to the courtroom theatrics, then proceeded to what, in their opinion, really made Steinberg a great trial lawyer. Steinberg, according to the *Journal*, began to battle the moment he took on a client. Meticulously prepared motions flew at judges and prosecutors like confetti at a Broadway parade. Every piece of evidence was challenged with two aims in mind: first, to exclude it from the trial; second, to establish a basis for appeal should his client be convicted. Expert prosecution witnesses were met with Steinberg's own, even more-expert experts. On one particularly memorable occasion, he'd found a Ph.D. from

Oregon willing to swear that lead fragments removed from the brain of a homicide victim might have come from a pencil.

Blake took a deep breath and kicked himself into gear. He put a little bounce into his walk as he crossed the room, a little confident athleticism. He needn't have bothered. Steinberg didn't look up until Blake was standing at his table.

"Mr. Steinberg? I'm Marty Blake."

Steinberg's eyebrows rose, sending the wig back a good two inches.

"*Boychick*, take a seat, please."

A waiter appeared at Blake's elbow, pulled out a chair, even managed a thin smile. Blake sat.

"Oscar, a brandy, please, for my friend, Martin Blake. We're drinking cognac this afternoon, Martin. By way of celebrating. This morning, I got a rapist off the hook. Good for the legend, bad for the world. *L'chayim*."

Blake nodded, took a moment to study the lawyer's face. It was homely, alright, just the way a *Daily News* reporter had described it— unkempt, salt-and-pepper eyebrows overhanging shrewd, black eyes; prominent fleshy nose dominating a thin mouth with a pronounced underbite. Blake made the lawyer for one of those sad kids who'd spent his childhood in the corners of the school yard. Hiding from the bullies, the jocks, the girls.

Oscar snapped his fingers and a second waiter appeared at his elbow. "Hennessy, for Mister Blake, Ryan."

Ryan nodded his understanding and both men walked away, confirming Blake's impression of his own status. He was worth a drink, but lunch was out of the question.

"Martin, you're Irish, yes? Maybe I should dispense with the Yiddish?"

Blake grinned, tapped the table with a forefinger. "Don't tell that to my mother. She's sure that I'm Jewish."

"Your mother's a Jew?" Steinberg's mouth dropped open. "Then you're a Jew. According to the law."

"According to whose law? Jewish law? Jewish law is not my . . ."

Steinberg's eyes narrowed. "According to Nazi law. Hitler law. And it doesn't stop, Martin. You see how the Germans are now? *Auslander raus!* Very nice. If there were still Jews in Germany, it'd be *Juden raus!* Maybe worse." He leaned across the table, touched Blake's sleeve. "In this country, the Jews are lucky. The blacks take the heat for us. But you wait, Martin. Our day will come."

Blake nodded thoughtfully, thinking, I better not tell this clown that my father's mother was German.

The lawyer sat back in his chair. He rubbed his eyes, shook his head slowly. "Do you care that I'm taking my time getting to the point? That I'm *plotzing* along like an old drunk?" He waved off Blake's polite reply. "But if you can't celebrate a victory, you might as well be dead, right? Today, I got a rapist off the hook."

The second waiter, Ryan, reappeared with the Hennessy. Blake took a sip, held it in his mouth for a moment, then swallowed dutifully.

"So, Blake, you know how I know this rapist was a rapist? He tells me, that's how. He comes waltzing into my office and says, 'The cops are looking for me. I committed a rape. Get me off the hook.'"

"Just like that?" Blake looked at his brandy, shuddered, turned back to Steinberg.

"Well, maybe not *exactly* like that. But words to that effect. Told me all about it, every detail."

"So what'd you do."

"Me? I rubbed my thumb across the tips of my fingers. 'Moolah, baby,' I tell him. '*Dinero, gelt.*' He dicks me around for a few minutes, pissing and moaning about his financial problems. 'Slow down a second,' I say. 'I wanna ask you a few questions. First, this woman you raped was your best buddy's girlfriend, right?'

"'Yeah,' he says.

"'And you went to her apartment intending to have sex with her. Whether she liked it or not.'

"'Yeah, well . . . uh.'

"'And she refused and she tried to fight you off. Correct?'

"'Yeah.'

"'And you fucked her anyway.'

"'I don't see what you're gettin' at.'

"'What I'm getting at is this: no discounts for rapists. You want off the hook, you gotta come up with the price of whatever freedom I can arrange.'"

Blake fought a revulsion bordering on nausea. Not every criminal lawyer accepted rape cases, especially from clients as guilty as the one Steinberg had just described.

"Once he understands my position, we have no trouble coming to an understanding. Seventy-five, large, plus expenses, which he gets from his rich daddy. Me, I start throwing money in all directions. I find two big-time MDs who'll swear the vaginal bruising could have come about through normal sex. And she's had plenty of that, been around the block so many times her head spins when she's standing still. The ex-boyfriends are ready to swear she liked it kinky and her being in analysis since she was thirteen isn't gonna help the prosecution's case one bit. Then I start with the evidence which mainly consists of torn underwear. Turns out the letter of transmittal from the duty officer at Midtown South to the forensic laboratories at One Police Plaza can't be found. Boom, out go the panties, out goes the bra. Now, I'm just waitin' for the bastards to blink."

Steinberg leaned forward, tapped Blake's sleeve again. His eyes narrowed to slits. "The cops started by charging my client with rape in the first degree, plus unlawful imprisonment. Add it up, it comes out twenty-nine to life, assuming the judges runs the two maximums consecutively which is exactly what the DA says'll happen if we force a trial. Meanwhile, because the prosecutor, in her infinite mercy, doesn't wanna put this poor girl through the ordeal of testifying, if we plead guilty to rape in the second degree, my client will get five years and do three of them.

"So, we go to the motions and I throw so much paperwork at the judge he nearly poops his pants. I challenge everything but the toilet paper in the mens' room. The judge doesn't even bother to set a trial date. He doesn't know when he'll make his ruling. He hates my guts and he makes it clear that his dislike extends to my client. What he doesn't know is that a client like mine, a middle-class kid with a big ego, can't see the difference between five years and twenty-five years. His knees shake if he thinks about five *minutes*. So, when I tell him, 'Relax kid, you're not gonna do a day,' he stands pat.

"Next deal: rape in the third degree. My client gets three years, does one, and passes the time in a special section they got reserved for sexual rehabilitation. I can remember the ADA telling me this as if it happened ten minutes ago. It was like she was biting off her tongue, that's how much she hated me. 'I don't think so,' I tell her. 'I haven't been in court for a long time. I need the action. Let's see how it turns out.'

"How it turns out is they finally give it up. Two days before the trial, they offer my client sexual misconduct, a misdemeanor. Three hundred hours of community service and two years of therapy. *No* time. Just like I promised."

FIVE

Blake shifted in his seat, toyed with an errant dessert fork. Wondering exactly what it was Steinberg wanted. What it is you're supposed to say when a guy you just met informs you that he spends his days emptying septic tanks with a soup spoon.

Gee, that's wonderful. And it's very nice of you to describe it lump by lump.

Meanwhile, the lawyer, his head cocked to the left, was staring at him through one narrowed eye. As if expecting a response.

Blake finally raised his snifter, managed a wink, reminded himself that he didn't have to take this job.

"*L'chayim*," he said. Let the fat prick figure out what *that* meant.

Steinberg straightened up. "*L'chayim*. By all means. To life. Because that's just what it is for a criminal lawyer. That's what life is. One sleazebag after another. And the more successful you get, the worse *they* get. Loan sharks, pimps, wise guys, rapists." Steinberg leaned forward, but this time he didn't tap Blake's sleeve. He grabbed Blake's wrist and squeezed hard. "One day, about four years ago, I'm sitting in my office. It was right after another victory. A victory with a celebration, like this one. I wouldn't say I was drunk, but I was feeling cocky. You know, like the prizefighter, John. L. Sullivan, who used to walk into bars and shout, 'I can lick any man in the house.'"

Blake pulled his arm back, started to say something, finally decided that discretion was, indeed, the better part of valor. He told himself to wait, that Steinberg would get down to business soon enough. It wasn't like they were about to do lunch.

"So, I'm sitting there," Steinberg continued, "feeling no pain, when I suddenly get this notion in my head: How many killers have I saved? How many dead bodies in my filing cabinets, on my balance sheet, in my tax returns? Could I fill my house with ghosts? Put a victim in every room? Under the beds? In the shower? The refrigerator? The medicine chest?"

"You're nuts, Steinberg." Blake shook his head in what he hoped was admiration. He sipped at his brandy, noting the onset of a very predictable recklessness. If he kept going, he'd pass through that recklessness, pass into belligerence. He put the glass down, resolved not to pick it up again.

"First," Steinberg continued, ignoring Blake's remark, "I say to myself, murderers only, but then I decide to count *any* homicide. I mean, to the victim it's all the same, right? So, I go to the filing cabinets and I thumb my way through. Any homicide where I'm sure my client was guilty, which happens to be *all* of them, I make a little mark on my fifty-percent Egyptian-cotton stationery. When I get to twenty-five marks, I give it up. The last client's name is Minelli, a wholesale butcher. He chopped up his business partner with a cleaver. Him, I couldn't get off the hook. Get it? The hook? The *meat* hook?"

Steinberg paused, sat back in chair. Blake knew he was expected to force a polite laugh, but he couldn't even manage a smile.

"Now, listen close, Blake, because I'm getting to the point. Right there, sitting on the carpet with the files spread around me, I make a decision. The next day, I start spreading the word: Give me an innocent man who's been convicted of a crime and I'll get that man out of prison."

"What, no innocent women?" Blake noted the wig begin to slide forward. A bad sign. "Just kidding, Mister Steinberg."

"Max, please. If we're going to have a relationship, it should be Max." The wig slowed, finally stopped. "What I'm getting at is this: I've got a lot of experience with innocent people who've been *convicted* of a crime they didn't commit. What I *don't* have is experience with an innocent person who pleaded guilty and waived his right to appeal. You know what I'm saying here, Martin? You know about trials?"

"Maybe you better refresh my memory." The truth was that Blake had never worked for a criminal lawyer.

"Okay, first you get busted, then you get arraigned, then you get indicted. That's all rubber-stamp, if you take my meaning. The client's first chance to fight back comes when both sides make pre-trial motions. By this time, you know what the prosecution's got, at least in the way of physical evidence, eyewitness identification, etc. And what you wanna do is get as much of it thrown out as possible. Are you with me so far?"

"All the way."

"Good. Now, this particular defendant, whose name is William Sowell, happens to have an IQ of 68. When the cops pick him up, they tell him they're just trying to clear his name, but they need his cooperation. That's the kiss of death, Martin. When they say they're just trying to clear your name, run for your fucking life. But what does this kid know? He's homeless; he's retarded; he's a drunk. Seventy-two hours later he gives them a statement. He *confesses*.

"Martin, you could take this to the bank—if *I* had been Billy Sowell's lawyer, that confession would've been so much toilet paper. Meanwhile, the kid's Legal Aid lawyer writes a brief that's almost incoherent and the judge lets the confession in. Likewise for a photo array and a lineup so biased they wouldn't get past a freshman law student. But the kicker is the hypnosis. Think of it, Martin, all the prosecution has is Sowell's confession and an eyewitness who puts him next to the body . . ."

"That's *all*?"

The wig began to move forward again. "Joanna told me you were experienced. Forgive me for saying this, Martin, but you seem a bit naive."

"I'm sorry, Max. It doesn't really matter, anyway."

"Why is that?"

"I'm an investigator, not a cop. What I do is report what I find, one way or the other." What he didn't add was that his field experience ran to undercover work in corporate computer rooms. That he had no street experience whatever. "Just go ahead. I'm not making any judgments here."

"Look, this kid has a mental age of ten years. The cops interrogated him for seventy-two hours. There's *no* physical evidence connecting him to the crime. They took samples of his blood and his hair, they took fibers from his overcoat, they tested his clothes for bloodstains— *nothing*. I ask you, Martin, if you were a judge, would you let a jury hear that confession?"

"No," Blake admitted. "Not if the kid's retarded. I wouldn't."

"Good. Now let's take the magic witness. It starts with her walking her dog at three o'clock in the morning. She comes out of her building and sees a man standing next to a car which turns out to have a body in the backseat. Two hours later, she describes the man like this—dark, curly hair, wearing an expensive overcoat. That's it. Somehow, between that first description and her testimony before the Grand Jury, she becomes one hundred percent convinced that Billy Sowell, a homeless drunk with a four-inch scar under his left eye, is the man she saw. The man she said she couldn't identify two hours after the original incident. You beginning to get the point, Martin?"

Blake looked at the brandy, then back at Steinberg. "You've got my attention here. Keep going."

"Okay, now to the kicker. To the *mystery*. Three weeks after the incident, the witness, one Melody Mitchell, undergoes hypnotic regression. You know what that is?"

"That's where you go back in time, right?"

"Exactly. Now, the cops have been using regression for a long time, decades, at least. And what the courts have discovered is that hypnotized individuals are very suggestible. You can put things in their heads; it's that simple. Most of the time, the prosecutor not only can't get the hypnosis admitted, he loses the witness forever. In fact, most of the time, the prosecutor doesn't even try. Especially in New York, where the judges are very strict about evidence."

Steinberg paused for a moment. He picked up his fork, toyed with a small chunk of now-cold lobster, popped it into his mouth. "But this judge admitted the whole ball of wax. And I'm not talking about some law-and-order freak. I'm talking about Judge John McGuire, who cut his teeth at the American Civil Liberties Union. John McGuire who has eyes for the federal bench. It's beyond belief, Martin. Beyond belief."

Blake looked at his hands, wondering what to do with them. He was at the point where even the Hennessy looked good. The cigarettes he'd given up two years before beckoned to him like the ghost of his first lover.

"You talking about a fix? Some kind of political pressure?" He picked up the snifter, drained it, set it back down.

"Hey, you're the detective, Martin. I'm saying what happened shouldn't have happened. And that's not the end of it. A couple of weeks before Billy Sowell's trial date, the prosecution offers him a deal. Manslaughter in the first degree with a six-year minimum. Remember, the original charge is murder in the second degree, plus attempted rape. The murder alone carries a mandatory twenty-five. Looks pretty good, right, because under normal conditions, you can appeal the motions while you're doing your time. The twist here is that the deal only goes down if Sowell waives his right to appeal. Which, on the advice of his lawyer, he does."

"From what you're saying, Max, it sounds like his lawyer oughta be taken out and shot. Or maybe you think he was part of the fix."

Steinberg grunted his disapproval. "You're putting the cart before the horse." He leaned forward, dropped his elbows to the table, dropped his chin into his hands. "Right now, the only basis for appeal is Billy Sowell's competency. What I'm gonna say is that he was too stupid to plead guilty, that he was so retarded that he couldn't appreciate the consequences of his decision. What I'd *like* to do is add that his attorney was also incompetent. Maybe he was a drunk or on cocaine. Or maybe he was having marital problems, or under investigation for a crime of his own. It doesn't matter. What the Appellate Court's gonna need is an excuse, a reason to grant Billy Sowell a trial. If you can make the kid's lawyer part of that excuse, you've already done your job."

"Yeah, well I don't see any problem here. I can work up a background check in a few days. If there's anything there . . ."

Steinberg shook his head from side to side. The wig, a half-beat behind, followed obediently. "That's not enough, Martin. I want you a hundred percent committed to getting this kid out of prison. Losing is not on my agenda. Likewise for giving it the old college try. You follow the trail wherever it leads. Remember this, Blake: Steinberg doesn't back down. Memorize it." He reached beneath the table, retrieved an attaché case, passed it across to Blake. "It's all in there—the cops' investigation, the Grand Jury testimony, the pre-trial briefs. Today's Tuesday. Friday morning, you've got an appointment with Billy Sowell in Columbia State Prison. I'll be in my office on Saturday morning. We'll talk."

Blake smiled at the dismissal. "Max," he said, "if I understand you correctly, you're doing this for nothing. *Pro bono.*"

"Right."

"Well, Max, don't take this the wrong way, but I'm not in the charity business. I can't *afford* to be in the charity business."

"I'm covering your fee. Assuming it's reasonable."

"What it is, Max, is three hundred dollars a day, plus expenses. By the time I get into your office on Saturday, you're gonna owe me a thousand dollars."

SIX

Bela Kosinski pried a green plastic swizzle stick out of a puddle of beer and stirred his drink. He did it slowly, solemnly, a half-smile on his face. The performance was part of a running joke between himself and Ed O'Leary, the bartender. The joke being that the transparent, tasteless, odorless liquid in the glass didn't need mixing. It was pure vodka.

"Stirred," Kosinski said, affecting a mangled British accent, "not shaken."

O'Leary managed a perfunctory grunt, then turned back to the Yankees, who were down by four runs. The bartender, as Bela Kosinski knew, couldn't have cared less about the Yankees. Or the Mets, or the Giants, or the Knicks. Ed supplemented his meager salary and the grudging tips left by the regulars at Cryders Bar & Grill with a little bookmaking. And "little" was the right way to describe O'Leary's handle. A fin here, a sawbuck there—not enough to interest the wise guys who worked the Whitestone area in northern Queens. Just a few extra bucks to, as Ed liked to say, "keep the wife in curlers."

A sudden, tinny cheer belched from the TV set, followed by a chorus of groans from the Cryders regulars. The Yankees were staging a typical late-inning rally. The regulars, or so Bela Kosinski, drawing on twenty years' of police experience, surmised, had backed the Red Sox. Perhaps they'd been counting their money.

He turned back to his vodka, recalling the years when he'd loved the juice, more years when he'd hated it, even what he'd come to call "the decade of sobriety." Now, he was neutral, believing there was no life without it and that was the end of that. That was *all* she wrote.

But then he'd once believed the same thing about the job, about the NYPD. He'd believed that once he left the job, his life would literally stop. He'd been wrong about that, because here he was, six weeks retired and still ticking. Like a time bomb.

He took a drink, felt the fire trickle into his belly, rebound up into his throat. Without thinking, he fished a roll of Tums out of his jacket and popped one into his mouth.

"No more water," he said to his nearest neighbor, Emily Caruso. "The fire next time."

Emily turned her beery breath on the ex-cop. "Looka this shit."

Bela Kosinski glanced around the bar, noting the scattered tables and chairs, the bowling machine, the broken jukebox.

"Looks like home to me," he announced.

"I'm talkin' about that kid at the end of the bar. Only he's too old to be a kid." She tipped a half-empty Bud up to her mouth, drained it in two quick swallows. "He's drinking Moussy."

Kosinski watched her larynx bob twice, then come to a stop. He listened to the reflexive belch. Thinking, this is where I'm going to spend the rest of my life. This is where I'm going to die. And the sooner, the better.

"So what?"

"Moussy, you jerk. Nonalcoholic beer. What's a guy doin' in a fuckin' bar if he don't wanna get loaded?"

Kosinski, his attention caught, looked down the length of the bar. Unlike Emily Caruso, he believed there was a place for nonalcoholic beer, a place in some Manhattan singles' bar. But not at Cryders. Kosinski was surprised that Cryders even *had* a bottle of Moussy in its ancient cooler. Maybe the jerk had brought it with him.

"Whatta ya think, Emily? Ya think he brought it with him?"

Emily Caruso laughed, then choked, then lit a cigarette. "You wanna take me home tonight?"

"Lemme think about it." Kosinski kept his voice neutral. Just as if Mrs. Caruso wasn't a seventy-plus great-grandmother. Just as if he had any interest whatever in sexual matters.

He lifted his glass, wishing that just this once he could really get drunk. Get happy or stupid or belligerent, the way he used to when he was a kid sneaking shots from his father's bottle. Nowadays, all he got was straight.

"Bell, you ready for another one?"

Kosinski looked up at the sound of his nickname. O'Leary was smiling.

"The Yankees winning?"

"They're even up."

"Would ya take a tie here, Ed?" The Yankee relief staff was notoriously weak.

"Forget it, Bell. No ties in baseball. Somebody's gotta win."

Kosinski nodded at his glass. "Fill the fucker." He waited while the bartender poured the ritual double, then raised the glass. "Who's the asshole at the end of the bar?"

"The one drinking the goddamned Moussy," Emily Caruso added.

"Never seen him before. Never served a Moussy before."

"I'm surprised you even carry that crap."

"We don't. The distributor left it about a year ago. No charge. Part of a promotion."

Kosinski turned his attention back to the man at the end of the bar, working him in typical cop fashion. He saw a white male, approximately thirty years of age, brown hair and eyes, light complexion, wearing a very loose short-sleeved shirt that tried, but failed to hide a weight lifter's chest. That failed to hide forearms damn near the size of Bell Kosinski's neck. Just as Kosinski finished his inventory, the man smiled and raised the bottle of Moussy.

Jeez, Kosinski thought, maybe my eyes are goin' now. Do I know this guy?

He looked closer, decided that it didn't matter whether he did or not, because the the jerk was already off the stool and walking toward him.

Inspired by a purely alcoholic whim, Kosinski stuck his thumbs into his ears, fanned the palms of his hands out, waggled his fingers. Much to his delight, the weight lifter stopped, tilted his head to the left.

What he looks like, Bell Kosinski decided, is a confused bulldog.

"I don't get it," the bulldog said.

"I'm tryin' to look moosy," Kosinski responded, deadpan.

"I still don't get it."

"Horns. Like on a fuckin' moose."

"You mean antlers, right?"

"Whatever."

"Well, I can accept the impression; it's the point that's giving me a problem."

"The beer, jerk." Kosinski noted the flinch, the underlying control, the funny lopsided smile as it emerged. "Moosy? Moussy? Get it?"

"Oh, sure."

"So, what could I do for you?"

"Are you Bela Kosinski?"

"The one and only."

"My name is Marty Blake. I'm a private investigator. Can I have a few minutes of your time?"

"You buyin'? Think twice before you make me an answer, because if you're buyin', I'm drinkin'."

"Does that mean if I'm not buying, you're *not* drinking?"

"It should only be." Kosinski turned to the bartender. "Keep 'em comin'. Eddie. We're gonna take a table."

He led the way, aware of his steady walk, the ease with which he controlled the rickety chair as he sat. Deciding the guy was all right. Controlled nasty, which meant they had something in common.

"So whatta ya want, Marty Blake?" He drained his glass, signaled to Ed O'Leary who was already crossing the room. "And how'd you find me?"

"I'm leavin' the bottle, Bell," O'Leary announced. "I can't be comin' every two minutes. The game's in extra innings."

Kosinski watched the bartender's back for a moment, then turned to Blake.

"So?" He refilled his glass, emptied it, then refilled it again.

"You asked me two questions?"

"True. And if you should take any longer to make an answer, I'm liable to forget what they were." He put on his best cop stare and drove it into Marty Blake's eyes.

"Why I'm here is simple enough. I'm here about a kid named Billy Sowell. How I found you is a bit more complicated."

"I like complicated. Remember, I used to be a detective."

"Okay." Blake took a deep breath. "I'll make it as simple as I can. I was reading the police file on the murder of Sondra Tillson. You were in charge of the case right up until Billy Sowell came into the picture, then you disappeared. That caught my attention, so what I did was use my computer to access a data base called the National Credit Information Network and give it your name and your occupation. A minute and a half later, I had all the header information on a credit-card application you made in 1979. I . . . ."

"*Header* information. What the fuck is *header* information?"

"Look, what I *can't* get—legally, at least—is a record of your actual transactions. When you used the card, what you bought, how you paid—like that. Everything else—the header information—is open to anybody who knows where to look. That includes your name, address, and phone number, among other things. What I did, when I called and you didn't answer, was enter your name, address, and phone number in a crisscross data base. Six minutes later, I printed out a list of your twenty closest neighbors, along with *their* addresses and phone numbers. Then I let my fingers do the walking. You know something, Mr. Kosinski? You have a neighbor who hates your guts. Told me you *live* in this bar."

Bell Kosinski, as he tried to digest the information being tossed in his face, felt his brain snap off like someone had thrown an electric switch. He was dimly aware of thoughts moving in and out of what should have been his consciousness, but they floated along at their own pace, like shadows in a dense fog. He couldn't stop them long enough to take a look, couldn't slow them down or speed them up.

When he came out of it, when something flicked the switch back on, Kosinski, who'd been through it before, was aware of the lapse in time. The question was how long and the answer was staring him in the face. The private eye (Blake, he remembered) was looking at him expectantly, but without alarm, so he couldn't have been out very long. Not this time.

"You investigated me?" It was the first coherent response he could make to what he actually remembered. He waited a moment, but when Blake didn't respond, added, "and now you're throwin' it up to me. Now you're *braggin'* about it. I hope you don't mind my sayin' so, but your bedside manner could use a little work."

Blake's smile remained in place, but his eyes sharpened. "What happened, Kosinski, is I got bored. Forty-eight hours reading Grand Jury testimony, police reports, autopsy reports? It could happen to anyone. Now, some people relax with a glass of vodka and some people relax with a computer. Me, I belong to the latter group, so just for the hell of it I bet myself ten bucks that I could run you down inside of three hours. That was at seven-thirty. It's now ten o'clock."

"Congratulations."

"Thank you. But like I said, it was only a whim. I didn't really expect you to answer my questions, but I didn't expect you to shit all over me, either. In fact, when you stuck out your fingers, my first reaction was to break them. One at a time."

Kosinski picked up his glass, spun it between his palms. "It's a good think you didn't. A neighborhood bar like this? You'd be lucky to get out of here alive."

"I did think of that." Blake dropped the smile. "You wanna talk about William Sowell?"

"What makes you think I know anything about it?"

"It was your case."

"One of how many thousands I handled while I was on the job?"

"A retarded kid was framed for a murder he could not have committed. You don't forget that."

"What makes you think he was framed?"

"You wanna start with the car?"

"Sure."

"The only blood in the vehicle was found on the backseat underneath the victim, whose throat was slashed. If she'd been killed in the front seat, then pushed into the back, which is the way it went down according to Sowell's confession, the inside of that car would've been *covered* with spray. It was not, therefore she was dead before she was put into the car. But you know all this, right Kosinski? You know there was no blood found *around* the car, either, which meant the car was driven after the body was put into it. Billy Sowell can't drive. He can't read well enough to fill out the application for a license. So, again, let me ask you—do you wanna talk about William Sowell?"

"I don't know anything about William Sowell." Kosinski picked up his glass, drained it, set it back down. "I wasn't there when it happened."

"You were there when his name first came up. According to the report you filed on December fifteenth, you and Detective Brannigan were in the squad room when you received an anonymous tip informing you that Billy Sowell killed Sondra Tillson."

"Is that what it said? It said I took the call?" Kosinski kept his voice neutral, but he was a good deal less than happy about his name being placed on a phony DD5 without his permission. Suppose he'd been called to testify? A little perjury might be good for the soul, but not when it's involuntary.

"You're telling me you didn't?"

"I'm not telling you anything. What's important here is that *you're* telling me. Telling me things like who hired you. Who's paying you. By the way, you got any ID? A business card'll do."

Blake, Kosinski noted, wasn't smiling any more. His face was serious, composed. As if he knew something Kosinski didn't. "I'm working for Billy Sowell's lawyer, an attorney named Max Steinberg."

"I thought the kid took a plea."

"A minor inconvenience." Blake tugged a card out of his wallet and passed it over.

"This Max Steinberg, is he the Max Steinberg with the fucked-up wig?"

"The same."

"Now, that's very interesting. Tell me, Blake, who's paying Steinberg?"

"Nobody. It's a labor of love."

"Pardon me?"

"He's doing the work *pro bono*. A matter of conscience is what he told me."

Kosinski looked down at his hands for a moment. He told himself it was time to get out, to get rid of Private Investigator Martin Blake before he said the wrong thing, got himself into the kind of trouble he didn't need. After all, who (or what) was Billy Sowell to Bell Kosinski? Why should Bell Kosinski give two shits about a homeless *retard* who got himself caught in a hurricane? These things happen in the course of a career and if you've got half a brain, you forget about them.

"Tell me something, Blake, you have a lot of experience with criminal cases?" Kosinski noted the quick blush, smiled inwardly. "That's what I thought. Well, you seem like a halfway decent kid, so I'm gonna tell ya somethin' here, somethin' you should already know. Watch your back at all times. At *all* times."

"You're admitting that Billy Sowell was framed?"

"What're you, taping this? Man, I'll shoot your ass right here in the bar." Kosinski felt a small tremor in the back of his neck, recognized it as fear. Which seemed altogether strange, considering that he was retired and his pension guaranteed. Considering that he fully expected to drink himself to death before he collected any significant amount of that pension.

Blake unbuttoned his shirt, taking his time about it. His chest was hairy, but not hairy enough to hide a tape recorder.

"No bug, Kosinski." He was smiling again. "Like I said, I came here because I was bored."

"Is that right? Well, I hope the trip improved your mood, 'cause I'm gonna end this right now. I was on vacation when Brannigan picked Sowell up. By the time I got back, the case was in the hands of the prosecutors. What happened in between is none of my business. None of yours, either."

"Is it Billy Sowell's business?" Blake paused momentarily, then continued when he got no response. "Because I'm driving upstate to see him tomorrow morning. If you like, I could ask him. Maybe he *likes* being in prison."

SEVEN

It was just a little past midnight when Bell Kosinski, after waving good-bye to the assembled regulars, stepped into the middle of a torrential downpour. He froze in surprise for a moment, still holding the door, and let the rain wash over him. Then he turned back to Ed O'Leary.

"The heat's breakin', Ed. It's gonna cool off." He noted O'Leary's indifferent shrug, understood that weather was a great irrelevancy in the bartender's world, that the faithful attended despite hurricanes and blizzards.

He let the door go and started off to walk the few blocks to his Fourteenth Avenue apartment, the one above the Cheery Day Laundromat. He wasn't usually given to nostalgia, but on this night, prodded by the sudden appearance of Marty Blake, his thoughts wandered back to his earliest days on the job. Days when, his honeymoon barely finished and a child on the way, he'd been entirely sober.

Once again, he was viewing the neon rainbow of nighttime New York through the smeared, greasy windshield of an RMP. (Only they didn't call them RMPs then. Back in 1969, they were still patrol cars.) His partner, Johnny Dedham, a ten-year veteran with the eyes of an eagle, tapped him on the shoulder and said, "Check out the two mutts on the corner, Bell. The ones in front of the bar."

Kosinski did as he was told, peering out between wiper strokes. The men were arguing. Their gesticulating arms, in quick, constant motion, jerked from streak to streak.

"Hit the siren, Bell. See if we can shut this off without getting out of the car."

It was already too late, but neither of them realized it.

The two men were silhouetted against a window outlined in violent red neon. Neon that, blurred by the rain, blurred again by the greasy windshield, changed the color of the blood, so that what Bell Kosinski saw, when mutt number one sliced mutt number two's throat, was a cloud of black smoke.

"What the fuck?"

"He cut him. He cut him, you idiot. Shit. Now I'm gonna have to get wet."

Kosinski moved fast, leaving his partner to worry about the wounded man. Propelled by adrenalin, he ran without fatigue, his gun drawn, his nightstick clenched in his free hand. Wanting the perp to come at him with the knife. Wanting an excuse to shoot.

But he didn't get it. When he finally came down that last alleyway, his own breath whistling in his ears, the perp, instead of leaping at him from a fire escape, was sitting with his back against a locked door. He was crying.

When Bell Kosinski came back to the present, he found himself staring at his own reflection in the darkened window of the Whitestone Unisex Barber Shop. The rain had flattened his blond hair, plastering it against his skull. Making it seem, he decided after a moment, as if he'd shaved his head.

What I look like, he thought, what with the nose and all, is a toy Kojack. Except that I don't have the trench coat. Except that I'm standing here in my shirtsleeves, freezing my ass off.

He put his head into the wind and walked down the block. The rain was nearly horizontal now, pushing into his face and eyes despite his bent head. Which was why he didn't see the figure in the doorway until it actually called out to him.

"Hey, Bell, I been lookin' for you."

Kosinski reached beneath his arm for the gun he no longer carried. He was puzzled for a moment, then recognized his old partner, Tommy Brannigan, standing in the shadows. Brannigan was sporting his shit-eating grin. The one that meant he wanted something.

"This a social call, Tommy?" Kosinski stepped under the canopy of Cho's Chinese Restaurant. Rain drummed on the canvas, dripped down through several small tears in the fabric.

"Jeez, Bell, you don't change. Still as hostile as ever."

The grin, much to Kosinski's amazement, actually widened. "What could I say, Tommy? It's my nature."

"So, how ya been?"

"Just great. I only been off the job a few weeks and already I found a new rhythm for my life. How 'bout you, Tommy? I heard you're workin' downtown, heard you made Detective, First. Now, if you could only pass the sergeant's exam, you'd have a real future."

The smile disappeared for just a minute, then re-formed. "Look, Bell, I didn't come here to trade insults. I . . ."

"That's too bad. Trading insults is the only thing I'm really good at." Kosinski stared at Brannigan's dark, curly hair. The rain, instead of plastering it against his skull, instead of making him look like an aging television detective, lifted it into a rich, dark halo. "And I hate your hair, too."

"What?"

"Nothing. Just tell me what you want, Tommy. I'm freezin' my ass off."

Brannigan took a deep breath, let it out. "Bell, you remember a mope named Billy Sowell?"

"Sowell? Lemme think for a minute. Oh, yeah, I remember. A *ret*ard. He went down for killing a broad over by Gramercy Park."

"That's the one."

"Didn't have much to do with that, Tommy. If I recall, I was on vacation when you picked him up."

"That's true. I won't argue with that. But you and me were partners on the first stage of the investigation. We caught the squeal."

Kosinski didn't answer immediately. He listened to the rain, watched drops of water zigzag down the window behind Brannigan's halo. Cars passed behind him. Strangely, he could hear tires hissing over the wet roadway, but the engines, muffled by the rain pounding on the canopy, were entirely inaudible.

"Somebody's making noises like they wanna reopen the case," Brannigan said. "People are gonna be nosing around. Asking questions."

"People? Somebody?"

"Yeah, look, there's something I gotta tell you. Something I should've told you a long time ago."

"You mean about putting my name on a bullshit five?" Kosinski paused, but Brannigan chose not to reply, though the smile was entirely gone. "Ya did somethin' really stupid, Tommy. But, then, smart was never your strong point."

"I had to protect the captain's informant."

"Fuck the informant. What you were doing was protecting the

captain. What was his name again? Oh yeah, Grogan. You were protecting Captain Grogan and you're still protectin' him. Only he's not a captain any more, is he?" Kosinski saw the truth in Brannigan's furious eyes. Saw the truth and laughed out loud. "So, what'd he make, Tommy? Inspector? Deputy Chief? You wouldn't by any chance be workin' under him, would ya?"

"You're a drunk, Kosinski. A miserable, fucking drunk."

"Clever choice of words, Tommy. Perceptive as hell."

Kosinski never saw Brannigan move. He didn't feel any pain, either. But there was no other way he could be sitting in the rain with the taste of diluted blood on his tongue unless he'd been sucker-punched.

"I tried to do this nice, Bell. I knew it was hopeless, but I tried."

"Thanks for the consideration." Kosinski struggled to his feet.

"What I'm telling you here—*telling*, not asking—is don't break the line. Don't sell out the job. Remember who you are and do what's right."

Kosinski wanted to say that he was retired and he didn't owe the job a goddamned thing, but Tommy Brannigan was already standing beside the Dodge sedan parked at the curb.

"Hey, Tommy, does 'what's right' mean putting a retarded kid in a prison cell?"

Brannigan pulled away without bothering to answer. Kosinski watched the sedan's blurred tail lights for a moment, trying to think of something else to say, then plodded off toward home.

Home, for Bell Kosinski, was a single, large room with a minikitchen at one end and a bathroom at the other. It was one of two above the Cheery Day Laundromat, the other being occupied by the laundromat's owner, a Mexican named Miguel Escobar who was saving to bring his family to New York.

Kosinski picked his way across the room, skirting the unmade bed, the ratty armchairs, the scarred formica table with its two rickety chairs. He opened the refrigerator and pulled a bottle of Smirnoff out of the freezer. His hand stuck to the cold glass, a sensation he some-how found comforting.

"Fire in the hole!" he shouted, putting the bottle to his mouth, sucking the fluid down.

And it *was* fire, no doubt about it. The vodka burned its way to his ulcer, then lay in a smoldering puddle.

Kosinski ignored the pain, counting on the vodka to numb all unpleasant side effects. That was why he drank in the first place.

He got up, crossed to the bureau, retrieved his .38, and carried it to the table.

"Haven't played this game in a long time," he muttered. "I missed it."

Kosinski popped out the cylinder, let the cartridges drop into his left hand, laid the gun on the table. Back when he was still a tough guy, when he was still sober, he'd really loved this weapon. There was a power to it, a power to holding life and death in his hands that had nothing to do with his own cowboy self-image. The power was in the weapon itself. He hadn't felt that power in a long time.

"Maybe," he said out loud, "that's because I never shot anybody. If I'd shot someone, it'd most likely be different."

But, of course, he knew the pistol still *had* that power. That it was still possessed by the same demons. That *he* was the one who'd changed.

Kosinski picked three cartridges off the tabletop, loaded one in every other chamber, snapped the cylinder back into the frame, put the gun into his mouth. He lingered over the taste and smell of gun oil on steel for a moment, finding it familiar, like one of the Cryders regulars on a weekday afternoon. Then he got down to business.

"Heads," he muttered, "I get the kid out of jail. Tails, I lose."

EIGHT

Bell Kosinski, standing in front of Marty Blake's apartment door, figured he looked pretty damn good. He actually thought the words— "pretty damn *good*." And why not? He'd taken his time with it, had stood under the shower until his nipples curled, run the razor across his face, soaped up, and run it again. He'd have blow-dried his hair if he'd owned a blow dryer—as it was, he'd trimmed his sideburns, snipped the little hairs in his nostrils and his ears. All with a rusted scissors so dull they'd have been better used as a pair of tweezers.

As luck would have it, his best suit, a tan, poplin beauty gleaned from an A&S clearance rack, had been waiting on a hanger in the closet. It was still covered by a dry cleaner's plastic bag, while his two other suits were lying on the floor next to several pairs of scuffed shoes. His luck had held as he'd searched his bureau to find one lightly starched white shirt, one stain-free tie, one laundered—though not, of course, *ironed*—handkerchief, two matching brown socks.

Unfortunately, none of it, he had to admit, would have come without a little help. No, without a little help, his hands wouldn't stop shaking long enough to knot the tie, button the shirt, zip his goddamned fly.

"But that was then," he said aloud, "and this is now."

He rang the bell, waited, rehearsed his opening lines. What he'd say if Blake answered, what he'd say if Blake's wife or girlfriend answered. But not what he'd say if a middle-aged woman with her right hand jammed into a shoulder bag answered. Not what he'd say if her hand was wrapped around a .38-caliber Smith & Wesson revolver.

"Could I help you?"

Kosinski stood stock-still for a moment, then his training took over. "You got a permit for that gun, lady?"

"You a cop?"

That stopped him again. "Not exactly," he finally said. "I'm retired. My name's Kosinski."

"Yeah? Ya know, my husband, he should rest in peace, was also a cop. But he wasn't one of those cops who thinks his wife is too delicate to hear about the job. No, he used to tell me all about it, about the blood and the bodies. About the rapes and the rapists. And I guess it must've sunk in, because now that he's gone, I'm very, very careful. Show me some ID, Kosinski."

Bell Kosinski fished out a set of photo ID that officially declared him, "NYPD, Retired." He held it up, tried to smile, said, "Ya know, I still have powers of arrest."

The woman read the ID, nodded, let the revolver drop into the shoulder bag. "If you wanted to arrest someone, you would have stayed on the job. Are you here to see my son?"

"If your son's name is Marty Blake, I am."

The woman stepped back. "C'mon in. Marty's takin' a shower."

As Bell Kosinski walked past Blake's mother, a door at the far end of the apartment opened and Marty Blake stepped into the hallway. He was wearing a terry-cloth bathrobe that'd been given to him by Rebecca Webber, a robe she appropriated every time she came to visit. He could still smell her powder in the soft cotton, which is what he was doing when he saw Bell Kosinski standing next to his mother.

"You here to see me?" he said, his nose buried in the robe's sleeve.

"I didn't spend two hours on a bus because I like the neighborhood."

Blake noted Kosinski's swollen lip, fought his own rising anger. "If you came here to warn me off, you can forget about it."

"I came here to help."

"Help?"

"Mr. Kosinski was twenty-two years on the job," Dora Blake said. "Show some respect. For your father, if for nobody else." Blake started to respond, thought better of it. He was opposed to tilting at windmills as a matter of principle. Much better to engage the clutch, let the vanes spin to no effect.

"Tell you what, Ma—why don't you entertain Mr. Kosinski while I get dressed. Get him a cup of coffee, fix him a bagel." Blake disappeared without waiting for an answer. Kosinski watched for a minute, then turned with a shrug.

"I don't think your son likes me," he said.

"You're saying there's something he *does* like? Besides himself?"

She led him into a small kitchen, sat him down, poured him a cup of coffee. "You should call me Dora," she announced.

"And you can call me Bell. Short for Bela." He slid a pint bottle of Smirnoff out of his jacket pocket and slopped half an inch into his cup. Thinking, What the fuck, might as well show 'em what ya got. Who says beggars can't be choosers?

"My husband, he should rest in peace, drank himself to death." Dora Blake filled her cup, then sat down across from Kosinski. "What is it with cops that they go to pieces the minute they retire?"

"Actually, I went to pieces while I was still on the job. That's why they retired me." Kosinski sipped at his fortified coffee, took a minute to evaluate the woman in front of him. She had her son's thick, curly hair, but there was nothing goofy about Dora Blake. Even surrounded by dark circles, her blue eyes were sharp and knowing. They complemented her strong nose and stubborn mouth, her trim, angular body.

"I suppose you've got a sad story. They've all got sad stories, the cops and the criminals."

Bell Kosinski bristled at the comment. "That's like comparing the fisherman to the fish. It doesn't make sense."

"You're saying it makes sense, good or otherwise, to drink vodka at eight o'clock in the morning? This is news to me."

Marty Blake, as he assembled his wardrobe and began to dress, could hear his mother slash at the ex-cop's psychic armor. Several clichés floated through his consciousness—better him than me; it couldn't happen to a nicer guy; as ye sow, so shall ye reap. Fitting payback for Kosinski's waggling fingers.

Still, despite his pleasure at Kosinski's battering, Blake couldn't help but wonder exactly what the guy was doing in his apartment. What he was doing and how he'd found it. Blake had made the ex-cop for a hopeless drunk, had used that conviction to control his own annoyance. Now, just twelve hours later, the drunk was sitting in his kitchen.

Blake tucked a white, short-sleeved shirt into navy-blue cotton trousers, buckled a narrow, gray belt, took a moment to assess his reflection in the mirror. The shirt was too tight, that much was obvious—Bernstein's French Dry Cleaning had struck again and his biceps were threatening to rip the sleeves apart. He was going into a prison to visit a retarded convict and the look he was trying for was fatherly, not bad cop in a precinct interrogation.

Rather than change the shirt, Blake decided to cover the whole thing with a wool-nylon jacket he'd gotten at a shop that specialized in fitting oddly shaped human bodies. An eggshell-white with just a touch of yellow, it was both too expensive and too sophisticated (in his estimation) for a prison visit, but it would have to do. His suits were too formal and his seersucker jacket, which makes him look like a complete schmuck and which would have been perfect, was in the cleaners.

Blake's mind shifted gears once the decision had been made. Shifted to Kosinski's cheap suit and cheaper tie. The drunk had made an effort to appear human, but that cut no ice with Marty Blake. Thoroughly conditioned by his father's last years, he wasn't about to be fooled by an off-the-rack cotton suit. A drunk was a drunk, a junkie was a junkie, a crackhead was a crackhead. In Blake's estimation, there was very little difference between them.

As he turned toward the kitchen, he heard Kosinski's voice. "I was everywhere in the detectives," he was saying. "Homicide, safes and lofts, organized crime, narcotics. Everywhere but Internal Affairs. That's where I drew the line. I mean, ya take the man's pay, ya do the man's job, but there's gotta be limits."

Dora Blake started to respond, then saw her son. "I think that's my cue, Bell. Time for me to go home."

"You don't live here?" Kosinski's surprise was sincere.

"Naw, I live in the building. Three flights up." She pushed her chair back, started to rise.

"Stick around, ma. I want a witness." Blake was convinced that Kosinski had come to threaten him in some way. The idea was both frightening and exhilarating. Or, at least, that's the way he felt it— warning bells announcing that he was into something much bigger than he expected, a rising excitement pricking at the hairs on the back of his neck. "All right, Kosinski, let's have the bad news."

Bell Kosinski looked up at Blake. Thinking, there was a time when I would have broken my nightstick over this jerk's head. Now, I'm coming to him as a beggar. No, not a beggar. A merchant. I'm here to trade.

"You remember that five you told me about last night?" he asked.

"Five?"

"He's talking about a follow-up report in the case file," Dora Blake interjected. "Right, Bell?"

"Yeah. Specifically, the one signed by me that says I got an anonymous phone call naming William Sowell as the killer of Sondra Tillson."

Blake, with no idea where this was going, managed a grudging, "Yeah, I remember. What about it?"

"Well, it didn't happen that way." Kosinski lifted his cup, took a long pull, flashed his best "in your face" smirk.

A silence followed, a silence in which Marty Blake found himself actually hating Bell Kosinski.

"Here's the truth," Kosinski finally continued. "The tip came through a captain named Aloysius Grogan. We, meaning Detective Tommy Brannigan and myself, received it from the mouth of Grogan's informant in a parking lot in Jamaica. I don't know who signed that five, but it wasn't me."

Marty Blake finally sat down. He folded his hands, dropped them to the top of the table. "You willing to swear to this?"

"I might be."

"Might?"

"Well, I want something for it."

"What is it, money?"

Kosinski shook his head, turned to Blake's mother. "Ya know, Dora, I don't wanna criticize, but you didn't raise your kid very polite."

Dora Blake flashed a wry smile, her eyes denying her lips. "What you're talking about is selling information that could get an innocent man out of prison. That's not nice, Bell. It doesn't call for polite."

"Did I say anything about money?" Kosinski looked into the depths of his empty cup, fought the urge to fill it from the bottle in his pocket. "Money has nothing to do with it. I came here to work on the case. You know, as a kind of assistant. And don't think I couldn't do any good, because as far as I can see, your son doesn't know squat about conducting a street investigation. Plus, I also have friends in the job. Friends like the one who pulled Martin Blake's file. Who told me, for instance, where Martin Blake lives. Who told me that Martin Blake's coming off a year's suspension for bugging somebody's apartment.

Who told me that he spent his whole career chasin' down corporate criminals."

Kosinski stopped abruptly, like a lawn mower that's just run out of gas. He looked down at his hands, wished he was anywhere but sitting at this table. Wished he was back at Cryders, watching CNN while Ed kept his glass full.

"Wait here a minute."

Kosinski raised his eyes. Blake was turning away, heading back into his bedroom. Dora's eyes, on the other hand, were looking right through him.

"You calling the lawyer, Blake?" he said. "You reporting to your master?"

Blake hesitated briefly, then continued on. The sound of Kosinski's voice followed him into the bedroom.

"Tell him I can prove what I'm saying. Tell him I can give it to him on a silver platter."

Blake had always prided himself on his objectivity. His work, as he saw it, inevitably put him in contact with people he didn't like. Some, maybe the majority, were paying clients. Others were people he needed for one thing or another. He could vividly recall an investigation where he spent night after night drinking with a man who spoke about women as if they were dogs. Who verbally undressed every female in every bar they walked into, describing things he wanted to do with them while their mothers watched.

"And ya know somethin', Blake, if the old cunt begs for it, maybe I'll give her a quick bang, too. While her kid licks my asshole. Whatta ya think of that?"

The man had been Blake's entrée into an extensive kickback scheme involving several hundred thousand dollars and half a dozen New York construction firms. At trial, he'd been the star witness for the prosecution. None of that would have happened if Blake hadn't listened to the sleaze, chuckled in the right places, paid for the drinks.

Blake fished Max Steinberg's card out of his wallet, punched the lawyer's number into the phone. The woman who answered took his name, then informed him that Steinberg was in conference.

"Mister Steinberg will call you back as soon as possible."

"I need to speak to him now. I'll wait."

"He may be quite some time, Mr. Blake."

"Just get him," Blake roared. "Interrupt him, tell him I have to make a decision about something and I can't wait."

"One moment."

The moment quickly stretched into two, then three, then four. Blake found himself wishing he'd never made the call, that for once he'd surrendered to impulse and thrown Bela Kosinski's drunken ass down the nearest stairwell.

"Short and sweet, Blake. And it better be good."

Blake took a breath, imagined the famous wig slipping down to cover Steinberg's forehead. "All right, according to the official record, William Sowell's name came to the attention of the police through an anonymous telephone tip. The detective who took that tip and who signed the report was named Bela Kosinski. You with me so far, Max?"

"Yeah, keep goin'."

"Right this minute, as we're talking, Bela Kosinski, who is now an ex-cop, is sitting in my kitchen. He says the tip came from a captain named Crogan. He also says he never signed that report."

Dead silence, then, "You're bullshitting me, right? This is a joke?"

"No joke, Max. And don't ask me to explain why Bela Kosinski is willing to swear to what he says. He claims he can prove it. Claims he didn't know anything about the report until I told him last night. My problem is that I don't know how important it is. Whether or not I should pay the price."

"Price? Is he actually demanding payment?"

"Not in money. He wants to become my assistant; he wants to work on the case."

"No shit?"

"And he's a drunk, Max. A straight-out lush with a nasty mouth."

"Welcome to the club."

"It's not funny. Look, Kosinski claims he was on vacation when Sowell was picked up, and by the time he came back, the deal was done. He can't tell us what actually happened to Sowell . . ."

"Forget it, Blake. I want him in my office tomorrow. What kind of a drunk is he? He fall down? Puke on himself? Tell me."

"How would I know? I just met him last night."

"Was he coherent last night?"

"Yeah, obnoxious in the extreme, but definitely coherent."

"Good. Don't let this guy out of your sight, Blake, because if you do, I got a feeling he's gonna disappear. Meanwhile, just so he doesn't get itchy, drown him in alcohol. Let him shoot his mouth off, listen to his troubles, keep your own mouth shut. You don't know he was on vacation. And even if he was, you don't know he didn't talk up the case after he got back. In fact, you don't know anything, except that your job is to get Bela Kosinski into my office tomorrow morning. Have a nice day."

"Look, Max . . ."

"And one more thing, Mister Blake—you should have known what to do without asking me."

NINE

Marty Blake, as he pushed his '91 Taurus north toward the Columbia Correctional Facility, chose to ignore his client's advice. It wasn't just that he was smarting over Steinberg's sarcastic remarks or peremptory tone. Blake was remembering his father and a boyhood filled with near-worship. For as long as he could recall, he'd always wanted to embody that mix of strength and kindness he'd seen in his dad. At fifteen, Marty would have been perfectly willing to blast the faces off Mount Rushmore and chisel Matthew Blake's features into the bluff. Right alongside those of Dirty Harry, James Bond, and Rocky.

At twenty, Blake saw it all come crashing down. Upon retirement, his father, who'd never had more than a single beer with dinner, became a straight-out lush. There was just no other way to put it; no other way Marty Blake *wanted* to put it. And it hadn't been the gradual slide of a man facing years of unstructured time—if that was the problem, Matthew Blake, all of forty-two years old, could simply have gotten a job. No, the fall had come with the abrupt finality of a Yugo slamming into the grill of an oncoming Peterbilt. One day he was Sergeant Blake, cool and confident; a month later he was citizen Blake, on his knees, hugging the toilet.

Blake had been a freshman at the John Jay College of Criminal Justice when his father turned in his papers. A year later, he was majoring in computer science at CCNY. By the time he reached his senior year, he'd found a girlfriend with an apartment and stopped coming home.

The weakness was the worst of it, he thought. That and my mother going about her business as if nothing had changed. It was like she was *trying* to kill him. Or better yet, to assist in his suicide, like the Michigan death doctor. Only pop didn't have multiple sclerosis or cancer or any disease of any kind. Not one you could actually measure.

It wasn't until Blake saw his mother wailing at the graveside that he began to understand that something far more complicated had been going on. By that time, his girlfriend was long gone and the apartment lease was in his own name. His mother, without a word of explanation, started coming down in the morning for a cup of coffee. They maintained their relationship by not mentioning Matthew Blake.

"Cheers."

Blake looked over. Kosinski was grinning at him, holding a pint of Smirnoff in his right hand.

"You enjoying this beautiful day, Marty?" He waved the bottle at the surrounding countryside. "'What is so rare as a day in June?' I'll tell ya what, Blake. A clear day in August in New York City is what. It's fuckin' beautiful out there."

"Maybe that's because we're not *in* New York City."

Properly chastened, Kosinski turned back to the open field. A small herd of cows cropped the grass on the crest of a hill. Silhouetted against a deep blue sky, they seemed as exotic to him as Columbus and his crew must have seemed to the Indians. He wondered, briefly, whether they were cows for milking or cows for eating. Or both.

"I just wanna go on record as saying that this has been a very liberating experience for me." He dropped the bottle into his jacket pocket, glanced over at Blake, decided there was something about the kid that made you want to ruffle his hair.

"Liberating? From what?"

"From the blue wall. From the fucking job. From the lies and the bullshit. Last night, after you left, I started thinking about all the times I looked the other way. Times I seen drug money go into somebody's pocket. Times I seen cops rob the dead. You know about cops robbing the dead, Blake? You know about that?"

Blake shook his head, reminded himself that listening to Kosinski was part of the job. That clients were always right, as long as they kept paying.

"Robbing the dead is not within my field of expertise, Kosinski. Why don't you tell me about it."

"Okay, suppose you're an ordinary patrolman taking jobs as they come in from Central. You get a 'see the man' call, nothing out of the ordinary, and it turns out to be some old geezer dead in his bed. We're not talkin' homicide here; we're talkin' about a body laying two days before anybody noticed. Now, the stink is ferocious, plus there's clusters of maggots around the ears and the eyes, so what you'd expect is for the cops to back out and call in the sergeant. After all, that's what the Patrol Guide says they're *supposed* to do.

"But that ain't what happens, Marty. No, what usually happens is that one or both of the responding officers go through the apartment. You know, look behind the cabinets, under the drawers, behind the toilet tank. For some reason, old people—especially if they live poor—don't trust banks. I hear it's got something to do with the Depression, but I wouldn't know about that. What I do know is that the money mostly goes in somebody's pocket. And remember, this money could be the difference between a real grave and potter's field.

"Now me, I never took a dime. Twenty-something years and I never took a dime from anybody. But what I did was look the other way. That's the blue wall; that's what it's all about for honest cops. I never went to the sergeant or the duty officer or the exec or the captain. I let it happen and I let a lot of other shit happen, too. I seen guys in handcuffs beat half to death because some cop *liked* to give out pain. I seen mutts walk away from their crimes because somebody got to somebody and the evidence disappeared. And I seen this kid, Sowell, put in prison for something he didn't do.

"The way I look at it now, Marty, is that I'm not a cop anymore and I'm never gonna be a cop again. I mean last night I asked myself, 'Bell, do you gotta take this blue wall shit to the fucking *grave?*' I can't see it. Especially because there's no honor underneath; there's no honor in protecting what's rotten. So that's why I decided to help get the kid out of jail. That's what I was thinking."

Blake didn't even bother to nod. Let the drunk rant, he thought. By tomorrow, he'll either produce or he'll be history. Better yet, he'll produce *and* he'll be history.

Still, for all his contempt, Blake couldn't help but compare Kosinski's ugly tale with Max Steinberg's introduction two days before. He found himself yearning for corporate criminals in Paul Stuart suits, Burberry trench coats, Ferragamo shoes. His father, he reasoned, must have spent his entire working life surrounded by that ugliness. Maybe he'd been overwhelmed by it. Not that that was any excuse. The realities had called for strength, not weakness.

They were off the Taconic Parkway by this time, passing up a gentle slope with fields of corn on both sides. It'd been an unusually wet summer and the nearly ripe corn, standing in sharp, straight rows, pressed to within feet of the roadway. The net effect on the two men was claustrophobic, as if the corn had been put there to conceal something else.

"Hey, Blake, you ever see that Stephen King movie, *Children of the Corn?*"

"Nope, must've missed it."

"Probably went to a Woody Allen movie that night."

"Whatever." Blake refused to take the bait.

"Well, anyway, that's what I keep expecting to come out of this corn. Kids with fangs. Something horrible."

In a way, Kosinski was right, because when Blake's Taurus crested the hill and the two men were able to see out over the planted fields, the meadows, and the orchards, they were greeted by the gray walls of the Columbia Correctional Facility less than a mile away. Forty feet high, capped at each corner with gun towers, and surrounded by the fruits of summer, the walls seemed a grim mirage. As if they couldn't possibly be there. As if it was time to recheck the compass, recalculate the journey.

"Jesus Christ," Blake muttered. "Welcome to hell." He glanced over to find his companion sitting straight up, a bemused half-smile just visible beneath that hawk's nose. "This seem funny to you, Kosinski?"

"I'm reliving an experience from my old life," Kosinski replied. He pulled out the Smirnoff, drank deeply, shoved the bottle under the seat. "It's like going into Rikers, only there's no walls at Rikers. But all them mutts in one place? You could feel it with your eyes closed. Doesn't matter about the walls."

"Feel what?"

Kosinski started to answer, then shook his head. "You'll figure it out the minute we get inside."

Blake cleared his throat. "There might not be any *we* to it. Steinberg set this up for one man. I'm gonna try to get you in, but . . ."

"Well, whatever," Kosinski muttered. "Say, you mind if I ask you a question?"

"Does it matter?"

"C'mon, Blake. Stop tryin' to play the tough guy. What's the point? I wanna help."

"Just say what you have to say, Kosinski."

"All right, I will. The question that occurred to me as we were dri-vin' up is exactly what it is you're doing here. I mean it's nice to visit your client and all, but we both know the kid didn't do it. Ask yourself: is guilt or innocence an issue? No, right? You could believe me, Blake, because I got a lot of experience in these matters, it's real important to know what you want to get out of an interview, *before* you go into it."

Blake kept his hands on the wheel, his eyes on the road. "What I'm doing here, Kosinski, and what I expect to get out of this interview, is three hundred dollars, plus expenses. That includes the tolls, the gas, and twenty-seven cents a mile on the car."

"So you don't think the kid could help you out?"

"Look, if Sowell could have provided himself with an alibi, he would have done it long ago."

"Yeah, that's probably right. So, tell me why the lawyer sent you up here? Aside from the fact that he likes puttin' out three hundred dol-lars a day, plus expenses."

Blake didn't bother to answer. They were a hundred yards from the guard shack outside the main entrance to the prison and he busied himself with arranging a proper face for the man inside. He needn't have taken the trouble. When the car pulled to a stop, a guard emerged, stepped up to Blake's window, demanded his name and business.

"My name is Blake. This is my associate, Mr. Kosinski. We're here to interview a prisoner, William Sowell."

"Yes, sir. I'll need some identification, sir." The guard's manner was military, from his polished brogans to the forest of half-inch spikes crowning his skull.

Blake fished out his newly minted private investigator's license, col-lected his companion's NYPD card, passed it over. He watched the guard disappear into the shack, saw him lift the phone. A minute later, he came back out.

"Sir, are either of you carrying firearms?"

Blake looked over at Kosinski who shook his head. "No."

"When I open the outer gate, please drive to the inner gate, then exit the vehicle."

Blake watched the guard retreat, watched the steel gate slide into the stone walls. He pulled forward, as instructed, trying to ignore the rising tension. Then he noticed a cluster of uniformed prisoners doing yard work and something close to dread rose through his spine to settle in the back of his neck. The Columbia Correctional Facility, he realized, as if for the first time, was a Max—A New York State prison. There were no shoplifters here.

"What they call it," Kosinski chortled, "is atmosphere. As in, this ain't the shit *you* breathe." He was grinning madly.

A second guard emerged from a cubicle inside the chain link fence surrounding the main gate. As military in his dress and bearing as the first, he went through the trunk, searched beneath the hood, found the bottle under the seat.

"This is contraband, sir. I'll have to confiscate it."

"Does that mean I get it back when I leave?" Kosinski's smile disappeared.

"No, sir, I'm afraid . . ."

Kosinski took a quick step forward. He snatched the bottle, unscrewed the cap, drained it in two long swallows, then handed it back. "Don't forget to recycle," he said. "It's good for America."

TEN

They never made it into the prison proper, the cell blocks, the work areas, the yard, the gym. After a thoroughly pissed-off correction officer opened the inner gate, they drove to a parking lot in front of the administration building and were directed to the office of Deputy Warden Paul Sheridan. To be sure, there were prisoners everywhere—behind the typewriters, bent over the filing cabinets, answering phones—but these were the tamest of the tame. These were trusties who'd demonstrated (to the satisfaction of the administration, if not the parole board) a long-term ability to control impulsive behavior. They worked in silence, each seemingly locked into his own carefully concealed thoughts. Nobody made eye contact, nobody smiled, nobody gossiped by the water cooler.

Kosinski, who understood the drill, was keenly aware of Blake's discomfort. He took energy from it, decided that it defined the difference between cops and citizens. That there was nothing in the vast memory of the most powerful computer to prepare you for the unique combination of violence and misery that characterizes every aspect of the criminal world. It was bad enough on the street, but when you compressed that atmosphere between four walls, it became powerful enough to suffocate the uninitiated. Like Martin Blake.

Deputy Warden Sheridan didn't bother to smile, didn't object to Kosinski's presence. He rechecked their identification, again asked about firearms, warned them about regulations prohibiting tape recorders and cameras. Kosinski watched Blake respond in the negative to each question. When they were alone for a moment, he leaned over and said, "A tape recorder doesn't do you much good if you don't know what it is you wanna record."

"You know what I'd really appreciate?" Blake responded. He spoke out of the side of his mouth, as if he was afraid of being overheard. As if he had something to conceal. "I'd really appreciate you keeping your drunken mouth shut. You're not running this show."

Kosinski started to answer, thought better of it, slid his hands into his pockets. If he was drunk, he didn't feel it. No, what he felt, when he examined himself in the following silence, was relieved. The way a game fish might feel after wriggling off a fisherman's hook.

Remember, he said to himself, the condition is decidedly temporary. Which is okay. Like being in remission after a dose of chemotherapy.

Deputy Sheridan, after a short absence, led them (Blake first, naturally; Kosinski trailing behind) to a small room set aside for attorney-client interviews. Everything about the space seemed begrudging, from the faded paint on the walls to the grimy tiles on the floor to the rickety metal chairs and table.

Blake, whose mind drifted to Joanna Bardo's collection of fake antiques, carefully wiped the chair seat before sitting down. Bell Kosinski, on the other hand, found the room luxurious in comparison with similar space in the precincts where he'd worked. At least nobody had pissed in the corner, which was a favorite pastime of cops who viewed lawyers as the only creatures on earth lower than the clients they served.

They waited in silence while Billy Sowell was summoned from one or another corner of the vast prison. Though neither measured the minutes, time dragged for both. Kosinski was tempted to speak, but held himself in check. What was the point?

Blake, for his part, was busy regretting his quick decision to accept Joanna Bardo's offer. Maybe, he speculated, he should have made the rounds of other firms specializing in corporate work. Because this wasn't right for him. He had no feel for the task at hand, no sense of how to proceed. To be sure, he understood the *mechanics* well enough, but the sixth sense that'd guided him when he'd worked undercover in corporate computer departments had now deserted him altogether.

The sudden appearance of Billy Sowell in a doorway at the far end of the room, a doorway leading into the depths of the Columbia Correctional Facility, did nothing to resolve Blake's self-doubt. The diminutive figure, no more than five-six, no more than a hundred and forty pounds, hesitated for a moment, then stepped out of the shadows and raised his head. Someone, perhaps an image-conscious correction officer, perhaps Sowell, himself, had made a halfhearted effort to wipe the makeup off his face. They needn't have bothered.

The end result—aquamarine streaks shot with greasy black mascara extending along both cheekbones—was even more bizarre than the original.

But Marty Blake's mind refused to make the obvious jump, refused to say homosexual or faggot or punk. Refused even to turn away in disgust. Instead, he let his eyes drop, noting the khaki shirt with its expertly shortened sleeves, the trousers tight enough to cradle Sowell's buttocks, to lift and offer them, two perfect hemispheres pushed into a soft, plump ball.

"Hi, Billy. Can I call you, Billy? My name's Bell. Bell Kosinski."

Blake watched Kosinski rise and take a step forward. Saw him smile, extend his hand, lead Billy Sowell to a chair. Saw him take a chocolate bar out his jacket pocket—the same pocket that'd held his Smirnoff—and hold it up for the correction officer now standing in the doorway to inspect.

"This okay?" He waited for the officer's grudging nod, then handed it over to Billy Sowell. "Billy, this is my friend, Marty Blake. We came here to help you get out of jail."

"Hello."

The soft hand Billy Sowell held out to Blake was tipped with perfectly manicured pink fingernails. Blake, fighting revulsion, took it briefly, let it drop, let his own hand fall into his lap. He wanted to be angry—with Kosinski for taking charge, with Joanna for putting him where he was, with Billy Sowell for being Billy Sowell—but he couldn't quite get there. What he was, was stunned.

"It's hard for you here, isn't it, Billy?" Kosinski was leaning forward in his chair, dominating Sowell's field of vision. "It's hard for you in prison?"

Sowell nodded. "Can you get me out of here soon?"

"No, Billy. Not real soon. You've got to hang in there." Kosinski reached out, took Billy Sowell's hand, cradled it in his own. "Billy, do you remember a man named Kamal Collars?"

"Kamal? Sure. He was my best friend. After my mom died, I mean."

"How did you know him?"

"We used to panhandle together. We were partners." He said it proudly, lifting his head to look into Kosinski's eyes. "And we drank together. How do you know Kamal?"

"I met him once. It was a long time ago, but he told me that he knew where you were on the night Sondra Tillson was killed. *You* don't remember where you were, do you, Billy?"

"No. I tried, I *really* tried. And since I came here I tried some more. But they didn't ask me right away. They didn't ask me for two weeks, so I can't remember."

"I understand. That why I want to ask your friend, Kamal. I want to ask him where you were, but I don't know how to find him, so I need your help." Kosinski dropped Billy Sowell's hand, took out a small spiral notebook and a pen. "Have you heard from Kamal since you came here?"

"No. But I'd like to."

Kosinski smiled. "I'll be sure to let him know. Now, what I want you to do is tell me where you used to live, where you used to go, friends you had together. Things like that."

Blake's first reaction was anger—Kosinski had held out on him; he should have mentioned Kamal Collars on the way up—but then, to his credit, he remembered that Steinberg had instructed him to pump Kosinski for all he was worth. He, Blake, had chosen to ignore the advice. The lawyer had been right and he'd been wrong; it was as simple as that.

What I have to do, he thought, is make up my goddamned mind. Maybe life in the sewer is too much for me. Maybe I'm not a tough guy. There's no shame in that, no shame at all. The shame comes from being half-in, half-out. Of course, I could stay with Steinberg while I look for other work. I could stay with the paycheck. But if I do that I have to do it right. I can't fuck around; I can't let myself be thrown by the ambience.

"I'm just back from my vacation and I don't mind telling you I'm hung over so bad I'm tryin' to crap and puke at the same time. I don't know anything about Billy Sowell yet, but I do know that the Tillson case is closed. Anyway, I'm at my desk and this giant walks into the squad room. Has to be six-six, two-fifty. Plus he's black as coal and wearin' a filthy jacket over six layers of shirts and underwear. Believe me, Blake, this is a guy who makes Park Avenue ladies pee into their bloomers. Which is probably why I remember him.

"As it happens, I'm the only dick in the squad room, so neither one of us had any choice in the matter. He walks up to my desk, tells me his name is Kamal Collars (which is a name you don't forget), and asks

for my partner, Tommy Brannigan. Naturally, I ask him what he wants
Brannigan for and he tells me that he called Brannigan about the
killing of Sondra Tillson and Brannigan told him to come down to the
house. He says he knows that Billy Sowell didn't kill Tillson because
he was with Sowell at the time. Now, as far as I'm concerned, it's none
of my business because it's not my collar, so I tell him Brannigan's in
the lieutenant's office and he'll be back in a few minutes. Meanwhile,
he should go by Brannigan's desk and take a seat."

They were on the Taconic Parkway, heading south at a stately fifty-
five miles per hour. Kosinski's head was starting to pound and he was
sweating, despite the air conditioning. What he needed was a drink,
but he read the set of Blake's face, the tight jaw and withdrawn
mouth, to mean that was the least likely of all the possibilities.

"Are you with me here, Blake?"

"Yeah, sure."

"You want me to tell you what I think?"

"I'm all ears."

"You know they turned the kid out, right?"

"Say that again?"

"Sowell. The kid. They turned him out. The wolves, I mean. A little guy like that? There's was no way he could fight back, even if he
had all his smarts. So what happened is they gave him a choice: put on
makeup and peddle your ass for us or die."

"That's very pat, Kosinski, but how do you know he doesn't like it?"

"Simple. If Billy Sowell was gay, he couldn't very well have killed
Sondra Tillson because he was sexually attracted to her. I mean, supposedly it was an attempted rape gone bad. Homosexuality would
have been a pretty good defense."

"Maybe he goes both ways."

"Guys who wear makeup don't go both ways, Marty. I shouldn't
have to tell you that."

ELEVEN

Marty Blake dropped Kosinski (at Cryders, naturally) just after four o'clock, then went off in search of a phone booth. It was Friday and he knew he didn't have much time. When he finally chanced upon a working booth on College Point Boulevard, he punched in the number of an old acquaintance.

I'm sorry. You have reached a nonworking number in the New York Telephone area. Please check the number and try again. I'm sorry, you have reached a nonworking . . .

He muttered the required, "Shit!", even though he wasn't surprised. All through what he liked to call "my exile," he'd stubbornly refused to calculate his losses. Figuring they'd become painfully obvious as soon as he went back to work.

"Time to take the long way around," he muttered, dialing Manhattan Exec's number.

"Manhattan Executive."

"Cynthia? It's Marty Blake."

"Hi, Marty. Joanna was asking about you. She wants you to keep in touch."

"Yeah, well I'll keep in touch some other time. Right now I need to speak to Conrad Angionis. That is, if he's still working for Joanna."

"Conrad practically lives here, Marty. Joanna would never let him go."

"I should have known. Listen, I'm in kind of a hurry. Can you put me through?"

A moment later, a hoarse, raspy voice muttered a clipped interrogatory. "Who?"

"You haven't changed, Conrad. Not even a little bit." Blake pictured the Greek, all six foot, seven inches of him, perched on a hard-backed chair in front of his IBM. With his desk raised six inches off the carpet by a wooden platform, he towered above the other techs, a fitting position for the man who ruled the computer room. Conrad wore his coarse, black hair in a long ponytail; a fierce beard sprouted from just beneath his eyes, rolled down his face, covered his collar and the knot in his tie.

"That you, Marty Blake?"

"It's me, Conrad. I'm thinking about asking for my old job back." Blake had run the department before he'd gotten his license and gone into the field.

"Yeah, and Joanna's gonna make me a full partner. What could I do for you?"

"I got a little problem, Conrad. I need to find someone."

"That's a problem?"

"For me it is. It's been a year and I've lost my contacts. Or, at least, I lost one of my contacts, the one I need right now. Look, I'm in a big hurry."

"You got a social security number?"

"No, but it wouldn't help if I did. The man I'm looking for is homeless. I need to get into HRA's files. Medicaid, food stamps, home relief, disability, like that. Maybe the Human Resources Administration can give him an address."

"If he's homeless, how can he have an address?"

"Glib, Conrad, but not clever. Look, the guy's name is Kamal Collars. Two years ago, he was living on the street. He might have gone into a shelter since then, or gotten a job, or moved in with relatives. If he's collecting welfare, he has to have an address, even if it's just a mail drop. If he's on Medicaid, maybe they'll have the location of a clinic he used recently. Look, it's getting on to five o'clock and it's Friday, which means we don't have time for the bullshit. Call your contact at HRA. I want whatever they have, including Collars' social security number. Remember, I'm a client now."

"So Joanna told me. How do you wanna write this up?"

Blake took a moment to think it over. He knew that what they were doing was entirely illegal, but that didn't mean his client shouldn't pay for it.

"Write it up as a search with negative results. And don't forget the discount."

Marty Blake, as he opened the door to his Forest Hills apartment, felt what he liked to call "clean fatigue." The polar opposite of what he felt coming off a twelve-hour shift in a yellow cab. Maybe it sprang from a sense (undoubtedly false) that he'd made peace with Bell Kosinski; maybe from the fact that Bell Kosinski had fallen asleep twenty minutes into the drive home; or maybe it came to nothing more than his conversation with Conrad Angionis, the first tangible thing he'd done to move the case forward. Angionis was an obsessive type. He wouldn't leave for the weekend until he'd exhausted every possibility, no matter how remote. All Blake had to do was stay by the phone.

He was still considering his day and how well it'd turned out, as he stepped through the door. Not thinking, really; he was too tired and too hungry for analysis. His mind was drifting from thought to thought, like a canoe on a sluggish river. Still, he was preoccupied enough to hear the grind of a motor and the slap-slap of running feet, and not recognize what they represented. The noise confused him at first, but then he finally realized that somebody was in his apartment, and that somebody was using his treadmill, and that somebody had to be Rebecca Webber.

Blake tiptoed into the bedroom and found Rebecca, her back turned to him, running at a steady pace. Apparently, she'd been doing it for some time, because she was wearing one of his cotton T-shirts over her own silk panties and both garments were soaked with sweat.

She did this for me, he thought. To please me. A special treat for her special pet.

Blake watched sweat drip from the ends of Rebecca's perfectly frosted, honey-blond hair, hair that now hung in wet, ropy tendrils, hair that would get a two-hundred-dollar reshaping at the Ted Orris Salon in the morning. He watched the drops run along the glistening down on the back of her neck, watched them disappear beneath the T-shirt plastered to the smooth muscles of her back. His eyes tracked the ridges of her spine, following them down to her small, round ass. To where the wet silk of her panties was little more than a beckoning shadow.

He waited until he couldn't stand it any more, until his lips ached for the dark hollows at the tops of her thighs. Quickly, quietly, he took off his own clothes, folding them carefully, knowing she wouldn't turn around, that even if she knew he was there, she was committed to the game. Then he yanked the plug.

When the treadmill stopped moving, she turned to face him, taking her time about it, her eyes flashing desire and triumph.

Screaming it, really. Blake glimpsed a future in which he wore a diamond-studded collar, in which he was led from place to place on a long, shiny silver leash.

Rebecca reached out to him, nostrils flaring, mouth somewhere between a sneer and a smirk. Blake grabbed her outstretched fingers, and spun her in a half-circle, imprisoning her wrists with his right hand. He twisted sharply and she cried out as she bent away from the pain.

"Don't hurt me," she said.

"Do I ever?"

He pushed her forward, curling her waist around the treadmill's railing, bringing her ass up against his crotch. Even with his eyes closed and that first touch of her sweaty flesh on his, he could feel her opening to him. A parting of waters into which he would descend, in which he would inevitably drown.

"I'm glad you came home when you did," she said as he pulled the crotch of her panties aside, as he slid inside her. "I don't have much time."

Afterward, as Rebecca showered, Blake sat, still naked, still sweat-soaked, on the edge of the tub, contemplating the discarded panties at the bottom of his wastebasket.

"Dior," she'd said as he dropped them in. "But definitely not *Christian*."

How much? he wondered. Two hundred? Maybe three with the matching bra and slip? Because she'll throw them away, too. She'll toss the ensemble out, or give it to her maid. When I go to the bureau, I grab one pair of socks, one pair of underpants, one T-shirt. Right off the top of the pile. Rebecca selects her lingerie as if she was expecting to perform a striptease for her gynecologist.

He'd watched her on the three occasions when he'd spent the night at her East-Side town house, the one tucked between the British and the South African embassies on East Seventy-eighth Street just off Fifth Avenue. In the morning, after her personal maid fetched the coffee, she'd lay out her wardrobe on a carved and gilded Empire sofa—hosiery, panties, bra, slip, skirt, blouse, sweater, shoes, necklace, bracelet, rings, watch. Then she'd step back to view the entire ensemble. As often as not, if she rejected one item, the whole outfit went back into the closet. Not that Rebecca was the one who *put* it back.

That chore was left to Sarah, the personal maid who'd been assigned to her on her tenth birthday.

The shower snapped off and Rebecca's arm emerged from behind the shower curtain. Blake got up and fetched the required towel. His reward: Rebecca Webber, elbows raised as she toweled her wet hair, stepping out of the mist with the brazen confidence of a harem queen.

"I've been meaning to tell you," she said. The towel moved from her throat to her breasts, cupping them as she patted the moist flesh. "William and I are going abroad. We'll be gone for some time. It's about the estate."

The estate in question involved ten thousand acres of what used to be East Germany. It had two unpronounceable German names (neither of which Marty Blake remembered), depending on whether you were referring to the property itself, or the seventeenth-century manor house that'd been in William (formerly Wilhelm) Webber's family for nearly three hundred years. Right up until 1944, when the advancing Soviet army had sent the family scurrying to the safety of the west. Somehow, William had become convinced that repatriation boiled down to little more than passing the right bribe to the right, former-Communist bureaucrat. Naturally, he'd dispatched a New York attorney to hire a Washington attorney to hire a Berlin attorney to find that man.

"When are you leaving?"

"Sunday morning."

"Nice of you to tell me."

"I'm telling you now, Marty. That's why I'm here. Things came to a head rather quickly, and William's afraid that if he doesn't act immediately, he'll lose his best chance."

"What does that have to do with you?"

"Please, Marty, don't be tiresome. It's really your only character flaw."

"Don't change the subject, Rebecca. You and William have led different lives for the last ten years. So, what does this trip to claim the ancestral homestead have to do with you?"

She put one foot up on the edge of the tub and began to run the towel along the inside of her left thigh. Her eyes were turned away from him and when she spoke, her voice was soft, almost wistful.

"I've always loved the continent," she said, as if that explained it.

TWELVE

"So you see what happened, Bell, is that all my problems with the diocese came to a head when I started talking to the Newman Club about St. Paul. I mean the guy was a flunky, right? A collaborating Jew who had the authority to arrest any Jew who invoked the name of Jesus. You can't get any lower than that, Bell. That's the muck on the bottom of the cesspool. Tell me, am I right?"

"You're right, Father Tim." Bell Kosinski listened with half an ear. He was feeling good, better than he'd felt in months. That was because he knew he wouldn't be taking the gun out tonight. Wouldn't clean it, touch it, even look at it.

"Okay, so he's traveling through the desert—this Saul who becomes Paul, this Jew who becomes a Greek—and he has a miraculous conversion. You know, struck blind, which maybe he deserved, then cured. A week later he's running the entire Christian show. I mean, when you think about it, the story doesn't make sense. Paul didn't even *know* Jesus—but before you can say, 'Holy Carpetbagger,' he's got Jesus' disciples running all over the Mediterranean converting the Gentiles. I'm telling you, Bell, if it wasn't for this collaborator, Christianity would be a religion of the Jews."

"And you told this to the Newman Club?" Kosinski took a drink, casually scratched his leg. The question was purely rhetorical. Father Tim, a retired priest and a Cryders regular, was obsessed with his own demise. Especially after his third drink.

"Yeah, the NYU chapter. And lemme tell ya, buddy, I definitely had their attention. That's the beauty of working with college kids. They're not afraid to think."

"Ya believe I used to confess to this guy?" Emily Caruso broke in. She shook her head in disbelief. "I musta been a goddamned jerk."

Father Tim winced at the blasphemy, but kept his attention focused on the ex-cop. "So, after a couple of sessions like this, I get a message that a certain Monsignor Cabella expects me to be in his office the next day at nine AM. When I get there, he's this little guinea with acne scars that make his cheeks into a mine field. 'Wha' you tella these kids?' he wants to know. Meanwhile, he doesn't offer coffee and I got one of those hangovers makes you think somebody divided your brain with a square of hot sheet metal. You know the one I'm talkin' about? You ever get that one, Bell?"

"I had every kind there is, Father."

"And that ain't all you had," Emily Caruso said. She waited until Kosinski turned to her, then whispered, "I used to tell this *putz* everything. I couldn't wash my tits in the shower, but I'd be confessin' it on Saturday afternoon. And all the time he's nothin' but a drunk. Word of God, Kosinski, I done a lotta stupid things in my life, but tellin' my sins. . . . Hey, whatta ya know, it's Moussy-man."

Kosinski looked up, his interest caught. It was Friday night, and the bar was packed with working men eager to part with a chunk of the old paycheck before tottering home to the wife and kids. It'd been this way ever since Bell Kosinski was old enough to get served, even back in the days when the wives weren't bringing home paychecks of their own.

They came from New York Telephone, Con Ed, UPS, Federal Express, a dozen construction companies. The unmarried among them had their girlfriends in tow, underage ladies in rhinestone jeans and halter tops. The only women in the place (besides Emily Caruso), the girlfriends stood in self-conscious knots, seemingly aware of their interloper status, even if their macho boyfriends were not.

The bowling machine was going strong, as was the recently repaired jukebox. The younger men were horsing around, pushing and joking while the regulars drank their boilermakers and pretended it was Tuesday afternoon. Bell Kosinski, on the other hand, liked the noise and the tension. It reminded him of his earliest days on the job when he'd walked a beat in Times Square. Day or night, The Deuce lived on anticipation. Of drugs, of sex, of violence—of some impending apocalypse that took many forms: a bloody civilian staggering toward an ambulance; a sleek hooker in crotchless panty hose working a razor back and forth across her pimp's face; a skeletal junkie in a doorway, his slate-gray features hardening under the onset of *rigor*.

"So listen, Bell." Father Tim grabbed Kosinski by the shoulder, tried to spin him around. When that tactic failed, he spoke directly into the back of the ex-cop's head. "I know I gotta tell the dago *something*, but I have this hangover and I can't concentrate. You know, like I made a big mistake trying to do the meeting without havin' a drink first and my hands are shaking so bad I've got 'em in my pockets. So what I do is run with the first thing that comes into my head. I tell him, 'You remember the Sermon on the Mount where Jesus commands the crowd to love their enemies? You remember that, Monsignor? Jesus said you should love your enemies two thousand years ago, so why is it that right now, after all this time, I don't know anybody who even *likes* their enemies? I mean it seems kind of strange until you really think about it. Then it becomes obvious. Jesus tells the crowd *what* to do, but He doesn't tell them *how* to do it. No, He doesn't tell the *crowd* how to do it, because the people in the crowd are merely called. They haven't been chosen, and how to love your enemies is a secret reserved for the chosen. That's why He had disciples. So He could tell them His secrets. Which leaves St. Paul in the dark, as far as I'm concerned; it makes him an organization man who could turn Europe into one big crowd. Everybody learning *what*. Nobody learning *how*.'"

Kosinski nodded automatically. "Say, Emily, where did you see this Moussy-Man? I can't find him."

"I seen his face in the window. There, he's comin' in the door."

Marty Blake's grinning face appeared, as if at Emily Caruso's command, in the open doorway. His shoulders, Kosinski noted, spanned the frame.

"Bell . . ."

"Not now, Father Tim. I got business." He signaled Ed O'Leary to fill the priest's glass, added Emily Caruso's as an afterthought, then waved to Marty Blake. "Hey, Marty, over here." He watched Blake edge through the crowd, muttering "Excuse me" and "Pardon me," and thought, I better warn this kid. Better tell him there's no water in the swimming pool. I better tell him you can't bounce on concrete.

"Kosinski, could I see you for a minute?"

"Sure, Marty. This private? You wanna go outside?"

"Yeah."

Kosinski snatched his glass off the bar top and followed Blake's retreating back. Once outside, his eyes swept the sidewalk in front of Cryders, noting several patrons catching a breath of fresh air while they drained their glasses. With two exceptions, their faces were unfamiliar. The exceptions were Cryders' resident bully, Tony Loest, and Cryders' resident (on weekends, when there were customers for his product) coke and pill dealer, Candy Packert.

Kosinski had never had a beef with Tony Loest, though he'd pulled him off a victim or two. Loest, Kosinski knew, wasn't physically afraid of him, but as a kid from the neighborhood, Loest was smart enough to respect the badge, the badge Kosinski no longer wore. Packert, on the other hand, was the kind of sleazebag Kosinski, in years gone by, would have slapped senseless. In years gone by, Kosinski knew, he would have run Candy Packert out of Whitestone.

"Hey, you with me, or what?"

Kosinsksi turned at the sound of Blake's voice, found him leaning one elbow on the roof of a sky-blue, 1979 Trans-Am. He heard a low grunt, like the chuff of a bull about to charge. "Hey, Marty, if I was you, I'd turn around."

It was too late. Loest, already in the air, came down on Marty Blake's back like a panther defending its cub.

Kosinski pointed at Candy Packert, shouted, "Just stay where the fuck you are," then started to move toward his partner. He needn't have bothered. Tony Loest, as if he'd willed it himself, spun around Blake's thick torso. His face slammed into the Pontiac's hood before Kosinski took a step.

"Jesus, Marty, what was that? Was that judo?" Kosinski put his body between Blake's and Loest's. Just in case Loest had any fight left in him.

"That was wrestling," Blake responded. He'd retreated several steps and was now standing behind Kosinski. "A reverse is what it's called. The spin, I mean. There's no move called 'face in the sheet metal.' I made that up on my own. Who is this jerk?"

"His name's Tony Loest. Works construction, so naturally he thinks he's a badass." Kosinski flashed his nastiest grin, even though he suspected that Loest couldn't see it through the blood. "Tony, I want you to go inside, wash your face, and have a drink. Tell Ed to put it on my tab."

"Fuck you, Kosinski. I ain't afraid of you."

Kosinski responded by slamming his fist into Tony Loest's chest.

Loest, who never saw it coming, doubled over and began to vomit enthusiastically.

"Packert, you hear me?" Kosinski kept his eyes on Loest, expecting him to revive, to live up to his reputation.

"I hear you." Candy Packert's voice was matter-of-fact. There was no disrespect in it.

"Take Tony inside, Packert. And keep him out of trouble. If you don't, I'm gonna see the narcs down at the One-O-Nine. Tell 'em what you and Tony are doing at Cryders."

"No problem. We're on the way."

Kosinski waited until Loest and Packert disappeared into the bar, then took Blake's arm and led him off down the street. "You were wonderful, Marty. I'm very impressed. Really, I'm not bullshitting here. I took you for an intellectual type. What with the computer and everything, you can hardly blame me."

"Cut the crap," Blake responded. "I didn't come here to be patronized by a drunk."

"Well, why *did* you come. Seeing as we're supposed to meet at the lawyer's office tomorrow morning."

"I came because I've got an address on Kamal Collars and I want to find him before we go to Steinberg's."

Kosinski started to respond, caught himself, grinned sheepishly as he realized that he really *was* impressed. Impressed and, in some way, proud. "You did that with the computer?"

"I did it with somebody else's computer."

"Yeah, whose?"

"Not your business, Kosinski. Look, Collars is on welfare. Disability, actually. Two weeks ago, a case worker paid him a home visit at the Chatham Hotel on West Twenty-ninth Street, near the river. I want you to go over there with me."

"That's great, Marty. Good timing. Most of those welfare hotels, if you're not inside by nine o'clock, you lose the bed." Kosinski felt a wave of gratitude wash over him. He raised a hand to his face, found his cheeks warm, thought, Jeez, I hope I'm not blushing. And if I am, I hope it's too dark for Blake to see it.

"What I want from you," Blake said, "is your expertise and your badge. In case we get some lip from the hotel rent-a-cops."

"That could be a problem, Marty. Seeing as how I'm not a cop any more and I don't *have* a badge."

"Kosinski, you look like a cop, you talk like a cop, you dress like a cop, you even smell like a cop. You make the right faces, you'll never have to show your badge."

"All right, Marty. Sounds good to me. Whatta ya say we swing by my apartment and I pick up my .38?"

"Why, you planning to shoot someone?"

"It's not about actually shooting anybody." Unless, Kosinski thought, it's about shooting *me*. "But there's nothing looks more cop than a shoulder rig under a cheap suit. What you do is leave the jacket unbuttoned; let 'em get a look at your .38. An ordinary citizen might still ask to see your tin, but street people think asking for ID is a sign of disrespect. I guess it's because they've gotten their faces slapped for doing it. Just keep in mind—getting some mutt to open his mouth doesn't mean the truth is what's coming out. In fact, for some of these people, lying to cops is a matter of honor."

THIRTEEN

"See, what I'm hoping, Marty, is that this alibi witness works out for Billy Sowell. Because if he doesn't, we're gonna have a hell of a time on our hands."

"Why's that?" They were passing over the Triborough Bridge and most of Blake's attention was occupied by the Manhattan skyline to the south. It was a clear night and the parade of skyscrapers, their lit windows gleaming like the diamonds in one of Rebecca Webber's better necklaces, seemed to retreat like soldiers into the deep black of a starless sky. In a matter of hours, Rebecca would be flying off into that sky. She would leave him without a moment's regret, would feel nothing but anticipation as she slid into her first-class seat. Which was only fitting. Why should she treat him like a man when he behaved like a stray mutt with a hard-on?

"It should be obvious, Marty. I'm surprised you don't know."

Blake turned to find Kosinski nursing the now-traditional pint of Smirnoff. "I'm getting real sick of you telling me what I don't know."

"Somebody's gotta do it. Because from what I can see, you don't know anything."

Kosinski's voice lacked detectable sarcasm; it was fatherly, concerned, sincere, which made it all the worse. Blake figured he should be pissed, but he actually felt pretty good. Most likely, Rebecca was packing her things, laying out various ensembles, wondering how much she could fit into several trunks and a full set of Luis Vuitton. He had no way of knowing when she'd come back; or if she'd still be interested when she did. Maybe she'd fasten onto some blond Bavarian stud with a full collection of whips and chains; maybe she'd stay in Europe, conquer the continent, flash the old world a little new world decadence. When he thought about it, Blake felt relieved. The weight was off and that made the question of who did what to whom entirely moot.

"You wanna know why I don't drink, Kosinski?" Blake said, the question surprising him even as he asked it.

"Astonish me. Tell me you're *not* an alcoholic."

"First, the truth is that I do drink. In this business, there are times when you can't refuse a social drink. But that's where I let it go. One drink, held in my hand until the ice melts. Now, I used to drink pretty hard when I was in my early twenties. That went on for about five years. Most nights and every weekend I'd make the bar scene on the Upper West Side. I'd have a few drinks and look around for someone who deserved to get his ass kicked. If I couldn't find a likely candidate, I'd keeping drinking until I didn't care about the 'deserved' part. I was a shit-kicker and proud of it, Kosinski. Thought I was the baddest motherfucker in New York. Then one day I picked the wrong bar and got myself worked over with a matched set of Louisville Sluggers. Spent a week in Mt. Sinai considering my fate while the fractures healed to the point where I could walk on crutches. Thinking about what a jerk I was and that I couldn't control what alcohol did to me. You following me here?"

"Sure."

"So, the question, for me, was do you learn from your mistakes? Or do you go right back out there and maybe this time get killed? Guess which one I picked?"

"Well, it seems to me like you're pretty belligerent even without the booze. You didn't start usin' dope, did ya?"

"Funny."

"Look, Marty, I'm not saying you're weak or stupid, but there's a few things you should understand. Go back to what I said before. About giving the kid an alibi. About what happens if we *can't* give the kid an alibi."

"I've already thought about it." Blake was steering the Taurus around a construction site on the Drive. Wishing he'd taken the Midtown Tunnel. He had to change lanes, but the yellow cab on his left was determined to keep him where he was. Blake watched the turbaned driver's lips move, wondered if he was being called the son of a profligate donkey. Or if the Sikh language had words like cocksucker and shithead.

"And did you come to any conclusions?"

"No, I didn't." Blake slid in behind the cab, began to inch forward. "Beyond the obvious."

"Which is what?"

"Which is that I'm being paid three hundred dollars a day plus expenses, some of which I mark up." Blake grinned, then realized that Kosinski wasn't going for it. Not this time. "If you can't put Sowell somewhere else when the killing went down," he said matter-of-factly, "then you have to find the actual killer."

"And that doesn't make you nervous? Being as the 'actual killer' was able to reach into the New York Police Department, the DA's office, and maybe the New York Supreme Court and Legal Aid to put someone else in prison?"

"It would, if I thought it was gonna come down to that. But it'll take a month before I get to the point where I have to admit that I can't provide Sowell with an alibi. By that time, Steinberg'll be ready to go into court with your testimony. He'll also be sick of parting with two grand a week. Remember, he's using his own money. No, Kosinski, I'm not worried about going up against the NYPD, because it's never gonna happen."

They drove the rest of the way in (from Marty Blake's point of view, anyway) merciful silence. It was Friday night and there were people about, but this particular slice of Manhattan, sandwiched between the sex and violence of Times Square to the north and the illicit glitter of Greenwich Village to the south, lacked both the focus and the crowds associated with New York nightlife. Blake was making his way crosstown on Twenty-ninth Street, carefully skirting Penn Station and its piggyback neighbor, Madison Square Garden. Though he knew the Garden, home to the Rangers and the Knicks, was usually dark in the summertime, he wasn't ready to chance a convention of Seventh Day Adventists or Jehovah's Witnesses.

The drive took him past the stolid prosperity of Murray Hill's carefully preserved brownstones, the newly renovated, low-rise office buildings clustered around Park Avenue South, the wholesale flower district, now shuttered, near Sixth Avenue, finally into a neighborhood of thoroughly neglected tenements.

The Chatham Hotel, a half block from the Hudson River, offered no surprises. A six-story, redbrick apartment building flanked by two identical six-story, redbrick buildings, it typified the decline of a once-proud neighborhood. Somewhere near the turn of the century, the landlord-owner had stood alongside his builder and surveyed the completed work with justifiable satisfaction. All three structures had elaborate cornices, complete with gargoyles at the corners. The lintels beneath the tall windows sported bunches of carved stone grapes and the broad stoops leading up to the front doors were protected by wrought-iron railings. It was good; it was solid; it would stand.

That pride was long gone, as long gone as the middle-class tenants who'd once lived here. The buildings on either side of the Chatham were abandoned, their windows closed-off with sheet metal, their doorways now solid walls of cinder block. The Chatham, itself, showed every indication of following its neighbors on the downward spiral from respectable housing to rubble-strewn lot. The mortar between the rows of brick had retreated so far, that it seemed, in the dim light of the single working street lamp, as if the bricks were actually floating. Broken windows, missing lintels, knots of ragged men sharing pints of Thunderbird, whores in day-glo spandex, drug dealers and their suburban customers—Blake felt slightly disoriented, as if he was again approaching the walls of the Columbia Correctional Facility. Meanwhile, Kosinski, already out of the car, was sucking in the night breeze like it was blowing across a field of tulips. Instead of the Hudson River.

"'It's a beautiful day in the neighborhood, a beautiful day in the neighborhood,'" he sang happily.

Blake, as he stepped out of the Taurus, watched the night birds drift away. They were fairly circumspect about it, floating down the block like styrofoam cups in a drainage ditch.

"Respect for the badge," Kosinski announced. "There's nothing like it. The darlin' mutts and the darlin' mopes all know we're not coming for *them*. Yet they slink into the night like assassins making their get-away. Admitting that it's our turf, in the end. Not theirs. Are we ready, Detective Blake?"

The lobby of the Chatham was predictably threadbare. Though, in Blake's eyes, reasonably clean, it smelled of booze, piss, and puke, as if the stench of despair was an unavoidable element in the atmosphere its inhabitants breathed. There was no desk, of course, no bellboys ready to help with the luggage—just two uniformed security guards seated behind a table set in the middle of the floor.

"Gentlemen," Kosinski walked over to the security guards, leaned on the table, let his jacket fall open in case they'd missed the hint.

"What you want?"

The guard who spoke was middle-aged, gray-haired, balding. His nameplate read "Jackson." The second guard, much younger, didn't bother to look up from the newspaper. His nameplate read, "Peterson."

"Well the first thing I want is to know if either of you boys are on parole?"

Blake saw the two heads snap to attention, felt a half-smile crawl over his face, knew that if he had to do this himself, he'd be entirely lost.

"Why you wanna mess with us, officer?" Jackson muttered. "Bein' as we ain't done nothin' to you."

"The nature of the beast," Kosinski returned. "It doesn't like to be disrespected."

"Well, that's interesting." Peterson folded his newspaper carefully, laid it in his lap. "Because I'm not on parole. Nor have I disrespected you in any way."

"Now, you jus' shut that college-boy mouth, Emil," Jackson said quickly. "I can handle this shit without no help. Y'unnerstand what ah'm sayin'?" He waited until Peterson went back to his newspaper, then folded his hands. "What can I do for you gentlemen?"

"We're looking for a man named Kamal Collars, Mister Jackson," Blake said. "We understand that he has a room here."

"No, sir," Jackson shook his head. "Ain't no Kamal Collars livin' at the Chatham."

"Look, we know he was visited here by a social worker less than a month ago. I can understand why you'd want to protect him, but he's not wanted for any crime. We . . ."

"Don't matter why you want the boy. He don't live here."

"This Collars' mail drop?" Kosinski asked matter-of-factly.

"What you say?"

Kosinski reached across the table, snatched the newspaper out of Peterson's hands, tossed it on the floor. Peterson looked at the paper, then started to rise. Blake, noting the smirk on Kosinski's face, took a step forward.

"We're not gonna have any trouble here," Kosinski said. "Because all we want is your cooperation. As good Americans, you owe us that much. Am I right, or wrong?"

Jackson put a restraining hand on his partner's arm. "Look, officer, I can't make the man be where he ain't. You could trus' me on this. If I had him in the closet, ah'd take him out and give him to you."

"That's too bad, Jackson, because what I'm gonna have to do is knock on every door in this fuckin' dive. I'm gonna have to roust the whores doin' business here, interrupt the dope deals, report whatever I see to the welfare people. By the time I get done, this hotel's gonna look like the buildings next door."

"Damn, officer. Ain't no need to do that. Mister Boazman, the manager, he's comin' in tomorra mornin', tell you anythin' you need to know."

"Glad to hear that, Jackson, but tomorrow's tomorrow and this is tonight and you're lyin' in my face."

"No . . ."

"Try to look at it from my point of view. See, I know that you know who Kamal Collars is. I know you know how to find him if his case-worker should happen to show up unannounced. I know that you know that Kamal Collars has to have an address in order to be eligible for welfare. I know that you know that he hands a piece of his check over to your boss in return for the privilege of listing this sleazy fuck-ing dive as his official residence. Now, truth be told, Jackson, I don't get a thrill out of harassing ex-cons tryin' to go straight. No sir, and if Mister Boazman was around, I wouldn't be botherin' you at all; I'd just go harass *him*, if you take my meaning. But Boazman ain't here and I can't wait for tomorrow morning, so if you don't give me the straight shit on Kamal Collars, I'm gonna tear the hotel apart lookin' for him."

Jackson met Kosinski's eyes for the first time. There was smoke in that meeting; Blake could smell it in Kosinski's thin-lipped grin, in the cop-hate radiating from Jackson's expressionless face. These were men who knew each other, who bargained on their own terms.

"Look, Mr. Jackson," Blake said, "like I told you before, Kamal Collars isn't wanted for anything. He didn't commit any crime that we know about. Help us locate him, and we'll be on our way. It's that simple."

Jackson glanced at his partner. "Get in the wind, college boy. I gotta talk private."

FOURTEEN

"See, gentlemen," Jackson said, once his partner was out the door, "what I got here is a problem. I ain't sayin' as I don't wanna help y'all out, but I do got a problem."

Blake sighed, shook his head, repeated himself. "We're not here to arrest Kamal Collars. Trust us on this. Collars'll be *grateful*."

"Ain't about Kamal." He pronounced it Ka-*mal*. "Old Kamal's just about through. Street done ate him up. Gettin' ready to shit him out, too. Kamal got the TB. Y'unnerstand what ah'm sayin' here? He got the kind they can't fix."

Kosinski circled the table, sat in Peterson's chair. He fished the Smirnoff out of his pocket, took a long drink, then passed it over to the security guard.

"Thank you, sir." Jackson matched Kosinski, sighed contentedly, returned the bottle after carefully wiping the rim on his sleeve. "See, the problem is that me and my partner—and I ain't talkin' 'bout ol' college boy—got a little thing goin' that ain't ezakly on the up and up. What we doin' ain' no crime or nothin', but if my boss find out about it, we gon' be shovelin' some serious shit."

"You takin' money from the whores, Jackson?"

"'The tricks sometime give us a tip to look out for they backs, but that ain't what ah'm gettin' to."

Blake, standing off to one side, knew that he was out of it. That's *if* he was ever in it to begin with. The hate had disappeared from Jackson's eyes, the impatience from Kosinski's voice and posture. Somehow, he'd missed the transition, and he felt slightly disoriented, as if he'd skipped a chapter in a spy novel.

"Well, it *is* gettin' kinda late, Jackson. And my partner needs his beauty rest."

"Okay, Im'a get to the point. Me and my man got forty cots set up in the basement. Charge two bucks a night to let folks sleep down there. What we givin' 'em is security, if you take my meanin'. Don't let in no crackheads, no knuckleheads. Don't allow no fightin', no stealin', no fuckin'. Mens and womens can sleep in peace 'cause they steady knowin' they gonna wake up with they goods where they left 'em. Plus, in the winter they could stay warm."

"Sounds like an okay deal. Is Kamal down there?"

"Yeah, he with us mos' every night."

"And you're afraid the manager—what's his name? Boazman, right? You're afraid Boazman'll find out and close you down."

"Nossir. Ah'm worried Boazman gonna find out and axe me for a piece. He ain't the owner, y'unnerstand what ah'm sayin? The owner don't come near the hotel; fraid he gonna get hisself busted for all the violations ain't been fixed. That's why he leave the managin' to Boazman. Now, I ain't greedy. Share and share alike, that's my thing. But Boazman, he already collectin' from the whores, and he ain't sharin' his shit. So, why I gotta take care of him?"

"No reason I can see," Kosinski said. "And no reason why me and my partner should ever speak to Mister Boazman. Being as he doesn't know anything about the work we're doing. You wanna take us down, now?"

"Yeah." Jackson stood up, stretched, snatched his flashlight off the table. "Y'all watch yo step."

They made their way, Blake trailing, across the lobby and down a narrow, winding stairway. Two low-wattage light bulbs screwed into ceiling fixtures provided some illumination, but not enough for Blake to actually see where he was placing his feet.

"This the only way out?" he asked. Imagining a fire, imagining humans jammed into the narrow passageway, roasting like pigs at a luau.

"There's a door out to the back." Jackson's disembodied voice floated past the back of Kosinski's head. "But it don't open no more. Rusted shut, plus Boazman got it locked. Yo, Screw-Boy, come on out here. Ah got peoples with me."

Blake stumbled coming off the last step. There was no light in the passageway except for the dim circle cast by Jackson's cheap flashlight. Suddenly, he found himself listening for scrabbling claws, the sharp protest of a disturbed rat; what he heard was muffled snores, humans muttering, coughing, crying in their sleep. He tried to imagine the actual room, the men and women lying on their cots, and wondered just what hell could have motivated them to pay for the privilege of sleeping in *this* hell.

"Jackson?" A uniformed guard stepped into the circle cast by the flashlight. He cradled an aluminum baseball bat across his chest.

"Yeah, it's me, Screw-Boy. These mens here to see Kamal Collars. Bring him on into the coal room. They got a light in there."

"What kind of men, Jackson? What do they want with Kamal?"

"Don't matter. We got to bring him out and there ain't nothin' more to it. Y'all jus' go fetch his ass."

Screw-Boy's mouth curled into a frown of disapproval. His eyes narrowed in momentary defiance, but he didn't argue, despite the baseball bat. Instead, he executed a perfect about-face and stepped off into the darkness.

"This way, officers." Jackson led them into a small room, then flicked on a light. The space was completely barren; the coal chute was sealed and the furnace had been removed sometime in the distant past. What remained was a concrete floor, plaster walls, a plank ceiling. "This the only room down here what ain't occupied. Y'all *could* do it upstairs, but there's liable to be peoples comin' in and out. I got no way to stop that."

"This'll do just fine," Kosinski said. "Leave the flashlight on your way out."

Blake, knowing that *he* wouldn't have walked into that darkness, expected Jackson to put up some kind of an argument, but the security guard simply handed the flashlight to Kosinski and left the room.

"You all right, Marty?"

"Never been better. Say, Kosinski, you think I could take a hit of that vodka?"

"Only if you promise not to kick my ass."

"What I promise is that I *will* kick your ass if you don't give me a drink."

"That's not a wise thing to say, Marty." Kosinski passed over the bottle. "Being as I'm armed and I'm afraid of you."

They heard Kamal Collars before they saw him. Heard the racking cough, the shuffling feet. Blake caught his partner's eye and shrugged. There was no getting out of it, now, but he found himself wishing for a diver's mask and a tank of oxygen. Or that he'd let Kosinski handle it by himself. The vodka rushed up into his brain just as Kamal Collars appeared in the doorway.

He'd once been a very large man, that much was obvious to Blake who'd known some true behemoths in his wrestling days, but only the bones were left now. Collars' filthy jacket hung on the points of his shoulders, collapsed against his sunken chest; his trousers, cinched with twine, dropped over his buttocks with barely a ripple. There were flecks of blood on his lips, more on a handkerchief held between his fingers. His eyes, to Blake, seemed utterly without light, or hope.

"You wanted me for something?"

"It's about Billy Sowell," Blake said. "I'm working for him."

"Billy?" A wistful smile pulled at Collars' mouth. "How long has it been now? Must be more than a year since he went away."

"More than two." Blake looked over at Kosinski, got a nod of approval. "Look, Mr. Collars, my name's Blake. I'm a private investigator." He fished out his credentials and tried to pass them over. Collars merely shook his head. "I've been hired by Billy's lawyer to help get him out of jail. I understand that you knew him back then."

"We were partners. We did everything together but fuck." Collars' voice was pitched so low it was barely distinguishable from his raspy breath.

"Partners in what, Mr. Collars? Could you explain that?"

"Old Billy was the greatest panhandler I've ever seen. He looked like something out of Charles Dickens. Folks just couldn't walk by. Me, on the other hand, being as I'm a big, dark, male African-American, white people used to shit their pants at the sight of me. Good for Billy; bad for me is the way you could look at it, I suppose. But Billy had his problems, too." Collars reached into his jacket, pulled out a pint of Thunderbird wine. He drank deeply, then grinned. "Don't suppose you'd want some of this?" The grin became a laugh when Blake merely shook his head, a laugh that ended in a coughing fit. "Oh, Lord, we do have fun, don't we?"

Blake fought off his annoyance, reminded himself that he had a job to do. "A laugh a minute is what I'd call it. Now, you were talking about your partnership with Billy Sowell."

"Yeah, well the thing was that Billy couldn't hold onto his money. All those qualities that got him the quarters in the first place worked against him when he was . . . when he was off-duty. He was little; he was retarded; he didn't know squat about the streets; he didn't have a violent bone in his body. No surprise he got ripped off three or four times a week. Me, I was living close enough to see what was happening, but I didn't do anything about it. Just felt it was none of my business, which is what comes of spending most of your life in prison. In fact, when I finally stepped in, it wasn't because I felt any affection for Billy Sowell. I was just tired of collecting aluminum cans from trash baskets.

"It was January and we had a fire going in a fifty-gallon drum. They were doing some construction work on the Drive and the city workers had stacked dozens of two-by-fours behind a fence. Me and the boys cut a hole through the fence on the first night; that gave us plenty of wood. I remember there were five or six of us around the fire, drinking and arguing about whether to let the fire die down before the cops showed up. It was very cold, icicles hangin' down off the roadway, ice on the river, wind blowing hard. If it wasn't for that fire, we'd all have to go into a shelter and that meant leaving our goods unprotected which nobody wanted to do.

"Anyway, I'm standing close to the barrel, trying to keep my feet warm, and I see Billy come walkin' up toward us. He's about fifty yards off when this knucklehead, Kilo Williamson, yokes him from behind. Billy, he gives up the money right away, but that's not enough for Kilo. He starts to yank Billy's coat off, so what I do is pick up a two-by-four, run up to Kilo, and hit him smack in the face. Never liked that motherfucker, but that's not the point. Kilo, he goes down hard, and I hit him while he's down. I hit him and I keep on hitting him until he starts to beg. Then I take the money and give it back to Billy.

"'You fuck with Billy, you fuck with me,' I say, and that's good enough for Kilo. He takes off for Bellevue and a couple dozen stitches. Me, I wait till he's out of sight, then I lead Billy to one side and make him a business proposition.

"'Look, here, Billy' I say, 'The fact is you can't cut it on your own. It's not your fault, but that's the way it is. What you need is a partner and I'm the man. I'll stay with you all day, teach you what you need to know if you're gonna survive out here, watch your back at night. We split fifty-fifty.'

"Now, Billy might be dumb, but he's not stupid. After I explain what fifty-fifty is, he takes the deal. We start off right then and there, split the change, and buy us a bottle of Thunderbird by way of a celebration.

"After that, we were together all the time. I got him his first woman, lady named Tonna worked out of a welfare hotel on Twenty-third Street. She took him on for nothing, claimed she'd never been with a virgin before. Me, I had to pay.

"I tried to teach him how to read and write, too, but he didn't quite get it. Billy liked history as long as I told it like a bedtime story and it had some kind of happy ending. Math was too much for him, but I taught him how to count money which was important. And I took him to the best soup kitchens, showed him where he could get used clothes and shower and find a clean toilet. After . . ."

Blake, his patience exhausted, finally interrupted. "You know, Mr. Collars, it's nice about you and Billy, but . . ."

"I know what you want. You're here about the alibi." Kamal Collars' expression didn't change. His features remained composed, his eyes remote and lifeless. "But I want you to hear the whole thing, so you can explain it to Billy. I never told the story before and it doesn't look as if I'm gonna get a chance to go through it again. I want you to tell Billy that I loved him and I want you to know you're telling the truth when you do. It won't take all that long."

Blake looked over at Kosinski, expecting some display of annoyance. He found the ex-cop leaning against the wall, arms folded across his chest, one hand gripping the pint.

"Just tell it the way you want to," Kosinski said. "But remember this—Billy's in jail and there're people who want to get him out. You've been in prison, so you know what's happening to him up there. I'm sure he'll be happy to hear that you still think about him, but he'll be a lot happier if you help get him back out on the street."

Kamal Collars gave no indication that he'd heard Kosinski. He sipped at his wine, then launched into his story.

"When I was a little boy—maybe three or four—my momma brought home a puppy, told me her name was Nefertiti. Funny giving a queen's name to a runt of a mutt, but my mother always liked to think big. Anyway, me and Nefertiti, we were together all the time. I didn't have any brothers or sisters and we, my momma and me, lived with my granny. Granny was an educated woman, had a college degree from a black college in South Carolina, and she was determined to teach me 'proper' English, which wasn't a whole lot of fun. But that's the way it was: momma brought home the bacon and set the rules; granny nagged at me not to become 'ignorant,' 'worthless,' 'trash,' 'shiftless' . . . hell, her life was filled with traps and over the years I guess I fell into every one of them. But Nefertiti, well, she became my friend.

"You know how kids are; they can make a stuffed toy come alive, especially if they live in neighborhoods where they can't go out and play. Especially if they have grannys who think the neighbors' kids are too no-account to associate with. Nefertiti was right there for me, as if she understood my loneliness, as if she chose to share it with me. At night she'd come into the bed and nobody, not my momma or my granny, was allowed into that room. Momma tried it once and got bit on her ankle. After that, if she wanted me, she'd call from the doorway.

"It went on that way for about a year, until one afternoon Momma took me and Nefertiti to the little playground they had in the back of the project. The city had fixed it up and everybody was going down to celebrate the reopening. I wasn't used to being outside and I was pretty much in awe of all the activity. I didn't play on the swings or the seesaw, just stayed on the edge of the sandbox with Nefertiti. Late in the afternoon, this boy came over. He was older than me, but I can't really say how much. He sat on the ground, asked me if Nefertiti was my dog, and I said, 'Yes, she is. She's my friend.'

The boy stared at me for a moment; he didn't say another word, just stared. Then he took out a knife and stabbed Nefertiti in the chest. Then he grinned and broke out laughing. Then he stabbed her again. Nefertiti didn't scream or anything; she rolled on her side and looked at me with that look dogs get when they're trying to understand something. I knew she was asking me to help her, but I was frozen. I couldn't do anything but watch.

"Now the thing about it was that beyond the grief, and there was plenty of that, I couldn't shake the feeling that I should have done something to stop that boy. It didn't matter that my momma told me the boy was crazy, that he'd been in trouble before, that he should never have been allowed to go off by himself. What I decided, as time went by, is that if I really loved Nefertiti, I would've put myself in front of that knife. And the reason I didn't was because I didn't deserve *her* love.

"I guess you could say that kids take notions and there's no getting past them. Just chalk it up to that. But what happened is I did the same thing with Billy. It's like I went through the wrong door in my life and I can't find my way back."

Kamal Collars paused, looked over at Kosinski as if to find confirmation. He sipped from his bottle, going about it slowly, deliberately, ceremoniously. Then he took a deep breath, coughed into his handkerchief, stared at the bright red blood for a moment.

"This is the way it went down," he said. "After Billy got busted, I went to the precinct and spoke to two cops, a white cop named Brannigan and a black cop named Cobb. I told them exactly what I'm gonna tell you now. On the night that woman was killed, me and Billy were caught in the middle of a riot at Tompkins Square Park. The riot was supposed to be about the homeless people sleeping in the park, but it was really a grudge match between the cops and the anarchists. It started with the anarchists screaming in the cops' faces, then jumped up to bottle and bricks. What the cops did, after they covered their nameplates and badge numbers with black tape, was go out and break heads. If you remember, the newspapers called it a police riot and the cops got blamed.

"Naturally, the two cops, Brannigan and Cobb, didn't believe me. Which is what I more or less expected. Why would anyone believe a homeless drunk with a prison record?

"'Look, here,' I said, 'I got a way to prove that Billy was at the riot. When the shit broke out, me and Billy tried to get away. We didn't have no more love for the anarchists and the punks than we had for the cops. Like, it wasn't our *business*, if you take my meaning. But no matter what direction we tried, we had to turn around because the cops were everywhere. Me and Billy, we were standing up against the liquor store on Avenue B, near Eleventh Street, when two cops grabbed this Hare Krishna dude, threw him down on the sidewalk, and started beatin' on his sorry ass. I thought they were gonna kill him, and maybe they would've, but a couple minutes into it, a photographer came running up and started taking pictures. When the cops saw him, they picked up the Hare Krishna and cuffed him. Now, the photographer was out in the street and me and Billy were standing behind the cops, so Billy has to be in those pictures. All you gotta do is find them.'

"Brannigan, he asks me if I know what paper the reporter worked for. I told him I didn't, but that the man was definitely wearing a press pass on his coat. Which is why the cops didn't kick his ass, too.

"'All right,' Brannigan says, 'we'll check it out. Where can we find you?' I told him I was staying down by the river, then I left. Walked right out the front door of the precinct, on my way to visit Billy in the Tombs. I didn't get half a block before Brannigan came up behind me. He yanked me into the precinct parking lot, and hit me in my face with the butt of the pistol. Didn't say a word, just started beatin' on me. I covered my head as best I could, but I didn't fight back. Figured I had to take it and that was that. Then I heard this *click* and I looked right up into the barrel of a cocked pistol. I remember that it was a revolver, like the ones the cops carry, but this piece had tape on the grip and around the trigger.

"When I started beggin'—'Please don't kill me, Officer, please don't kill me'—Brannigan got this big grin on his face, a real shit-eater. 'Nigger,' he said, 'I don't wanna see your ugly black face again. Not ever again. You hear what I'm saying, nigger? I see your face again, you're gonna breathe through your fucking forehead.'

"Now, the thing about it is that I could've gone to Billy's lawyer. That's what I thought of when the fear wore off. But then I started thinking if Brannigan would pull a piece in the precinct parking lot, if he'd pistol whip me right out there in the open, he wouldn't stop at nothin'. So what I did was stay out of it. I let Billy go down. Like I let Nefertiti go down. Like I'm goin' down, too. Fair is fair, right?"

FIFTEEN

In his dream, Blake searched for Rebecca Webber. There was something he had to tell her, something important, and as the search proceeded, as it stretched out, becoming more and more hopeless, his mood shifted from determination to anxiety to near panic.

The search began in Rebecca's town house, amid William Webber's personal collection of art-nouveau furnishings, Postimpressionist paintings, and modern sculptures, then jumped suddenly into the basement of the Chatham Hotel. Blake called out Rebecca's name as he groped his way along a darkened hallway, paused to listen for the sound of her voice, her quick, sardonic laughter. At times, he thought he heard an answering call, but her voice, filtered through the moaning, the snoring, the shuffle of feet somewhere in the distance, was too faint to pin down. Maybe it came from here, maybe from there, maybe it wasn't her at all.

Along the way, he ran into Bell Kosinski, Jackson, the security guard, Kamal Collars, Billy Sowell, Max Steinberg. He knew them, despite the gloom, and asked each for help. Their apologetic refusals were filled with pity.

"You one of us, boy," Jackson declared. "Might jus' as well get used to it. Y'uunerstan' what ah'm sayin'?"

Kosinski handed him a stiff drink; Sowell made an obscene proposal, added: "I'm prettier than that bitch, and a *lot* more faithful."

Kamal Collars offered to trade Rebecca for Queen Nefertiti. "Fair deal, fair deal," he explained.

Blake left them all behind. He proceeded into a space without sound or light, a space where consciousness was the only measure of his own existence. He knew that Rebecca couldn't be present, because there was nothing here, but himself. Then he stumbled into a closed door, yanked it open, was blinded by the unexpected glare.

"Marty, wake up. Marty, Marty. Wake up."

Still half asleep, Blake opened his eyes, thought he saw Rebecca silhoutted against the window, realized it was his mother. His heart sank, even as the dream fled.

"Don't you have an appointment with the lawyer this morning? It's nearly ten o'clock."

Blake sat up in bed, muttered something about working late.

"Well, the coffee's made," Dora Blake said. "I wouldn't have come in, but there's something I want to tell you before you leave."

"All right, all right. What's the weather today?"

"Hot. You won't need a jacket."

Twenty minutes later, Blake, his hair still wet, slipped into a pair of gray cotton slacks, buttoned up a sky-blue silk shirt, jammed his feet into crepe-soled moccasins. He left the bedroom without looking at himself in the mirror.

"So what's the big deal, Ma? And where's the coffee?"

"The coffee's on the stove. And what I have to say isn't a big deal. It's just something I think you need to be aware of."

Blake poured himself a cup of coffee, knowing his mother wouldn't be rushed; he sat down at the kitchen table and stirred a spoonful of sugar into the black liquid.

"I checked out the cop."

"Pardon?"

"Bell Kosinski, I checked him out with your Uncle Patrick. I thought you'd want to know before you got in too deep."

"Ma, he's not my partner. You shouldn't have bothered Uncle Pat." Patrick Blake was an NYPD captain, an insider's insider who worked out of Personnel at 1 Police Plaza.

"Then what is he?"

"A temporary inconvenience is how I try to look at him."

"Being a wise guy isn't gonna help you here, Marty. The reason I know is because I also asked Patrick about Sondra Tillson."

"Why am I not surprised?"

"If you're not interested, we could always go back to the weather."

"Uncle Patrick knew about Sondra Tillson?" It was as close as he could get to an apology.

"Not off the top of his head. I called him yesterday morning and he called me back last night. Apparantly, it wasn't that hard to find out."

Blake drained half the cup, glanced at his watch. "I don't have a lot of time, Ma."

Dora Blake sat down next to her son. She held her cup between her palms, rolled the handle back and forth. "Kosinski was a good cop. Clean, sober, a definite up-and-comer. He made Detective, First, before he was thirty-five. Went along that way for another six or seven years. Then something happened, something at home, his service record doesn't say just what it was, but he started drinking. Patrick said it didn't interfere with his performance rating, which actually went up a little. In fact, if he hadn't taken to boozing openly on the job, nobody would have noticed. As it was, all they asked was that he take a tour on the farm. You know, dry out a little, get it under control. He refused and they eased him out with his pension. No muss, no fuss."

"Is that it?"

"Yeah, Marty, honest and good. That's it." Dora Blake was clearly pissed. "Tell me something, my only son, did you ever stop to think that Kosinski was planted on you?"

"I found *him*, Ma. It wasn't the other way around."

"And the next morning he showed up on your doorstep."

Blake shook his head firmly. "It doesn't matter what I think. The lawyer said to use him and the lawyer's paying the bills. And by the way, if he's a plant, he's not a very good one. I couldn't have gotten as far as I have without Kosinski's help."

"I'm glad you can see that."

"I'm not an idiot, no matter what you believe. Why don't you tell me about Sondra Tillson?"

Dora Blake laid the cup on the table, started to stand, thought better of it. "Patrick can't help you there."

"Can't or won't?"

"Both. Look, we're talking about the job, Marty. Patrick won't betray the job and neither will any other cop. He as much as admitted that cops were involved."

"I already know that." He told her about Kamal Collars, his alibi for Billy Sowell, Brannigan's reaction.

"Why am I not shocked?" She took her son's hand, a gesture that surprised them both. "You've got to be careful, Marty. These crooks carry guns and badges, not pencils. They won't go down without a fight."

Blake stared at his mother's long, bony fingers. He wanted to come up with a typical wise-guy remark, felt that it was expected, like the next step in a tango, but he couldn't do it. "It's not going to come to

that," he said. The pat response sounded like so much wishful thinking, even to him. How many times had he used the same line?
Sometimes it got to the point where even if he was right, he was
wrong. "Are you telling me to drop the case? Get out while I can?"

She drew back. "You have to do the job, Marty. You took it and now
you have to do it."

"So, how do you find these guys, Max?" Bell Kosinski, comfortably
seated in Max Steinberg's office, sniffed at a water glass half filled
with brandy. He let his gaze wander over the lawyer's office, noted the
southwestern motif, the kachina dolls, the eagle feathers, the pottery,
the worn blankets, the antelope skull. "I mean the innocent ones. You
get letters from convicts, or what?"

"Letters?" The wig hopped as Steinberg's mouth opened into a
huge grin. "I get letters by the ton. You wouldn't believe the letters.
'Dear Mister Steinberg: It wasn't me on that videotape in the liquor
store. I admit the robber has an uncanny resemblance to me, but I was
in Hong Kong on a business trip at the time.'"

Kosinski laughed appreciatively. The bouquet of the smoky liquor
was so intoxicating, he almost didn't want to drink it. Almost. "What
about Sowell? How'd you find him?"

"Spoken like a true cop." Steinberg's tone was admiring; the wig
remained still. "Well, he didn't write me a letter. And he still hasn't
figured out that he was framed. To him, it just happened, which is the
way he looks at his whole life."

"After talking to the kid, I can appreciate what you're sayin'. The
poor bastard never saw it coming."

Kosinski's attention drifted to a painting on the surface of a small
wooden table set beneath a window. He wondered why the artist had
chosen to work on a piece of furniture, then realized the design
had been executed with grains of brightly colored sand. "Jeez," he
said, "whatever you do, Max, don't open that window."

"Why? I could always do another one."

"Yeah, you did this yourself?" Kosinski got up to take a closer look,
pausing, as he rose, to drain his glass. The liquor smelled good, tasted
better, hit his empty stomach with the intensity of a Szechuan chili
pepper in an infant's mouth. He dutifully fetched the roll of Tums,
swallowed two, continued over to the table. "This is really great.
How'd you keep the colors apart?"

"The trick, Kosinski, is not to breathe hard while you're working."

"Yeah, I *knew* that. So, tell me, how'd you latch onto Billy Sowell?"

"Joanna Bardo, you know who she is?"

"Uh-uh."

"Blake's former employer. She founded Manhattan Executive Security. A fantastic woman, brilliant, ambitious, cultured . . . very New York, if you take my meaning. Joanna cornered me at a party, a benefit for the Guggenheim Museum. Ran the whole thing down. I had Legal Aid send the original case material over, read it through, and that was that. The kid was framed; I was between causes; all systems were go."

Kosinski nodded as the lawyer told his story. The wig, he noted, was absolutely still, a good sign as far as he was concerned. Steinberg was probably telling the truth.

"Where did Joanna . . . what's her name? Bardo? Where did *she* get it from?"

"Let me think a minute, while I pour you a refill. Wonderful stuff, by the way. Hennessy VO. During the week, I never drink until after the courts close. Saturdays and Sundays . . . well, that's another story."

Kosinski handed the glass over, sat down again. "You know you're in deep here, right? But do you know *how* deep?"

Steinberg's jaw tightened, his lower lip slid up until it touched his nostrils. The transformation was startling. "I don't care if the fucking *mayor's* part of it," he shouted. "I wouldn't give a shit if it was the goddamned *president*. Steinberg doesn't back down."

"But you do understand? You know?"

"Yeah, so what?"

"The kid, Max. Blake hasn't figured it out yet. What's the word they use these days? Denial. The kid's in denial."

Steinberg's expression softened. He shrugged, took a drink. "I might have made a mistake there. Joanna led me to believe Blake was a lot more experienced. See, the thing of it was I didn't wanna hire an ex-cop, because cops were involved in the frame. I had no way of knowing who could be reached and who couldn't."

"You still don't."

"True."

"So where does that leave me?"

"Kosinksi, that leaves you giving me a sworn deposition that'll prove fabricated evidence was employed against my client. Now, as I fully intend to use this evidence to nail the NYPD in general and your ex-partner, Tommy Brannigan, in particular, the way I see it is that once you put your John Hancock on the dotted line, you're committed. Whether you know it or not."

When Marty Blake showed up fifteen minutes later, Kosinski moved off to one side of the room. He let his hands fumble through a book of photographs while Blake made his report, figuring why steal the kid's thunder? Why not let the kid shine? That was why he hadn't mentioned Kamal Collars in his conversation with Steinberg. That was why he'd steered away from any discussion of the case.

It was Blake's evident professionalism that surprised him, the bound interim report, the concise verbal presentation, the demand for payment before the report was turned over. Kosinski couldn't have been more pleased. He celebrated by draining his glass.

"Normally," Blake was saying, "I'd have asked for a retainer, in advance. I didn't because you were recommended by Joanna, but now I'm getting close to the end of the puzzle. In fact, from what I'm giving you today, you could close it off without me. So . . ."

Steinberg was working his way through the statement, peering at it, running the tip of one manicured fingernail down the column of figures. As he worked, the wig crept forward. The movement, oddly formal, was slow, but steady. When the wig covered his upper forehead like a street demon's bandanna, he looked up.

"Two thousand dollars? *Boychick*, you gotta be kidding me."

Blake shook his head slowly "Joanna taught me never to joke about money. I think the statement is clear. I billed you for my time, my expenses, and my associate's time."

"Your associate? This Kosinski is now an associate?"

"I couldn't have gotten this far without him. Why shouldn't he get paid? I mean, look at it this way, Max, I think we can wrap this up in a couple of days. Without Kosinski it might have dragged on for weeks. At three hundred dollars a day, plus expenses. The way I see it, you're getting off easy."

SIXTEEN

Blake never doubted that he'd find the photograph, never doubted that Collars was telling the truth, didn't even bother to add "if the photo exists." He accepted Steinberg's check, then made the suggestion he'd been prepared to make all along.

"I want you to get on the phone, Max. All these newspapers have morgues and I'm gonna have to get into them. It'd go a lot faster if you could pull some strings. Cut the red tape, so to speak."

Steinberg, having read Blake's report, having paid Blake's bill, readily agreed. Naturally, as a New York celebrity, he admitted to knowing everyone.

"In fact," he said, "if you come up with that photo, I'm gonna call in the media. Put a little heat on the courts."

"There's some people ain't gonna like that," Kosinski said. "You might wanna think about doin' this on the quiet. Not make any more waves than necessary."

"Steinberg doesn't back down."

"That's all well and good, Max. I mean, it's nice to be macho, but there's another way to look at it: if Billy Sowell didn't kill Sondra Tillson, folks are gonna wonder who *did* kill her. Now, if we go about our business nice and quiet, certain people could let Billy go and just forget about it. If we make a lot of noise, on the other hand, the cops're gonna have to reopen the investigation. You can see how that might cause some problems for whoever killed her. Likewise for the folks who covered it up."

Blake barely heard the conversation. His mind was already forming a plan of attack, looking for an organizing principle. In addition to four major dailies, New York had a dozen weekly papers, some of them very small and very local. Add six television stations, a handful of magazines, the wire services, and the distinct (and very disturbing) possibility that the photographer Collars remembered had been one of hundreds of New York independents, a free-lancer looking for the big break, and it became obvious that the situation demanded structure.

As always, Blake would turn to his computer for answers. Or, rather, he'd turn to Joanna Bardo's computer. As far as he knew, there was no data base for newspaper photographs, but if he could pull up the various articles written the morning after the riot, he might get a hint as to which papers had reporters present when the shit hit the fan. Collars had remembered one photographer taking Billy's picture, but, in fact, Billy Sowell's face might appear in the background of any photo taken that evening. Hopefully, there was more than one needle in the haystack.

"Look, I'm gonna take off." Blake stood abruptly. "Max, call me when you get through making those calls. If I'm not home, leave a message on the machine. What I'm gonna do is get on the computer and check a few things out. And don't worry, being as it's Saturday and I'm in a good mood, you won't get charged." He took a deep breath. It was time to bite the bullet, and, to his surprise, he wasn't looking forward to it.

"Bell," he said, consciously using Kosinski's first name, "it's been great. I'll get your money to you as soon as Max's check clears." He noted Kosinski's surprise, the way his eyes dropped to his hands. It was too bad, really. Because he liked the ex-cop, knew he could have used him in a thousand ways. If he wasn't a hopeless drunk.

"Yeah, great," Kosinski muttered. "You know where to find me."

Blake wasn't surprised to discover Conrad Angionis in Manhattan Exec's computer room on a Saturday morning. Cynthia Barret hadn't been exaggerating when she'd insisted that Conrad "practically lives here." Joanna Bardo's presence, on the other hand, was totally unexpected. Joanna, a tireless self-promoter, usually spent her weekends in the Hamptons or Connecticut, brownnosing former, present, and prospective clients.

"Marty, it's so nice to see you again. It's been a long time." She was sitting in Cynthia Barret's chair, her smile every bit as nasty as her tone of voice.

"You come in just to see me, Joanna? I didn't think I was that important." Blake, who could have done the work from the modem in his own apartment, had called ahead, just to be sure Conrad was in the computer room. Conrad, apparently under orders, had run to Joanna with the news.

"If Mohammed won't come to the mountain . . ."

"I've been busy."

"Too busy to make a phone call?"

"You're *not* the client, Joanna. Max Steinberg is happy with my work, if not with my fees, and that's all that counts."

"I like to be kept informed, Marty. I like to know what's going on."

"Yeah? Well, you're definitely gonna be disappointed here, because I'm not gonna tell you anything beyond that fact that I should have the case wrapped up in a few days. You need more than that, you might wanna give Max Steinberg a call. He loves to bullshit and right now, even as we speak, he's chugging Hennessy like there's no tomorrow."

Joanna's right hand fluttered up to her face, reached for an invisible cigarette. Blake smiled, remembering that Joanna had once described her two-pack-a-day habit as "my single weakness."

"You might want to remember that you're going to need me in the future."

"It's a matter of professional ethics, Joanna. As in client confidentiality being the only bit of ethics in the whole damned profession. Don't take it personally."

Joanna stood up, managed a smile. "You're right. After all, it's not like I'm guaranteeing payment. You really think you'll be able to wrap this up soon?"

"Very soon."

"Then I'd better get busy finding something else for you."

She was wearing a violet blouse and a pair of very plain, very tight cotton pants. Blake, as she turned to leave, was aware of something different, something changed. She was nearly out of the room, before he figured it out.

"Joanna," he called. "What happened to your ass?"

"My what?" She turned to face him.

"Your ass, Joanna. As in, half of it isn't there any more."

"Liposuction, Marty. I finally went and did it. What do you think?"

"What I think, Joanna, is that now you're finally perfect."

Blake found Conrad Angionis installed on his throne in the computer room. One look at his face told Blake that Conrad wasn't about to apologize for jumping through Joanna's hoop. Why should he?

Conrad's love for the computer and what he could do with it naturally extended to Manhattan Executive and Joanna Bardo. Blake didn't sign his paycheck.

"You working this afternoon, Conrad, or playing?" Blake asked after ' the ritual handshake.

"Both. I'm teaching Maggie to take a social security number and run it through every data base in her memory, from the most to the least likely. The problem is which is most and which is least. More or less would have been easier."

"Doesn't that get expensive? Who's gonna pay for it?"

Conrad sniffed, crossed his legs, folded his arms over his chest. "Someday, we'll need the capability. When that day comes, we'll have it. Besides, Maggie likes to learn."

"Maggie *likes* to learn? Buddy, you've gone over the edge."

"You never understood, Marty. That's why you went into field work. It's not your fault, really, but that's the way it is. Now, did you come here to work, or to ridicule me."

Blake outlined the project, giving as little information as possible. Conrad, who could negotiate the maze of data bases in half the time it took Blake, was to key in the day, November twenty-eighth, the year, and the word "riot." Blake would review the printouts, try to guess which papers were on the spot and which were merely putting up a brave front.

Conrad, with a small gesture of contempt for the simplicity of the task, went to work immediately. Blake sat back, watched Conrad's long fingers dance across the keyboard, roll the mouse over its pad. He felt removed from the sordid activities of the past few days. With Kosinski's help (he had to admit), he'd come through his first battle-field experience, a victory, no doubt about it. It was just a matter of mopping up.

Blake's thoughts drifted to Billy Sowell in his prison cell. He began to imagine Sowell's life, thought better of it, realized, to his surprise, that this was the first time his work had dealt with protecting an individual. Up to now, he'd protected property, and usually the property of corporations that were little better than the individuals or companies ripping them off.

He pictured Billy Sowell walking out of prison, walking past the correction officer with the crew cut. There would be nothing remotely resembling freedom on the other side of the gate. Not for a retarded kid with no resources, no friends. What would he do? Go back to Kamal Collars? Find another giant to protect him and his packing-crate home?

What *I'm* gonna do, Blake decided, is push Steinberg into finding the kid a place to live. There's gotta be a city program somewhere that hasn't been gutted and I'm gonna make sure that Billy Sowell gets into it.

"Martin, you still here?"

"Huh? Oh, yeah, Conrad. I'm here. What'd you come up with?"

"The New York Times. Daily News to follow."

Blake scanned the predictably small *Times* article, then tossed it away in disgust. According to the grand monarch, the police "alleged" that the rioters' conduct demanded a response, that the response was necessary to maintain "order." The rioters "alleged" that the cops had covered their badges and nameplates with black friction tape as part of a well-developed plan to "punish the homeless." Local residents "alleged" that the police had attacked them without provocation as they were making their way home. The *Times* article had appeared on page two of the Metro section; there wasn't a hint of personal observation in its matter-of-fact tone.

The reporting in the *Daily News*, when Blake finally got his hands on it, was a lot more promising. The reporter, Brad Cooper, was claiming that the cops had thrown him through a storefront window. The term "police riot" appeared several times in the article.

The *Post*'s coverage was predictably brief, but that didn't mean anything. Photos were the *Post*'s specialty. There might be a half dozen to go along with the few paragraphs of print. *Newsday*, also predictably, had the most extensive coverage. With two stories on the riot, a separate piece on the long-term conflict between cops and self-styled anarchists, a history of the homeless in Tompkins Square Park, *Newsday* had covered the story like they owned it.

"Anything else, Marty?"

Conrad was clearly bored. He sprawled in his chair, sipped at a mug of tea, calmly picked his nose. Blake knew it was time to bow out, that he could accomplish nothing to justify the bill he was running up. The problem, he thought, is that it's Saturday, it's two o'clock in the afternoon, and I don't have a damn thing to do. Well, maybe I'll hit the weight room later on. Pump some iron, bullshit with the gym rats. Work off the tension.

"Tell you what, Conrad, kick out the follow-up stories for, say, the next ten days. Let's see where it goes. Also, get me issues of the *Village Voice*, the *East Village Other*, and the *Soho Spirit* for the same period. Let's see who did what. Meanwhile, I'm gonna call the client."

Although Steinberg was not at his office, the message on Marty Blake's answering machine was succinct enough:

> *Steinberg here. Look, bubbe, we got real lucky. The papers don't hang onto photos unless they're printed, but in this particular case, the DA's office professed an interest in prosecuting the cops (which, by the way, never actually happened), and subpoenaed all the photos and every inch of videotape shot the night of the riot. Tomorrow morning, go down to the DA's office, see an ADA named Benny Green. Benny's an old friend of mine. He'll have the package ready for you.*

PART TWO

PROLOGUE

Billy Sowell lies quietly on his bunk. He is trying to make a decision, but decisions do not come easily to him. He sits up and looks around his cell, notes the bare concrete walls, shakes his head. He feels the walls should be decorated, like the walls of other prisoners, though he will not put up photographs of spread-eagled women. Something about the open mouths, the gaping vaginas, the legs pulled back into the chest—Billy is not aroused; he is afraid.

But he thinks the whole thing is too much for him anyway. The sex thing. There are no pictures of naked men on anybody's walls, not one single picture. So why do they come to him for sex? Why do they come to a boy if they want sex with a woman?

He thinks that maybe it's because he *is* a woman. Now that he knows how to put on the eyeliner, the mascara, the lipstick. Now that he knows enough to make the men do their business quickly, which is something only a woman could know.

Billy hears the CO making his way along the catwalk. The CO's name is Tompkins and he walks with heavy steps. Thud, thud, thud—not like the convicts who glide over the concrete like ghosts. Like cat ghosts.

"Sowell?"

"Yes." Billy has learned not to look at the COs. He's been told that it's okay to look at them, as long as you don't look in their eyes, but he doesn't trust himself not to make a mistake.

"You gonna stay in your cell until the count?"

"Yes, I'll be here." He does not add the fact that he's not allowed to leave, that he'd like to go out to the yard or to the movie, but Jackie Gee wants him to stay in his cell except for meals or work or to visit Chaplain Squires, which he does on Wednesday nights. Jackie Gee is Billy's pimp. Billy is Jackie Gee's property.

Billy listens to CO Tompkins' retreating footsteps for a moment, then returns to his problem. The pictures in his book, *Bible Stories for*

Children, would be perfect for his walls. Only he's not sure that Chaplain Squires, who gave him *Bible Stories for Children*, won't be mad at him for cutting the pages out. It's a difficult decision for Billy; it requires every bit of subtlety he can bring to the problem.

The book was a gift. Chaplain Squires said he wouldn't have to give it back, that it was *his* book. If it's *his* book, he should be able to do anything he wants to it. Right?

Somehow it doesn't work. Billy's made too many mistakes in his life, even after he thought about things for a very long time. He has no way to predict the outcome of any but the simplest actions.

"Backfire," he says out loud.

Kamal once explained what a backfire was, that you hold the gun and press the trigger and it shoots back at you. It kills *you*.

Billy looks down at the open page, runs a finger along the binding. The twelve apostles are huddled together in a small boat. The wind has torn its tiny sail to shreds and even Billy can see that the bearded figures are at the mercy of the storm. The sea boils around them; huge waves loom high over their heads, ready to come crashing down.

Billy imagines himself in the boat, helpless and afraid. He closes his eyes, not wanting to see Jesus yet. Wanting to see the darkness first. Chaplain Squires told him the apostles meant to use the stars to guide their boat, but the clouds covered the stars and they got lost.

That's the way he felt after his mother died, when they put him in a shelter. He felt lost. Everything was bigger than he was. Stronger. He didn't know what to do or where to go. When he left the shelter and began to drink, things only got worse. People took his money, his clothes, his wine. And there was nothing he could do about it. Nothing. He was as helpless as the apostles in their small boat.

Then Kamal found him.

Billy remembers telling Chaplain Squires that Kamal was something like Jesus. Only he wasn't *really* Jesus, because Kamal couldn't help him after the cops came.

Chaplain Squires hadn't gotten mad, like Billy was afraid he would. "The real Jesus never goes away," he explained. "Once He enters your heart, He's there forever and ever. But you've got to want Him, Billy. Jesus can't do it by Himself. You have to open your heart to make room for Him."

Billy opens his eyes, looks down at the page. Jesus, in His white robe, surrounded by light, approaches the apostles in their boat. He isn't really walking on the water, like Chaplain Squires said. He's float-ing just above it, as if He didn't want to get His toes wet. One hand points at His heart, the other to the sky above.

The apostles are looking right at Jesus, but as far as Billy can tell from their faces, the apostles are still afraid. And that doesn't make sense, no matter how Chaplain Squires tries to explain it. Why aren't they happy? Now that they're going to be rescued?

Billy puts the book down, lies back on his bed. The Screamer has started up again. "You fucking bitch, you dirty fucking bitch. I'll kill you, I'll kill you."

Jackie Gee says it's only a matter of time until the Squad takes The Screamer away to the psych annex. Jackie Gee also says that Billy will be taken to the psych annex if he complains to the COs. Which is kind of funny, because the COs must already know from the makeup and the way he moves around the prison. But what's not very funny is that Jackie Gee has said that before he goes out on parole, he will sell Billy to the highest bidder.

Footsteps sound on the catwalk outside his cell. Soft footsteps. Billy wonder if it's Jackie Gee come to get him. He is very surprised when a CO stops in the open doorway.

"Hello, Billy. Do you remember me?"

Billy looks directly at a CO for the first time in two years. His memory is much better, now that he can't drink, and he recognizes Officer Brannigan right away. Officer Brannigan looks just the same, with his big smile, except that he's wearing a CO's uniform instead of a regular suit.

"Yes, I remember you," Billy answers. "What do you want?"

"I'm going to take you out of here. I know you didn't kill that woman."

"I know I didn't kill her, too." Billy does not believe the cop has come to help him in any way, though he can't imagine what the cop wants.

"Your lawyer, Max, he sent me to get you."

"Mister Steinberg?"

"Yes, that's right."

"I spoke to Mister Steinberg today. On the telephone. He told me that I had to stay here for a while."

"Are you afraid of me, Billy? Did I ever hurt you?" Brannigan steps into the cell, sits down next to Billy, puts his arm around Billy's shoulder.

Instead of answering, Billy shuts his eyes. He wants to open his heart to Jesus, tries with all his might. When nothing happens, when the pressure of the cop's hand on his shoulder increases, Billy wishes for Kamal Collars, then Jackie Gee. From off in the distance, he hears the rush of booted feet, the terrified howl of The Screamer in his cell. The Squad has come for The Screamer just as the cop has come for him. Somehow it makes sense.

"Billy? Are you with me here?"

"Yes."

"I have some medicine for you. To make it easier."

"But I'm not sick."

"I know, Billy. This isn't for sickness. It's to make your mind rest. I was going to give it to you later, but I think it'll be better if I do it now."

"I don't want it." Billy pulls away from the cop. He stands up and looks around, wondering if he should run out onto the catwalk. Or call for help. He knows what happens to convicts who disobey the COs, has seen merciless beatings with his own eyes. But is a cop a CO? Could a cop get into a prison if the COs didn't want him there?

He can't decide. It's the same problem all over again, the problem that doesn't ever go away. Deciding, deciding, deciding.

"Jesus, help me," he whispers, but it is not Jesus who spins him around. And it is not Jesus' fist that sends him crashing onto the bed.

"Shit," Tommy Brannigan says aloud. "All this trouble for a fuckin' *re*tard." He jams the syringe into Billy Sowell's shoulder, jams it right through the shirtsleeve, depresses the plunger. "Here, this'll slow your faggot ass down to a crawl."

He watches Sowell's eyes flutter, lets him drop, hopes the little prick'll die on the spot, though it's not supposed to come off that way. But, no, slowly, very slowly, Billy pulls himself to a sitting position.

"Now, listen up, Billy. What's gonna happen here is that you and me are gonna take a walk. Just you and me, real sweet, like I was one of your fucking boyfriends. You get that?"

Brannigan doesn't wait for an answer. He grabs Billy by the arm, digs his fingers into Billy's flesh, reminds himself that he doesn't have to be here. That he wanted to do it himself, that he volunteered for the job, that he intends to enjoy it.

"Up ya go, motherfucker."

They make their way along the catwalk, down the stairs, past the first and second tiers, into the bowels of C Block. It's a warm evening and most of the population is out in the yard. The few prisoners in their cells refuse to so much as glance at Sowell and Brannigan. Brannigan doesn't bother to speak, either. There's no point; Sowell is too stoned to resist; he follows alongside like a fawning puppy. When they reach the long tunnels connecting C Block to the other buildings in the prison complex, Brannigan stops to get his bearings.

"Where are we going?"

To hell, is what Brannigan wants to say. He looks at Billy, shakes his head, again wonders why Steinberg would lift a finger to save this retarded piece of shit. Why Bell Kosinski would turn on the job, on his whole life.

Well, he decides, Kosinski's doing it because he's a drunk and Steinberg's doing it because he's a Jew. But this time the bleeding-heart routine is gonna backfire. It's gonna blow up right in their faces.

"I'm taking you out of here, Billy. You're goin' far, far away."

Brannigan starts up the tunnel, notes Billy hanging back, slaps him in the face.

"Jeez," he says to no one in particular, "the echo is amazing. I gotta remember this."

He starts out again, fingers wrapped in Billy Sowell's hair. The corridor, as far as Brannigan can see, is deserted, as it's supposed to be. At the far end, a hundred yards and two sharp bends away, three COs man a regular post. They will keep all foot traffic bottled up for the next ten minutes. Plenty of time for what Tommy Brannigan has in mind.

When he reaches the second utility room, he pauses, listens for a moment, then turns the handle. The room is dark, but this doesn't surprise him. He pushes Sowell inside, closes the door behind him, gropes for the light switch.

"Well, *Señor* Officer Brannigan, we meet again. How you like my world?"

"Cut the shit, Hinjosa. We don't have a lotta time."

Hinjosa laughs softly, wipes his mouth with the back of his hand. "No time? I got mucho time, Officer Brannigan. I got fifteen years to life."

And you deserve it, too, Brannigan thinks, knowing that Hinjosa, an NYPD sergeant, murdered his wife and that it wasn't a crime of passion, that the prick had been after the insurance money. His confession had bought him ten years less than the maximum.

"Tell me something, Hinjosa, the other cons know you're an ex-cop?"

"We call ourselves *offenders*, not cons." Hinjosa laughs softly. "You got to stop livin' in the past, *maricon*."

Brannigan sneers at the insult, decides to ignore it. "So, how do you survive? Most cops do their time in protective custody."

Hinjosa holds up a brick. "Look, *mamacita*, no fingerprints." He smashes the brick into Billy Sowell's skull. "No mercy, either. Tha's how I survive, Officer Brannigan."

"Yeah?" Brannigan refuses to give an inch. "Well, if I was you, tough guy, I'd watch out for that blood. Most likely, the faggot's got AIDS."

Hinjosa tears at Billy Sowell's uniform. Metal buttons fly across the room, rattle on the concrete floor. Pieces of torn khaki flutter to the ground like tan butterflies. When he is satisfied, he pushes Billy, chest down, onto the top of a table and mounts him.

"We gonna need more than one sample, Officer Brannigan. To make it look good. If you ain' got the heart to take a piece of his ass, maybe you could jus' jerk off."

ONE

"You know, Bell, there is nossing ze poor boy can do about hiss feelings. I knew his papa well and ziss is how Tony Loest was raised: if there is a problem in your life, you must to punch that problem in ze face. You, Bell, haf embarrassed ze poor boy und he simply cannot agzept it. If I wass you, I would watch my step."

Kosinski nodded in what he hoped was a thoughtful manner. Heinrich Werther was a Cryders regular and therefore entitled to a certain amount of respect. He was entitled, for instance, to his moon face, his round, wire-rimmed glasses, his Aryan know-it-all manner. He was even entitled to play the psychiatrist when he'd spent the bulk of his working life as a forklift operator in a now-defunct Long Island City warehouse.

"So, what do you think I should do, Heinrich?" Kosinski glanced at the far end of the bar, the end nearest the door. Tony Loest was eye-fucking him over the heaped bandages covering his nose. This after bragging to Ed O'Leary that he was going to "kick that fucking cop's fucking ass."

Werther's eyebrows rose, a pair of thick, gray crescents. He drained his eighth beer in one long gulp, then launched into his sixth explanation of the night. "By far ze simplest solution," he insisted, "is to allow Tony Loest to beat you into submizzion. That will restore hiss ezzential dignity."

"What about *my* essential dignity?" The question was purely rhetorical. Kosinski slid his hand in his pocket, fingered the sap he'd been carrying since his and Marty Blake's visit to the Chatham Hotel. He'd dumped his .38 after leaving Max Steinberg's office, put it on a closet shelf behind a box of long-unused Christmas lights, as far from his hand as he could get it. But he'd forgotten about the sap.

What I've gotta do, he thought, is use it fast. Whack this jerk the minute he talks out of line. Because there's gonna be insults here. Tony'll run his mouth before he runs his fists. I can use that to my advantage. Pretend I'm afraid, then turn his ribs into fucking dominoes.

"You must not to come down to ziss level. You are better than Tony. Besides which it would not do you any good. You see, Tony must to redeem hiz honor. Und he can only do it wiss violence. That is his ezzential nature. For you to humiliate him once again vould necessitate an escalation of zis violence."

Kosinski drained his glass, motioned to Ed behind the bar. "So whatta ya think, Ed? Ya think if I kick Tony's ass, it'll lead to nuclear war?"

"Don't worry, Bell, he ain't gonna try nothin' in my bar. I already had a word with the jerk."

"That's great, Ed." Kosinski (and every other Cryders regular) knew that O'Leary kept a sawed-off .12 gauge and a baseball bat next to the lemon wedges. "But what happens when I go outside?"

O'Leary flashed a wicked grin. "You could always call a cop, Bell. I mean, if you're worried about it."

"You see, Bell? You see how zey always return to that macho bull-shit? Zey are nossing but monkeys fighting over the big banana. That is all they know."

"How 'bout another beer, professor?" O'Leary asked. "To sharpen your psychological insight."

Heinrich managed a withering "peasant" before nodding assent.

What I think I'm gonna do here, Kosinski mused, is work up a little advantage for myself. What I'm gonna do is keep drinking, let Tony try to match me. By the time we get outside, he'll be lucky if he can stand.

Still, what Bell Kosinski was hoping, in his heart of hearts, was that Candy Packert would show up to diffuse the situation. Despite the fact that Packert was unlikely to appear on a weekday when the bar was patronized exclusively by committed booze hounds. Candy was a businessman and his business was cocaine: he might be out in Bayside, working the nightclubs on Bell Boulevard; or in Forest Hills, working the Queens Boulevard circuit. Anywhere but Cryders.

Kosinski glanced past Tony Loest, glanced at the door as it opened, looking for Candy Packert and seeing Marty Blake step into the bar. He saw Blake lock eyes with Tony Loest, saw Loest's expression slowly drift from out-and-out savagery to out-and-out fear. The transition, though it couldn't have taken more than a few seconds, seemed to

LAST CHANCE FOR GLORY

occur slowly, with confusion at its center. Tony's narrowed eyes gradually widened, then his head slowly dropped, then he spun on his stool to face Ed O'Leary on the other side of the bar.

"You ready for another, Mister Loest?"

Blake, when he turned back to Kosinski, was grinning madly. Up on his toes, eyes glittering, he stepped over to the ex-cop, shot a contemptuous glance at Heinrich Werther, said, "I gotta talk to you a minute, Kosinski."

"Marty," Kosinski said, astonished, "are you drunk?"

"I don't see how that's any of your fucking business."

"Yeah, you're right, Marty. It's not. You wanna take a table?"

"Naw, this'll do just fine." Blake plopped himself down on the stool deserted by Heinrich Werther, pulled several crumpled sheets of paper out of his pocket, tossed them onto the wet bar. "Take a look at these. Got some real interesting pictures here."

Kosinski flattened the sheets, then leaned back to get a good look before they disintegrated in the puddle on the bar. There were four of them, each a photo of the riot in Tompkins Square Park. Kosinski saw cops swinging nightsticks, punks throwing bottle and rocks, citizens running for their lives. In each, Kamal Collars towed an almost bemused Billy Sowell away from the action.

"So whatta ya think, Kosinski? Proof positive, right? Can't be in two places at the same time, right?"

Kosinski looked up at Blake, wondered if Blake had come to brag. If that's all there was to it. "What I think is that it's time for congratulations. Looks like the kid's gonna get out."

"The kid's *already* out. Ain't that amazing?" Blake brought his face to within inches of Kosinski's. "Even as we speak, Billy Sowell is lying on a slab in an upstate morgue, the victim, so the authorities say, of a common sexual assault that went too far. Beaten to death, so they say, with a common red brick. Do you think that was Billy's problem, Kosinski? Do you think he was just too common?"

"Look, take it easy, Marty." Kosinski's voice was deliberately soft, the way he'd pitched it when passing the bad news to a victim's family. "It's not like it comes as a big surprise."

"No? You were expecting this?"

"I was expecting *something*. That's what I've been trying to tell you all along. The people who set this up—and I'm not saying I know who they are—these people are not goin' down without a fight." Kosinski heaved a sigh of relief as Marty Blake leaned back. The kid was unpredictable, that was for sure. All along, Blake had been making noises like freeing Billy Sowell was just a job, like the only point was Max Steinberg's autograph on a check.

"So tell me," Blake demanded. "I mean we all know you're a great detective—it's common fucking knowledge—but how do you know that Sowell's death has anything to do with us?" He ran on before Kosinski could answer. "Not that it matters. Whoever put Billy Sowell in prison is responsible for his death, right? No matter who actually did the killing, right?"

"I can't argue with that, Marty." Kosinski drained his glass, waved to Ed O'Leary. "And it's good that you can see it clearly. Because we're never gonna get in that prison to find out what happened."

"That's what I told Max, but I couldn't get through to him. He's mighty pissed, Bell. He thinks . . ." Blake stopped abruptly. "What are you grinning at?"

"Was I grinning? Sorry, I didn't realize. Go ahead." Kosinski couldn't think of any way to explain why Blake's use of his first name affected him so deeply. In truth, he didn't want to explain it to himself.

"Yeah? Well, button your lip and hang onto your balls, Kosinski. Max Steinberg wants revenge, and he wants the both of us to help him get it, and there's only one way *to* get it, and that's what you've been warning me about all along. Steinberg wants to find Sondra Tillson's killer."

"And what about you, Marty? What do *you* want?"

Blake actually flinched at the question. Which didn't surprise Kosinski who'd come to accept the fact that people often didn't know the most obvious things about themselves. It wasn't a question of dishonesty, either. Blake just couldn't see the contradictions.

"Well, you know . . ."

"I *don't* know, Marty. And I—or we—don't have all that much time to find the answer. You have to be in or out here. Look, if they reached into that prison to whack Billy Sowell, what makes you think they'll hesitate to hit *us*?"

"How do you know they killed Billy Sowell? It might have happened just the way the administration says it did. A little rough sex got a little too rough. Nothing more to it."

"Marty, I know it like I knew that Billy's makeup didn't mean he was gay. You got to reach out a little, open up your mind. Billy Sowell was a prison prostitute, a valuable commodity. You *steal* property, you don't destroy it. Look, you said Billy was beaten to death with a brick. Why would that happen? Because he resisted? Because he fought for his honor?"

"Maybe the killer was a sadist, maybe . . ."

"Wrong on two counts. First, a sadist would've done it slowly, with a shank, one slice at a time. This was out-and-out murder. Second, Billy's pimp had to have had enough juice to protect his property; that's what pimping is all about, in the joint or on the street. I'm not saying there's *no* possibility that it went down like you said. What I'm saying—and you could believe me because I got a lot of experience in these matters—is that you should think twice before you step into this. You should know exactly what you want to get out of it. You should know what's in it for *you*."

Bell Kosinski was right about one thing—Marty Blake had greatly exceeded his single-drink limit. But Kosinski was wrong if he thought alcohol was responsible for Blake's anger. Much to his surprise, Marty Blake had felt it rise in him even as Max Steinberg outlined the reported facts over the telephone. By the time he'd replaced the receiver, he was ready to smack someone, anyone. Rebecca Webber's face had floated up in his mind, followed by Billy Sowell's, Joanna Bardo's, Matthew Blake's, Bell Kosinski's.

The feeling itself, divorced from any object, was thoroughly familiar. Marty Blake wanted to hurt someone and he wanted to be hurt; he wanted the utter chaos of a barroom brawl with chairs, bottles, and boots flying in all directions. You were *supposed* to come out of it with a torn ear, a swollen eye: anything less was dishonorable. Anything less meant you'd wasted your time on an unworthy opponent. There was no glory in squashing a bug.

Blake, who'd been blaming his temper on alcohol for more years than he cared to admit, had wasted no time getting to a neighborhood bar in Kew Gardens. The Scotch hadn't made him any more angry than he already was, but it did short circuit further introspection. Now, sitting next to Bell Kosinski in Max Steinberg's office, considerably more sober, but no less enraged, he found himself disgusted by everything within his field of vision.

A horse-faced clown and a drunk, he thought. What the fuck am I doing here? Sitting on a mission chair, staring at baskets filled with painted gourds, bleached animal skulls, eagle feathers. And who does he think *he* is, Max Earp? Talking to Wild Bell Hickok. About Billy the *fucking* Kid? Shit, what I'd like to do—what I'd love to do—is walk over to that sand painting and blow it away like I was blowing out the candles on a birthday cake. One quick whoosh and call for the vacuum cleaner. See what the jerk has to say about it.

Steinberg was going on about the lack of detail coming out of the Department of Corrections. "They're investigating is what they say. The rest is none of my business. They're only notifying me because Billy hasn't got a next of kin and do I want to pay for the funeral when the ME gets through with the body. Otherwise, they're gonna dump him in a graveyard they got up there for indigent cons. I tell ya, Bell, I got so pissed-off I called a reporter I know at *Newsday* and asked him if he'd do the story. I wanted to put it out there."

"And he turned you down, right?" Kosinski seemed perfectly content. Sitting there with his fist wrapped around a glass of the lawyer's booze.

"Yeah. A maybe-innocent dead con who can't even tell his own story? From this you don't make a Pulitzer. 'Bring me the real killer,' he said. 'And make sure it's the mayor. Then we got a story.'"

"So that's what you wanna do, Max? Find the real killer?"

"Damn right. Steinberg doesn't back down."

"And how 'bout you, Marty. What do you want?"

"What do I want?" Blake grinned. "I wanna put on eagle feathers and do a war dance."

"That's not good enough. Not even close."

"Well, it's gonna *have* to be, Kosinski, because that's all you're gettin'."

Kosinski nodded wisely, a gesture that raised the hair on the back of Marty Blake's neck, then turned to face the lawyer. "Whatta ya say, Max? Should we talk about the case?"

TWO

"I see it as your basic crime of passion," Kosinski began. "She says something; he says something; she says something. Whoosh, whoosh, whoosh, whoosh. Two defensive cuts, third one's the charm. It slices down to the bone—opens the jugular vein, the carotid, laryngeal, and thyroidal arteries, the esophagus and the trachea. She falls away, maybe clutching her throat, definitely spurting blood across the room; she falls onto her back, and now he's sorry. So sorry that he tries to make it better. He drops to his knees, takes the edges of the wound and pinches them together like a faith healer in a revival tent. It doesn't help, of course, doesn't restore Sondra Tillson, but it does force blood down into her lungs. Enough blood for her to drown before she bleeds out."

Kosinski stopped, drained his glass, wondered if he was being too dramatic, too positive. Wondered if he was having too much fun. He filled his glass, filled the lawyer's, filled Marty Blake's despite the *pro forma* protest.

"Now he's in a panic. Crime is not his thing, neither is physical violence. He's not a mob guy with a disposal site in a Staten Island swamp. And he can't just walk away, because he killed her in his own home.

"He mops the floor, wipes most of the blood off her body, changes his clothes, takes her out through the garage, lays her on the backseat of her own car. All he knows is that he has to be rid of her, as much because he's killed the proverbial 'thing he loves' as from fear of getting caught. And believe me, he *does* love her. He loves her much too much to dump her in the woods or in a vacant lot. No, what our killer does is drive into Manhattan, at great risk to himself, and leave her two blocks from the apartment she shares with her husband. He takes her *home*."

Steinberg's head moved slowly back and forth. A half-smile split his lips, but his eyes were glittering with the fervor of a born trial lawyer facing an impeachable witness.

"You'll excuse me, Mister Kosinski, for being a skeptic, but in my opinion, it's just this kind of tunnel vision that puts innocent people in jail. I read the case file from cover to cover and I can make a dozen scenarios out of it. You're pushing this one like it was chiseled on the tablets."

"It's job description, Max," Blake interrupted. "As in it's Bell's job to find criminals and your job to get them off the hook."

Steinberg reacted sharply, the wig bouncing forward as he spoke. "Whatsa matter, Marty? You don't like defense lawyers? You think Shakespeare was right? You think maybe we should kill all the lawyers? Did you hate the lawyers when it was your own ass on the line?"

"Whoa! Slow down a minute." Kosinski to the rescue. He looked over at Marty Blake, nodded as he spoke. "Max's got a right to question me here, because it *isn't* in the case file. Why should it be? If I put my own theory in the case file and it turned out to be wrong, some defense counsel, like Max Steinberg, would beat me to death with it. Facts go into the file; theories you keep to yourself.

"So, let's run through it. We know that Sondra Tillson wasn't killed in the car, because of the blood—or the lack of blood—which lack also points to another piece of the puzzle: she was probably murdered in a single-family home. How else could he have gotten her into her own car? There's no way you can picture him dragging a naked body down a hallway to an elevator. And there's no way he could have cleaned up a motel room, so don't even suggest it.

"Sondra Tillson's throat was badly bruised. At first, I thought she'd been strangled as well as stabbed, but the pattern of bruising was inconsistent with strangulation. The bruises were clustered at the edges of the wound and were probably made with the tips of the fingers alone. That is, the perp was trying to repair the damage, to put her back together.

"Apparently, he didn't try very hard, because her lividity was consistent with her position on the backseat of the car. He didn't dress her, and the only fibers found on her body came from her own clothing, which I take to mean that he didn't cover the body with a sheet or a blanket. I also take it to mean he didn't have to go very far. The ME found minor abrasions packed with dirty motor oil on both heels. Perfectly consistent with being dragged across a garage floor.

"Now, let's go through the deal: he kills her, tries to fix it, can't, puts her body into the backseat instead of the trunk. He's in a total panic, thinking what am I gonna do, where can I go, how can I get away with it? Thinking like an ordinary citizen who made a big, big mistake. But then something happens, something you wouldn't expect. Instead of heading out to the boonies, maybe dumping her body where it won't be discovered until spring, our perp drives his lover home. He puts her where she'll be found and buried before she starts to decompose. You wanna call it sick, call it sick, but I make it for an act of remorse. I make it for an act of *love*."

Steinberg sat up in his chair, clapped his hands enthusiastically. "Very nice, Bell. Very, *very* nice, but let's try this one on: the killer owns a business in Manhattan. He invites his cutie in for a quickie—you like that? cutie? quickie?—but then something goes wrong and he kills her. Of course, like you said, he's gotta dump the body, but there's another problem, too. Her car is parked in front of his place of business. So, he does what he *has* to do—he pulls an overcoat over his bloody clothes, stuffs her in the backseat of her own car, abandons the car close enough to her apartment to throw suspicion on the husband."

Bell Kosinski shrugged his shoulders. "You want to put them in an office somewhere, an office that just happens to have oil-stained concrete next to it, that's fine with me. In fact, you can take it one step further and say they were both nude when the fatal blow was struck. That eliminates the bloody clothes problem altogether. But what you can't take out is the fact that they knew each other and that he loved her. What you can't take out is that the case would've been a dunker if somebody with ultimate juice hadn't stepped in. Tell me something, Max, tell me how Grogan, or whoever started the ball rolling, got Billy Sowell's name?"

"I don't know," Steinberg answered. "It's been bothering me, too."

"You know what we're talkin' about, Marty?" Kosinski shifted his gaze to Marty Blake. "Billy Sowell lives in a box. He has no ties with any city agency. Doesn't get welfare, disability, food stamps. How the fuck does anyone know enough about his life to set him up?"

"Why don't we cut to the chase, Bell? Why don't you tell us what we're gonna do about it?"

Blake's voice was dead neutral, which didn't bother Kosinski at all. If Blake wanted to pretend to play his cards close to the vest, that was perfectly okay. Eventually, Blake would come around and he . . .

"Hey, Bell, you still with us?" Steinberg's voice, more concerned than condemning. "You fall asleep?"

Kosinski opened his eyes, grinned sheepishly. "I was reminiscing," he explained. "Blame it on the booze. Anyway, I only spent a few days on the case before I took my vacation. Tommy and I canvassed the neighborhood around Gramercy Park, spoke to the husband twice, interviewed as many friends and relatives as we could locate. The neighborhood gave us nothing, except for Melody Mitchell. At the time, I was a hundred percent convinced that she couldn't make a positive ID, but I had Brannigan take her into the house to look at the mug shots anyway. According to him, it was a complete waste.

"The husband, Johan, had an ironclad alibi for the time of the murder. He was on a plane, halfway between Stockholm and Manhattan when his wife was killed. Returning from a business trip. Tillson Enterprises is the largest importer of Scandinavian furniture in the country; the two of them, Johan and Sondra, ran the outfit together. I caught up with him as he came off the plane, told him his wife had been murdered, hit him with it as hard as I could. What I wanted was a reaction, and what he did was fall down. Just like that—he hit the carpet like a sack of potatoes.

"By the time I came back for the second interview, I was sure that Sondra Tillson hadn't been hit by a professional, that it was an impulse crime. Now, I was looking for the lover, and I put it to Johan in no uncertain terms. 'If your wife was sleeping around, I want to know it,' I told him. The statement took him off guard and what he did, the prick, was lie to me."

"You know that for a fact?" Steinberg demanded. "Or are we maybe looking at a cop hunch?"

"Call it a hunch if you want to. I don't really give a shit. Sondra Tillson was having an affair and Johan Tillson knew about it. Likewise, the girlfriends and relatives. You wanna hear something funny? Nobody—not one single individual—would admit to having any contact with the victim in the forty-eight hours preceding her death. I tell ya, Max, another couple of days and I would've had the lover's name—I would'a got it by squeezing Johan Tillson like a tube of toothpaste—but then my vacation came up and I took it. I figured I'd put the pieces together when I got back."

"Aren't you forgetting something?" Blake asked. "Aren't you forgetting about Grogan?"

Kosinski tried to shrug, tried to get mad, failed in both attempts. He knew where Blake was going and in his heart of hearts, knew he deserved it. "Yeah," he admitted, "there was that, too."

"Because the fact is," Blake continued, "the frame started *before* you went on vacation. The fact is that you let Billy Sowell hang."

"Look, Marty . . ."

"Look at what? Look at Billy Sowell's corpse? Should I check out the size of his asshole? See if it's bigger or smaller than the Lincoln Tunnel?"

"For Christ's sake, Marty, I'm not your damned father." Kosinski's first reaction was to wish he could take the words back. His second reaction was to brace himself against an all-out attack. He slid his hand into his pocket, fingered the sap, decided that, come what may, he wouldn't let Marty Blake tie him into a pretzel. Meanwhile, Blake hadn't flinched, hadn't moved a muscle. "Look, what's done is done. You know your bible? 'When I was a cop, I spoke as a cop.' Now I'm wearin' a different hat and there's nothing more to be said about it."

"He's right," Steinberg declared. "This is bullshit. You should please save it for your psychiatrist. The *both* of you." He tapped the table with his index finger. "Because the point is that Max Steinberg is going to be doing all the paying. I'm the cash register and I don't open for psychodrama. The question here is what we're gonna do about Billy Sowell and Sondra Tillson."

"That's two questions," Kosinski said. "Because I'd bet my pension against a nickel that the man who killed Sondra Tillson had nothing to do with Billy Sowell."

THREE

Blake stared at his untouched drink, half-listened to the babble, bided his time. He was no longer angry, no longer drunk. Something inside him had shifted and was now hardening. It had happened to him several times in the past: when he'd moved out to avoid his drunken father; when Joanna Bardo had summoned him to Manhattan Executive; when he'd left the computer room to go into the field. Looking back, he saw this sequence as inevitable, though at the time he'd assumed it was all just happening. No more than random events to which he reacted.

Blake let his attention fall back into the conversation. They were arguing about the target, whether they should content themselves with Billy Sowell's killer. Or did conscience demand that Sondra Tillson also be avenged?

"Excuse me for saying this," Kosinski insisted, "but you didn't see Sondra Tillson's body."

"Big deal," the lawyer said. "I didn't see Billy Sowell's, either. Look, you wanna wag weenies, I got file cabinets *stuffed* with crime-scene photographs. I tell you, when it comes to murdered people, black and white is worse than color."

Steinberg, his cheeks flushed with alcohol, black eyes glittering maliciously, turned to Marty Blake. "How 'bout you, Mr. Blake? You ever come eyeball to eyeball with a corpse?"

Blake smiled, felt himself drift back to his father's funeral, envisioned himself standing over the open casket, remembered that, of course, his father's eyes had been closed. "Guess not, Max. Can't say as I've had the privilege."

"Well, you didn't miss nothin'," Kosinski said. He lifted the empty bottle of Hennessy, frowned, looked over at an uncaring Max Steinberg. "Guess it's time to get down to business, right?"

"Right," Steinberg said. "Past time."

Kosinski set the bottle on Steinberg's desk, eyed Blake's untouched drink. "We have to start with the human beings. Sondra Tillson was killed; Billy Sowell was framed. They stand at the center, like all victims. Surrounding them, we've got the husband, Johan; the witness, Melody Mitchell; Billy Sowell's attorney whose name we don't even know . . ."

"David Ferretti," Steinberg interrupted. "He's writing wills now. Out in Brooklyn."

"Plus the Honorable John McGuire who passed judgment; Detective Tommy Brannigan who conducted the investigation; Captain Aloysius Grogan who put Billy Sowell's name in Brannigan's ear. We can forget about Brannigan and Aloysius Grogan. You're not gonna crack those two nuts. As for the lawyer, Ferretti, it's possible he was just a jerk, that he thought the deal he got for Billy Sowell was too good to be true. Likewise for Melody Mitchell. If they were gonna bribe Melody Mitchell, they wouldn't have bothered with the hypnosis, which actually hurt the case. Now, Johan Tillson knew Billy Sowell didn't kill his wife. Would he let an innocent man go to prison without getting something in return? I doubt it, but even if he let Billy Sowell hang because he was too embarrassed to admit his wife had a lover, he knows who actually killed her. Judge McGuire, on the other hand, is guilty beyond a shadow of a doubt. He knew the kid was being framed; he could have stopped it; he let it happen. It's that simple."

Steinberg stopped Kosinski with a wave of his hand. "Okay, fine, for this you don't have to be a genius. The husband and the judge. What do you plan to do? Beat it out of them?"

"Marty, you're up." Kosinski, unable to contain himself, slid Blake's drink across the surface of the desk.

"It's not very complicated, Max." Blake pushed his full glass over to Kosinski. "The first week, I investigate the targets— bank and credit records, deeds and mortgages, tax returns, like that. What I'll be looking for is enough ammunition to start a panic. Meanwhile, Bell's gonna check out their homes and offices, look for the easiest way in, who's got an alarm, a wife, a dog. The next step is to wire them up— believe me, by the time I get finished you'll be able to hear sugar hit the Frosted Flakes—then have Bell pay a visit, hit them with the facts of life. Me, I don't think there's gonna be a problem finding the bad guys. The problem is what we're gonna do with the proof. That's where you come in, Max. You and your press connections. You're gonna play Deep Throat in the Billygate investigation."

Max Steinberg's face turned petulant. His eyes and mouth squeezed down; his nose wrinkled up. For a moment, Blake was sure the lawyer was going to cry. Which didn't surprise Blake all that much. It's easy to be a hero, he reasoned, when heroism means writing a brief. Or a check.

"You know how many felonies you want me to commit?" the lawyer asked. "Federal and state?"

"Actually, I haven't counted. I started to, but I ran out of fingers and toes."

Kosinski laughed softly. "Don't be nasty, Martin," he advised. "It's too early for nasty."

"What's that supposed to mean?" Steinberg demanded.

"It means you haven't turned us down. Yet."

Steinberg folded his arms across his chest. "What you're talking here is disbarment and prison. There's gotta be another way. A *legal* way."

"We could always forget about it," Marty said. "Hey, look, you're a defense lawyer. You've dedicated your life to getting criminals off the hook. Maybe you could look at Billy Sowell's killer as another notch on the old gun."

"That's *enough*, Marty."

Blake looked over at Kosinski, noted the narrowed eyes, the thin, disapproving mouth. "Yeah, maybe so," he admitted.

"See, Max," Kosinski said, "and you could trust me here, because I got a lot of experience in these matters, without badges, we got no hope of doin' it the right way. We'll never get court orders for the taps and bugs, never get permission to go into financial records. No, either we do it Marty's way and try not to get caught, or we just walk away. Me, I'm a lazy drunk. I don't like to walk."

"Let me explain a few things," Blake interrupted. "You're not gonna do shit, Max, except supply the money. Not in the beginning. Me and Bell are gonna set it up, collect the evidence, then *retrieve* the hardware. The idea is to get in and out before anybody knows what's happening. Bell's gonna be the target, of course. He'll be the one asking the questions and the one they're gonna go after if things get rough. What *you* have to do is pick your reporter carefully, make sure he'll stand up, protect his source. Because the whole idea is to force the cops to investigate the cops, which is like asking politicians to tell the truth. It doesn't happen unless there's real strong motivation."

Steinberg, his mouth set in a tight, determined line, pushed the chair away from his desk and crossed the room to a three-drawer, oak-paneled file cabinet. He opened the top drawer and removed a .32-caliber automatic. "I had a client," he announced, "two or three years ago. A crazy man. Talked to himself, heard voices, but smart, too. Sly is a better word for it. I pled him insane for the murder of his wife and two children, got him off the hook, at least as far as prison was concerned. Somehow, I failed to make it clear that when the jury said, 'Not guilty,' it only meant that he was going to the crazy house instead of jail. *He* thought he was gonna walk out of the courtroom. A free man, so to speak.

"Well, *boychicks*, as you might expect, when he figured it out, he flipped. Threatened to cut my head off was what he did. I admit the jerk was scary, but I'd been threatened before, so I didn't think much of it. Until he escaped on the way to Mattewan. I bought this gun twenty-four hours later, carried it in my coat pocket; I was that sure the prick was coming after me, that any minute he'd appear with an ax in his hands. As it turned out, he headed north after his escape and never came within a hundred miles of Manhattan.

"Still, it taught me a lesson: better to keep so far away from the line that you can't cross it by accident. I stopped taking cash payments from clients, started reporting all my income to the IRS, stopped encouraging witnesses to perjure themselves. What I didn't want is that I should be hunted again—not by an individual, not by the government. Now, I'm being asked to risk going to prison."

Steinberg paused, held up the automatic for inspection. "Not much of a weapon, it's true. Fifteen-year-old gangbangers wouldn't spit on it. But, for me, it made a big difference." He paused again. "Look, it's easy to say, 'We'll investigate the targets, wire up the houses, retrieve the hardware.' I mean, you don't have to worry about the consequences of everything going right. That much is obvious. But what about the consequences of things going wrong? What if they catch you going into the houses? What if they find the bugs? Like I told you before, Steinberg doesn't back down. But that doesn't mean Steinberg's a moron, either. Marty, you said something about money. How much do you need and what are you gonna do with it?"

Blake saw the question as a command, which is what it was. He forced himself to react calmly. "Somewhere between five and ten thousand dollars. Information costs money. It's not like in the movies where a ten-year-old can break into any computer in the world. If you wanna get into the IRS computer, for instance, you have to find somebody with access to rent you a little time. And like any other black-market operation, illegal time costs a lot more than legal time. The same principle applies to the hardware. I have to buy it on the black market, because if I buy it legally, the serial numbers will come right back to me if it's found."

"Enough." Steinberg waved the little .32, a conductor cuing his musicians. "Here's what's gonna happen. First, I'm gonna write you a check for seventy-five-hundred dollars. Second, you're gonna write me a receipt for services rendered. That's in the past tense, in case you missed the point. Third, you and Mr. Kosinski are gonna go out and do your thing. When you're finished—when *all* the bugs and taps are in your possession—you're gonna come back. At which point I will pay you for your time, evaluate the material, then decide what to do next. Any comments?" He paused briefly. A grin sucked at his protruding lower lip. "And by the way, boys, you might wanna consider that I have another role to play besides the role of banker. Like, if you should maybe happen to get yourselves arrested, you're gonna need a lawyer and I'm the best."

FOUR

"I have a decision to make, an interesting decision," Blake explained as he and Bell Kosinski drove the short distance to Manhattan Executive's Soho offices. In another season, they would have walked the half mile, but a merciless August sun had reduced city life to a mad dash from one air-conditioned space to another. "Steinberg claims that Joanna Bardo first told him about Billy Sowell. What I'm wondering is who told Joanna?"

"Sounds like you don't trust her."

Kosinski wanted a drink. As usual. He saw no particular reason, outside of the fact that Blake was driving the car, to resist the urge, but he knew that his end of the bargain would eventually call for him to drive a car. If he was going to do that (without, for instance, wiping out half the pedestrians in New York), he'd have to cool the drinking. It was that simple.

Not that he was at all sure he *could* slow down. Which was funny because, at the same time, he had no doubt that he'd do what was expected of him. Kosinski was coming to understand that his relationship with Marty Blake might be more than a temporary reprieve. That it might be a beginning, assuming he didn't fuck it up. Or got himself killed. Or massacre a crowd of preschoolers standing at a bus stop.

"Joanna came up the hard way. Her mother died when she was seven, left her to raise three younger sisters. Plus she had to deal with a father who liked to use his hands. Now she's finally got something and the way I see it, she'll probably give me up before she gives up Manhattan Executive."

"Probably?"

"I can't say for sure, Bell. Maybe she came by the story innocently. Then it wouldn't matter."

Kosinski nodded, closed his eyes, let his head fall back. He remembered his first days in Homicide and the forty-eight-hour rule. The one that insisted if you didn't clear the case within forty-eight hours, it'd most likely never be cleared. What it meant, in practical terms, was that you had to have the instincts of a starving wolf. You didn't pace yourself, didn't settle in for the long haul, didn't bother to eat your Wheaties in the morning. No, what you did was run through potential witnesses like a bowling ball through a set of pins. You followed trails with maniacal intensity, practiced an unavoidable tunnel vision that sometimes missed your legitimate prey altogether.

Most of those conditions, Kosinski knew, couldn't be applied to a case that was more than two years old. Still, the scent of blood was the scent of blood and when you were starving, nothing else mattered. He recalled his first summer job—sweeping out a small, rat-plagued warehouse in Flushing. The owner had just bought three Fox Terrier pups and was keeping them in a storage room during the day. From time to time, he'd open the door and toss them a dead or dying rat. "So they know what they're supposed to do in life." Six months later, the warehouse was rodent free.

"You still here, Kosinski?"

"Yeah, I was just thinking about what you said. Tell me something, why do you have to say anything at all to Joanna Bardo? I thought you were in business on your own?"

Blake smiled, turned his head to face Kosinski. They were on Greene Street, just below Spring, stopped at a light. "Did you always work with a partner, Bell?"

"Almost always."

"Well, I *never* worked with a partner, so you have to give me time to get used to the idea. I think Steinberg's suggestion, to investigate the judge who admitted the bullshit confession and the husband who lied to you is reasonable. According to Steinberg, John McGuire was a liberal, an ACLU guy who sold out his principles to put Billy Sowell behind bars. Maybe we can appeal to his conscience, use it as an extra wedge. That is, if we get something to go with it. As for Johan Tillson, from what you said, he has to know that Billy Sowell didn't kill his wife. So, why has he kept his mouth shut all these years? Why wouldn't he talk to Max Steinberg? Believe me, Bell, if money changed hands, I'm gonna know it."

Kosinski stifled a smile, glanced out the window, noted the deserted streets, the storefronts shimmering like desert mirages. He could almost hear the hum and drip of air conditioners, almost feel the heat rising from the sidewalks. There was a time when he'd walked streets very similar to these. Enveloped by a thin membrane of sweat, hoping he wouldn't have to chase some fifteen-year-old kid through the backyards.

"Do you really think it's gonna come to that? Caribbean bank accounts? Sounds too big to me."

Blake stared straight ahead; his voice, when he spoke, was matter-of-fact. "You're probably right, but we have to be ready to follow the paper trail wherever it leads. We're not looking for some street mutt with a rusty .38. It's not a problem for you, anyway. The main thing is to keep what we're doing absolutely quiet while the hardware is in place. The kind of surveillance we're gonna set up is easily detected. *If* you're looking for it. It's also illegal, but if we get the hardware out before anybody knows what's happening, it's a crime that's very hard to prove. By the way, you might want to apply for a PI's license. It'd give you a little more credibility, especially with the cops."

"Well, actually . . ." Kosinski found himself blushing, tried to remember how long it'd been since he'd been embarrassed by anything, failed utterly. "Actually," he admitted, "I already did."

"Dead? Just like that?" Joanna Bardo perched on her chair like a bird of prey looking for a careless mouse. "Some people have no luck in life. I suppose that sounds callous."

"Yeah, 'callous' is the word for it," Blake said mildly.

"But it's *true*, isn't it? Haven't you seen it yourself?" Her round Mediterranean eyes widened, her small mouth turned down; she somehow managed to look indignant and petulant at the same time. "It's the one fate I always wanted to avoid. I'd rather go down in flames than be a Sad Sack. Billy Sowell didn't live a life. Not his own life, anyway. He was led through his days like a dog on leash. I suppose you can't blame the dog for having a sadistic master. But if the dog never fights back? Never bites, never growls?"

"Billy Sowell didn't have the teeth for biting. His fangs were pulled early in the game." Blake smiled, waved his hands. "But it's over, anyway. I have a few details to work out—the lawyer wants to get Billy a posthumous pardon—but I'm basically looking for work, so if there's anything out there . . ."

Joanna folded her hands, laid them on the desk. She was all business, now, Kosinski could see that much. She seemed relieved, as well, to be off the subject of Billy Sowell. Blake was taking his time, maintaining his usual sarcastic demeanor, concerned (but not *too* concerned) with Billy Sowell as an individual. As a human being.

"As a matter of fact," Joanna said, "I have a small job, if you want it. A Senior Vice President at Bower and Bower thinks his wife is cheating on him. He asked me to put her under surveillance for a week or so, then report back. There's no divorce in the works, so he doesn't need videos or photographs; he just wants to know what she's doing. It's a softball, really, but the client has plenty of money and he's willing to pay standard daytime surveillance rates. Just make sure you get a decent retainer, because the man is sixty-nine years old and his wife is sixty-seven. We may be looking at premature senility here."

"After Max Steinberg," Blake laughed, "I could use a little senility."

"It's all an act," Joanna declared. "Steinberg knows exactly what he's doing. In fact, you could make a decent case for the theory that all he's done with his life is make the best of a bad situation. I mean, when you take his appearance into consideration. That's probably why he goes on these crusades. It's just part of the act."

"But why Billy Sowell?" Blake shook his head. "It's the only question I forgot to ask him."

"Well, that's easy enough. As you know, I belong to any number of charitable organizations. It's purely business, of course. The boards of these organizations are studded with potential clients and you can approach them informally at the annual dinners. As it happens, a Reverend Abner Squires was the guest speaker at a meeting of the Osmond Society—they're involved in prison reform—and he told me what'd happened to Billy Sowell, before and after Billy went to prison. Reverend Squires is the Protestant chaplain at the Columbia Correctional Facility. I'd already met Steinberg and listened to him brag about his various crusades on behalf of the innocent, so I put them together. Do a favor, get a favor—that's all it came to."

Bell Kosinski stared at his freshly poured drink, listened to the ice crack. In some ways the anticipation was as good as the actual hit, which was ironic. He'd begun drinking in order to shut his brain down, and now he drank to get it going. He sipped at the vodka, felt the little neurons in his skull split and crack, felt pathways open, drained the glass.

"No time like the present," he muttered.

"Pardon me?"

It was nearly five o'clock, late for a Cryders regular to be as close to sober as Bell Kosinski. Father Tim, for instance, was feeling no pain whatsoever.

"No time like the present," Kosinski repeated. "To plow into the future."

Kosinski watched Ed O'Leary add an ice cube, then fill his glass. "Gettin' fancy, Bell," the bartender said. "I mean with the ice and all. Next you'll be askin' for an olive."

"It's kind of a celebration."

"Yeah?" O'Leary grinned maliciously, cocked his head to one side. "That's pretty amazing. I didn't know you had anything to celebrate."

"I'm celebrating my onrushing demise." Kosinski raised the glass. "Last drink of the night."

The bartender's mouth dropped. "I hope you're not gonna do nothin' stupid, like go on the wagon. Shit, Bell, I can't afford to lose the business."

"Well, I'm not exactly going on the wagon, but I may tie myself to an axle and let it drag me around for a few weeks." Ed O'Leary took a moment to digest the information. He started to reply, checked himself, walked away.

"Ed's a calculating man," Father Tim said. "Ruled by profit and loss."

"Haunted by profit and loss, Father." Kosinski tasted his drink. One more and then off to bed? It didn't seem possible. "Ed's a worrier."

"A charitable observation." Father Tim pulled on the cross around his neck. "But not undeserved. What's this about 'going on the wagon?'"

"It's not a big deal, Father. I have to drive a car and I can't do it drunk."

"And you think you can do it sober." It was a statement, not a question.

"Time will tell." Kosinski glanced around the room, noted the dingy, fly-specked walls, the dust covering every unused surface. If he had a few more drinks, he knew, Cryders would undergo a miraculous transformation. It would slip into a state most people associated with home. It would become downright cozy.

"Father Tim, can I ask you a theological question?"

"Certainly." The priest's face brightened. "I don't pretend to be Thomas Aquinas, but I'll give you the best answer I've got."

"Suicide is a mortal sin, right?"

"That's right. The taking of life is not the business of human beings. Except in self-defense. Or in war. Or when you're frying some low-life, scumbag murderer."

"But never suicide, right?"

"Never. Not in the Catholic Church."

"All right, now look at this for a minute. Suppose I make a decision to cross every street I come to without looking. I don't care if the light is red or green; I don't care about the traffic. When I get to the corner, I just keep on going. Is that suicide?"

Father Tim smiled. "Bell," he replied, "it's not something you need to worry about. Even if it *is* suicide, the truly insane are always forgiven. When you meet Saint Peter, just plead diminished capacity."

FIVE

Marty Blake slid his Ford Taurus into a parking space on Liberty Avenue directly across the street from Eternal Memorials Incorporated, but instead of shutting down the engine, he flipped the air conditioning to maximum and settled back in the seat. He'd been to Eternal Memorials a number of times in the past, been to it in winter and summer, and it'd always seemed to occupy a space of its own, as if it was impervious both to the vagaries of the weather and the violent despair of the South Jamaica slums that surrounded it. Maybe it was the stone, the granite, and the marble slabs, the blind angels, the gray crosses, the inscribed lilies. The place looked and felt as eternal as its name. As eternal as the man who ran it.

Last chance, Blake thought to himself, last chance to change your mind. To return Steinberg's money, go chase Joanna's adultress. Hell, it might even be fun. Maybe this sixty-seven-year-old corporate wife has a trio of bodybuilders stashed in an apartment somewhere. Maybe she's running with a motorcycle gang. Maybe a *lesbian* motorcycle gang—Butch Bikers from Hell.

The worst of it was that he couldn't shake the conviction that he was putting Bell Kosinski's life on the line. Never mind his own career. Or the fact that their best chance of escaping prosecution lay in his, Blake's, remaining in the background. Kosinski hadn't been exaggerating the physical danger. Whoever substituted Billy Sowell's life for the life of Sondra Tillson's actual killer wouldn't hesitate to add another life to the bottom line. Whoever did it would have nothing whatever to lose.

The question of the day, he told himself, is Kosinski's question: What's in it for Marty Blake? Sure, Billy Sowell's life, if you can call the way he lived a life, was taken away, was actually stolen. But when you look around and see the misery out there, Billy Sowell's life and death come to no more than a quick blip on an overloaded screen. The rest is all ego.

A phrase drifted up—blood in the water. Just the faintest taste of an organism in distress. Marty Blake had never hunted anything more dangerous than facts, but he knew, as he sat in his car, that the potential ferocity of his enemy was as important to him as all the rest of it put together. He recalled seeing a film in which a young Masai warrior proved his manhood by facing a lion with a spear. The kid had been shit-scared—you could see it in his face—but he'd done it and survived. Afterwards, he stood before the photographer, proudly displaying his two trophies: the skin of the beast he'd killed and the four parallel scars running across his chest.

As he opened the door and stepped into the heat, one final thought occurred to him: Where's the glory in giving the spear to Bell Kosinski? If you want to wear the lion's hide, you have to hold the spear yourself.

Blake hustled across the street, wasted no time stepping into the air-conditioned showroom. He was wearing his best off-white linen jacket over a dark gray silk shirt and he didn't want to get either sweated up.

"May I help you?"

The gray man in the gray, three-piece suit fit the room perfectly. His name was Regis Dodd and he was exactly what he appeared to be. Or, almost what he appeared to be. Dodd, Blake had come to know, *did* sell tombstones. He played no part in Eternal Memorials' other business, but his original name—the one he'd been born with—was Mikhail Kasprazk.

"You don't remember me?"

"Sir? Have we met?" The salesman leaned closer, peered at Blake for a moment. "Oh yes, Mister Blake. Nice to see you again. It's been quite a long time. I don't suppose you've come about a memorial?"

Blake shook his head. "Sorry to disappoint you, Regis, but my loved one is healthy at the moment. Maybe next time."

"I see." Regis Dodd's expression never changed. His bloodless white skin echoed a droopy mouth and pale, watery, eyes. Dignity, Blake guessed, was what he strived for; death-warmed-over is what he actually achieved.

"Mr. Patel is in his customary place. Through the workroom. I assume he's expecting you?"

"You assume right."

As Blake made his way through Eternal Memorials' storage room, he quickly prepared himself for an encounter with the great man. The great genius. There was a story about Gurpreet Patel, a story that'd been circulating for so long it'd come to assume the power of fact. According to the rumor, Patel had surivived as long as he had because the CIA, the FBI, the State Department, and the Department of Justice all used him for operations that were too hot to go through their own computers. In return for his cooperation (and discretion), they protected him and gave him access to all but the most sensitive information.

Blake didn't know if the rumors were true or false, deliberately refused to make a judgment. Reasoning there was no way he could be sure and it didn't matter anyway. Because nobody (at least, nobody Blake *knew*) could gather information as quickly as Gurpreet Patel. He didn't use the telephone lines available to home hackers; Patel claimed he could tap into the special networks set up by the telephone companies to serve corporate giants and government agencies. He further claimed that he had access codes for every large data base in the western world and more than a few for the Far East.

Some of it was bullshit, Blake assumed. It had to be. But Gurpreet Patel had never failed Marty Blake. Assuming he'd taken the assignment. That was the other thing about Gurpreet Patel, the part that had to be prepared for. Patel had his own ethical standards. He rejected as many jobs as he accepted, and there was no way to predict what he'd do in advance. You had to carefully kiss his ass while you carefully spelled out the details and carefully hoped for the best.

Blake took a deep breath and knocked on the door.

"Yes?" The single syllable was deep and resonant, even through the closed door.

"It's me, Gurp. Marty Blake."

"You must please to say the password."

Blake reached for the doorknob, then withdrew his hand. Knowing it was going to be locked. He took another breath, wished he'd used his other option, that he'd gone to Joanna's bounty hunter, Vinnie Cappolino. Vinnie had the connections, but lacked the patience (and the subtlety) necessary for financial investigation. Both he and his partner preferred straight lines.

"I didn't come for a gravestone," he shouted. "I came for the bloody mausoleum."

Bzzzzzzzzzzzzzzzzzz.

The door popped open and Blake stepped into Gurpreet Patel's personal nightmare. The four walls of the windowless room were covered with a continuous mural depicting an anonymous city after a nuclear holocaust. The artist, at Patel's direction, had painted it so that the room's floor appeared to be in the center of the city, a tiny oasis from which devastation stretched in all directions. Smoke issued from countless fires; water spouted from ruptured mains; charred bodies littered the streets. On the ceiling, white storybook clouds floated above a dozen soaring vultures in an indifferent azure sky; at ground zero, a black, marble desk sat in the center of a grass-green carpet.

"Welcome, Marty Blake. A glass of plum wine?"

Gurpreet Patel was so old as to appear ageless. His long, snow-white hair framed a full, equally white beard. Above the beard, his cheeks and forehead were a deep mahogany, his eyes large and dark.

"No wine, Gurp. I'm working."

"Espresso, perhaps. Freshly brewed, of course."

"Fine. Espresso." Blake watched Patel disappear through a door in the back, a door so carefully worked into the mural that it was all but invisible until it opened. Patel's IBM R/6000, fifty grand worth of speed and memory, sat on a table against the wall. Blake hadn't worked with a machine that powerful since coming out of college and the sight made him jealous.

"You see? It did not take so long as all that." Patel appeared in the doorway bearing a silver tray laden with two tiny cups and saucers, an equally tiny sugar bowl, and a steaming espresso pot.

"It shouldn't, considering the fact that you saw me coming. That your video surveillance units cover every inch of the building."

Patel frowned. "You have spotted them?"

"Didn't have to. I've been here often enough to judge your character."

"Ha! Bloody well said, Marty Blake." Patel filled the two cups, added sugar and a twist of lemon peel without asking. "Let's drink to the success of your enterprise."

Blake drank, smiled. "The success of my enterprise depends on you, Gurp."

"I am sorry to hear that, Marty Blake. You should not put all your eggs in one box."

Blake started to correct the Indian, noted the confident smile, thought better of it. "It's not the information, Gurp. I could get the information myself, but it'd take me three months."

"Ah, yes. 'Ars longa, vita brevis,' as they say."

"'Art is long, life is short,'" Blake dutifully translated. "The long and the short of it according to Horace."

"Quite. Now, in deference to this singular truth, we must get immediately to working. If you would please to tell the story."

Blake took his time about it, carefully detailing Billy Sowell's life and fate, before outlining his strategy and naming his targets. Patel listened closely, frowned in all the right places, groaned when Blake described the final atrocity.

"Infamous," he declared when Blake was through. "You know something, Marty Blake? I have never before worked on a murder, I am very much looking forward to it and I will lower my fee accordingly. For you and for Mister Sowell I will charge only ten thousand dollars."

"Three."

"Monstrous." Patel's eyes widened, flashed fire. "You are insulting me with your bloody western arrogance. In the truth, it is not a wise thing to do."

"It's an easy job," Blake said, unperturbed. "I could do it in a few hours if I had your access and that IBM."

Patel glared for a moment, then his face softened. "Well, it is not, after all, so terribly difficult. The briberies must have occurred soon after the murder. That limits the dimensions of the search. Still, if the briberies were paid with something other than money, we may have a bloody hard time finding them. I will do this job for nine thousand dollars."

"Gurp, have I ever haggled before?"

"Yes, Marty Blake. You have haggled me every single time. Unmercifully, I might add."

"That was just for fun." Blake sipped at his espresso, let the bitter coffee bite his tongue. "But this time it's different. This time there's no rich corporation to put up the money and I haven't worked in a year, so I'm dead broke. All the money's coming from the lawyer and his pockets just aren't that deep. Believe me, Gurp, I checked him out myself. Max Steinberg's credit is worse than Saddam Hussein's."

"Eight thousand. And I do it as a boy scout. For the damn good deed of it."

"It's not a good deed if you get paid."

"Please, Marty Blake. I am not a Judeo-Christian. Do not trouble me with your ethics."

Blake leaned back in his chair, laced his fingers behind his skull. "Take the three thousand, Gurp. We'll talk about the rest of it after the search."

"And if I find no irregularity? Will you then come to me and pay your debt?"

"You know I will. I have to, because if I don't, you'll freeze me out and I won't have the pleasure of letting you bust my balls in the future."

Patel thought about it for a moment, then nodded. "All right, okay. I will do it for only you. Three thousand will be my retainer. Now, you said to me that you haven't worked in one year. There must be a bloody good story to explain that one, because as we both know, you are addicted to activity. I will fetch pastries and you will tell me all about it. That, Marty Blake, is the civilized way to proceed among friends who do business."

"Thank you," Blake said, "for sharing that with me."

SIX

The train was in motion. That was the good news. Gurp Patel was busy turning the economic lives of John McGuire, Judge of the Appellate Court, and Johan Tillson, bereaved survivor, inside out. Kosinski, as obsessive as Patel if Blake judged him right, was in the field, preparing for the second stage of the operation. All in all, it was as right as Blake could get it.

The bad news was that until Patel finished his research, there was nothing for Blake to do but sit on his hands, a clearly impossible task. What was it Patel had said about him? That he was addicted to activity? Alone in his apartment, he thought of Rebecca Webber and quickly realized that the only part of him that missed her was safely tucked into his briefs. Too bad. In some ways, he'd be happier if his memories made him miserable.

Tomorrow morning, he'd go out for a long run, pay a visit to the gym, pump iron until he was exhausted. Tomorrow night, he'd pace the floors of his apartment, wish again and again that his own fingers were tapping at Gurp Patel's keyboards. By the end of the week, he'd be one step from insanity.

Compulsive, Blake thought, is what the shrinks call it. I have to stay busy, even if that means taking risks. The Curse of a Scheming Mind is what it *should* be called. If we can locate our prime target— the killer, the fixer, whatever you want to call him—before we approach McGuire and Tillson. . . . If we could actually tap his phone, see where the first call leads. . . .

Blake slipped out of his gym shorts, slid into his pants, pulled on a freshly laundered Izod knit. He thought, briefly, of Steinberg's forty-five hundred dollars, the forty-five hundred he hadn't given to Gurp Patel. That money was going to be used to buy the bugs and taps he'd need to do the job. Because the truth (which he hadn't bothered to share with Bell Kosinski or Max Steinberg) was that he had no equipment of his own and couldn't very well borrow Manhattan

Executive's without alerting Joanna Bardo. Of course, there'd be hell to pay when Gurp presented his bill; when he, Marty Blake, went back to Max Steinberg with his hand out.

Ten minutes later, Blake was sitting at his mother's kitchen table, staring down at the scarred formica. He'd grown up with that blue marbeled pattern, had put any number of the chips and scars there himself.

"What's with the scrapbook, Mom? I saw it open on the chair when I came in. It's not like you."

Dora Blake shrugged, busied herself with a strawberry cheesecake. "Sometimes it gets lonely. What could I say? It doesn't happen every day, but when it does, I go back and visit the good times." She hesitated, shrugged. "I wonder how many people can look at their lives and say, 'This is exactly how I thought it was going to be. This is just the way I planned it.'"

"Christ, Mom, you sound like you're eighty. Instead of fifty. It's not your fault about Pop."

"How do you know that?"

Blake didn't answer immediately. Instead, he accepted a plate, scooped the strawberries off the top of his cheesecake, studied the odd look in his mother's eye. "This isn't what I came here to talk about," he said, knowing she wouldn't be diverted.

"I always thought I was gonna wait until you asked me." She looked down at her hands. "But you won't do it. You're stubborn, hard-headed. And I feel bad enough to make you feel bad, too. It's that simple."

"I was afraid of that."

"And smart-mouthed." She leaned forward. "Addicted to cheap, *unearned* cynicism."

"Damn," Blake returned, "and I thought I was addicted to activity. I must've missed something. Look, Mom, before you get started. I came up to ask for a favor. I'd like Uncle Patrick to do something for me, something he won't wanna do, and I was hoping you could get him up here. So he can look me in the eye when he turns me down." Blake leaned back, crossed his legs, laid his fork on the plate. Just as if his heart wasn't pounding in his chest.

"Your father worked Queens Homicide his last couple of years on the job. You know that, right?"

"It was a long time ago, but now that you mention it, yeah, I remember."

"You remember that he was good at his job? That he was decorated twice in the last year?"

"I don't get the point here, Ma. Pop was good at his job, but he quit and fell apart. That's what I've been *led* to believe."

"That's what you wanted to believe. It's not what you were told."

"I wasn't told *anything*. Remember?"

"And you never asked." She waved a hand in his face, stifling any further response. "Your father was doing a routine canvass. Burning shoe leather is what he called it. Anyway, he knocks on this particular door and a young woman opens it. Matty's about to ask the questions when he sees—or, he claims he sees—a large bag of cocaine, a kilo as it turns out, lying in plain view on a table behind her. He thinks it's a gift from heaven, a good clean collar that just fell out of the sky, and he puts the woman—her name is Chantel McKendrick—under arrest. Takes her down to the house, does the paperwork, ships her off to Central Booking. I remember him telling me about it when he came home that night. Laughing about it. 'If they weren't so stupid,' he said, 'I might have to work for a living.'

"I was surprised, of course. A kilo is a lot of cocaine to leave on a table, but Matty said she was so stoned she barely knew her own name. Plus, he figured it wasn't hers, that some dealer was using her place to stash his dope and she was taking her cut off the top.

"Two days later, Chantel McKendrick's attorney—and he wasn't legal aid, either; McKendrick's lawyer was your new friend, Maxwell Steinberg—told an entirely different story. According to Steinberg, Matty pushed his way into Chantel's apartment, found the cocaine, offered to let her off hook if she had sex with him. When she refused, he forced her, then arrested her anyway."

Blake shook his head angrily. "This is bullshit, Ma. There isn't a detective on the job that hasn't been accused somewhere along the line. It comes with the territory."

"Maybe so, Marty, but when Max Steinberg does the accusing, the brass down at the big house listens. And not because they believe him. They listen because Max Steinberg has the juice to make the job look bad.

"So what happened is that somebody downtown shipped it over to Internal Affairs. And the headhunters ran with it, interviewed women your father had arrested when he worked Vice, came up with half a dozen accusations. Now, understand, Marty, I pieced the story together as best I could, because once it got rolling, Matty wouldn't talk about it. He said there was no point, that it wouldn't make any difference, and he was right. Every cop gets offers and more than a few take advantage.

"It was the use of force that made it so bad, of course. That made it more than an indiscretion. *If* he was guilty. Nobody knows exactly how the headhunters conducted the investigation. Maybe they pressured the other women, maybe . . . ."

Blake pushed the chair away from the table, started to stand. He wasn't getting ready to leave. No, what he wanted to do was pace the floor.

"I know how it works," he said. "If they want you, they get you. That's all there is to it."

"Does that mean you think they were out to get your father?"

The question stopped Blake in his tracks. He leaned down on the table. Wanting to say, Of course they were after him. Pop wouldn't do that. My father wasn't a rapist. . . . The words froze in his mouth.

"There's no way to be sure," he finally admitted.

"That's right, Marty. That's the way it is with the headhunters. You never know why they're doing anything. You never know who's pulling the strings." She took a deep breath, let it go slowly. "They did have some evidence, though. One of the five women who accused him had been treated for cuts and bruises two days after her arrest. At the time, she claimed that her injuries came by way of a jail-house fight. When IAD found her, she told a different story. She said that Matthew Blake had beaten, then raped her, then threatened to have her killed if she told anyone."

"That's not proof," Blake insisted. "Proof is a DNA match on semen, proof is an objective eyewitness. . . ."

"You're right, Marty. There was no proof. Chantel McKendrick was never examined. But proof in a court of law was never really the point. In a way, Matty would've been better off if the papers had picked it up. Then the job would have defended him as a matter of principle. As it was, they offered him a clear choice: retire or face departmental charges and the possible loss of his pension. Matty retired."

"And then fell apart."

Dora Blake nodded, gathered Blake's empty plate, turned to the sink. "He didn't do it without help," she said matter-of-factly.

"Meaning what?"

"Meaning most of his cop buddies stopped coming around after word got out. Meaning they stopped inviting him to Emerald Society meetings, Holy Name Society breakfasts. Meaning his wife never truly believed in his innocence, that she couldn't resist her own doubts."

SEVEN

Bell Kosinski couldn't remember a time in his life when he was so lucky to be so stupid. He was parked on Twenty-fifth Street, just off Madison Avenue, staring out at the main entrance to the building that housed New York's Appellate Court. It was nine-thirty in the morning and he'd fought a great deal of traffic to get to his position. That was the stupid part. Stupid to think the exalted judges who sat on the Appellate Court would be anywhere near Manhattan in the month of August. The building was locked tight; the court was not in session.

Which was just as well, because Marty Blake, for all his arrogance, was never going to bug Judge John McGuire's chambers. It might have been possible in the chaos of the criminal court buildings downtown. Their halls teemed with lawyers, defendants, witnesses, clerks, court buffs, reporters . . . a constantly changing set of exotic characters (like Maxwell Steinberg) to provide the necessary cover.

The Appellate Court was entirely different—defendants rarely attended; witnesses were almost never called; court buffs soon discovered that the appeals process dulled even the juiciest murder. Blake would be challenged by the court officers within minutes.

Kosinski sipped at a pint of Smirnoff, took a minute to admire the two story building. Despite its small size, the architect had packed it with ornamentation. Two marble statues flanked the broad steps leading to the main entrance. One, a hooded figure out of the Old Testament, read from a large book. The other, a Roman warrior in battle gear, held a sword on his lap and glared at oblivious pedestrians. The implication, Kosinski guessed, was that if the right hand doesn't get you, the left one will.

He rolled up the window, started the tiny rented Datsun, flipped on the air conditioning. The city was heating up, absorbing heat like clay in a baker's oven. By the time the sun reached its zenith, spit would sizzle on the hoods of parked cars. Even Central Park would be deserted.

HONK!

Kosinski jerked his head to the left, saw a uniformed brownie in a Traffic Department Plymouth wave her hand contemptuously. He watched her mouth the words "Move it, asshole," before indulging himself in the violent fantasy most common to New Yorkers, imagining himself assaulting a Traffic Agent with the nearest blunt object. Then the brownie picked up her summons book and he drove away like a good little boy.

His next scheduled stop was in the Riverdale section of the Bronx, an upscale neighborhood rarely mentioned in the media where the Bronx had become synonymous with dark faces, drugs, and violence. Riverdale had been home to Johan Tillson since shortly after Sondra Tillson's murder and Kosinski was supposed to sit on the importer's residence until he had a thorough picture of who lived there. But something was bothering him, something so obvious that he should have seen it long ago.

He found a pay phone on Madison Avenue, dialed a number, got lucky.

"Dunne here."

"Bobby?"

"Is that you, Bell Kosinski?" Robert Dunne asked. "Do I recognize your besotted tones?"

"Not too besotted at the moment, Bobby. In fact, I'm perilously close to sober. You think I might come over and talk to you for a few minutes. I need a favor."

"A favor? Bell, please."

Sergeant Robert Dunne, Kosinski knew, was reacting as any good veteran cop was certain to react whenever the word "favor" was mentioned. Without at least an implied *quid pro quo*, a favor was inevitably seen as an imposition, a breach of etiquette. Kosinski, with nothing tangible to trade, had decided to offer himself. Knowing that Robert Dunne maintained his own tenuous sobriety by preaching it to any alcoholic cop who'd listen.

"Look, Bobby, what I'm tryin' to do here is start a new life. And I could use a little help."

A brief silence, then: "Are ya really sober, Bell? You're not puttin' me on?"

"Not exactly sober, but not drunk, either. And I'm not jokin' about tryin' to start a new life. I'm working for a PI now, and if I don't fuck things up, it could be permanent. I mean, let's face it, Bobby, it's hard to get straight when you wake up to nothing every morning."

"Then it's over between you and Ingrid? For good and forever."

"It's been over between us for a long time, Bobby. I told you that a couple of years ago."

"Never give up hope, Bell. Hope springs eternal."

Kosinski paused, considered the fact that he never wanted to see his wife again; that he didn't know where she lived or what she did with her days; that the job took her alimony out of his pension check every month and reading the stub was as close as he got to missing her.

"Yeah, I guess that's so. And what I hope is that you'll give me a few minutes of your time. So I can ask my favor."

"C'mon up, boyo. It never hurts to listen. Isn't that what I've been tellin' ya for years?"

Half an hour later, the Datsun safely tucked away in a parking lot, Kosinski was seated in Bobby Dunne's Washington Heights living room. Trying to explain himself.

"So, ya see, Bobby, I haven't actually *decided* to quit drinkin'. It's something I'm workin' up to. In the meanwhile, I'm tryin' to run down this captain and what I figure, being as you're Treasurer of the Emerald Society, is you could look up his command. Point me in the right direction, so to speak."

Kosinski, looking directly into Robert Dunne's sad, compassionate eyes, tried to forget the fact that he hated compassion, especially when it flowed in his direction. Dunne's broad, square, heavy-boned face reeked of inner conviction. Its small, inoffensive features were widely spaced, as if they had nothing to do with each other. As if his personality was perfectly expressed by the shape of his skull and the individual features had been added in a kind of biological retro-fit.

"Would ya pray with me, Bell?"

"It wasn't exactly what I had in mind. Maybe we should save it for when I actually *decide* to quit." Kosinski, though he had no real hope of diverting Bobby Dunne, didn't want the man turning up at his door with a bible tucked beneath his arm. "You know, like when I make a *final* decision."

Dunne dropped to his knees, and Kosinski reluctantly followed. Hoping against hope that Dunne wouldn't pull out a rosary, put him through a half hour of punishment.

"Oh, Lord," Dunne began, his eyes raised to the ceiling, his hands steepled beneath his chin, "we pray here for the heart and soul of Bell Kosinski. I've known him for a long time, Lord, since before he became a drunk, and I can vouch for him. Bell Kosinski is a good man who's seen his share of trouble and now humbly begs for Your divine aid. Let us pray."

Five Hail Marys and an Our Father later, Kosinski and Dunne faced each other across a low coffee table. Dunne seemed relaxed, almost fulfilled, but Kosinski's hands had begun to tremble. A sharp pain jabbed at his right eye, demanding immediate medication. He thought about going into the bathroom, realized that Dunne had seen every alcoholic dodge in the book.

"Take it out, Bell. Before you fall apart."

"Huh?" The words caught Kosinski off guard.

"When you decide to cut out the booze, let me know. I'll send you upstate. The job has a place near Albany where they dry you out without killing you. In the meantime . . . well, let's just say I'd be happier if you didn't try to con me."

Kosinski nodded, took out the bottle, sipped at it judiciously. "I wasn't kidding about finding work, Bobby," he said after a moment. "This is a big chance for me."

"I know all about it," Dunne said without smiling. "Believe me, I've been there and back. Often enough to know that you can't control it. If you're not entirely sober, you'll soon be entirely drunk. Now, what is it you wanted?"

"I hate you when you're right, Bobby." Kosinski paused for a response, but Dunne maintained the same cement-block expression. "Okay, the first thing is that what I tell you, and it won't be much, has to be kept confidential. Even if you turn me down."

"Understood."

"I'm serious. It's gotta stop here."

Dunne finally smiled. "I swear it on my faith, Bell. Just do me a favor and *don't* confess to murder."

"If somebody gets killed, it's gonna be me." Kosinski was all business, now; figuring that he'd paid for his favor, that he had an absolute right to ask. "I'm trying to run down a cop named Grogan. Two years ago, he was a captain. He might have been promoted since then, might be a deputy inspector. Grogan is about as Irish a name as you can get, which means he has to belong to the Emerald Society. Being as you're the Treasurer, I was hoping you could pinpoint his command."

"That's it?"

"That's it. I want to know who Grogan works for."

"Damn, Bell, I thought this was gonna be juicy."

"Life is filled with disappointments."

"And you can't give me any more information?"

"Not a word."

Dunne shook his head. "What you're askin' me to do is go against the job. You know that, right?"

The question came as no surprise to Bell Kosinski. "I'm not sayin' you should testify against him. I just wanna know what—or, who—I'm up against. If you tell me to drop dead, I'll understand. I'll understand, but I'll find out some other way."

Kosinski could see the gears turning in Bobby Dunne's head. His first instinct was to protect the job, but if he followed that instinct and refused Kosinski's request, he'd lose his convert forever. Lose him to no good end.

"Grogan's a pretty common name, Bell. You couldn't be a little more specific?"

"*Aloysius* Grogan. Maybe that'll narrow it down some."

"I was afraid that's what you were going to say."

"You know him?"

"That I do, Bell. And you were right. He's Inspector Grogan now."

"Who does he work for?"

"I don't suppose it'd slow you down if I tell you that you're over your head?"

"I been drowning for years, Bobby. I'm not afraid of the water."

"You should be. This time, you should be."

"Yes or no?" Kosinski almost licked his lips. He could taste the blood, the way he'd tasted it so many time in Homicide. He'd nearly forgotten how good it was. That's how long it'd been.

"Alright, Bell. It's not like it was a secret. Inspector Aloysius Grogan works directly under Chief Samuel Harrah."

"Is that supposed to mean something to me? I never heard of Chief Samuel Harrah."

Dunne shrugged and grinned. "You're not supposed to, Bell. Not unless you're ambitious enough to study the job. Chief Harrah has commanded the Intelligence Division of the New York City Police Department for the past twenty-five years. He took the job when his father retired."

"How old is he?"

"Sixty-five or so."

"That's five years past mandatory retirement."

"I guess nobody told him, Bell."

Kosinski took a second to put it together. When he'd first come on the job, Intelligence had been in the news quite a bit. That was in the era of the Black Liberation Army and the Weather Underground. Cops were being assassinated at the rate of one a month; they were being sniped at almost every day; the tension had been nearly unbearable. At the time, Kosinski had been convinced, like nearly every other cop, that it was only a matter of time until the country drifted into guerilla warfare. But then it'd all died down, just burnt itself out like a fire that'd run out of fuel. The Eighties had been relatively peaceful, at least from a cop's point of view, and the Intelligence Division had faded into the background.

"Weren't the spooks in trouble a couple of years ago?" Kosinski finally asked.

"Yes, they were. For routinely taping a black call-in radio station." Dunne stood up, motioned for Bell to do the same. "And that's all I've got to say on the matter. Except that you might wanna think it over, Bell. Hope may spring eternal in the human breast. But not if the heart stops beating."

EIGHT

The preliminaries were over—the hug for Dora, the manly hand-shake for Marty, the "how are you, it's been a long time, what have you been doing" . . . all the bullshit. Patrick Blake was sitting at his sister-in-law's kitchen table, nursing a glass of Scotch and smiling at his nephew. His shirt collar was loose, his black tie pulled down, his uniform jacket draped over the back of a chair. Forty pounds overweight and nearly bald, he looked every inch the moderately successful professional drifting into retirement. Or a fatal heart attack, whichever came first. His cheeks were their usual apple-red, a tribute to his blood pressure and the rolls of fat that hung over his belt and his collar.

"So, Marty, what's the bad news?"

Patrick Blake's dark eyes, Marty noted, were still shrewd, still wary. They carried the lessons he'd learned thirty years ago on the streets. The lessons in survival he'd dragged up through the ranks. At first glance, Marty could find no point of vulnerability, but time would tell.

"How much has Mom told you about what I've been doing?"

Patrick Blake glanced at his uniform jacket, then back at his nephew. "She told me you're tryin' to get some mutt off the hook. Claimin' he was framed."

"Does that mean you think it *can't* happen? A man *can't* be framed?"

"They all claim they're innocent, Marty." He waved a pudgy hand in dismissal, chuckled softly, shook his head. "They don't know how to tell the truth. It's why they're called criminals."

"You mean like my father? Like your brother when he claimed he was innocent? Just another subhuman piece of shit trying to get off the hook?" Marty glanced at his mother, noted the clenched jaw and stubborn half-smile. He wondered, briefly, what it'd been like for her, a Jew marrying into a family of Irish cops, then turned back to his uncle.

"I tried, Marty. I did everything I could to help your father. But when the headhunters get hold of a case, there's no controlling what they do."

"That's not the point, Uncle Patrick. Unless you think your brother was a rapist . . ." Marty let his voice fall off. Knowing full well that Patrick Blake, no matter what he thought, couldn't very well call Matthew Blake a rapist. Not in front of his wife and his only child. "I mean I'm not a cop, so it's hard for me to understand. It sounds like you're saying the job is *never* wrong. That no cop *ever* crosses the line. I don't see how you can hold that position without believing that your own brother was a rapist."

"Now, look here, Marty . . ."

Patrick Blake was starting to heat up. Which came as no surprise to Marty. His uncle had always been volatile; he'd ruled his family the way he'd ruled the men under his command.

"But, in any event," Marty calmly continued, "this is one convicted criminal who's definitely not trying to wriggle off the hook. Billy Sowell is dead. He was murdered in prison."

Blake watched a tremor flow upwards from his uncle's belt, imagined it as a chill running up the spine. He'd pierced the armor and he knew it. Time to drive the sword home.

"You know, Uncle Patrick, I must have been ten or eleven when I first heard about police corruption. That's when the Knapp Commission was doing its work and bent cops were all over the TV screen. Before then, I believed that cops were good and pure; I literally imagined them as angels of the Lord. Maybe I had too much imagination—Catholic school can have that effect on you—but I was upset enough to go to my father and ask him if he was on the take."

"You said that?" Patrick Blake half-rose out of his chair. "You accused your own father?"

"Relax, Uncle Pat. I was ten years old. And I wasn't accusing him. Believe me, the last thing I wanted to hear him say was 'Yes.'" Blake hesitated long enough for the information to sink in, but not long enough for his uncle to work up a head of steam. "The thing about it is that he wasn't pissed off. Not at all. He took me into my room, sat me down, then explained the reality of being a cop. Some cops never took anything; some cops took little things like free lunches; some cops took with both hands. But no cop, not unless he was lower than the criminals he arrested, turned his back on rape or murder. That's where the line was drawn and if you crossed it, you weren't a cop any more. It was as simple as that." Blake leaned back, smiled at his thoroughly pissed-off uncle. "Was he bullshitting me, Uncle Patrick? Was he telling a stupid kid what the stupid kid wanted to hear?"

"You're a smart-mouthed prick, Marty. Your father should have slapped your face instead of trying to reason with you."

"I've seen the evidence, Uncle Patrick, the whole damned file. Billy Sowell didn't kill Sondra Tillson. Which means somebody else killed her and that somebody else is walking the streets. Is that okay with you, Uncle Patrick? If it is, just tell me and I'll go away."

Patrick Blake looked over at his sister-in-law. Marty wasn't certain that his uncle was asking for help, but if he was, he'd have to look elsewhere. Dora Blake was wearing her stone face, the one that wasn't remotely interested in questions or excuses.

"Look, Marty," Patrick Blake finally said, "you don't know what you're getting into."

"I understand that, Uncle Patrick. That's why you're here. To tell me what I'm getting into. To tell me, for instance, about a captain named Aloysius Grogan. What he does, who he works for, like that."

"And there's nothing I can say to slow you down?"

"Nothing."

Patrick Blake took a deep breath; his jowls fluttered as he blew it out. "Alright, Marty. I'll give you what you want, but then we're quits. Don't look for any more help, because I won't risk the career of my son. The one who's named after your father, if you remember. He's five years on the job and if he's gonna move up, he'll need my help." He waited for Marty to nod agreement before continuing. "Now, I'm gonna tell you this in my own way, and I don't want to be interrupted. When I'm finished, you'll know what you need to know." He paused, got a second nod, hurried on. "Last week, Aloysius Grogan—he's an inspector, now—shows up at my office unannounced. I don't know who he is, but when an inspector comes calling, you make yourself available. He asks me if you're my nephew, if you're the son of Detective Matthew Blake. When I tell him you are, he asks me if I have any influence over you.

"'Because if you do,' he says, 'you better slow him down, Captain. He's workin' for a sleazeball lawyer, tryin' to hurt the job. People don't like it and they're not gonna sit on their hands much longer.'

"Then he walks out before I can answer him. Now, understand this, even though Grogan technically outranks me, it doesn't mean the bastard can bull his way into my office and order me around. You don't get assigned to the big house unless you have friends in high places and the both of us know it. So, what I have to figure is that his highly placed friends somehow outrank my highly placed friends, which is why I didn't throw him out of my office two minutes after he got there.

"What I do is head for the computer—remember, I work in personnel—and punch in Grogan's name. When his command turns out to be Intelligence, I know what I'm up against. I'm sure you're old enough to remember the story about J. Edgar Hoover, that he stayed FBI Director as long as he did because he had something on everybody. Well, that same rumor applies to Chief Samuel Harrah, Grogan's boss. He's commanded Intelligence under five different commissioners, and what they say is that you don't *get* to be commissioner without his approval.

"To tell the truth, Marty, though I'd been hearing the rumor for years, I never thought much about it. Most of the time, Intelligence doesn't have anything to do with the rest of the job. They collect information on subversive groups or organized crime, but they don't make any arrests. If Samuel Harrah and his spooks happen onto something important, they take it directly to the Commissioner and he parcels it out to the appropriate division. I guess that's the biggest difference between Samuel Harrah and J. Edgar Hoover. Hoover couldn't stay out of the spotlight. Harrah operates in total darkness.

"Just after your mother phoned this morning, I was called up to my boss's office. My *rabbi's* office, a man who's helped me along in my career for the more than twenty years. He throws your father's file on my desk, tells me the headhunters are thinkin' about reopening the case.

"'For chrissake, Solly,' I tell him. 'The man's *dead*.'

"'They don't care,' he says. 'His widow's collecting a pension and they wanna take it away.'"

Patrick Blake pushed the chair back and shoved himself to his feet. "Dora," he said, "I'm sorry to have to tell it to you like this, but I also wanna say that your son should have better manners. He's a little nothing, a cockroach going up against a lion. Maybe you can talk some sense into him. Before he gets stepped on."

It should have been an exit line. At least, from where Marty Blake sat. But his mother was much too quick. She'd been standing quietly by the sink and now she moved forward until she was a couple of feet from her brother-in-law.

"What you oughta be, Patrick," she said, "is pissed off at Aloysius Grogan. He's the man who came into your office and spit in your face. Instead, you're taking it out on Marty who hasn't done a damn thing to you. I tell ya, Patrick, if I didn't know better, I'd think what you're doing is hating the man who scares you the least."

"Now, wait a second . . ."

"That's a good idea," Marty Blake said, "let's all take a second to think it over. First, they're *not* gonna go after Pop's pension. No charges were ever filed at the time and a dead man can't confront his accusers which is a basic constitutional right. It's a bluff and a bad bluff, at that, which I have to admit makes me very happy. These people are scared, because they know they can get hurt here. It doesn't make them less dangerous, but it might make them stupid. Uncle Patrick, I have another favor to ask. I want you to look up Inspector Grogan. I want you to tell him you talked to me and I told you that Steinberg pulled out. Being as Billy Sowell's dead and buried, it's gotta make sense."

Patrick Blake hadn't taken his eyes off his sister-in-law. Nevertheless, he replied without hesitation.

"Tell me why I should do you a favor."

"Actually, there's two reasons. First, because it doesn't make any difference. My father's pension isn't on the line. No, it's your career—and your son's career—that's up for grabs. If I keep going, you're gonna take the blame. Nobody's gonna give a shit whose side you're on. You're supposed to stop me and if you don't, they're gonna punish you. It's as simple as that."

When Patrick Blake turned to face his nephew, the truth was written all over his scarlet face. When he spoke, his voice was dead flat. "You said there were two reasons. What's the second?"

"If you cut the head off, the body dies."

NINE

"So ya see how it is, Bell? I'm the kinda dude could admit he done somethin' fucked up when he done somethin' fucked up. I mean ya friend should'na sat on my car, right? Like I just *waxed* it and shit. But that don't give me no right to jump on his fuckin' back like I done."

Tony Loest shook his head, lowered his eyes, flicked his lashes.

"These things happen, Tony. Everybody's got a temper, right?"

Kosinski tried to put some feeling into it. After all, resolution was resolution; an apology was an apology. Even if Tony Loest was so coked up he was spitting the words between clenched teeth, he'd most likely remember the next time they met. Most likely.

"Yeah," Loest replied, "but with me a temper is a curse. I mean I could'a done good wit' my life. Instead of endin' up haulin' bricks like what I'm tryin' to do. Only there ain't no fuckin' work out there, ya know what I'm sayin? So now I'm like doin' crimes to feed my family. All because I got this temper and I one day clocked this bitch math teacher gimme a hard time about chewin' some fuckin' gum. Ya believe that, Bell? In fronna the whole class she hadda make me an example. How could I take that shit, I . . ."

"Jeez," Kosinski interrupted. "I don't see how you could've accepted something like that. It must've been awful." He was hoping the sarcasm would slow Tony down. Hoping against hope.

"Awful ain't the word for it, Bell. Like it was totally fucked up. That's why I had'a smack her in the face. I mean, I couldn'a held my head up if I didn't waste her a little bit. It was only human, right?"

"Yeah, wait a second." Kosinski raised his glass, signaled Ed O'Leary, endured the bartender's pitiless smirk.

"What's up, Bell? You maybe need a little more tomato juice in your vodka? Did I mix ya *cocktail* a bit too strong?"

"Fuck you, Ed. I feel like I'm gettin' it from both ends. And why? Just because I ordered a Bloody Mary? Tell ya the truth, I'm thinkin' about takin' my business somewhere else."

"Business?" O'Leary scowled. "Shit, now that you reformed, you ain't got no business. Not that I can see." Despite the bravado, he filled Kosinski's glass with equal measures of vodka and Mott's tomato juice.

"What I can't figure out," Kosinski said to Tony Loest, "is how a man with the personality of a junkyard dog has any customers at all. Why do we come back?"

"Beats me," Loest agreed. "Listen, I gotta go to the toilet. It's like an emergency."

O'Leary watched Loest retreat, then leaned over the bar. "Whatta ya think, Bell? Think he's got a nervous bladder?"

"I couldn't say about his bladder, Ed. But his *nose* looked pretty nervous."

The bartender laughed, shook his head. "I can remember a time when I would'a took a junkie like him and put my sawed-off in his face. Tell him to get the fuck out and stay out. Now, my weekend customers'll go somewheres else if they can't buy cocaine. They *expect* it. Like it's just part of life."

"Times change, Ed. I guess ya gotta go with the flow."

"Maybe that's why I love drunks so much. Guys like Bell Kosinski *used* to be. They're committed. They don't got time for this other bullshit."

"I'll drink to that." Kosinski hoisted his Bloody Mary, saw Marty Blake walk through the door. He drained the glass and hustled over, figuring they better get out of Cryders before Tony Loest came back and started apologizing.

"C'mon, Marty," he said, taking Blake's arm, "let's go for a little walk. It's stuffy in here." He waited until the door was safely closed behind them before continuing. "It's lucky you stopped down," he said, "because I got somethin' I wanna tell you. I did a little research, found out who Grogan works for. Thought it might be important."

Kosinski saw it as a test. He'd gone beyond Blake's instructions, maybe jeopardized the both of them if he'd spoken to the wrong person. The question was whether Blake trusted his judgment.

"That's funny, Bell. Because I did the same thing. And what amazes me is how stupid we were not to see it before this."

"Yeah?" Kosinski felt his cheeks light up, hoped Marty couldn't see him blushing. "Myself, I blame it on the booze. What's your excuse?"

Blake managed a grin that died as quickly as it appeared. "Why don't you tell me what you came up with," he said.

Kosinski waited until they were inside Blake's Taurus before detailing his conversation with Sergeant Dunne. When he finished, Blake nodded his agreement.

"A big problem for us," he said. "A *very* big problem."

Kosinski, who couldn't see what difference it made, started to agree, then checked himself. "It doesn't hurt to know who you're up against," he offered.

"Tell you the truth, I wish it was Homicide or Narcotics. Something simple. Intelligence? Lemme ask you a question—when you called this sergeant, did you use your home phone?"

Kosinski felt the blood rush into his face again. This time he was sure Blake would notice. He felt like he was on fire. "Actually, I didn't. I was on the road when the idea came to me. You figure the phones are tapped, right?"

"From what I understand, surveillance is all the spooks do. We have to assume they're good at it. The problem is that our strategy depends on keeping our strategy quiet until we're ready. If Grogan, say, or Brannigan, already warned the judge and the husband, we're wasting our time. Now, you say you never spoke about it on the phone or in your apartment. Maybe it's just blind luck, but I didn't, either. Which makes Steinberg's office the point of vulnerability."

Blake drove the rest of the way to Kosinski's apartment in silence, but instead of pulling into an available parking space directly in front of the laundromat, he slid by without slowing down.

"You see that van there, Bell?" Blake asked.

"Sure."

"You recognize it?"

"Recognize? Marty, who looks at parked cars?"

"I'm talking about the name on it. Packer Brothers Plumbing. You ever heard of 'em?"

"You telling me you think the van is full of cop spies? I don't think we're that important."

When Blake finally pulled over, they were two blocks away. "Here's what I want you to do, Bell. I want you to walk back to your apartment and turn on the radio or the television. Make it as loud as you can. When I come by, just run with whatever I say. I've got an idea and it's something I wanted to talk to you about anyway."

Kosinski managed to get inside his apartment without looking at the van in question. He turned on the radio and raised the volume. One drink later, Blake knocked at his door.

"Hey, Marty, what's up? I wasn't expecting to see you again." He felt like a complete fool, like a character in a very, very bad movie. "How 'bout a mixed drink. I got vodka and ice."

"You go ahead, Bell. I'm driving tonight. But do me a favor, okay? Would you shut off the TV. There's something I wanna talk to you about."

Kosinski wasn't altogether surprised when Blake opened his briefcase and pulled out an instrument that looked like the two-way radio he, Kosinski, had carried while on patrol. Nor was he surprised when Blake flipped it on, extended the antenna, started running it along the wall. But he was completely shocked by the story Blake told as he methodically went about his business. It was a story about his cop father being accused of rape and the part played by a lawyer named Maxwell Steinberg. A story about a good cop's slow, steady disintegration. Kosinski wasn't drunk enough to confuse it with his own story, but the downward progression was close enough to keep him riveted.

"And you just now found out about this?" he asked when Blake finally stopped talking.

"Yeah. I caught my mother in a bad mood and she took it out on me. Maybe she thought she was gonna shake me up, but I only wish I'd heard it before. While my father was still alive and I could've done something about it." He paused long enough to motion Kosinski over. "All day I've been trying to tell myself that my father wasn't a rapist, but I can't make it stick." He pointed to a small hole in the cracked drywall, mouthed the word "microphone," then knelt down. "I mean what kid really knows his father? Fathers are either heroes or bums. Or both, like my old man." He began to pull at the strip of plastic that served as a wallboard. "Anyway, Bell, what I finally decided was I had to know. One way or the other. And what I was hoping was that you'd help me out. You have to have connections in the job, even if you're retired. Plus, when I put the question to Max Steinberg, I want someone there who can be objective. Someone who can pull me away if I lose my temper."

When Kosinski saw the transmitter, it was as if he'd been transported back in time. Back to his early days on the job when he could still become angry at the wicked ways of wicked men. He knew exactly what that small black box was, had used one just like it when he'd worked Organized Crime.

"I'll do whatever I can," he muttered. "You got a right to know."

Blake replaced the plastic. "Look, don't take this the wrong way, but I'd like to talk about what we're gonna do and this apartment's a little depressing. Whatta ya say we go out for a drink?"

Ten minutes later, they were in Blake's car, driving toward Manhattan. Blake was going on about transmitters and parabolic microphones. As if their previous conversation hadn't taken place.

"We got a lucky break here, Bell. Steinberg's office is on the twenty-fifth floor. There's no way they can use a line-of-sight transmitter like the one in your apartment. Most likely, they're using a tape recorder, which means if they haven't retrieved the tape yet, we've got a chance. Personally . . ."

"Wait a second," Kosinski finally interrupted. "What you said about your father—was it true or were you just making it up? And don't tell me you were making it up or I'm gonna think I'm dealin' with an emotionally disturbed person."

"It's true, as far as it goes."

"And you still wanna do something about it? You still wanna know what really happened?"

"Yeah, but not right away. I'm not gonna confront Steinberg until I don't need him any more. Until I don't need his money. For now, I'm too pissed off to think about anybody but Samuel Harrah. This guy believes he can't be taken down, that he's invincible, but times have changed. In his day, the cops had all the hardware. Now, it's *my* day."

TEN

In some ways, Kosinski decided, you have to admire Steinberg as much as Marty Blake. For one thing, he's a lot freer with the booze. Take right now, for instance. Whereas Blake wouldn't pop for a glass of stale spit, Maxwell Steinberg has a sixty-dollar bottle of Hennessy sitting smack in the middle of his desk. Unrepentant to the point of defiance.

The other thing was that Steinberg kept asking irrelevant questions. Much to Kosinski's amusement and Blake's increasing annoyance, Max the Bulldog simply wouldn't be deflected.

"An RF detector? Is that supposed to mean something? Please, I'm not a technical man. I'm a nineteen fifties, I Like Ike, man-of-letters. Not only can't I program my VCR, I'm intimidated by the play button. Believe me, I have to consult my analyst before I plug it into the wall. So tell me what you're doing in words I can understand. If you don't mind."

Blake took off his headphones, let them dangle from his fingers. "I'm looking for a transmitter, Max."

"Then they should call it a transmitter detector. A thing should be called what it is."

"I'll buy that." Blake started to replace the headphones, but he was a little too slow.

"So, please, what does RF stand for?"

"Radio frequency."

This time Blake got the earphones over his head, forcing Steinberg to tap him on the shoulder.

"Look, Max, I don't have time for this bullshit."

For a second, Kosinski was sure that Blake was going to lose control. Maybe invoke his father's name before sending Max Steinberg into orbit. But, no, Marty Blake, though his lower lip trembled and his eyes narrowed, slowly pulled it together. He even managed a smile.

"For Christ's sake, Max, your breath is melting the silver in my fillings."

"That's because I'm drunk, Marty. Being as I didn't expect to work tonight, I thought it was an appropriate way to observe Billy Sowell's death."

"It *is* appropriate. And I need you to talk. Talking activates the bugs. But it'd be a lot better if you'd talk to my associate, Mr. Kosinski. Go ahead. Ask him about Intelligence and the NYPD. Decide if those two words can appear in the same sentence without creating an oxymoron."

Steinberg looked hurt. He watched Blake for a moment, then came back to the bottle on his desk. "I guess you're the only game in town."

"Looks like it, Max."

"So what do you know about Intelligence?"

"Well, I'd have to agree with Marty. It doesn't have a lot to do with cops. Or robbers, for that matter."

"Please, I'd appreciate if you'd take this seriously." Kosinski filled his glass, raised it to show his intentions, drank deeply. "In the Thirties, when Intelligence was known as the Red Squad, they tracked commies. In the Forties, they tracked Nazis. In the Fifties and Sixties, they tracked commies again. In the Seventies, they tracked Black militants, Puerto Rican nationalists, and white revolutionaries. In the Eighties . . . ? Who knows, Max. Things got quiet and I can't remember anyone in the Detectives ever mentioning Intelligence except in connection with organized crime. Not in more years than I want to count."

Steinberg nodded. "Well, it might interest you to know that the old Red Squad is still in action. Me, I like to call it the Red Squad because my father, who considered himself a socialist, was investigated by the Red Squad in the Thirties. But that's another story for another time. Today's story goes back to 1988 and a client named Boyd Harrison. A real blueblood, this Harrison, *senior* vice president at Smyth, Smyth, and Paulson. You look at him, you see the Rock of Gilbraltar. Like in the television ad where it comes sailing over the water."

"I know the type," Kosinski said. "I loved puttin' the cuffs on a guy whose suit was worth more than my car." He set the glass down, let himself enjoy the memory. "See, when you bust a street mutt he mostly looks resigned. Maybe once in a while pissed off, but *never* surprised. The jerks with the suits nearly go into shock."

"Shock is a good word for what happened to Boyd Harrison. It turned out he was a degenerate gambler who'd embezzled half a million dollars. Innocence was not in question; they had him cold and my job was to cut the best deal possible. Of course, the first thing I'm looking for is leverage, some way to put the DA in a mood to bargain. Which is not gonna be easy, because the case is like the *real* Rock of Gibraltar. Plus, the jerk made admissions to the suits who arrested him.

"Me, I don't bullshit the clients. I tell Harrison the facts of life and ask him if there's anything he could tell me about himself that might be useful. Like, for instance, he volunteers three times a week to clean toilets at a homeless shelter.

Steinberg paused as Blake came over to the desk, put one instrument away, took out another, left without a word.

"Bell, your friend is a snot," Steinberg declared.

"True," Kosinski replied, "but he does good work." Steinberg took so long to think about it, Kosinski figured the lawyer had to be adding up the numbers, weighing Blake's cost against his worth.

"Anyway," Steinberg finally said, "the story my client told me, and which I originally thought was so much crapola, went like this. A month before his arrest, Boyd Harrison receives a visit from a cop who calls himself Lieutenant Anthony Carabone. My client never asks to see formal ID, but he does get a look at the badge, which doesn't prove much. This Carabone lays out Harrison's entire scheme, complete with figures, then demands a ten-thousand-dollar payoff. Harrison agrees, but naturally, being a degenerate gambler, he doesn't have a penny when the day of reckoning comes around. About a month later, he finds himself behind bars.

"Anthony Carabone? Sound more like the mafia than the cops, but I decide to check it out, mostly because it's the only game in town. Not that I'm so stupid I report the blackmail and hope the cops investigate on their own. No, the first thing I do is call in some favors and track Lieutenant Carabone to his lair, which turns out to be Intelligence. This gets my back up, because, naturally, I'm thinking about my father and how he couldn't hold a job because somebody in a suit always came around to pass the word to his employers. So what I do is file a motion demanding anything Intelligence has in its files relating to my client. Now, what I'm expecting is a flat denial that any such files exist, but, instead, the prosecutor cites national security, claims that releasing the files would send the country right down the tubes.

"The judge, naturally, puts off any consideration of trial while he reads the briefs and considers the verbal arguments. He says it'll take him from six to nine months because of his crowded calendar and the five hundred pages I've tossed in his face. Bell, for me it was seventh heaven, because now I've got my wedge and I fully intend to pound it home. 'Make me a deal,' I tell the prosecutor. 'And make it good, because I'm telling you my client's family has plenty of money and, just in case the judge should happen to rule against me (which he won't because Steinberg is never wrong about technicalities), I'm prepared to go into the federal courts.'"

Kosinski shook his head, remembered how much he'd hated defense attorneys when he was a cop. "Probation, right? That's what they gave you?"

"That's what they gave my *client*, Bell. I wasn't on trial."

"And it doesn't bother you that this criminal, who stole five hundred thousand dollars, got off the hook?"

Steinberg folded his arms across his chest, let the wig slide forward. "That's my job. That's what I do." He glared at Kosinski.

"You didn't have to become a *criminal* lawyer. Nobody forced it on you."

"From you, Kosinski, I didn't expect naive. What attorneys do is advocate their clients' positions. It doesn't matter if the client is a human or a corporation; it doesn't matter how bad those positions are. A lawyer's job is to make the best of the worst."

Blake interrupted before Kosinski could return fire. "Come over here," he said. "I've found it." He was standing beneath a mounted buffalo's head, pointing at something neither man could immediately see. "There, right there. That black dot. That's the microphone."

"Looks like a cockroach's ass," Steinberg observed.

"If you check a little closer, you can see the wire running through the fur. See it?"

"Son-of-a-bitch, they bugged my office. I swear I'm beginning to take this personally, and when Steinberg takes it personally, hold onto your ass."

"Bell, let's see if we can get the head down without disturbing the wire. I wanna make sure it goes back exactly the way it was."

Once the head was lying on Steinberg's couch, the setup became painfully obvious. The reels of the tape recorder, mounted in a hollow space inside the enormous skull, turned whenever they made a sound.

"It's kinda big, isn't it?" Kosinski asked. "I was expecting something the size of a credit card."

"For a tape recorder that'll carry ten hours of conversation, it's *very* small, believe me." Blake wrapped his fingers in a handkerchief, rewound the tape, started to work his way through it. Through Steinberg on the telephone, Steinberg yelling at his clients, Steinberg yelling at his secretary, Steinberg moaning while a female voice shouted, "Faster, Maxwell, faster, faster, faster."

"So, *nu*," Steinberg said, stopping the tape, "for me the only sin is that she charges two hundred dollars to work me to death."

"Don't worry, Maxwell," Blake observed, "we're not gonna be judgmental here. Me and Bell, we always advocate our client's position. You wouldn't happen to remember when you took that position, would you?"

"Two days ago. After hours."

"Good. That means the conversation we had yesterday has to be on here. I'll go through it when I get home to make sure." Blake pulled the cassette, replaced it with a blank tape and turned the recorder over. Using a rubber-tipped screwdriver, he removed the back plate. "No scratches," he said. "It's important, because they'll look for signs of tampering." He found a small red wire leading from the motor and worked it loose with his fingertips. When he pressed the play button and nothing happened, he grinned and said, "Defective merchandise. Curse of the dishonest spook. They might guess, but they can't know."

Steinberg looked at his drinking partner. "Okay," he said, "I'm admitting it. The boy does good work. Expensive, but good."

"Like that hooker, for instance?" Kosinski let his voice rise an octave. "'Faster, Maxwell. Faster, faster, faster.'"

"What could I say, Bell? My doctor tells me I gotta get more exercise and treadmills are boring. Likewise for stationary bicycles."

Blake held up the tape recorder. "You think we could go over a few things?" When there was no answer, he continued. "From now on, unless I tell you different, you should assume that big brother is listening to every word. Understand?" He waited for both men to nod. "The way I see it, Harrah can't use all his resources. That's why we don't have personal tails and that's why there's only one surveillance van. Max, the blackmail story you told? How did Intelligence discover that your client was embezzling funds unless he was part of some larger investigation?"

"We thought about that, of course," Steinberg answered. "At first, it didn't make sense—Harrison was a Ronald Reagan conservative and a decorated Vietnam veteran. His wife was as straight as he was, except that she spent a lot of her time doing volunteer work for children. One of the places where she volunteered was called the Bedford-Stuyvesant Children's Center. According to her, the center was on the up-and-up, which might have been the case, but the supervisor, Ramon Tavares, was indicted for stashing a hundred M16s in the basement. The way I heard it, the cops thought he was part of the FALN, the Puerto Rican terrorist outfit. It's possible that she and her husband just happened to be in the wrong place at the wrong time and got themselves targeted."

"Sure," Blake said, "but where does the blackmail come in? Unless Samuel Harrah does a little business on the side. Which is why I don't think he can use all his assets. Not unless every single cop in the Intelligence Division is bent."

"It'd be too expensive," Kosinski interrupted. "To cut all those cops in. Too expensive and too dangerous. He'd never do it."

"Excuse me," Steinberg said, "but I don't see what blackmail has to do with Billy Sowell getting framed. It sounds like a straight payoff to me."

Blake held both hands up. "At this point, it doesn't matter. The field's in motion and we're gonna follow the bouncing ball wherever it goes. It's just nice to know we're not up against thirty thousand cops. Bell, do me a favor. Take the bus over tomorrow morning. We'll go out together."

"What about my car?"

"Drive the car back to the rental agency and turn it in. I swept my own car and it was clean, but I don't know about yours and I don't want to check it on the street. Look, the way I see it, Samuel Harrah is dead meat. He's right out in the open and he doesn't have any idea what we're gonna do. Plus, he's scared shitless, which is why he's watching us. Believe me, boys, it's only a matter of time until we have what we need to put him away. Unless, of course, he kills us."

Kosinski looked into Blake's eyes, noted the mad grin. He was about to say something about maintaining control when Blake spoke again.

"But, don't worry, the way I'm gonna work it, they'll go to jail even if they *do* kill us."

ELEVEN

Marty Blake sat in his car, listened to the rain pound on the roof, stared through a shifting gray curtain at the front door of Eternal Memorials, Inc. The way he saw it, this was his last chance at reflection. The last chance to back off, change his mind, run away. His Uncle Patrick had made that point abundantly clear. Had arrived unexpectedly at his door, been cautioned with a gesture, then led upstairs to Dora Blake's apartment.

"Bugged?" Patrick Blake had said. "I don't believe it."

"And tapped." Blake had managed to keep a straight face. With difficulty.

"Jesus Christ."

"No, Uncle Pat. Not Jesus Christ—Jesus doesn't need hardware to know what I'm up to. Samuel Harrah, on the other hand, has yet to attain godhood. I hope."

As far as Marty Blake was concerned, that was the high point of the conversation. Uncle Patrick had come to call his nephew off "before it was too late." He'd been so persistent, so desperate, that Blake had finally become suspicious.

"You didn't rat me out, did you, Uncle Pat? Didn't put your nephew's head on the block?"

The accusation had sent the older man running for the door. Huffing his indignation through clenched teeth.

"Just tell me one thing, Marty. Just tell me what's in it for you. What's in it for *anybody*." Patrick Blake had paused in the open doorway, had actually filled the frame. Resplendent in his captain's uniform, he'd jammed his peaked cap on his head, then fired one last volley. "There's no win here. There's no *upside*. If you take a cop down—even a dirty cop—you'll pay for it as long as you live in New York. Remember Serpico. Remember that honest cops hated him, too."

When the door had closed (more softly than Blake would have predicted) he'd turned to his mother, expecting support. No such luck.

She'd poured out the ritual mugs of coffee, observed a few minutes of nearly mandatory silence, then fired her own volley.

"What I told you the other day about your father? About how I didn't know if he was guilty or not? It wasn't true. I know he didn't—couldn't . . ." She'd hesitated, looked down at her feet. "I know that your father—my husband—was not a rapist. But I couldn't convince him. Couldn't reach him. He decided to walk away from his life and that's just what he did. Men are only strong when their fears are out in front of them."

Blake had watched his mother for a moment, noting her discomfort. Enjoying it, if the truth be told. Thinking, maybe she hadn't reached him because she was too busy keeping his disgrace a secret.

"My father's gone," he'd finally said. "And if I get sidetracked here, I'm gonna be gone, too. But I promise you this, Mom—once I'm finished with Samuel Harrah, I'm gonna convince Max Steinberg to tell me the truth. Let me know if you wanna hear it."

He'd returned to his apartment, tried to put Matthew Blake out of his mind, discovered a letter from Rebecca Webber in his mailbox as he left the building.

> *Things have gone very badly here. We cannot leave the hotel without being called* auslander *by some ragged beggar.* Schlafsitz des Rabes *is lost to us. We return on September 2nd.*
> REBECCA

Schlafsitz des Rabes? There was no, I love you. No, I miss you. Not even, I'm hot for your body. Still, the message was clear enough: We return on September second. Be ready.

Marty Blake, in his own estimation, needed Rebecca Webber about as much as his Bally loafers needed the sudden downpour. September second was nearly a week away. Time enough to end the investigation, brace Max Steinberg, prepare for Rebecca's return. Maybe he'd go to Bloomingdale's and find a pair of silk pajamas with a bunny tail sewn into the seat. It was the least he could do.

The strangest part was that everything in Blake's professional life was going smoothly. Steinberg had been angry enough to write a five-figure check; Johan Tillson's apartment and business phones had been tapped; John McGuire's suburban home had been wired so thoroughly that Blake was sure he'd hear the judge singing in the shower. Best of all, Gurpreet Patel had come through, summoning Marty Blake with a terse, self-congratulatory telegram, while Joanna Bardo had called to tell him the middle-aged client with the wayward wife had backed out at the last minute due to the wife's filing for divorce. Apparently, she'd been sneaking out to see a lawyer, not a lover.

Blake pushed the door open, stuck his umbrella outside. The water was running along the pavement in sheets. If he blocked the flow, it would crawl up the side of his Ballys, maybe even slosh down over the top.

"Fuck it," he said aloud, "a man's gotta suffer for his art."

He was wrong about the back wave. Not content with his loafer, it surged up the side of his calf, cresting at the knee. The sensation, he decided, wasn't all that bad. But his cuffs would drip and shoes would give off wet sucking sounds until he managed to get home and change. And, of course, Gurp Patel would notice.

"How wonderful, Marty Blake. You have added a babbling brook to the tableau." He waved his arms, indicating the mural surrounding them. "With wonderful sound effects."

"What could I say? I was too itchy to sit it out."

"This is not wise. This is the time for patience. You must wait like the praying mantis in the tall grass. You must . . ."

"Cut the crap. You're not Buddha."

Gurp Patel stroked his beard. "Not even a Buddhist," he admitted. "Too many 'Kung Fu' episodes." He rolled his eyes up into his head. 'Ah, so, Grasshopper. As the bud becomes a rose, the boy becomes a man.'"

Blake countered with Jack Webb: "Just the facts, Gurp."

"The facts, the facts. *Always* the facts. That is the main problem with you Americans. Substance without style. Facts are so . . . so damned blatant."

"Yeah? Well, they pay for *your* style." Blake glanced at the mural, the painted ceiling. "They support you in the insanity to which you've become accustomed."

"True," Gurp Patel countered, "and that is bringing us directly to the point. Money. You will be very sad to know that I am charging you eight thousand dollars for doing what you could have easily done by your own self."

"Is that eight thousand over and above the three thousand I already gave you?" Blake ignored the last part. His reasons for not doing the preliminary groundwork himself were none of Patel's business.

"Your teeth should rot from asking this question."

"I take that to be an affirmative."

"Quite."

"And you're not going to give me the information until I pay you?"

"Also quite."

"It's too much for what 'you could have done by your own self.'"

"You should be seeing it as a lesson. Also, while you could have done it by your own self, it would have been most difficult, most time consuming. Nothing was where it was supposed to be. I had to become a true detective."

"As opposed to a *false* detective?"

"Quite."

"How do I know you have anything worthwhile?"

"This is not in question, because you are paying for effort, not result."

"Paying for style and not substance?"

"Quite."

Blake haggled for a few minutes, found he had no taste for the game. His thoughts drifted to Rebecca Webber in his apartment, of the two of them drowning in lust while the tape recorder turned. The images excited him, especially the very end of the scenario when he told Rebecca that someone was listening. Would she become angry and storm out of the apartment? Or would she laugh, become excited, demand video cameras?

"Look here, Gurp. You originally asked for seven thousand and that's what I'm willing to pay. You shouldn't have told me that I could have done it without your help. Me and you, our lives are about information and that's just the kind of information that encourages haggling."

Patel straightened in his chair, pushed his enormous belly in Blake's direction. "I have been a good friend to you, Marty Blake. Perhaps too good. You should remember that I can also be an enemy."

"The way I feel, it doesn't matter." Blake folded his arms, held his ground. "I'm not worried about what's gonna happen after I do what I have to do, because one way or another, I'm not gonna be running the show. I'm going down and that's all there is to it."

"In that case you will have no need for money. In that case you should be giving me *all* your money." Despite a bantering tone, Patel's expression softened. "Why are you doing this, Marty Blake? Is it for the justice? I have thought I knew you well, but this cannot be the case. You are not a wonderfully cynical American as I believed. Justice? No, I revise my opinion and now say you are a wonderful American *romantic*. It does not bother you that your victim is dead. You do it for the principle."

Blake told himself to let it go at that, but he found himself responding anyway. Maybe, he told himself, it's because I've been asked the damn question so often by so many people. Maybe I have to find an answer that'll shut them up.

"It's not about justice," he said evenly. "It's about the arrogance of Samuel Harrah. It's about me being even more arrogant. Call it the Mount Everest Syndrome. I want Samuel Harrah because he's there."

Patel took a moment to think it over. Finally, he shook his head and smiled. "Then you will be very disappointed to know that I have found no direct connection between Samuel Harrah and either John McGuire or Johan Tillson."

"Does this mean you've settled for the extra four grand?"

"I do it out of the goodness of my heart." Patel head-bowed modestly before accepting, then counting his money. "All very good. Now, I am beginning with Johan Tillson's bank records, thinking there must be a very significant bribe because Johan Tillson is a wealthy man who would not be leaving his wife's killer to walk on the street for a few pennies. Nothing there, Marty Blake, no large deposits, no series of small deposits. Also for his credit cards—everything is normal; he pays each month with an ordinary check. His stock portfolio is extensive, but inactive for the period in question.

"Well, I am naturally thinking that maybe Samuel Harrah applied the stick and not the carrot. Very depressing because threats do not leave paper trails. Still, I persist. Perhaps the bribe went through the Tillson business. If so, it is very fortunate that his business records are computerized. If I had to search through file cabinets . . ."

Blake sat up in his chair, half-smiled. "Gurp, are you telling me you burglarized Tillson's business office?" The image of Gurp Patel hoisting his bowling ball of a gut through a second-story window was too good to resist.

"Not personally, of course." He leaned forward, tapped his nose with a forefinger. "You know, in my day, I was dubbed the Asian James Bond. Quite the dashing and daring fellow, I assure you."

"But now . . . ?"

"Now, I pursue . . . my pursuits. But we were speaking of Tillson Enterprises. Initially, I am looking for a large business transaction with no deletion from inventory. A purchase order, perhaps, from a ficti- tious corporation. But the accounts are depressingly normal, except for one item. Five months after the murder of Sondra Tillson, Johan Tillson purchased the Long Island City warehouse he'd been leasing. The total amount of the transaction: two hundred thousand dollars. The seller: Landsman Properties.

"Now, I am admitting not to be an expert on New York real estate, but this seems quite cheap for a four-story, forty-thousand-square-foot building. Especially because Mister Tillson had been paying six thou- sand dollars each month for the use of only two floors. So, I am further researching the deed and finding the property last changed hands two months before Johan Tillson bought it. The price: eight hundred thousand dollars.

"Well, there it is. The bribe on one of your silver platters. All a matter of public record and something you might easily have attained for yourself without my help. Tell me, please, Marty Blake, how you will be justifying this expense to your client?"

Blake looked down at his watch, tapped it, held it up to his ear. "Time marches on, Gurp. Unless I'm running fast, I've got an hour to wrap this up and get out to Manhasset with my associate. As for the client, well . . . as far as you're concerned, *I'm* the client. Now, tell me about Landsman Properties."

"Landsman Properties was a Delaware corporation. It . . ."

"Did you say 'was'?"

"Yes, I did. Now please to listen. It was formed exactly one month before the purchase of the warehouse. It went out of business one month after the property was transferred to Johan Tillson. The sole stockholder of the now defunct Landsman Properties is a man named Alan Green, father of Edward Green."

"The Borough President of Manhattan? *That* Edward Green?" Even though the information fit neatly into the puzzle, Blake was taken off guard. Figuring the last thing he needed was another powerful enemy.

"Yes, they are being one and the same people. This, of course, is not meaning that Edward Green is the killer and lover of Sondra

Tillson. Perhaps the father did it all by himself. True, Alan Green is seventy-eight years old and paralyzed on one side by a stroke, but . . ." Patel stopped in midsentence, waited for and received a smile from Blake. "As Borough President, Edward Green cannot be making the payoff by himself. Each year, he is forced by the law to make financial disclosure; any questionable transaction would be surely examined. But his father is under no such an obligation, Marty Blake. Plus you must also be considering that the father has been one of your . . . your American wheeler-dealers for nearly fifty years."

Blake nodded, thinking credit where credit is due. The old man had wrapped it up nicely. "I assume you have a printout with the dates and figures."

"You assume correctly. Now, as for the Honorable John McGuire, his finances are absolutely in order. He is a man with few assets except for his home which is valued at five hundred and fifty thousand dollars, but which he purchased in 1971, I tell you, Marty Blake, no money was changing hands."

"Maybe I was wrong about McGuire," Blake conceded. "Maybe he was up for reelection and decided that discretion was the better part of valor. After all, Billy Sowell was charged with murdering a white woman. Letting him off on a technicality wouldn't have gotten McGuire any votes."

"No, you were right, but the answers were not being found in John McGuire's financial records. They were in the newspapers where you could easily be finding them had you taken the trouble to look. According to *The New York Times*, John McGuire's son, Bradford, was arrested for selling four ounces of cocaine to an undercover cop three months before Billy Sowell was appearing in the judge's courtroom. This is Bradford's third arrest, the first being a misdemeanor, the second a C felony. For these indiscretions he was receiving both times probation. Now he faces mandatory imprisonment, but two days after John McGuire's ruling against Billy Sowell, the charges against his son are dropped for lacking evidence. The cocaine has somehow disappeared from the laboratory."

There was nothing more to say. Blake started to rise, paying the necessary compliment as he did. "It's perfect, Gurp. But now it's time to stampede the cattle. Past time."

"Before you are going, please to tell me how you figure this case."

"Simple, Gurp. Edward Green killed Sondra Tillson and Samuel

Harrah covered it up. I . . . Gurp, are you curious enough to spend fifteen minutes checking Billy Sowell's birth certificate?

"We will do it in ten."

Twelve minutes later, they had the document on the monitor. Sowell had been born in Columbia Memorial Hospital on March 16, 1973. He'd weighed six pounds, four ounces at birth. His mother was listed as Barbara Sowell. His father as Edward Green.

"That's the connection," Blake said. "That's how Barbara Sowell got the money to keep Billy locked up in that apartment. That's why there was no money when she died. The info on the birth certificate comes from the mother. Green could have denied it, but he wanted—still wants—to be mayor, so he decided to pay off. Shit, I'll bet my left testicle that he was paying off Samuel Harrah as well as Barbara Sowell. See, the thing that kept bothering me was how Billy Sowell got set up. How'd they find this homeless retarded patsy? Now I have the answer: Edward Green killed his lover, then sacrificed his son, so he could become mayor of all the people in New York instead of doing fifteen-to-life in a New York State correctional facility." Blake stopped abruptly. "You know the best part, Gurp? The best part is that Green and Harrah think they're safe. Green's counting votes and Harrah's counting his money. But, as LBJ said of Hubert Humphrey, I've got their balls in my pocket."

TWELVE

"So that's the last piece," Blake said to his partner. "Edward Green slices up his lover, then asks Samuel Harrah to get him off the hook. Green's a big-time politician, so maybe he knows Harrah well enough to ask a favor. Or maybe Harrah's been blackmailing Green all along and the frame-up just adds to the premium. Either way, the incorruptible Bela Kosinski is on the case and they know Tillson's gonna fold if they don't find somebody in a big hurry. But who? It's not like there's a hundred candidates waiting for the chance. If they pick the wrong guy and he comes up with a lawyer and an alibi, they're worse off than when they started. Well, it turns out that Edward Green, fearless killer, has the perfect patsy in his own family. He's got drunken, retarded, homeless Billy Sowell living in a packing crate by the East River. His illegitimate son."

"It works, Marty." Kosinski touched the butt of his .38, his personal version of knocking on wood. "And I have no doubt whatsoever that we're gonna be able to prove it. But lemme ask you a question. Whatta ya think Samuel Harrah does with the money? I mean all the blackmail over all the years. He's gotta put it *somewhere*, right?"

"Right."

"And finding a big stack of money Harrah can't explain would be the ultimate proof, the proof that'd send him to prison."

Blake drummed on the steering wheel for a moment, then turned to his partner. "I thought of that, Bell. And I could probably find Harrah's stash by myself if that was all I had to do. But I've spent seven thousand dollars getting the information we already have and the money's running a little tight. Plus I've gotta handle retrieving the hardware, getting the tapes out to the right people. Face it, there's only the two of us here. We can't do everything. If we strike out with McGuire and Tillson, or if they find the equipment, then we may have to go after Harrah directly, but for now I think we should stay with what we've got."

They were sitting in a rented U-Haul van outside a liquor store on Northern Boulevard in Manhasset. Kosinski was sipping contentedly at a pint of Smirnoff, seeming, to himself, like an overfed infant clinging to a bottle of cold formula. It wasn't the worst feeling he'd ever had. "If that's the case, why am I sorry for Goliath?"

Answering by starting the car, Blake drove east, taking his time, enjoying the red lights, the anticipation. Kosinski stared straight ahead. In his own way, without showing anything on the outside, he was working himself up. Getting ready for the Honorable John McGuire, the former ACLU liberal who'd substituted Billy Sowell's life for a few years in the life of his son. The life of an innocent for the life of a dope-dealing mutt.

"We never talked about it," he said without preamble. "In Homicide. We never talked about what made it different. I guess it must've been the same in Sex Crimes, but I never worked the unit. What I'm sayin' is that in Homicide you always had a victim lying on a slab. It wasn't like bustin' out whores and junkies. I know everybody says you're not supposed to feel sorry for them, but when you put the cuffs on some street whore with tracks runnin' up and down both arms it's not the same as reading a killer his rights. Anybody who ever worked in Homicide will tell you that. I mean most cops hate the job, the job and all the bullshit that goes with it. In Homicide, the only thing I hated was not closing a case."

Blake turned left onto Onderdonk Avenue. The commerce of Northern Boulevard quickly gave way to a neighborhood of sprawling private homes surrounded by dense green lawns and manicured shrubbery. August flowers—asters, snapdragons, dahlias, hollyhocks, zinnias—blossomed behind neat borders of marigolds, imapatiens, or alyssum. A soft mist, reinforced by a dead gray sky, muted the brighter colors, melted them down, ran them together. The densely packed leaves on the Japanese maples seemed, to Marty Blake, like solid sheets of dull red brick.

Paradise, he thought. That's what it looks like. Split-level paradise with the humans in complete control of everything but the children. Somehow, despite the exalted status of their professional fathers and mothers, some of these kids grow up to be junkies and dealers. That's when the law-and-order bullshit drops away. "Oh, please, your honor, he's a good boy. Just give little snookums one more chance. I know I only vote for judges who send purse snatchers away for life, but give my little baby another shot. You can see he's not a nigger."

Blake pulled to the curb in front of 2115 Andrew Street. The house, one of the few ranch-style homes in the neighborhood, spread across a square, half-acre lot. Its backyard was hidden by a seven-foot-high redwood fence, a fence required by both the municipality and John McGuire's insurance company to prevent small children from wandering into the free-form swimming pool behind the house.

The fence had served a far different purpose on Blake's previous visit. Lost in its shadows, he'd been able to take his time with the alarm, open the rear patio door without tearing the lock apart, enter and leave without a trace. It'd enabled him to bury a receiver/tape recorder in a bed of pachysandra, to check it for defects without worrying about the neighbors, passersby, wandering dogs. Blake, like all burglars, loved a high fence.

"You up for this?" Blake asked.

"Yeah," Kosinski said, "I am. It's been a long time."

"Shit, I wish I was going in." Blake slid into the back of the van, toyed with the dial of a receiver/tape recorder identical to the one buried in the backyard. He wanted something tangible in case Harrah was smart enough (or paranoid enough) to check for possible surveillance. He knew he wasn't going to get it from Johan Tillson because Tillson lived on the nineteenth floor of a high-security apartment building in the Riverdale section of the Bronx. Blake had managed to work a tap into the basement phone lines, but the apartment itself had represented too great a risk for too little return.

"I know how ya feel, Marty." Kosinski opened the door, dropped one foot to the asphalt. "So what I think you should do is use the opportunity to work on your own technique. Consider what you would have said, then compare it to what the master says."

"Thanks, champ. And good luck."

THIRTEEN

Luck, Kosinski thought as he made his way up the walk, has nothing to do with it. When you've got what I have, your only challenge is to keep the perp talking. Which ain't gonna be that hard because I'm not a cop and which doesn't matter anyway because I'm not lookin' for him to confess. Even if it *is* good for the soul.

He rang the bell, then unbuttoned his jacket to let the butt of his .38 show plainly. When the door opened a minute later, he systematically wiped all trace of expression off his face.

"Judge John McGuire?"

"Yes?"

"My name is Bela Kosinski, I'm a private investigator." He held out his ID, waited for McGuire to get a good look. "I represent an attorney named Maxwell Steinberg who represents a man named William Sowell. If you remember, Sowell pleaded guilty to manslaughter in your courtroom." He waited for a response, accepted McGuire's grudging nod. "The thing of it is, Judge, there's real serious doubt about the boy's guilt. I mean I'm retired now, but I was one of the detectives assigned to the original investigation, so I'm very familiar with the case from a cop's point of view and I don't think he did it."

"Are you preparing an appeal?"

McGuire's small gray eyes revealed even less to Bell Kosinski than the matter-of-fact tone of his voice. Maybe fifty years old, McGuire carried an extra thirty pounds, mostly on a belly that overhung his belt, yet he stood with his shoulders thrown back, his neck straight, as if ready for an attack.

"We feel that his attorney was incompetent. That's what I want to speak to you about. If you got a few minutes." Kosinski noted the hesitation, caught the rapid blink as McGuire searched for a decision. "Look, Judge, I was a detective for fifteen years. I've heard every dirtbag lie a criminal can tell and I just don't think this particular kid is guilty. If you could give me a few minutes to go through it with you,

I'm sure you'll feel the same way. I mean I visited Sowell a few days ago and you can believe me when I say he's serving hard time. The kid's a pure victim."

McGuire shuffled his feet, looked back into the house. "Yes, well I suppose a few minutes won't hurt, but we'll have to keep it quiet. My wife is ill. She's resting in her room." Kosinski followed the judge through the deserted living room into a small office at the back of the house. McGuire closed the door after them, gestured for Kosinski to take a chair. "You know," he said, "I accepted Sowell's plea bargain with some misgivings. The state's case was weak and his attorney seemed a little too anxious to strike a deal. Still, my hands were tied. I . . ."

"Save it for the newspapers, Judge. Which is exactly where you're gonna find your name."

McGuire's eyes snapped up to meet Kosinski's, then abruptly dropped to the blotter on his desk. "I think you had better explain yourself." He managed to put a little muscle into the first few words, but his voice fell off at the end.

"I lied before," Kosinski said. "Deliberately. To get you in here." He paused, expecting some kind of response. When he didn't get one, he decided that McGuire was suffering from a guilty conscience. "Billy Sowell's not planning to file an appeal. You know why? Because *dead* men aren't allowed to appeal."

"Dead?"

"Yeah, as in killed in the course of a sexual assault. The medical examiner seemed to think it was unintended, that he wouldn't submit and his assailants—there was more than one, by the way—hit him a little too hard. Me, I think it was part of the kick. As in: hit him, fuck him, watch him squeal, make him beg, put him down. You gotta see it as a package."

McGuire swiveled his chair to face the window. He stared at his swimming pool for a moment, then turned back to face Kosinski. "I assume there's more."

"Oh yeah, Judge, there's a lot more. You don't really think I came here to bullshit about Billy Sowell's attorney, do ya?" Kosinski paused, took McGuire's silence for acquiescence. The lamb begging for the butcher's knife. "Tell me something, Your Honor, what does the ACLU think about hypnotically induced memory enhancement? Is it high on their list of admissible evidence? I mean you were a big-shot liberal, right? Champion of the little people? Protector of the constitution? So what happened to the fucking constitution when you admitted Melody Mitchell's testimony after she'd been hypnotized?"

"We held a special hearing on the hypnotism. The material uncovered was not relevant. It had no bearing on Mitchell's identification."

McGuire's voice was a little stronger, as if he was remembering the arguments dredged up at the evidentiary hearing. Maybe he'd been repeating them to himself over the years, trying to edge away from the truth of what he'd done. Kosinski wasn't sure, but as he wasn't ready to fire his big guns, he was perfectly willing to debate Sowell's guilt. He stood up, let his chair fall over backwards, leaned across the desk.

"Let's have a little talk here. Heart to heart so you know where I'm comin' from. I interviewed the witness, Melody Mitchell, a few hours after the body was found. She saw exactly nothing. You can believe me because I got a lot of experience in these matters. Melody Mitchell was coached all the way. But, of course, you knew this, right? You saw the photo spread and you knew it was biased. You saw the hypnotic session on videotape and you knew Mitchell was looking for the scar, the scar that happened to show up on Billy Sowell when they put him in that lineup. You knew it all and you let it happen when you, all by your miserable fucking self, could've put a stop to it." He was shouting now, letting the cords stand out on the side of his neck. It was all so familiar, so practiced. His face would be red, flecks of dried spit would cling to the corners of his mouth, his eyes would be as narrow and focused as those of a charging pit bull.

McGuire pushed his chair back, looking for a little breathing room. "There was a detailed confession. Don't overlook that."

Kosinski smiled, then let his anger drop away. He could feel the muscles along his cheekbone and forehead drop like the curtain at the end of a play. It was a little early for the move, but, then again, McGuire wasn't a hardened criminal. It took a long time to soften hardened criminals.

He circled the desk, then crossed his arms and sat on the edge. "Sign of a guilty mind, Judge. You should have thrown me out—that's what an innocent man would've done—but you wanna know if I found out about your deal. You wanna know how much I have on you." He shook his head, repeated, "Sign of a guilty mind."

"I think I've had enough."

"Listen to me." Kosinski ignored McGuire's remark, kept his own tone intimate and cordial. "People with IQs in the mid-sixties don't give detailed confessions. That's because they don't have the details to give. But you knew that, right? Just like you knew there wasn't a shred of evidence to put him at the scene. Not a shred. Just like you knew the kid had been interrogated for seventy-two hours without a lawyer present." He laughed out loud. "Jesus Christ, the prosecutor must've shit his pants when you drew the case. John McGuire, the super-liberal. John McGuire, every criminal's dream. Hell, you let killers go back out on the street because some cop forgot to cross the ts. Prosecutors with airtight cases got diarrhea when they had to step into your courtroom. Tell me, Judge, what'd your ACLU buddies have to say after you sentenced Billy Sowell to hell?"

McGuire reached around Kosinski to pull the phone into his lap. Kosinski responded by opening the left side of his jacket. He watched McGuire's gaze drop to the .38 nestled in its shoulder rig. "Don't worry, Your Honor. I'm not gonna shoot. But there's something I have to show you, just in case you're still . . . still *confused*." He pulled a photocopy from his jacket pocket, pressed out the creases, then passed it over to John McGuire. "Now, the first thing I want you to notice is the date on the page. It's up in the right hand corner. See? November twenty-eighth, the morning after Sondra Tillson was killed. Now look at the photograph. You see the face I circled? That's Billy Sowell's face. The picture was taken just about the time that Sondra Tillson's throat was being slashed."

"Then why didn't he say so?" McGuire's voice was soft, nearly a whisper. He was holding the phone against his belly, cradling it with his arms.

"Ya know, Judge, I never got the chance to ask him, but the way I see it, there's three basic reasons why he didn't alibi himself. First, nobody asked him where he was until two weeks after the fact. Second, he was retarded and he didn't have a real good sense of time. Third, he was a hopeless drunk. But someone who knew the truth *did* show up. Guy named Collars. He went down to the precinct and Detective Brannigan put a gun to his head. Told him not to come back."

"Do you think I knew that?" McGuire set the phone on the floor. He straightened up in the chair, began to button his cardigan. "If I made a mistake, then I'm sorry. I suppose you can always file a complaint with the Chief Judge's office. I wouldn't be surprised if they censured me, but . . ."

"Stop, already. Please. You're breakin' my heart." Kosinski stood up. "You know, letting in the witness and the confession wasn't the worst thing you did. Far from it. The worst thing you did, the sellout of the fucking century, was when you let Billy Sowell waive his right to appeal. I mean, it *did* turn out to be a death sentence." Kosinski took off his jacket, twirled it over his shoulder, let it drop to the floor. "Now, before we get into the good stuff, I wanna show you that I'm not wired. I believe standard procedure calls for me to strip."

He had his shirt, his tie, and his shoulder rig off before McGuire stopped him with a wave. "Enough," McGuire said. "Enough."

"Enough?" Kosinski hummed to himself as he dressed. Taking his time about it. When he finished, he took the pint bottle of Smirnoff from his outside jacket pocket, drank deeply, then offered the last couple of inches to McGuire. "Go on, take it," he said. "What you did wasn't so bad. If I'd been in your shoes, I might have done it myself. Your kid's future was on the line."

McGuire's head jerked at the mention of his son, but he took the bottle, sipping once, then draining it. He might as well have announced his desire to make a clean confession. Kosinski felt what he could only describe as elation flood his body. As if he was a marathon runner approaching the finish line with his nearest competitor still out of sight.

"The prosecutor told me that Sowell was guilty," the judge said. "Off the record. He indicated that he had several confidential informants who corroborated Sowell's confession."

Kosinski resumed his position on the edge of the desk. "He may have told you that, Judge, but that's not the reason why you let Billy Sowell go to jail."

"I didn't say it was the reason." He looked at his interrogator for a moment before continuing. "You see, I really believed that Sowell was guilty. I know you don't want to accept that, but I did. Oh, I knew that his guilt couldn't be proven, that if I tossed out Melody Mitchell and Sowell's confession, he wouldn't be convicted at trial. And I didn't forget that I'd taken an oath to uphold the constitutions of New York and the United States. I wasn't unmindful of my responsibility, but I didn't knowingly send an innocent man to prison."

"They had you by the short hairs, didn't they? Your son, Bradford, your only child, was facing mandatory state time. A middle-class kid like him? The sharks up in Attica would've had his asshole for breakfast. I mean, what else could you do?" Kosinski hesitated, then launched smoothly into a lie. The ease with which he made the transition pleased him immensely. "Me, I got a kid nineteen years old. He's pretty good for a New York teenager, but not *that* good. If he got in trouble? If he was facing hard time? Hell, I'd do just about anything to get him out."

McGuire took a deep breath. His hands were folded and still in his lap. He looked at them for a moment, then made his decision. The decision Kosinski expected, that he'd seen any number of criminals make. He decided to get it over with, to put it behind him. He'd regret it later on, of course. They all did.

"My son, Bradford . . . he's not a bad kid. He needed treatment, not prison. But the DA charged him with criminal sale of a controlled substance in the second degree. That's an A2 felony, Mr. Kosinski, and it carries a mandatory minimum of four years to life. The idea of Bradford spending four years in Greenhaven or Attica or Clinton . . . well, it scared me half to death, because I knew if that happened, my boy would be gone forever." He unbuttoned his cardigan, let it fall over the back of the chair. "I've made a lot of enemies in my life, especially among law-enforcement personnel."

"In other words, the cops and the prosecutors hated your guts."

"Well put, Mr. Kosinski. Technically, Bradford was guilty of an A1 felony which would have carried a minimum of fifteen years. Four years to life was the prosecutor's idea of a plea bargain. The situation was impossible. I couldn't communicate with the prosecutor's office for obvious reasons and my politician friends were unwilling to help because Bradford's arrest had been widely reported in the media."

"In other words, you were helpless."

"That's right."

"But then an angel came from heaven to make it all better. Tell me, was it Samuel Harrah himself? Or did he send his errand boy, Aloysius Grogan?"

"Harrah called me on the phone. He told me he could help Bradford, but he didn't spell it out. Grogan showed up the next day. He was quite blunt: admit the evidence, accept Sowell's plea bargain, and my son goes free. The prosecutor—his name was Andrew Boyd— came after Grogan. He never mentioned Grogan or Harrah by name, but his intentions were clear enough. Boyd told me that Sowell was guilty, claimed he had information that couldn't be introduced at trial.

He showed me a transcript of an alleged conversation between an undercover cop and an informant. The informant stated that Sowell had confessed to him on the day after the murder, had actually shown him the bloody knife and the bloody clothes, had asked the best way to get rid of them."

"And you bought it?"

"Yes, I believed that Sowell was guilty."

"But now you don't? Now you know he was innocent?"

"Yes."

"So the only question is what you're gonna do about it. If anything."

"If the man is dead, there's nothing I *can* do about it."

"You can put Samuel Harrah and his buddies in prison."

Kosinski was just getting warmed up when the door to McGuire's study flew open. The middle-aged woman who stepped into the room wore a flannel bathrobe over a blue, cotton nightgown. Her steel-gray hair stood away from her skull, a perfect complement to her blazing eyes and clenched jaw. And to the automatic she held in her hand.

"You stupid bastard." She spat the words at her husband. "I told you to let Bradford go. I told you he was a good-for-nothing drug addict. I told you he was a loser and he wouldn't stop being a loser until you *let* him lose. Just look what you've done to us. And for what? Don't you know that Bradford's out there smoking cocaine while our lives are burning up?" She paused briefly, stared at her cringing husband. Then she turned to Kosinski. "You've got sixty seconds to get out of my house. If you're not gone in that time, I'm going to kill you, claim I thought you were a burglar, and take my chances with the local police."

FOURTEEN

Bell Kosinski made it in thirty seconds, made it out the door, down the path, and into the U-Haul. He was about to turn the key dangling from the ignition when a familiar voice brought him to a halt.

"It's gone far enough, Ann," John McGuire said. His voice, strained through a tiny speaker, seemed to come from much farther away than the rear of the van. "We must allow the chips to fall where they may."

"Spare me the dramatics, John McGuire. I swear to God I think you left your manhood with Samuel Harrah. Traded it for a boy who had no manhood to begin with. Why should you be afraid of this pissant private detective? Or his shyster client? Call Chief Harrah, give him the details and let him take care of it. You won't be any worse off than you are now."

Kosinski half-listened to them wrangle, thinking how right Ann McGuire was in her assessment of the situation. Calling Harrah was their only hope; they had nothing whatever to lose.

Still, McGuire continued to resist. "Ann, Billy Sowell is *dead*. And it's my fault. Without me it couldn't have happened."

"You're right, John. It *is* your fault. But it's not *my* fault, understand? It's not my fault and I don't want to go down with the ship. Call Chief Harrah, then go to confession. Tormented as you are, I'm sure Jesus will forgive you."

They went at it for another few minutes with Ann McGuire reminding her husband that he'd made the original decision against her advice, that Billy Sowell was dead and therefore beyond help, that by doing nothing he was merely adding another item, namely herself, to an already swollen collection of mortal sins.

McGuire's phone began to beep a few seconds later. A man picked up on the second ring, announced, "Intelligence, Sergeant Caton." The judge identified himself, asked for Harrah, got put on hold.

"Make it quick, McGuire. I'm in a meeting."

It was the first time Kosinski had been able to ascribe any human quality to the man he hunted. In fact, he realized with a jolt, he didn't even know what his enemy looked like. Whenever he closed his eyes, he saw his old partner, Tom Brannigan. Or Aloysius Grogan. It was as if Samuel Harrah was beyond his imagination.

McGuire wasted no time; he listed the information, named Kosinski, then asked Harrah to do what he could and to do it fast. His voice, to Kosinski, seemed surprisingly strong, the voice of a man firmly resolved to do his duty.

"I'll check it out," Harrah said when McGuire finished.

The click of the phone was followed by a dead silence. Kosinski looked into the back of the van, watched Blake work a dial on the receiver.

". . . what you asked. Please, leave me alone now."

"So you can contemplate your sins?"

"It's really not your problem, Ann."

"No, it's not."

Kosinski listened to the sound of squeaking hinges, the slam of a door, then more silence.

"Bell, take off. There's nothing else here."

"In a minute, Marty. I gotta see how it comes out."

How it came out was more than evident a few seconds later when the sharp crack of an automatic echoed through the metal-sided van.

"The way I see it," Kosinski said to his partner as they drove Blake's recovered Taurus west on the Long Island Expressway, "is that nobody wants to be responsible. I don't care who it is. They break a law; they get caught; they don't wanna pay. Even if it's the President doing it in the best interests of the country, the idea is to get off the hook. I mean did Clarence Thomas step up to the dock and say, 'Yeah, I loved the way Anita Hill scrunched up her mouth when I described Long Dong Silver's dick?' How about Ronald Reagan selling those guns to Iran? Did Reagan say, 'Fuck the Congress; fuck the Constitution. I did what I had to do and I'm ready to pay the price?' How about Clinton and the Flowers broad? I'm tellin ya, Marty, nobody wants to be responsible, from the lowest street mutt to the President of the United States. That's why McGuire killed himself. He didn't wanna stand up for what he did and he knew I was gonna make him."

Blake nodded his head in the right places, but he was thinking about McGuire. Reminding himself that the judge's testimony was crucial to his overall strategy.

"How do you know he's dead, Bell? How do you know he didn't shoot his *wife*?" Blake half-turned to stare at his partner's impassive face.

"What are you getting at, Marty? The wife wasn't even in the room. As for McGuire surviving, I saw the piece. It was Browning nine millimeter. If the judge lives, he's gonna be a vegetable."

"Maybe he jerked the gun at the last second."

Kosinski grunted, shook his head, missed his partner's point altogether. "It's not your fault, Marty," he said. "You didn't pull the trigger. In your field, I guess you never got used to dealin' with death . . ."

"What the fuck are you talking about?" Traffic on the expressway was heavy, but moving. As usual, the muscleheads were cutting in and out, creating a constant hazard that demanded most of Blake's attention. At the moment, a Bronco with oversized tires and more lights than a semitrailer was tracking within two feet of his rear bumper. Blake glanced at the driver's reflection in the mirror, noted the furrowed brow, the narrowed eyes, the mouth contracted into a stiff snarl. He wondered if the guy was on drugs? Or drunk? Or just plain crazy? And why were there so many of them out there? Once upon a time, the parkway lunatics had been an aberration. Now they were an expected part of the New York landscape, another human hazard to be avoided whenever possible.

Blake found an opening in the traffic. He was just about to signal and move over when the Bronco jumped into the right lane and blew by. The driver, as he cut back in front of the Taurus, extended an arm, then a finger.

"I just can't figure guys like that," Kosinski said. "He challenges us without knowing anything about us. I mean I'm packin' a .38, you're packin' a nine millimeter, and we both have permits. We could make this jerk dead in a big hurry."

"I think I've had enough 'dead' for one day." Blake slapped the steering wheel with the palm of his hand. "Christ, Bell, we've got exactly nothing here. All Harrah said was that he'd check it out. What can we do with that? I mean someone was supposed to get back to the judge—maybe Grogan, maybe your old partner, Brannigan. They would've been forced to make contact, even if it was just to be sure McGuire wasn't about to fold. We needed that, Bell, because the way it is now, there's no point to retrieving the hardware. What are we gonna get, funeral preparations?"

Kosinski was caught off guard. "That tape'll have the reporters coming in their pants, Marty. Which I thought was the point."

"Yeah, maybe so, but if you remember, the press was supposed to put the heat on the cops, force the NYPD to conduct an investigation. If McGuire's dead . . . I think I made a mistake, Bell. I think I should've tried to wire Harrah's apartment. We had no hope of getting into his office, but I could've tried to get into his home."

"How do you know he does business out of his apartment?"

"I don't."

"How do you know he doesn't check his apartment for bugs?"

"I don't."

"Marty, lemme ask you a question?"

"Shoot."

"Do you think we could pull off the highway, maybe find a liquor store? I'm not used to seein' you second-guess yourself and it's makin' me nervous."

FIFTEEN

An hour later, Kosinski and Blake were parked across the street from the Oxford Arms, Johan Tillson's apartment building, staring through double glass doors at the security guard behind the concierge's desk in the lobby. Neither man was fooled by the rent-a-cop's gold-braided uniform or the carefully arranged flowers on his desk. The guard was clearly a professional, acknowledging residents with a nod, challenging visitors with a sharp look. Blake had been inside less than a week before, had been carefully inspected even though he wore a phone company uniform. He'd passed over his forged identification, noted the video monitors covering the garage and side entrances, waited patiently while the information on his ID was copied into a logbook. He'd signed the logbook, then waited again while the guard compared signatures before allowing him access to the switchboard in the basement.

The security had come as no surprise to Blake. The Riverdale section of the Bronx, a narrow tongue of land extending north along the Hudson River, was among the wealthiest New York neighborhoods outside Manhattan. Like virtually all such areas, Riverdale (and its closest neighbor, middle-class Kingsbridge) was surrounded by miles of tenements and public-housing projects, desolate slums that (according to the good citizens of Riverdale, anyway) spawned the endless parade of merciless criminals. The fact that Riverdale was a low-crime neighborhood, that it was heavily patrolled by NYPD cops as well as a half-dozen private security firms, had no effect on a pervasive fear that, in many ways, circumscribes the lives of all wealthy New Yorkers. According to the standards imposed by that paranoia, the single guard at the Oxford Arms left the building's residents seriously unprotected.

"Wait or go?" Kosinski asked.

Plan A called for Bell Kosinski to confront Johan Tillson the way he'd confronted John McGuire. To show up on Tillson's doorstep, stick his foot in the door if he was denied admission, and hit the

importer with the facts of life. But if Kosinski had to be announced by
the guard, there was a decent chance that Tillson would simply refuse
to speak to him, especially if Chief Harrah had decided to warn the
principals.

"Wait," Blake said. "Sooner or later, the guy's bound to take a
break. Maybe you can follow somebody in."

Time proved Blake right. After forty very slow minutes, a middle-
aged man in designer sweats came out of the elevator to man the bar-
ricades while the rent-a-cop went off in search of a bathroom and a
cup of coffee.

"A goddamned citizen," Blake observed. "Doing his civic fucking
duty."

"Take it easy, Marty. He's makin' the right move."

"And what's the right move for us, Bell?"

Kosinski took a second to consider the possibilities. He sipped at
the bottle, shrugged his shoulders. "What I think I have to do is bluff
the amateur before the pro comes back. If that doesn't work—if I can't
get a face-to-face—then I'll try calling Tillson on the phone. If I can't
get him on the phone, I guess I'll have to mail him a letter. Figure it
this way: If Tillson won't even talk to me, it's because Harrah's got
him scared shitless. If Harrah called him, it's on tape which is all we
were after."

He waited until Blake nodded agreement, then got out of the car,
opened his jacket, and crossed to the outer doors of the Oxford Arms.
Once again, he wiped all expression from his face before pushing the
doors open and striding directly to the concierge's station.

"May I help you?"

Kosinski flashed his ID, snapped the billfold shut, announced:
"Kosinski. To see Johan Tillson."

"John Tillson?"

"Whatever."

"Is he expecting you?"

"Unless you're him, it's none of your business." Kosinski paused
long enough to flash a thin, triumphant smirk. "And you're *not* him."

Directly challenged, the man let his eyes drop away from
Kosinski's. Unfortunately, they fell to the revolver tucked beneath
Kosinski's armpit. "I'll announce you," he said. "Would you repeat
your name?"

"Kosinski."

"And your first name?"

"Mister."

The man picked up an ordinary telephone receiver, then punched three digits into the console on his desk.

"John, it's Augie. There's someone here to see you. Says his name is Kosinski." He covered the mouthpiece with his hand. "Mr. Tillson wants to know what you want."

Kosinski leaned over the desk and took the receiver from Augie's hand. "Why don't *I* tell him. It's a lot more efficient that way." He turned his back, smiled to himself. Now that he'd gotten this far, he was sure he'd be able to talk his way upstairs. It was only a matter of applying the right pressure. "I don't know if you remember me, Mr. Tillson. I was one of the cops who interviewed you after your wife died. The reason I'm here is because some new facts have come to light and I'd like to run through them with you. I mean, as the victim's husband, you definitely got a right to know."

Kosinski pictured the short, dumpy, moon-faced businessman on the other end of the phone. He remembered bracing Tillson in Kennedy airport on the night of his wife's murder. The man had collapsed into the arms of a Port Authority cop. Yet, despite the grief, he'd refused to reveal the name of his wife's lover, even on that first night when he was yet to speak with Edward Green or Samuel Harrah. Maybe he was simply embarrassed. Or maybe the fact that Sondra Tillson, the woman he loved, had died in another man's bedroom was too painful to be spoken aloud.

"I don't believe I want to hear what you have to say, Mr. Kosinski. As far as I'm concerned, it's over and done with."

Kosinski dropped his voice to a whisper. "Ya know somethin', Johan, I can appreciate your position. Believe me, if I was in your shoes, I wouldn't wanna hear the truth either. Unfortunately, you're faced with a nut case—namely myself—who's gonna speak his piece whether you like it or not. If you won't see me face-to-face, I'll say what I have to say right here in this lobby. And I'll say it very fucking loud, Johan. I mean it's the least I could do for Uncle Augie here. The jerk's leanin' so far over the desk, he's gonna wind up with a crease in his dick."

"I don't appreciate being threatened," Tillson muttered. "But, if you must . . ."

Kosinski handed the phone to Augie, then took off for the elevators. He was peaking, now that the end (*his* end, at least) was in sight. The funny part was that he was sure his soon-to-be conversation with Johan Tillson was entirely unnecessary, that he didn't have to provoke Tillson into calling Harrah, because they'd already spoken. The importer had been far too calm and collected for Kosinski's appearance to have come as a surprise.

As the elevator rose, Kosinski found himself wishing he knew exactly where apartment 19E was. He wanted to step out of the elevator, stride directly to the importer's door, and pound away. Instead, he'd be peering at every number, fumbling his way to the big confrontation.

The elevator came to a stop with a sudden thump. Kosinski glanced at the lighted panel, saw that number 19 was lit, turned back to find his old partner, Tommy Brannigan, standing in the open doorway. Standing there with a vintage Colt .45 in his left hand.

Kosinski smiled to cover the surprise, noted that his heart was pounding against his rib cage like a demented speed bag, that he could feel the blood drumming in his temples and throat. Terrified, he realized, was the obvious word for it. So why was his mind clear and sharp? Why did he feel relieved? What did his body remember that his brain had forgotten long ago?

"I guess this means that Johan doesn't wanna speak to me. Too bad, Tommy. Because I was looking forward to asking him if he found out that his wife was fucking Edward Green before or after Green slashed her throat."

Brannigan motioned Kosinski into the far corner of the elevator, then stepped inside and pressed the door-open button. "Christ, that's a big hole," Kosinski said, pointing at the .45. "That barrel is what I'm talkin' about. It's impressive—I admit it—but wouldn't a .22 have been more practical?"

"You're sick, Kosinski. You need help."

"I wouldn't argue the point, Tommy, but I gotta say the therapy here is a bit radical. And not real, real effective. I mean whatta ya think's gonna happen if you pull that trigger? How many fingers'll dial nine-one-one in the first thirty seconds? This ain't the ghetto, Tommy. These folks still believe in law and order. That's because they don't know you."

Brannigan shook his head, smiled his familiar shit-eating grin. "Credit where credit is due, Bell. You broke the case wide open. The thing I can't figure out is *why*. It can't be the money, because you could get ten times as much from us."

"Well, Tommy, I'm not entirely sure myself, but I think it has something to do with penance." He hesitated, gave it a second to sink in. "But you're not gonna kill me, are ya?"

"Not here," Brannigan admitted, "for all the reasons you just named. But I did wanna show you the gun that's gonna do the job." He held up the .45 for Kosinski's inspection. "Nice, right? Pre-war. It'd be worth a lot of money if it had a serial number."

"Are you supposed to be scaring me, Tommy?" Kosinski found himself wishing he was wired. They'd tossed it around, he and Blake, and decided to go without it. The decision had been a mistake, a mistake his partner was sure to take badly.

"Hey, Bell, you can't blame a guy for tryin', right?" Brannigan's smile dropped away. "I wasn't kidding before. About credit where credit is due. And I have to admit, like everybody else, I thought you were a hopeless drunk. But now that it's done, now that you proved you're still the best, why not let the deal go? Your partner and your boss are smart enough to accept reality. Blake's out there beggin' his old boss for scut work and Steinberg's petitioning the governor to have Sowell posthumously pardoned. But you, Bell, you keep on pushing, like you could raise the kid back from the dead by taking me down."

"You sayin' if I walk away, Sammy Harrah will just forget the whole deal? Because, being as I can bury him any time I want, I find that hard to believe. Men like Harrah, they can't live with a sword hangin' over their heads. Not if they've been the ones wielding the sword for as long as he has."

"Nobody's lookin' for revenge here. If we had to . . . to silence you just because of what you know, then we'd have to go after Blake and Steinberg, too. It doesn't take a genius to see where that leads." Brannigan stepped out of the elevator. "Give me something, Bell. Something I can take back to my boss." He put his foot against the door to keep it from closing. "I don't want to kill you—it's not in my nature to kill another cop—but you're not leaving me with a whole lot of options."

"No option means no decision to make. You should be grateful. And thanks for the information."

"What information?"

Kosinski folded his arms across his chest and leaned against the back of the elevator. "How many cops are there assigned to the Intelligence Division, Tommy? Four hundred? Five hundred?" He took a step toward Brannigan, let his hands drop to his sides. "See, I was a *little* worried that Harrah might send an army after me. I say a little worried because it didn't seem likely that Harrah would've let a whole lot of people know about his blackmail scam. But now I don't have to worry at all." He took another step, grinned his nastiest grin. "Because there's no way on the face of this holy fucking Earth that Chief Samuel Harrah, if he had anybody at all, would send a complete jerk like Tommy Brannigan to kill a man."

SIXTEEN

"It's baffling, Marty. Really. It's right outta 'Unsolved Mysteries.' I mean, the minute I saw the gun, my body started to pump adrenalin. Like I thought my heart was gonna squeeze out between my ribs, that's how bad it was. So how come the adrenalin didn't get into my brain? Being as the same blood that goes to my heart goes to my head?"

"No mystery," Blake said. He was threading the Taurus through the perennial construction on the Cross Bronx Expressway, marveling at the layers of dirt and debris on the steep hillside beside the sunken roadway. New York had been a dirty city for as long as he could remember, but parts of the Bronx seemed absolutely abandoned.

"Then maybe you can explain it." Kosinski held his right hand in front of his face. "See, I'm still shakin'."

"Simply a case of vapor barrier. That's all it is. When the alcohol evaporates in your brain, it sets up a barrier that kills adrenaline. And any other normal response to somebody putting a gun in your face. I thought everybody knew that."

"And I thought you were finished with the booze jokes."

Blake, to his surprise, found himself taking the question seriously. His relationship with Bell Kosinski had come full circle, that was obvious enough, but something else had changed as well. As his admiration for the pugnacious Kosinski had grown, the anger directed at his father had diminished. It wasn't a reaction he'd decided to have (any more than Kosinski had decided not to be afraid), but he couldn't deny it either. He knew if he explained it to his mother (which he definitely wouldn't), she'd call it growing up. And she'd use her snottiest voice to make the point.

"You were unbelievable," Blake announced. "With McGuire. You were just fucking great. I won't say I wanted the judge to do what he did, but you went through him like a tornado through a trailer park."

Kosinski saw no reason to comment. His part was over and, win or lose, he'd done his job. Which didn't mean there wouldn't be any consequences. He felt the tension sliding away, wondered where the bottom was.

"What's going on, Marty?"

"Pardon?"

"You took the wrong exit. We should be goin' over the Whitestone Bridge, not the Throgs Neck."

"That depends on where we're heading." Blake glanced at Kosinski. He could sense the ex-cop's warning antenna begin to vibrate. *Bullllll-shit, Bullllll-shit, Bullllll-shit.* That was something else Kosinski and Blake's father had in common. Whereas Marty Blake had always been able to con his mother, despite her generally cynical nature, he'd never been able to fool Matthew Blake.

"Tell me something, Bell. Do you believe Brannigan?"

"About what?"

"How do we know he wasn't throwing up a smoke screen?" Blake slowed for the toll, fished a token out of the ashtray. "Suppose they've already found the tap in Tillson's basement. Harrah would have to know you didn't put it there. That you aren't his only problem."

Kosinski rolled down the window, let the cool air wash over his face. "I don't think it matters. If Harrah comes after me, he's gonna have to come after you and Max, too. Brannigan as much as admitted it."

"That's why you have to vanish." Blake flipped the token into the basket, then accelerated onto the bridge. "Because Harrah's not gonna make a move against me or Max until after he takes you out. Remember, I only need a few days to put it all together. Once it hits the papers, there's nothing Harrah can do but grin and bear it. I spoke to Steinberg this morning. He thinks there's a good chance Harrah will try to contact him. If that happens, Max is gonna promise to call you off. Or, at least, to try. Add it up, Bell—you disappear; Steinberg kisses some ass; we buy the time we need."

"When did you make all these decisions?"

"The last day or so."

"And you made 'em without me bein' there?"

"It's not what it looks like."

"What's it look like?"

Blake glanced at his partner. Kosinski's face was flaming. "You were pumped, Bell. I didn't wanna do anything to bring you down." He hesitated, finally said it. "I couldn't take a chance."

"But you did, Marty. You did take a chance."

Kosinski was right, of course. Blake knew there was *every* chance that his partner would simply refuse to hide. That Bell Kosinski's attitude was genuine and the final confrontation was the only part that really mattered to him. The rest of it was just foreplay.

If that's what it takes, Blake thought, to see it through to the end, then so be it. He's got as much right to his motives as I have to mine.

Blake exited the Clearview Expressway at Northern Boulevard, made a left at the light, began to work his way east. Kosinski sat quietly, waiting for the bottom line to become clear. He'd left the job convinced that he had nothing more to lose, but the day's events had rekindled a supposedly dead appetite. And the worst part was that he hadn't stumbled, that he couldn't hide behind failure. Blake had ordered him to stampede the cattle and that's exactly what had happened. That was why Tommy Brannigan, for all his breezy attitude, had been frightened enough to show a gun in a public place.

"Home Sweet Home," Blake said.

Kosinski looked up to find Blake's Taurus parked in the courtyard of the Adriatic Motor Inn.

"At least you could have picked a motel with hot and cold running whores," he said.

"Sorry, Bell. You're gonna have to settle for HBO and a case of Absolut. The room's paid for the next three days. Hopefully, it won't take longer."

Blake led the way up a flight of stairs and along a ramp to room 9B. He unlocked the door, handed the key to his partner, and walked inside. The single room was done entirely in brown. Chocolate rug, beige walls, tan bedspread, mahogany-stained bureau.

Kosinski looked around, then shook his head. "I'm wearin' a blue suit," he said. "It don't go with the room."

Blake responded by taking a roll of bills out of his pocket and dropping it on the bureau. "Courtesy of Max Steinberg's conscience. You need anything, shirts, socks, another suit, just hoof it up to Bell Boulevard." He walked over to the bed and sat down. "Do me a favor. Pour us both a drink. I left the bottles in the bathroom."

Kosinski (to his credit as far as Blake was concerned) obeyed without further comment, fetching two plastic tumblers and a bottle of Absolut, filling both glasses to the brim. Blake sipped at the clear liquid, thought about it for a second, then drained half the glass. He waited for the heat in his belly to blossom up into his brain before he began talking.

"I never worked with a partner before," he said. "My work never called for it. Not that I wasn't part of a team. Hell, sometimes there'd be seven or eight of us between the field investigators, the hardware technicians, and the computer people. But that's not the same as a partner." He stopped, looked up at Kosinski. "Anyway, I liked seeing myself that way. *The Kid Rides Alone*—that'd be the name of the movie. And that's probably why I gave you such a hard time in the beginning. I just didn't wanna share the glory."

"And don't forget your father." Kosinski's face showed no emotion beyond ordinary cop curiosity.

"Yeah, there was that, too. I didn't think a . . ."

"A drunk?"

"Why don't you make it hard for me, prick?"

Kosinski started to laugh, a typical drunk's phlegmy rattle. After a moment, Blake joined in, thinking, there's nothing I like better than acting out a cliché. Maybe that's why the main thing I feel, right at this minute, is embarrassed.

"Whatever I thought, I was wrong," he said. "That's the important point. I'm not kissing your ass, here. I couldn't have gotten this far without you and that's all there is to that."

"So what you're saying is that you need me. Like you need your computer and your tape recorders." Kosinski filled his glass, offered the bottle to his partner who waved it away. "Maybe you could keep me in a closet."

Blake shook his head. "I'm gonna say what I have to say, Bell, so you can drop the attitude. What it is, I think, is that I'm getting too old to go it alone. It gets harder and harder when you can't even remember why."

Kosinski raised his glass. "There's one point I won't argue."

"The bottom line is that I don't wanna lose you. Not by having you deliberately walk into a bullet. And let me emphasize *deliberately*. Because you can't blame it on the alcohol, or on Chief Harrah."

"I know that, Marty. But you might wanna consider that I'm not walkin' around unarmed. Brannigan thinks I'm gonna paint a bull's-eye on my forehead. He thinks I'm just gonna stand there with my eyes closed. The way I see it, that's all to my advantage." He scratched the side of his head, then let his hand fall into his lap.

"Brannigan won't be the one, Bell. Harrah hasn't survived all these years because he's stupid. Look, I'm not asking for the rest of your life. Just give me a couple of days. Once we get through this, we can deal with whatever's bothering you."

"Whatever's *bothering* me? Somehow, I don't think I like the sound of that. What'd you do, have me checked out?"

"Not me, Bell. My mother did it without asking. You met her, so you know I'm not bullshitting."

Kosinski nodded thoughtfully. "The first time I saw your mother, she had her fingers wrapped around the butt of a .38. That's usually the sign of a person who gets her own way. So, what'd she find out?" Changing topics abruptly was a standard interrogative technique. As was the slightly sharper tone. Kosinski suddenly realized that he was pissed off. Which, in light of the fact that all Blake wanted him to do was stay alive, seemed entirely inappropriate.

"For Christ's sake, Bell, she didn't show me your file."

"That's not an answer."

Blake took a deep breath, decided the conversation wasn't going where he wanted it to go and there was nothing he could do about it. "According to my Uncle Patrick, you were a good cop for most of your career, then you ran into some personal problems and lost it."

"That's it?"

"Yeah, that's it."

"He didn't tell you about Reggie the Veggie?" Kosinski drained the plastic tumbler, filled it up, socked down another two inches of vodka. Figuring if he couldn't entirely blame his anger, he could always blame the booze. Knowing that when he was finished, he was going to have to blame something, that he couldn't admit that he *wanted* to recite his story to Marty Blake.

"The floor's yours, Bell. I got no more punch lines."

"The first thing you gotta know is that I came from a family of drunks. Both my parents, mother and father, as well as assorted uncles and aunts. Which is like having to spend your life dancing on the edge of an open mine shaft. Whether you like to or not, whether it's *fair* or not, your life is a disaster waiting to happen.

"Still, I was pretty good. I was very religious, an altar boy and all that, until the juices started to flow. I fucked up as a teenager, like most of the kids in the neighborhood, but I never got into anything heavy. After high school, I joined the army and spent two years stationed in Berlin, which is pretty amazing all by itself, considering that I enlisted because I wanted to go to Vietnam. Maybe that's why I joined the cops six months after I was discharged. If I didn't prove myself in Vietnam, I could still do it on the mean streets.

"By that time, I was married. To Ingrid Horst, a German girl I met in Berlin. I'd like to think she wasn't crazy when I met her, but I have to admit there's no way I can be sure. Maybe it was the language and the culture that confused me. Or maybe I was too busy to notice, too busy trying to make cop of the century. I swear to God, Marty, at one point in the year, I had more collars than my whole squad put together. I worked like a dog, donating my overtime to the city, prowling the streets on my days off. By the time I started my fifth year on the job, I had the gold shield, which is what I wanted from the beginning.

"Three cheers for the conquering hero, right? Especially when Ingrid announced that she was pregnant after six years of trying. I remember she told me right before Sunday mass at St. Joseph's, told me to say an extra prayer for the baby. Which I did, Marty. I said a lot of prayers over the next nine months, but somebody upstairs forgot to listen, because my son was born with the top half of his brain missing. The *top* half. He could breathe, drink, chew, swallow, digest, piss, and shit. He couldn't see, hear, smell, taste, or think. Nice, right?"

Kosinski told his story as if he was reciting a memorized poem to an audience of bored tenth graders. He continued to drink as he went along, working the bottle and glass as if they were props. His voice remained dead calm, though he began to slur his words.

"The docs," he continued, "told us to put him away, that there was a building at Pilgrim State Hospital where they cared for . . . lemme see how he put it. Oh, yeah, he said for people in a 'persistent vegetative state.' I think that's when the name first came to me. Ingrid had already decided to call the baby Reginald. I hated the name, of course, but under the circumstances I didn't put up much of a fight. If you saw the kid, you'd know exactly what I'm talkin' about. It was like his head just stopped about halfway up. He was as flat on top as an anvil.

"I was devastated, Marty. No joke. The baby was supposed to start the perfect family, the one that went hand in hand with being the perfect cop. When he came out Reggie the Veggie, it was like gettin' blindsided by an ocean liner. I mean if you spend your whole life tryin' to take control—which is the only way children of alcoholics can survive—hopeless situations aren't a whole lot of fun. But it wasn't like I loved this baby. Or like there was anything there *to* love. The kid was a monster.

"So, whatta ya do when you're faced with a situation like that? Whatta ya *have* to do?"

Kosinski stopped abruptly. He looked into Blake's eyes, kept his gaze fixed until Blake realized that the question wasn't purely rhetorical. He was expected to answer.

"I guess you have to bite the bullet," he said after a moment. "You have to give the . . . the child up and get on with your life."

"Yeah?" Kosinski laughed, a single sharp bark that echoed briefly in the small room. "Well, Ingrid had other ideas. She decided to develop her Reginald's full potential. Decided that the doctors were wrong, that prayer could overcome science, that love conquers all. I tried to talk to her, the docs tried, the nurses tried, the goddamned hospital social worker tried. I can still see her in the bed holding this baby, her eyes staring somewhere off in the distance. You remember those saint books the nuns used to give out in grammar school? Ingrid looked just like one of the martyrs in those books. Like she'd found her cross and she wasn't giving it up. Like the cross was the whole point.

"Naturally, I thought about walkin' out on her. Not because of Reggie. I was gonna walk out because I knew she was crazy. But I didn't do it, Marty. First, because I was religious all my life and when I said 'For better or for worse,' I meant it. But it was also because the docs said Reggie couldn't live more than a year, that he'd probably be dead within a few months. Maybe then, I figured, we could get it back together.

"As it turned out, Reggie the Veggie lived for nine years. And for nine years I continued to do my Christian duty. I didn't drink, except for the occasional beer. I stopped putting in all the overtime so I could help Ingrid around the house. I listened to her read bedtime stories to a creature with all the understanding of an artichoke. That's where the name came from. Reggie the Veggie. It popped into my head one day and I couldn't get it out again."

Kosinski stopped, took a deep breath, stared at the drink in his hand for a moment. "So, that's the way it went for nine years. On the job, I was a good cop, but not the super cop I wanted to be. At home, I was an appliance, a vacuum cleaner, a dishwasher. I swear, Marty, over time the house seemed to get colder and colder. No matter what it was doing outside, there was a damp chill that washed over me the minute I opened the door. You think I'm exaggerating? I'd invite you to talk to our friends, only we didn't have any.

"The final act began the day Reggie was buried. As we walked away from the grave, Ingrid turned to me and said, 'You haff killed him, Bell.' Just like that, in a thick German accent. And she didn't stop. Faith would have saved Reggie, but I didn't have faith. Love would have saved him, but I didn't have love. Prayer would have saved him, but I'd refused to pray. It all added up to the same thing: Reggie the Veggie would've grown up to be Albert Einstein if it hadn't been for my failings.

"Two weeks later, Ingrid's lawyer served me with divorce papers and a restraining order keeping me out of my own house. The bank accounts had already been emptied. A year after that, when the divorce became legal, she married a postman from Howard Beach. Last I heard, they had three kids, two girls and a boy."

Kosinski felt the vodka for the first time. He looked down at the bottle, saw that it was within four inches of being empty. He hadn't done this in a long time, hadn't drunk himself into what would soon become a stupor.

"So ya see, Marty," he said, trying to get the words out as quickly as possible, "what I did was step into that mine shaft I already mentioned. I mean it was always there, right, so it wasn't much of a problem. All I had to do was close my eyes and jump."

SEVENTEEN

Blake's first inkling that events were not about to unfold on schedule came at nine o'clock the following morning when he looked out his kitchen window to find a white Ford Econoline parked across the street. The vehicle itself wouldn't have aroused any suspicion—it was as anonymous as any of the other vehicles lining either side of the avenue—but the overweight middle-aged man with the bent nose and the brush cut leaning against the Ford fairly screamed cop. As did the occupied black Dodge sedans parked behind the van.

Blake stood watching for a moment, sipping at his coffee while he digested the information. Curiously (to himself, at least), he felt no emotion whatever; his mind was clicking away, calculating the possibilities. The cop—he assumed it was Aloysius Grogan, based on Kosinski's description—was making no attempt to conceal himself.

At first glance, it seemed an attempt at pure intimidation, the neighborhood bully just waiting for some little kid to head out to school. But there had to be fear behind it, too. Kosinski hadn't simply recited his lessons to Brannigan the night before. He'd used the facts the way a mugger uses a lead pipe.

Blake tried to put himself in his enemy's shoes. He began by assuming that Samuel Harrah—a man he'd never met and knew very little about—would have the cold objectivity to act in his own self-interest. In that case, he couldn't afford to accept the carefully presented scenario that had Bell Kosinski operating on his own. The stakes were too high. At the same time and for the same reason, Harrah wouldn't simply order his (Blake's) and Steinberg's executions. Steinberg was too important, too high profile. If he disappeared, there'd be hell to pay. Too much hell if Blake and the lawyer were simply going about their business. If, as advertised, they'd decided to back off.

But there was another side to be considered. This one involved a power-crazed cop who'd been having his own way for a long time.

Blake recalled a psych course he'd taken at Columbia. The class (as were all classes, according to the instructor, a woman named Cynthia Williams) had been fascinated by descriptions of the criminal psychopath. Professor Williams, after a long, technical discussion, had advised that the simplest way to understand the mind of the psychopath/sociopath was in terms of control. Control over his or her own life as well as the lives of others. When that control was threatened, when the facade was pulled down, the psychopath's response was almost certain to be aggressive, rather than passive. Aggressive and, as often as not, irrational.

Blake glanced out the window. The rear doors of the van were open and the cop with the crew cut was talking to someone inside.

Too casual, Blake thought. They're out there to harass me, to remind me. And to watch. Maybe they found the hardware in Tillson's basement, or the transmitters in McGuire's house. It doesn't really matter, because it doesn't change anything. Time is working against them.

He went into the living room, dug out John Coltrane's "My Favorite Things," popped it into his CD player, and set the volume high enough to cover the sound of his own movements. Then he quickly gathered the still-uncopied tape of McGuire's confession, Gurp Patel's written report, and an RF detector, stuffing everything into a briefcase before quietly opening the door and slipping into the hallway.

"You look like you're running away from home."

Blake's head jerked down between his shoulder blades; he felt the muscles in his back tighten, announcing that they, at least, hadn't discarded the possibility of a bullet.

"Christ, Mom, you scared the hell out of me."

"Is it that bad?" For the first time, Dora Blake's face showed evidence of concern.

"That depends on whether you ask my cerebral cortex or my hypothalamus. They seem to have conflicting opinions on the subject." He ran through the details as he led his mother back up the stairs to her apartment. Inside, he swept all five rooms, looking for bugs, finding nothing. Even so, he flipped on the TV and turned the sound up high enough to drown casual conversation before handing the briefcase over to his mother.

"I want you to take this material over to Sarah Tannebaum's apartment, see if she'll hold it for a couple of days. I haven't made a copy of the tape yet, so be careful with it." Blake paused, remembering Bell Kosinski's ugly tale. Last night (when he *should* have been attending to business) he'd run through the story again and again, vacillating between condemnation of what he understood as weakness and a growing conviction that once Kosinski had made that first, basic decision—to stick by his wife and his child—he was doomed. Bell Kosinski could not be blamed for having been struck by lightning, not even by an arch-moralist like Marty Blake. Sometimes there were no bad guys.

Dora Blake took the briefcase from her son and set it on the floor. "Should I get in touch with Patrick?" she asked. "If he knew what was going on, he'd have to do something."

"Like what?"

"Spare me the sarcasm, Marty. I'm not blind. I saw the way you jumped when I spoke to you in the hallway."

"For once, I'm not being sarcastic. I don't see what Uncle Pat can do, assuming he wants to do anything, which I doubt. But if you wanna call him, it's all right with me. Tell him everything I've told you; tell him I can prove it. But don't let him get his hands on that tape. No matter what. Don't even let him know that it exists. Assume that your phone is tapped and watch what you say. I don't want you to become a target. If you sound like a scared mother trying to help her son, that's fine. But if Harrah thinks you're in possession of evidence that could incriminate him, he'll have to come after you. He won't have any choice."

"Didn't you just check the apartment?"

"Yeah, and there are no transmitters or tape recorders *inside*. But that doesn't mean that Harrah's people haven't tapped into the phone line somewhere between here and the Woodhaven Boulevard switching station. Hell, they could be in an apartment across the street with a parabolic mic and a long-distance video camera. Better warn your lovers." Blake glanced at his watch. "Look, I have to get moving. I've got an appointment with Joanna Bardo in an hour and I'm gonna be late. Remember, Uncle Pat's been an ass kisser all his life. That's how he got his desk job in Personnel. Don't expect much and you won't be disappointed."

Twenty minutes later, when Marty Blake stepped out of his air-conditioned apartment building, the sun slammed into his body as if it had been waiting for his appearance, as if it recognized him. He looked up into a sky drained of color, a sky that seemed nothing more than an extension of the blazing white sun.

A line from one of the Rolling Stones' first songs popped into his mind. "And the time is right for fighting in the street, boys." All over the city, tenement dwellers, desperate for relief, were deserting their apartments. The radios would boom, the beer and wine would flow, the reefer, the dope, the crack and, before very long, the blood.

"You, Blake, get over here."

Blake glanced at the crew-cut figure across the street. Grogan was standing in shadow, yet beads of sweat stood out on his forehead. He looked like he'd rather be anywhere else.

"Pardon me?" Blake whispered a quick prayer to the spirit of Robert DeNiro, then slipped into his sunglasses, put one hand on his chest, and cocked his head. "You talkin' to me?"

Instead of answering, Grogan crossed the street. As he did, a tall cop with a mop of bushy hair, Tommy Brannigan, undoubtedly, scrambled out of the front sedan and hurried to follow.

"What's your game, huh? What the fuck do you think you're doing?"

Blake stared at the twisted features of Aloysius Grogan. Thinking he'd been right in expecting an irrational response, but he'd picked the wrong psychopath. He cautioned himself to be careful, to play the cowed noncombatant. To not, under any circumstances, lose his temper.

"You wouldn't consider telling me who you are and what you want?"

Blake saw the punch coming. Saw Grogan curl his right hand into a fist, slowly raise it to the level of his shoulder, throw it ponderously forward. It was the blow of a fat, middle-aged man, yet it seemed almost petulant to Marty Blake, the act of a frustrated child, a brat. Nevertheless, it hit his left cheekbone with enough force to knock him backward into the side of the building.

"If I had my way, I'd take you down to headquarters and break you." Grogan's spat the words between clenched teeth. "Do you understand? I'd break you like any other common criminal."

The message delivered, he spun on his heel and led his two much more formidable companions back to their respective vehicles. A minute later, both sedans pulled away from the curb and headed off down the street.

Blake picked himself up, checked his linen jacket for tears and smudges, refused to touch the swelling on his left cheek. His schedule called for him to visit Manhattan Executive, to plead poverty, to beg Joanna Bardo to throw him a little work. The charade seemed more important than ever. Steinberg was doing the real work, searching out a reporter willing to write up the story. He hoped to interest a *Newsday* columnist named Jack Patchen who had a reputation as a cop basher, but there were other possibilities. Certainly, the tale of blackmail and murder that led from Sondra Tillson's corpse to the Borough President of Manhattan to the head of NYPD Intelligence to an Appellate Court judge to a dead, homeless patsy had to qualify as the story of the decade, if not the century. Somebody would pick it up, somebody would run with it. It was just a matter of time.

Half an hour later, Blake was driving west on the Long Island Expressway, poking along in the right lane while he considered just what it would feel like to be taken downtown and broken. Grogan was a cop from the old school. He'd probably use a rubber hose instead of a stun gun. That way it would take longer.

Virtually everybody was passing the Taurus, most after a few choice words and an angry gesture. That was the only reason he noticed the maroon Buick trailing some fifty yards behind. His first reaction was annoyance; he should have spotted the tail long before he did. He left the LIE at Greenpoint Avenue, made a left, and drove until he found a small deli. Joining a line of double-parked cars, he slipped inside, bought a container of coffee, then resumed his journey. He was in the exact-change lane at the entrance to the Midtown Tunnel, ready to toss his token into the hopper, when he again saw the Buick.

In a way, Blake thought, it's too good to be true. After all, there's not much point in putting on an act if you haven't got an audience. I'll have to shake him before I meet Steinberg at Emilio's, but that shouldn't be a problem either. Not in Manhattan. No, the trick is to lose him without arousing suspicion. To lose him, then let him find me again when I'm finished with the lawyer.

Blake took the simplest route to Joanna's office, working his way down Park Avenue to Broadway, then down Broadway into Soho. He drove as if he hadn't a care in the world, waddling along while cabs and small trucks darted around him like a swarm of ants around a puddle of oil.

The Buick paced him, a half-block behind. At one point, when a red light brought them bumper to bumper, Blake glanced in the mirror, saw a young man with shoulder-length hair and a hoop earring in his left ear; he memorized the face as a matter of reflex.

As he pulled away from the light, Blake began to calculate the moves he'd have to make if Steinberg was being shadowed. Their business supposedly completed, there was no legitimate reason for them to meet. Somehow, Blake would have to find a way to observe the lawyer as he arrived for their rendezvous.

From Steinberg, his thoughts drifted to Bell Kosinski stashed away (*hopefully* stashed away) in a Bayside motel. Kosinski wouldn't stay put for more than a couple of days. The ex-cop (in Blake's mind, at least) was the ultimate tough guy; there was no way he could play the frightened rabbit for any length of time. If Blake couldn't bring Harrah and his co-conspirators down in a New York hurry, Kosinski was going to do a little hunting of his own.

EIGHTEEN

"Stunning, Cynthia, absolutely stunning." Blake had never been above a little false flattery—paying the right compliment to the right client's wife or girlfriend at the odd cocktail party came with the territory—but this time he was being sincere. Cynthia Barret wore a tan, silk, scoop-neck blouse surmounted by a finely spun gold necklace and matching earrings. A tribal scarf draped her right shoulder, falling in gentle folds across her chest. Its rich oranges, browns and yellows complemented her cinnamon skin tones, added depth to her yellow-brown eyes, accented the thrust of her breasts.

"Thank you, Marty." Cynthia Barret offered both hands to Blake. "Joanna decided to give out midyear bonuses. Business has gotten a lot better."

"And you spent your bonus on clothing and jewelry, correct?"

"Actually, I used it to pay off my MasterCard so I'd have room to charge the clothes and jewelry. Citibank likes it better that way. They offered to increase my credit limit."

"Somebody oughta warn 'em. Before the regulators catch on."

Cynthia's laughter was rich and warm, as always. "Joanna's expecting you."

"I hope she's in a good mood, because I want her to throw me a little work."

"Oh, she is, Marty. Joanna just bought . . . she just *acquired* a new piece. You might want to throw her a compliment or two."

Blake stuck his hands in his pockets. "Out with it, Cynthia. Let's hear the pedigree."

"Well, my dear." Cynthia lifted her nose in the air, looked down its length at Marty Blake. "My sainted employer has purchased a Chippendale figured maple linen press, circa 1780. It features an elaborately molded cornice over two arched paneled cupboard doors, and three shelves flanked by fluted pilasters." She paused, dropped her chin. "I swear, Marty, it's the ugliest thing I've ever seen."

"Is it too ugly to be a fake?"

That got a another laugh. "I don't know, Marty. Why don't you ask Joanna?"

"Because I don't have the *cojones*?" Blake admitted. "I never did."

Blake didn't have to worry about identifying the antique in question, because Joanna Bardo was posed in front of it when he entered her office. Her gold dress with its lace-trimmed collar was clearly designed to complement the yellow tones of the blocky maple chest. As he entered the room, she gently closed the cupboard doors.

"Damn, Joanna." Blake paused in the doorway. "I don't know which piece I like best, the chest or the woman who's standing in front of it."

"We've got a problem, Marty. Why don't you sit down."

Blake, momentarily silenced by the unexpected turn of events, complied. He had no choice at that point, but he did wonder why she'd bothered to pose if she had bad news for him. The answer became obvious when she continued to posture in front of her latest triumph.

"Last night," she began, her back half-turned, one hand raised as if to caress the piece, "I received a phone call from a new client, a client I've been after for the better part of a year."

"And the phone call was about me."

"That's right, Marty."

"Who was it from?"

"It was from an aide to Borough President Edward Green."

Blake slumped in the chair, reminded himself to watch his temper. "What'd this aide want?"

"He claimed that you've been prying into Green's affairs, that you've been conducting an illegal surveillance. Your license, apparently, is about to be pulled. The question, of course, was whether or not you still work for Manhattan Executive." She paused, then turned to face him. "The question was whether or not *I* sent you."

"And did you?"

"That's not funny."

"It's not meant to be." Blake crossed his legs, let his hand drop to his knee. "Think about it, Joanna. You *did* send me to Max Steinberg. I'm not going to apologize for doing my job. In fact, to tell you the truth, I'm proud of what I accomplished. I produced absolute proof of Billy Sowell's innocence and that's all I did. I haven't seen Max

Steinberg since our meeting just after the kid's murder. We were both drunk, if I remember right."

Joanna Bardo finally deserted her new toy. She walked over to her desk and sat down. "Marty Blake, you're full of shit."

"That bad, is it?" Despite the bravado, Blake was disheartened by the out-of-character profanity.

"This morning, shortly before you arrived, I was visited by a detective named Brannigan. He was carrying a box filled with hardware—bugs, taps, transmitters, and recorders. Brannigan claimed the hardware had been used to conduct an illegal surveillance and he wanted to know if Manhattan Executive had supplied it. Had supplied it to *you*."

"Manhattan Executive didn't, so I can't see what your problem is."

Joanna leaned on the desk. "My problem is twofold, Marty. First, you and I had a deal that included use of Manhattan Executive's hardware, but the material I saw was brand new. If you spent that kind of money when you could have used our stock, you did it because you didn't trust me. It's that simple. Second, you came to me a few days ago, you and your new colleague, begging for work, work you apparently didn't need. That visit was purely an attempt to deceive me."

"So, I'm convicted without trial, convicted on the word of a cop and a politician?" Blake's mind was spinning furiously. He knew he'd made a mistake bringing Kosinski with him to Joanna's. The question was whether or not he could still deny his partner. "Are you recording this conversation?"

The question brought a quick blush, followed by an even quicker frown. "Do you know how hard I worked to get this account? Do you have any idea? Edward Green's going to run for Mayor next year. His campaign committee's become our biggest single client and we've only gotten started." She stopped, glanced over at the maple chest, shook her head. "I did everything I could for you. I set you up, found you work, allowed you access to the computer. In return, you deceived me. I tell you, Marty, it hurts."

Blake stood up, started to leave, then decided to make a final statement. "I don't know a goddamned thing about Edward Green. Nothing, understand? But what I do or don't know isn't really the point, is it?" He took a step back toward Joanna's desk. "Fuck you,

Joanna. Fuck you and fuck your maple linen press and your miserable ambition and your pitiful pretensions." He stopped abruptly, let his voice drop off, managed a sneer. "How does it feel to live with your nose up someone's ass? To sacrifice an old friend because a client's aide makes a phone call? If some high roller said, 'Get the nigger out of the front office,' would you fire Cynthia, too?"

Blake noted Joanna Bardo's composed features and realized that she wasn't buying his act. She'd report back to Edward Green as soon as he was out the door, maybe even messenger him a copy of the tape she hadn't denied she was making. But that was all to the good—his denial would be on the record; his anger, though it hadn't fooled Joanna, would at least confuse Samuel Harrah. Joanna had said they were after his license, not his life, which meant they hadn't made up their minds about his intentions. Or maybe they assumed he'd been rendered harmless by their recovery of the assorted bugs and taps he'd planted. Either way, it worked to his advantage.

"You've lost your smile, Marty. Your beautiful smile." Joanna's tone was almost wistful. She pushed her chair back a few inches, then folded her hands and laid them in her lap. "There was a time when it could light up the room and now it's gone. I feel like I'm talking to another person. You're rougher now, meaner. Have you asked yourself where you're going?" She stood up, crossed the room, opened the door. "Good-bye, Marty. I won't be seeing you again."

Blake carried Joanna Bardo's final comments with him as he made his way uptown. He began by slipping out through the basement into an alleyway that led to Wooster Street, then hailing a cab and ordering the driver to circle the block and come back up Greene. Sure enough, the maroon Buick was still parked in front of Joanna's building. The long-haired cop was slumped behind the wheel, his earring just visible behind the pages of the *Daily News*. Blake nodded with satisfaction, then let his mind drift.

Manhattan Executive had been home to him for a long time. Joanna Bardo, as resident mother, had nurtured him (and used him) while he'd learned his craft one step at a time. Now the tit had been abruptly withdrawn and he should, he supposed, be feeling some kind of separation anxiety, some sense of loss. But the only thing he really felt was the trickle of sweat running down into his collar. The cab, even with its windows open, was pumping out a greenhouse effect all its own.

Just a few weeks ago, Blake realized with a start, he'd been driving a yellow beast very similar to this one. He glanced at the driver's hack license. Francois George. Or was it George Francois? The Taxi and Limousine Commission had a way of screwing up foreign names. He was Haitian, anyway, as were so many New York cabbies.

Blake had a sudden urge to ask Francois George about life in his home country. Had he driven a cab in Port-au-Prince? Had he left his family behind, his wife, his children, just to get to a country where most people despised him on sight? What had driven him, politics or poverty? Or maybe the politics *of* poverty. Haiti had been poor and the Haitian people oppressed for so long that separating the two was little more than a game played by American politicians to keep Haitians out of the country.

"Hey, check this out, man."

Blake followed Francois George's bony finger to a pair of middle-aged women strolling arm and arm along Houston Street. "Fuckin' dykes. I hate fuckin' dykes." He snorted, shook his head. "Pussy-bumpers. It's disgusting."

Having destroyed Blake's illusions, the cabbie made a quick left in front of a city bus and swept uptown on First Avenue. "Francois George, where are you from?" Blake asked.

"Harlem," he replied. "West 152nd Street."

"This your cab?"

"Me and the bank, we share it." He chuckled softly. "I bought the medallion fifteen years ago, paid it off in eighty-nine, then borrowed on it last year and bought a laundromat which I'm lettin' my woman run. We doin' okay, between us. Lookin' to move out, though. Out of Harlem to someplace safe." He laughed again. "If we can figure out where that is."

Blake left the cab at First Avenue and Seventh Street, half a block from Emilio's Ristorante and twenty minutes early for his meeting with Max Steinberg. He went directly to a coffee shop across the street, took a stool near the front window, and ordered coffee and a slice of coconut custard pie. He was on his second cup when the lawyer stepped out of a cab and walked into Emilio's. Ten minutes later, convinced that Steinberg was alone, he paid the check and strolled across the street.

"Marty, sit down." The lawyer spoke without raising his eyes. "We gotta talk."

Blake took in the slumped shoulders, the flat voice, and the lowered head. The famous wig lay motionless, like a golfer's divot on a bleached white rock.

"You don't look so good, Max." He ordered a dry Manhattan, watched the waiter retreat, wondered why he was surprised, why his heart felt like a ball of lead in his chest.

"I've felt better." Steinberg sipped at his drink, took a deep breath, then finally met Blake's eyes. "Let's make this short and sweet," he said. "I'm pulling out. I got no choice."

"Really? And what happened to, 'Steinberg never backs down'?"

Blake caught a glimmer of Steinberg's customary fire, watched it die out as quickly as it had appeared. The lawyer was so thoroughly beaten that Blake actually felt sorry for him. Steinberg would carry this defeat to the grave.

"I don't have a choice," he repeated. "They got me by the balls."

Blake leaned back as the waiter set his drink on the table. He looked at it for a moment, then drained the glass and ordered another. "I take it you haven't contacted a reporter, haven't gotten started."

Steinberg shook his head. "No, nothing. They've been on me since right after the last time we spoke." He looked down at his hands. "Something I did a few years ago. With a client. Before I decided to clean up my act. I shouldn't have, but I took a chance. Christ, Marty, I thought it was forgotten, but the bastards had it all the time."

"Then why didn't they try to blackmail you? Isn't blackmail part of their game?"

"They said . . ."

"Who, Max. Name the name."

"Thomas Brannigan."

"Then you didn't even rate a visit from the big man."

"No, not even that. They swatted me like a fly." Steinberg finished his drink, signaled to the waiter for a refill. "You wanna know why they didn't put the screws to me before now? Because they checked me out and discovered that I'm in hock up to my ears. If I'm not mistaken, you don't get blood from a stone."

"But they held the information."

"Two more years, Marty. Two more years and the statute of limitations kicks in. Two more years and I would've been free."

"'Free and clear?'"

The waiter appeared with their drinks. He set them on the table, asked if they were ready to order lunch.

"I'm drinking mine," Steinberg declared, waving the man away. "Look, Marty, if you think Harrah doesn't know what you're up to, think again. I'm here to warn you off, that's part of the deal. If you make a move on Harrah, he takes me down, me and your boss, Joanna Bardo. I'm talkin' about the first sign of a move."

Blake took a minute to look around while he gathered his thoughts. Emilio's was one of the last of the old-time Italian restaurants in the neighborhood, a hangover from the days when Italians actually lived on the Lower East Side. The walls were covered with yellowing photographs, many of them signed. Carmen Basilio was there, and Jake LaMotta, and the Rock, of course, Rocky Marciano. Vic Damone had a place of honor above the polished cappuccino machine, next to Robert DeNiro, Sly Stallone, and Lou Costello. Oddly, Frank Sinatra was missing from the pantheon.

"So where's the Chairman of the Board?" Blake asked, a half-smile playing at the corners of his mouth.

"The what?"

"The Chairman of the Board, Max. Frank. Where the fuck is Frank?"

Steinberg finally lost his temper. "You're crazy, Blake. I expected it from the drunk, Kosinski, but I thought you had more sense."

"I guess I fooled the both of us." Blake pulled his chair into the table and leaned forward. The smile had become a sneer. "So what's the deal, Max. If I decide to forget, what's in it for me?"

"You get to keep your license. The bugs and taps are forgotten."

"And Bell? What's in it for Bell? Or do we have to turn our backs the day he comes floating up in the river?"

When Steinberg didn't reply, Blake changed the subject. "Max, you remember a cop named Matthew Blake. I believe you ran into him eight or ten years ago."

"Did I represent him? Was he related to you?"

Blake took a moment to study the lawyer's expression. Steinberg's hooded eyes were meant to conceal, that was obvious enough, but the edge of a smile played at the corners of his mouth.

"You've known about it the whole time, isn't that right?" Blake expected a *pro forma* denial, but Steinberg's face remained set. "The thing is, Max, you shouldn't lie to me here. The way I'm feeling, I'd just as soon make you eat that wig."

Steinberg shrugged, spread his hands. "At first I didn't make the connection—Blake, it's a common name—but then it came back to me, so I checked it out and discovered you were the son. Life is full of surprises, right? Still, when I asked myself what difference it made, I came up blank, so I kept my mouth shut. You're not your father."

Blake drained his glass, paused to allow the fire in his belly to flare up into his hands and face. "Your client, the druggie, what was her name?"

"Chantel McKendrick."

"She said my father raped her."

"That's right."

"And you pressed the complaint."

"Whatta you think, Marty? You think I just took her word for it? Anything to win a case?" Steinberg put his hands on the table, leaned forward until his face was a foot from Blake's. "The first thing I did, *boychick*, was put her on a polygraph and make her repeat every detail. *Shtup* by fucking *shtup*. Then I made her do it again; then I took her through it backwards."

"And she passed?"

"With flying colors." The lawyer's eyes glowed triumphantly. It was the look of an athlete who's somehow managed to salvage victory out of defeat, a battered fighter amazed to find his opponent on the canvas. "But, hey, why should anyone be surprised? It's a common occurrence, right?"

Blake stood up. "Yeah," he admitted, "it happens every day. Well, duty calls."

By the time he was safely installed in a cab, Blake was already contemplating his next move. He wouldn't go back to pick up the Taurus. What was the point? No, what he had to do was find a car-rental agency that'd accept cash, then get out to Kosinski and break the bad news. Kosinski wouldn't sit still, of course. He couldn't, now that the end had drifted out of sight. Well, maybe a kevlar vest would give him a fighting chance. And maybe he could try a rosary blessed by the pope.

NINETEEN

"Ya know that guy with the white hair?" Emily Caruso asked Bell Kosinski. "I used to see him on the television sometimes."

Father Tim pondered the question for a moment, his fingers reflexively stroking his chin. "Bishop Fulton J. Sheen," he finally said, pronouncing each word carefully as he approached the end of a typical Cryders evening.

"For chrissake, Bell, would ya tell this booze hound to shut his face?" She turned away from Kosinski, turned to glare at the retired priest. "Do I look like I'm talkin' to you? Do I look like the kinda person would waste their breath on an old rummy who never even one time in his life got laid?"

Father Tim chuckled. "I forgive you, Emily. As I have in the past, I do now. I forgive you, Emily, and I bless you."

His remark had the desired effect. Emily Caruso, every wrinkle on her face jiggling with outrage, swung back to Bell Kosinski. "He's mockin' me, Bell, like he mocked his vows when he was a priest. The man has no shame." She raised her eyebrows, drew herself up for the final thrust. "He used to drink in the *confessional*. I smelled it on his breath. What kind of absolution could you get from a drunk?"

Bell Kosinski nodded thoughtfully. "So, why didn't you find another priest? It's not like he was the only one."

He watched the old lady's mouth draw up into a sly smile. Her giggle was surprisingly girlish, a sound that seemed to echo up from the school yards of his adolescence. He closed his eyes, saw Andrea Fischetti, his first love, heard her soft laughter as his fingers slid between the buttons of her pure white blouse.

"I kept goin' because I could tell the jerk anything," Emily Caruso declared, "and it was like there was nobody there to remember. I mean if no one's home, you're just talkin' to an empty box, right?"

"I remember every word, Emily. I could recite a list of your transgressions as accurately as Gabriel reading from the book."

She shook her head, willing the priest away. "So that guy with the white hair, you remember who he is, Bell?"

"Not really."

"Yeah, you do," she insisted, tugging at his arm. "The albino-lookin' geek. The one said everybody's supposed to get fifteen minutes of fame. That's who I'm talkin' about."

"Andy Warhol," Father Tim said.

"Right, Bell, Andy Warhol. So what I wanna know is what happened to my fifteen minutes? I mean, look at me. If I gotta wait much longer, the only way I'll get a turn is if my goddamned hearse runs over a little kid on the way to the cemetery." She paused, her smile dissolving as she thought it through. "Better make it a *crowd* of little kids, a crowd of little kids waitin' for a school bus. One kid wouldn't do it in New York."

Kosinski shrugged. "Guess Andy was wrong."

"He would've been," Father Tim declared, "if that was what he actually said."

"Did anybody ask you?"

"Andy Warhol said that everybody was *entitled* to fifteen minutes of fame. Entitlement is no guarantee."

Emily Caruso turned on him in a fury. "You don't know shit about it," she began. "He never said anything about entitled, not a damned word."

Kosinski let his mind drift away from what had become a nightly Cryders ritual. Emily Caruso's voice would continue to rise; Father Tim would respond evenly, refuting every point she made; Ed O'Leary would finally stride the length of the bar and threaten to ban them from Cryders forever. Both would pretend to take the threat seriously, though each knew that Ed would never willingly suffer the economic loss. If they failed to show up two nights in a row, he'd be knocking on their doors, ready to drag them in by the collar.

Kosinski watched them with a bemused expression. Thinking the strangest part of the whole business with Max Steinberg and Marty Blake was how happy he felt right at this moment, like a traveler home from a long and difficult journey, a successful journey. Somehow, it'd all been worth it; he'd not only come through unscathed, but in some real way increased. And that was ridiculous; stupid beyond stupid. How could it be over when he was sitting there with his chest wrapped in a kevlar vest and a Smith & Wesson Model 10 tucked into his waistband?

He looked over at Tony Loest sitting on a stool near the door. Tony had been hired to lay bricks on a two-year commercial project, a high-rise going up in downtown Brooklyn, and was officially out of the cocaine business. He was downing boilermakers like he'd been sentenced to death and this was his last chance to repent.

"You ready, Bell?"

Kosinski looked up at Ed O'Leary. The bartender, having issued the ritual threat to Emily and the good Father, was hovering over him, bottle in hand.

"Always," he said. "Always ready."

O'Leary filled the glass, then leaned across the bar. "I'm gettin' killed here," he confided. "The Mets are up, eight to one. That fuckin' *yam*, Bonilla, all year he's been a stiff, tonight he hits for the cycle. Go figure."

Kosinski watched the bartender walk away. He wanted to return to his reverie, wanted to immerse himself in this odd, unexpected joy, but Emily Caruso was already plucking at his sleeve.

"Ya know what I think, Bell?" Her eyes had lost focus. She was weaving on her stool like a wheelchair athlete running a giant slalom. "I think Andy Warhol was full of shit. How could *everybody* get fifteen minutes? There's like too many people." She paused, finally said. "And not enough time."

Kosinski nodded. "Yeah, you add 'em up and there's five or six billion candidates. If they all got famous, there wouldn't be any audience."

"Maybe," Father Tim declared, "we could have an all-volunteer audience, a core of selfless individuals who renounce their fifteen minutes in the interests of a greater good. We could hook them up to battery-operated television sets for sixteen hours a day, then parade those desiring fame in front of a camera." He stopped long enough to drain his glass, then belch softly. "Of course, we'd have to have an entitlement commission to decide who is and who isn't entitled, who's worthy and who's not. Violent felons and successful politicians would be automatically excluded."

Kosinski glanced at Emily Caruso, noted that she was past responding to Father Tim's jibes. "There's lots of ways to become famous," he observed, "and not all of them are good." Like, he thought, being a white ex-cop whacked in a white neighborhood. Between the event, the investigation, and the funeral, he might even be worth half an hour.

"Fame ain't what you get." Emily shook hear head, then fought to control the motion before it dragged her off the stool. "Ya know what ya get, Bell?"

"Tell me, Emily."

"What ya get is one sad story. Dead kids, a husband who kicks your ass, foster homes, an uncle with an eye for twelve-year-olds . . . whatever it is that cuts you down. You get that so you can see your way through to the end. I mean everyone knows you're not supposed to actually *tell* it, but at least nobody gets denied. Every single human being on the face of this planet gets one sad story."

"Even Father Tim?"

Emily Caruso responded by sliding off the stool, Father Tim by catching her with practiced ease.

"I better take her home," he said. "Better get myself home, too."

Home, for Emily Caruso, was a room in her daughter's house three blocks away.

"You think she can make it?"

"She did last night." He put his hand around her waist, pushed his hat down over his head. "And the night before. God be with you, Bell."

Kosinski stayed in the bar until there were no more customers, until Ed O'Leary had washed the last glass, wiped the bar, rinsed the empties and dumped them in the redemption bin. He wasn't afraid; he didn't dread the empty streets. As far as he could tell, he was looking forward to the confrontation. He'd never fired his .38 in the line of duty, never been shot at though he'd busted many a vicious mutt in his day.

It's the novelty, he finally concluded. When I left the job, I gave up the idea of change. Everything was supposed to stay the same, a lake of booze with the days floating on top like paper sailboats in a puddle.

He looked down at the wet surface of the bar, counted the black cigarette scars in the wood. "You know what the problem is?" he said to nobody in particular.

"No, Bell, what's the problem."

Kosinski stared at Ed O'Leary for a moment. The bartender was standing in the doorway to the back room. "The problem is that you're not in charge, but you can't help acting like you are. The problem is that you never get to throw the first punch, but you keep trying."

He stood up, found his body solid and centered, his hands steady as he tugged the revolver out of his waistband. He cradled the weapon in his palm for a moment, held it with his thumb over the hammer and the front site, his index and middle fingers along the two-inch barrel, his ring finger curled outside the trigger guard. Then he let his hand drop to his side.

From a distance, in the dark, the gun would be invisible. That was Plan A, Plan B, and Plan C; the strategy, he had to admit, of a drunken ex-cop utterly committed to throwing the first punch.

"That bad, is it, Bell?" Ed O'Leary was back behind the bar. He was standing in front of the open cash register with a sawed-off .12 gauge in his left hand. "You want, I'll walk you over to your place."

"I don't think so, Ed." Kosinski started for the door, then caught himself and turned back to O'Leary. "These bad guys are cops. It's not a battle you could really win." Again he started to turn away, again he caught himself. "They know I won't stop on my own. If they thought I'd stop, they might let me off the hook, but they know I won't because that's what I told them. I got only myself to blame."

It was just after two o'clock when Kosinski finally left Cryders. The air was cool and wet, the sidewalk already slick with dew. He took a deep breath, felt the moisture begin to build on his hair and eyebrows. The streets were empty. Off in the distance, he heard a truck work through its gears, the roar of the engine, the sudden silence as the driver shifted, the deep, guttural blast when the transmission re-engaged. The sound struck him as slow and plodding, which was the way he imagined himself right at that moment.

He crossed the avenue, his eyes moving from doorway to doorway. New York was never dark, not with four streetlights on every block. It was a place of shadows, shadows that gradually brightened, revealing their secrets as you closed in on them.

A car turned onto the avenue and swept past. Kosinski imagined Tommy Brannigan wearing a reversed Raiders baseball cap and a red bandanna, imagined him leaning out of a rear window, Uzi in hand. Grogan would be in front, pulling the trigger of a semiautomatic .12 gauge, while a steely eyed Samuel Harrah kept the car straight and steady.

The idea of an all-cop drive by amused Kosinski and he continued to spin it out as he made his way down the street. Maybe the car would be one of those low-rider Chevies, the kind that go up and down when the driver pushes a button. But, no, that was too west coast. In New York it would have to be a black Mercedes Benz, its radio spitting out

Ice T's "Cop Killer." The rap would grow louder and louder as the car slowed for its final approach; he would spin, raise his .38, get off a few defiant shots before the report of his small revolver was overwhelmed by the deep boom of the shotgun, the repetitive crash of the Uzi.

The really important question, he said to himself, is should I jerk and dance like Bonnie and Clyde at the end of that movie, or should I be lifted by an onrushing wall of lead and slammed through a plate-glass window?

He kept moving while he weighed the merits, kept his right side close to the parked cars lining the block. He'd never been hunted before, but he'd played the part of the hunter often enough. What you learned to do, propelled as you were by absolute terror, was keep your eyes moving. You learned to search the interiors of parked cars, the blank, rectangular doorways, the deep shadows at the end of the alley. To scan the rooftops, the windows, even the trees, your eyes jerking from object to object while your heart jumped furiously in your chest.

What I'll do is take the broken glass, he finally decided. The furious fusillade will pick me up off the ground, slam me backward through a window. Slivers of glass will flash like a shower of diamonds as the light dies in my eyes.

Dies in my eyes? No, too much. Let it be as the light *fades* in my eyes. Fades is better.

Without warning, Kosinski was overwhelmed by an onrushing wave of nausea. He staggered over to the curb, began to retch, felt his mind begin to slow even as his body was wracked by a series of deep, relentless spasms.

He was a block away from home when his brain snapped back into place. His knees were wet, his scalp cut and dripping blood. He started to reach up, to explore the wound, then saw the gun in his hand and remembered why it was there.

I wonder, he speculated, if I would've used it. I wonder if whatever brought me here would've known what to do. Something made me stand up, something got my legs moving, something knew where home was. But did something know about combat? About fear?

He willed his eyes back into the shadows, dropped his hand to his side. The unlit sign above the Cheery Day Laundromat beckoned to him, whispered a story about home and safety, a story he refused to acknowledge. Instead of rushing toward the locks and bolts of his apartment door, he stood motionless, drew in breath after breath, allowed the cool evening air to embrace him.

Two blocks away, a maroon Buick turned onto Fourteenth Avenue, made its way up the block, stopped in the intersection. Kosinski saw the driver's head swivel briefly, then the car accelerated, crossed into the wrong lane, and came to a stop less than ten feet away.

"Say, buddy, I'm trying to get up on the Whitestone Bridge. I must've taken a wrong turn, because every way I go brings me right back here." The driver's long blond hair glowed in the light from the street lamp. It swept back along the side of his head to reveal a gold earring that, as Kosinski saw it anyway, neatly matched the shine of his glistening white teeth.

"Make a u-turn, go back to 162nd Street, then take a right onto the Cross Island Parkway." He let his palm drop down onto the butt of the revolver, slid his finger inside the trigger guard, instinctively hid the Smith & Wesson behind his leg.

"Gimme that street again." The smile widened.

"It's called the street of your dead dreams."

The driver's smile disappeared as the gun he carried, a large-caliber automatic, jumped into the open window. Kosinski stepped to the left, watched the pistol slide toward him, raised his .38, and fired three times. The sound, unimaginably loud in the cool night air, covered the approaching footsteps so that Kosinski's first knowledge of a second assassin came from a bullet slamming into the back of his vest.

Center of mass, he thought, a perfect shot.

He was hit twice more as he spun to face his attacker. The first shot slammed into the vest hard enough to crack a rib, the second tore through his left arm, shredding flesh, shattering bone. He felt no pain, no urge to turn and flee; instead, he watched his mind shrink down into a hard, black ball, a point of darkness that held reserves of outright hatred he hadn't known he possessed.

"Last chance," he told the fat man in the Yankees baseball jacket. "Last chance for glory," he told himself.

TWENTY

After Marty Blake dropped his partner off at Cryders Bar, he made a deliberate decision to lose himself in what he termed "operational details," a decision that proceeded directly from his own feelings of helplessness. He'd begged Kosinski to remain in hiding, dredging up every argument he could think of, but the ex-cop had remained adamant, determined, it seemed, to put his head on the block.

"But, Marty," he'd patiently explained, a soft smile brushing the corners of his mouth, "the thing about it is that I'm not afraid. How can you hide if you're not afraid?"

Blake hadn't been surprised, but his dilemma, as he understood it, was that Bell Kosinski's willfulness didn't get Marty Blake off the hook. If Bell Kosinski went down, Marty Blake would pay for not being there when it happened.

After all, he *had* run away from Matthew Blake; he'd allowed his father to disintegrate into a puddle of Bushmills. Certain consequences had followed, just as they'd follow from a slaughtered Bell Kosinski. It wasn't a matter of justice; the word *rapist* had no meaning here. This sequence was purely mechanical, one thing leading to another and . . . well, if you didn't like it, you could just go fuck yourself. Couldn't you?

Blake did have a valid excuse for leaving Bell Kosinski to his fate; he knew the only way out, for either of them, was to keep pushing. Steinberg's withdrawal and the loss of the tapes at McGuire's and Tillson's weren't fatal blows. The material already in his possession would surely interest the right reporter. The problem was that most reporters had pipelines into the NYPD—developing contacts was just part of the job—and some were bound to be more loyal than others. Avoiding a setup would take time, which was exactly what Bell Kosinski didn't have.

In the meanwhile, there was work to be done. From Cryders, Blake drove back to Forest Hills, entering through the back of a building adjoining his own, then crossing the roof to reach his apartment. His main objective was the material stored at Sarah Tannebaum's, but there was something he had to do first. He turned the key in the lock, eased the door open, slid inside without a sound. It was seven o'clock and nearly dark.

He tiptoed over to a window, peered at the white van across the street. Its presence energized him, as if he'd just come face to face with Samuel Harrah. As he pulled away, he suddenly realized why Kosinski had gone back to Cryders. The chess game was being played in the dark, with both sides making covert moves. Tommy Brannigan had pretended to believe that Kosinski was operating on his own while his bosses orchestrated an all-out assault on Max Steinberg. Steinberg had caved in, but Steinberg didn't know that Blake had recorded McGuire's confession. Kosinski had yearned for resolution, something solid, a brisk wind to blow away the smoke, reveal the mirrors.

Well, that was the difference between Marty Blake and his partner. Blake wanted to win and if winning required patience, then so be it. He knew that he wasn't going to get resolution; he had no magic piece to leap over the defense and checkmate Samuel Harrah. There was, however, one very solid move on his immediate horizon. He opened the bottom drawer of his bureau, removed the Llama M-82 lying beneath a stack of neatly folded T-shirts and stuck it in his belt. Thinking the touch of cool metal and the smell of gun oil is about as solid as it gets.

He left as quietly as he'd entered, then made his way up the stairs to his mother's apartment, wanting only to retrieve the tape and the paperwork and be on his way. Still, he wasn't surprised to find Patrick Blake sitting on the couch; no, what surprised him was the sound of Judge John McGuire's voice on a portable tape player.

"How . . ." He stared at Dora Blake, unable to find words to describe his sense of betrayal.

For once, Dora Blake had no answer; she stood mute, unmoving.

"Your mother's looking for a way out," Patrick Blake said. "You can't blame her."

"Wanna bet?" Blake turned to face his uncle. "I'm taking the tape." He noted the sheaf of papers in Patrick's lap. "And the report."

"I won't try to stop you."

"Smart move."

The cop's face reddened as his mouth pulled down into a sharp, straight line. "Damn your arrogance," he muttered.

Blake took the papers from his uncle's hands, pulled the tape and tucked it into its plastic case. "What's the next move, Uncle Pat? Now that you know what actually happened to Billy Sowell."

"I've been thinking about that for the last two days." Patrick Blake's features finally relaxed. "And I can't see a sure thing anywhere."

"I'll settle for the kind of public disclosure that'll take the heat off Kosinski. At this point, that's the *only* point." He hesitated, as if resolving his intentions for the first time. "Once the evidence is out there, Harrah has nothing to gain by attacking my partner. It's really that simple."

Patrick Blake grunted, shifted his weight, took a sheet of paper from his jacket pocket and passed it to his nephew. "Marcus Fletcher is an Assistant DA. Those are his office and home phone numbers."

"Did you speak to him about the case?"

"No, Marty, I didn't."

"Then what's the point?"

"Marcus Fletcher is black, a law-and-order freak, and very, very ambitious. Robert Morgenthau, the District Attorney, is an old man. The city's changing, Marty, and everybody with half a brain knows it. All Fletcher needs is a little publicity to light the fuse on his political rocket. The feeling, in the job, is that he likes prosecuting cops, but, me, I think he's on some kind of a religious crusade. I sat next to him at one of the Mayor's fund-raisers and all he talked about was moral pollution. Movies, TV, rap music, the schools, the liberals . . . there was no end to it."

"Yeah, well, I'll keep him in mind." Blake tucked the sheet of paper in his pocket. Despite a lingering paranoia, he couldn't bring himself to believe that Patrick Blake would set him up. Not with his mother watching. "Tell me something, Uncle Pat. Did you come in through the front door?"

"Of course."

"Of course?"

"Get to the point, Marty."

"The point is that you've been off the street too long. Harrah's got a surveillance van parked outside. Your visit tonight will not go unnoticed." Blake watched the blood drain from his uncle's face. "Remember what I told you last time, Uncle Pat. You cut off the head and the body dies."

Satisfied with his exit line, Blake pecked his mother on the cheek, then returned to his car without further comment. He drove to a drug store on Queens Boulevard, made a dozen copies of Gurp Patel's report, stocked up on basic toiletries, manila envelopes, and yellow legal pads. From there, he made his way down the boulevard to a discount appliance store in Rego Park where he bought a dual cassette deck and ten blank tapes. His last stop, a Gap store in the Queens Mall, yielded jeans, two oversized Hawaiian shirts, underwear, and socks.

Back in his room at the Adriatic Motel, he opened the windows as if to rid the space of Bell Kosinski's ghost, then sat down to work. He popped the tape of McGuire's confession and a blank cassette into the recorder, set the controls for hi-speed copying, watched the reels spin for a moment before turning to the yellow legal pad on the small desk.

He wrote steadily for the next two hours, pausing only to change tapes, making draft after draft until he was satisfied that what he'd written would spur some reporter somewhere into action. If worse came to worse, he was prepared to do a mass mailing to the ten nastiest columnists in New York. His mental list included the likes of Jimmy Breslin, Jack Neufield, Sheryl McCarthy, Amy Pagnozzi, Peter Noel, and William Bastone. Others would follow. Surely one of them . . .

He picked up the pad and read the opening paragraph for the fiftieth time.

On November 27, 1991, Sondra Tillson, a New York City resident, was brutally murdered. Her throat was slashed and her body left in a car near Gramercy Park. On December 12, 1991, William Sowell, a retarded man with a proven IQ of 68, confessed to the crime. The enclosed material will prove that the actual killer, Edward Green, Borough President of Manhattan, conspired with Chief Samuel Harrah, head of the Intelligence Division of the New York City Police Department, and Supreme Court Judge John McGuire, now dead by his own hand, to frame William Sowell.

As a hook, he concluded, it wasn't bad. He tried to picture Jimmy Breslin reading those words, then tossing the entire package into a wastebasket, but the image wouldn't materialize. Breslin would act all right—out of fear that one of his competitors would beat him to the story, if for no other reason—but the process would be tedious. Every fact would have to be checked, including Blake's later assertion that the voice on the tape belonged to John McGuire. In the meantime, there'd be less and less reason for Samuel Harrah to hold himself in check.

Blake pushed himself away from the desk and began to pack. He'd rented the room in his own name, though he'd paid for it in cash. Harrah could find him simply by assigning a dozen men to work the phone book. It was time to move.

On his way out, he grabbed the phone and dialed Rebecca Webber's number. When she picked up on the third ring, he smiled to himself. She wasn't due back for another three days.

"Rebecca, it's Marty Blake."

"Marty." Her voice was light and sexy at the same time, a seemingly impossible combination that had Marty Blake salivating like Pavlov's dog at the sound of a dinner bell. "I flew back early."

"This I already figured."

"To be with you," she concluded, ignoring the sarcasm. "It's been a long time."

"Almost two weeks." He paused. "I was expecting to speak to Sarah." Sixty-year-old Sarah Thomas was Rebecca's personal servant.

"What about? You're not having an affair, are you?"

"Would that make you jealous? Or turn you on?" Blake visualized Rebecca's quick smile, wondered if she was actually thinking it over. "Look, Rebecca, I don't have a lot of time. Stay away from my apartment. It's being watched and I won't be there anyway."

"Are you in trouble, Marty?"

"Trouble isn't the word for it." He paused, tried to think of a word that actually described his situation. *Fucked* came to mind, followed by *desperate*, followed by *stupid*. "Look, I have to go."

"If you need a place to hide, you could stay here. With me."

"What happened to William?"

"He's still in Germany."

"And you're back."

She hesitated for a moment. "It was grubby, so grubby. Seedy aristocrats; miserable, violent workers; refugees huddled in collapsing tenements; pensioners begging in the street. I . . ." She stopped again, managed a short, bitter laugh. "If I have to have an ancestral home, I'll take the Rainbow Room."

"Good choice."

"Does that mean you're coming to me?"

The Last Temptation of Marty Blake: strike a deal with Harrah, then lose himself in Rebecca's flesh. He could taste the soft hollow in her throat, the salty moisture beneath her breasts, feel the grip of her thighs, the insistent, demanding thrust of her hips. If he walked away now . . . If he walked away now, he'd be free of her.

"I can't, Rebecca." To his own disgust, he sounded like a whipped puppy instead of the free and independent man he'd just imagined. "I have to see it through."

"I don't understand. What does one thing have to do with the other?"

From her point of view, he supposed, the question was reasonable. Or, at least, he didn't have a ready answer that would take less than two or three years to communicate.

"Listen, Marty, we're not without influence in this city." The words came quickly, smoothly. "William is very close to the Borough President, Edward Green."

Blake choked back a laugh. "That's good to know, Rebecca. Maybe you can pull some strings, put Humpty back together again."

"You're still in one piece, as far as I can tell." Her throaty laugh poured through the receiver. "I'm cold, Marty. I just came out of the shower and I must have put on a few pounds because the towel doesn't seem big enough to keep me warm."

"Try turning down the air conditioner. I've gotta go."

As he made his way through eastern Queens toward La Guardia Airport, Blake considered Marcus Fletcher, the Assistant DA mentioned by his uncle. Patrick Blake had described Fletcher as an ambitious law-and-order freak with a hard-on for the cops. All well and good, but, as far as Blake knew, the investigative staff assigned to the DA's office was composed entirely of NYPD personnel, any of whom might be in Chief Harrah's pocket. Still, as long as he didn't put all his eggs in Fletcher's basket, it was a shot worth taking.

Twenty minutes later, he checked into the Continental Motel on Ditmars Boulevard under the name Martin Reid. The Continental was a step above the dirty-movie motels that dotted Queens, but not such a big step that the clerk bothered to ask identification from a man checking in at three o'clock in the morning. He took Blake's money, handed over the key, went back to the flickering black-and-white television without ever changing expression.

Inside his room, Blake quickly addressed one of the manila envelopes to his uncle, stuffed it with Gurp Patel's report, his own letter, and a copy of McGuire's tape, then sealed it. Tomorrow, when he put it in the mail, it would serve two purposes. If his uncle decided to take his comment about the head and the body seriously, if he decided that Samuel Harrah, defanged, could do less damage to his career than Samuel Harrah, enthroned, he might just pass the material on to Marcus Fletcher. Even if he didn't, he'd have the evidence in hand. Maybe, if his nephew met a sad fate on the streets of New York, he'd act out of conscience. Maybe Dora Blake would make him.

TWENTY-ONE

By nine the next morning, Marty Blake had showered, shaved, dressed, and was out the door. It was September 1, a Saturday, and nature, as if noting the end of the traditional summer season, had thrown a rare early fall day at the city of New York. The temperature was twenty degrees cooler than it had been on the prior morning (this without benefit of rain, a second miracle). A few thick white clouds marched briskly across a deep blue sky, the air smelled clean and crisp, even the litter on the street, polished by the sun, failed to offend.

Blake, caught off guard, paused for a moment to collect his bearings. Like every other citizen, he'd been fighting nature all through the dog days of August. Now a sharp breeze cut through his light cotton shirt, curled the hairs on his chest, puckered his nipples.

"Chilly day, mister. Winter's comin'. You got any spare change?"

Blake wasn't surprised by the beggar's ragged appearance, the two ripped trash bags he carried, or even his white skin and blond hair. What shocked him was the panhandler's youth. The boy couldn't have been more than a year or two out of high school, yet he looked more than beaten. He looked like he'd been hammered.

"Yeah, wait a minute." He jammed his hand into the pocket of his new jeans, dug out a quarter, and dutifully passed it over. "Wish me luck, man," he said. "Earn your money."

The boy looked up at Blake for the first time. His light blue eyes, though devoid of hostility or aggression, were reproachful, announcing that citizens who could afford a roof and three squares a day didn't need luck. They didn't need it because they already had it.

"Good luck, sir. Thank you, sir." He turned, dropped his eyes to the sidewalk and shuffled away.

Blake watched him for a moment, then crossed the street to a small delicatessen in the middle of the block. Inside, he ordered a regular coffee and a toasted corn muffin, stood back to wait for his order,

glanced down at the headline of the *New York Post*: EX-COP
WHACKED IN WHITESTONE.

Blake grabbed the paper, opened it to page three, and began to read
the body of the story. The ex-cop named in the headline was not Bell
Kosinski. That was the good news. The bad news was that Bell Kosinski
had been charged with second-degree murder and was now in Bellevue
Hospital's prison ward. His condition was described as critical.

The dead ex-cop, whose Buick had meandered half a block before
crashing into a parked car, was named Anthony Carabone. In 1989,
he'd sold a gram of cocaine to an Internal Affairs precinct spy. His
felony indictment had eventually been plea bargained down to a misdemeanor and he'd been sentenced to five years supervised probation,
but his job, of course, had been lost forever.

"A drug deal gone bad," was how Detective Hank Norris had
described the shoot-out to the reporter covering the story. He'd gone
on to say that a third, apparently wounded man, had fled the scene
and was being sought.

"Hey, buddy."

Blake looked up at the counterman. "What'd you say?"

"Your order's ready."

"How much?"

"A buck seventy-five. With the paper."

Blake took the bag and the newspaper back to his car. Inside, he
read the story over and over again, trying to glean some piece of information that didn't have Bell Kosinski lying helpless in a locked prison
ward. When he finally understood that he couldn't will his partner out
of harm's way, he felt the last pieces of the puzzle click into place.

He drove into La Guardia Airport, parked by the Delta Terminal,
and went in search of an indoor pay phone. The first step was to buy
Kosinski a little time and the best way to do that was to offer himself.
He got the phone number of the Intelligence Division from the phone
book, reached the switchboard operator, and asked for Samuel Harrah.
A minute later, Harrah's secretary, a very male cop named O'Brien,
fielded his request to speak directly to the Chief.

"About what?"

"About an ex-cop whacked in Whitestone."

"I think you want Homicide."

Blake took a deep breath, reminded himself to control his temper.
"Is Chief Harrah in his office?"

"It's Saturday."

"That's not what I asked you."

It was O'Brien's turn to hesitate. "Yeah, he's in." The admission was grudging.

"You tell him that Marty Blake is on the phone. Tell him if he doesn't wanna speak to me now, I won't be calling back. This is his first, last, and only chance."

After several minutes of silence, Blake heard a familiar voice.

"Whatta ya want, Blake?"

"Grogan?"

"*Inspector* Grogan."

Blake smiled, thinking the great man, Samuel Harrah, remained as anonymous as ever.

"I'll make it short and sweet, Grogan. In about two hours, you're gonna receive a package by messenger, some written material and a tape recording. I'd advise you to read the material and listen to the tape very closely, because your fat ass depends on it. My feeling is that we can do business, but not if my partner dies. You understand what I'm saying here? Kosinski is part of the deal. If he goes, you go. I'll be in touch."

An hour later, the package dropped at a messenger service in Flushing, Blake parked the rented Nissan in a lot on Hillside Avenue and walked down the block to the Jamaica library. Inside, he located a copy of *Who's Who In New York*. Chief Samuel Harrah's profile included the names of his wife, Margaret, his two sons and a single sibling, a brother. The sons, George and Owen, were both attorneys. The brother was dead. A Manhattan telephone directory provided office addresses for the two lawyers.

On impulse, Blake turned to the library's computerized periodical files and located a *Daily News* story on the NYPD's Intelligence Division. The story, written in 1989 and stored on microfilm, included a blurred photograph of Chief Samuel Harrah standing behind Mayor Ed Koch and Commissioner Benjamin Ward. Blake stared down at the photo, looking for some sign of malevolence (horns, perhaps, or at least a wicked leer), but the carefully composed features, the small eyes, pug nose, slightly receding chin, remained unthreatening. Samuel Harrah looked like any other man approaching his senior years. Like any other man looking forward to retirement and his grandchildren.

It was only a few blocks to Gurp Patel's headquarters on Liberty Avenue. On the way, Blake considered what he'd do if Patel wasn't in his office. Fortunately, what he'd do if Patel had taken the weekend off was the same thing he'd do if Patel had disappeared off the face of the Earth. Eternal Memorials, in defiance of its name, was gone; nothing remained, not even the sign. A Buildings Department form, glued to the front door, announced that the very building had been condemned.

Blake turned away from the empty building, saw two boys walking along the sidewalk, stopped them on impulse.

"Do you boys live around here?" he asked.

"I ain't no boy," the taller of the two replied fiercely.

"Ain't no boy," the younger one echoed.

Blake grinned for the first time in weeks. The older boy came up to his waist, the younger seemed just out of the toddler stage.

"I stand corrected," he said. "Do you *gentlemen* live around here?"

"You the po-lease?"

"The po-lease."

Blake shook his head. "Not a cop, a businessman. I had an appointment with the people in this building, but they seem to have disappeared."

"Yeah," the younger boy exclaimed, "we seen it. A . . ."

"Shut up, Marcus." The older boy, jaw set, legs apart, stared defiantly at Blake. "We ain't the public library, mister. Public library's free."

Blake dug a five-dollar bill out of his pocket and held it up for inspection.

"Ain't enough. It's gonna cost ya twenty."

"Yeah, twenty."

"Forget it, kids. I'm not that curious." He shook the bill. "Going once, going twice . . ."

"Okay, man, we tell ya." The older boy snatched the bill out of Blake's hand. "We're unemployed," he announced. "That's why I'm doin' it."

"Unemployed from what grammar school?"

The boy ignored the question. "Yesterday morning two trucks pulled up here. Me and Marcus, we seen 'em on the way to school. One was the kinda truck that moves furniture. The other was a big motherfucker. Long, with no top on it."

"A flatbed?" Blake asked.

"Don't know what it's called, but if you gon' be interruptin' me, I gotta get paid for my time." The boy waited long enough to make his point, then continued. "They was still here when we come back home, so we stopped to watch. The stones went on the big truck. Had a machine to bring 'em out. The office stuff went in the van. They was still workin' when we left."

"Any cops around?"

"Not that I seen."

"How about a computer?"

"Don't know, man. A lotta that stuff was in crates. Look, me and Marcus gotta go. We ain't home for lunch, Pop's gonna come lookin'."

Blake watched the boys for a minute, then went back to his car and drove to an outdoor pay phone. He dialed Patel's number, let the phone ring thirty times, finally hung up. Patel and his computer were gone, but the legend, the mystery, was still growing. He smiled to himself, touched the automatic tucked beneath his belt, imagined putting it up against Joanna Bardo's skull. It wasn't the most unpleasant fantasy he'd ever had, but it wasn't the answer, either.

As he made his way through the slums of South Jamaica, a procession of unwelcome thoughts flashed through Blake's mind. Irrelevant and useless, from his point of view, their power was nonetheless irresistible. He should not have allowed Kosinski to expose himself, should have worked up a contingency plan (like, for instance, the one he'd come with now) to keep his partner behind locked doors. At the very least, he could have kept Max Steinberg's defection to himself. That would have bought Kosinski an extra couple of days.

But, of course, Bell Kosinski was his partner and his friend, an adult and not a child. Lying to him for his own good was nearly as repulsive as the image of his broken body sprawled on a Whitestone sidewalk. Besides, there was no way Blake could have anticipated the lawyer's cop-out. Hadn't Steinberg lectured them on how careful he was to stay on the right side of the law? But, at the same time, the lawyer had also reserved the right to desert the ship, a possibility that should have been factored into the equation. Instead, Blake had just assumed that Steinberg would come through.

Bad mistake, Blake thought. Almost *fatal* mistake.

It was the "almost" part that made it so hard. Blake had prepared himself for the worst, but not for the "almost" worst. Kosinski dead gave him all the time he needed. Time to prepare a scenario that left him unscathed, time to put it into effect, time to plan a revenge that wasn't tantamount to suicide. Kosinski alive, on the other hand, demanded immediate action, conferred obligations that couldn't be put off in the name of self-preservation.

Honor is what it is, he told himself. There's no other word for it. And it has nothing to do with the penal code or the Ten Commandments. Honor is self-taught; it's not sitting out there on a pair of stone tablets. It's not created by politicians, either. You know it when you feel it and not before. If you ignore it . . . Well, my father tried that one and it didn't really work out for him.

He stared out through the windshield, swept the sidewalk as if searching for Kosinski's body as he made the turn from Forty-eighth Street onto Barnett Avenue. A hundred yards into the block, he pulled to the shoulder, shut down the engine, stared across the street at the new home of Joanna Bardo's exiled bounty hunters. And at the man sitting on the motorcycle parked in front.

Woodside Investigations looked more like a hideout than a home. Stuffed into a one-story brick building between Jane and John's Used Auto Parts and AAAAAAAAA (WE'RE FIRST IN THE PHONE BOOK) EXTERMINATORS, it was a long way from the determined ambience of Manhattan Executive's corporate offices. The differences seemed almost deliberate.

Blake, of course, knew that the bail bondsmen who used Vinnie Cappolino and Walter Francis didn't give a damn about abstractions like ambience. Why should they? Out anywhere between twenty and two hundred thousand dollars, what they wanted was the Terminator. Vinnie Cappolino may not have been Arnold Schwarzenegger, but you couldn't really tell the difference by looking. The black leather vest, the military-green T-shirt, the greasy jeans, the stripped-down Harley-Davidson . . . as far as Vinnie was concerned, the movies were imitating *him*.

"That you, Marty Blake?"

Blake stared at the figure on the motorcycle for a moment before replying. He and Cappolino had gotten into it once, both mean-drunk, both anxious to resolve months of verbal jousting. The fight had quickly degenerated into utter savagery, into kicking, biting, gouging, a contest of wills that'd ended in a thoroughly unsatisfying draw.

"Yeah," Blake said, "it's me."

Cappolino got off the Harley, stretched his tall, wiry frame, then walked over to Blake's Nissan.

"Got a phone call about you."

"From Joanna?"

A grin split Cappolino's narrow mouth, revealing a set of tiny, yellow teeth. "The one and only. Told me you was on the shit list. Wha'd ya do, boy? You forget to curtsy?"

"Yeah. I forgot to kiss her liposuctioned butt." Blake stared into Cappolino's black eyes. "I need some information, Vinnie, and I need it fast. Tax returns mostly."

"You got money?" Vinnie Cappolino, his smile now curled into a triumphant smirk, leaned down into the window. "See, what happened is that Walter up and married an accountant name of Linda Horstmann. Linda runs a tight ship, Marty. No freebies is where she's comin' from. Just for the fuck of it don't work no more."

TWENTY-TWO

It ain't the beeps, Kosinski thought, or the green television with the spiked line moving across the screen. It's not the cast across my chest, or the tube where my throat used to be, or the hiss of the respirator, or how cold it feels when they put the new blood in. The dope takes care of all that, the dope and not movin' a muscle.

He felt like he was floating in his own personal lake, a lake with no horizons, a lake of morphine. The objects in his room—including the sharp burst of pain following any shift of his body—were little more than fellow travelers, vessels adrift in the darkness. They might disappear at any time, simply vanish, leaving him to the warm, enveloping waters.

I don't know why I wasted my whole life on booze, he thought, when I could've become a degenerate junkie.

It was supposed to be funny, but his thoughts seemed as far away as the IV pole with its dangling plastic bag or the metal bedpan on the small table next to the bed.

Thank God for the snake, he said to himself, the snake in paradise. If it wasn't for that snake, I wouldn't have any reality at all.

The snake lived in the circular steel lock on the metal door at the other end of the room. He made a sound, the snake, whenever he was disturbed by a turning key, a sharp, metallic snap that echoed in the small space, cutting through the morphine, the pain.

"Just a little blood," the male nurse announced. He paused at the foot of the bed, as if expecting an answer. Kosinski tried to oblige, couldn't produce more than a hoarse croak. Not with half his throat torn away, his jaw splintered.

"Now, now, don't you try to talk. You're goin' for an operation."

The nurse probed at Kosinski's right wrist for a moment, then raised a bloody plastic vial in triumph. "Got the good hands," he bragged. "Velvet fingers. You ready for a pain shot?"

When Kosinski nodded, a bolt of fire (which he should have anticipated) shot from his jaw into his brain, leaving him dizzy and disoriented. The morphine brought him all the way back, running into every cell in his body. Smoothing the wrinkles. He knew that any one of the hourly injections might contain a lethal dose, had attended the bodies of overdosed junkies hundreds of times.

Hell, he thought, every junkie's seen another junkie die. It doesn't stop 'em, doesn't even slow 'em down. Why should I be different?

He closed his eyes, felt his mind light up with dreams, images from the past that, no matter how gruesome, entertained him. He saw small charred bodies scattered about the top floor of a crumbling tenement; the boy in the closet, chained there for days at a time by his crack-addicted parents; a stripper-whore at a department racket bouncing from lap to lap; a dusty photograph in a black metal frame, a wedding photo taken in Berlin. He stared at the photo for a moment, held it in his mind. The soldier, a goofy smile plastered to his face, looked back at him; the blond woman stared off into space.

I should have known!

The words echoed in the empty spaces—*should have known, should have known, should have known, should have known*. They repeated until he realized they were coming from Marty Blake's mouth.

Kosinski opened his eyes, looked around. The room was empty.

Well, he concluded, it doesn't matter whether Marty Blake should have known or not. Knowing doesn't have shit to do with it.

He closed his eyes again, saw his wife, Ingrid. She'd grown up in the hell of post-WWII Berlin, told of crawling through the rubble in search of food, her older sisters trading themselves for canned hams, sacks of sugar.

Knowing doesn't have shit to do with it, he repeated.

A key turned in the lock, roused the snake until he shouted his annoyance. Kosinski wondered if it was time for another injection. Could an hour have gone by? Maybe they were coming to get him ready for his operation. Or for new X rays.

He saw Tommy Brannigan standing in the open doorway and thought, Or maybe they don't like me any more.

Brannigan closed the door, walked over, stared into his eyes. "It's always sad when partners part," he said.

Kosinski wanted to answer. He framed a number of snappy comebacks, selected, "You can't get more together than this." But when he tried to speak, all he managed was an odd hum: *uhhhhhhhhhhhhhhhhhh-hh*. The sound struck him as purely mechanical, a complement, really, to the regular hiss of the respirator as it pumped life into his body.

"Can't talk?" Brannigan shook his head. "Too bad, too bad." He sat on the edge of the bed, folded his arms. "But maybe we can work something out. Maybe worse doesn't have to come to worst. If you understand what I'm sayin', blink once."

Kosinski took a minute to think it over, then blinked eight times, the comatose man's version of a snappy comeback. Brannigan shrugged, then nodded.

"How did I know?" he asked before slapping Kosinski in the face.

The pain was ferocious, a rabid animal gnawing its way through his skull. It ate until it was no longer hungry, until Kosinski could open his eyes, see through the tears, hear Tommy Brannigan's soft laughter.

"Somehow I think I already know how you're gonna answer this question, but let's do it again for the record. If you understand me, blink once."

Kosinski wanted to say, That's not a question. Instead, he blinked once.

"Good." Brannigan stood up, began to pace the room. "Christ, what a mess. Look at yourself, Bell. Look what you did to yourself. I'm not gonna ask you why because you couldn't answer anyway, but you still oughta think about it. I mean in these last few minutes of your miserable fucking life."

But there was nothing to think about. There were no moves to be made, no maneuvers, no manipulations; Bell Kosinski was absolutely helpless. Not that he minded all that much. Not that he was surprised. The way he figured it, he'd already gotten more than his share of extra time. He'd already gotten his fifteen minutes and the rest was pure gravy.

"See," Brannigan explained, "it's not about good guys and bad guys. That's because the good guys don't exist. Good guys are something bad guys made up to keep the assholes in line. Ya know what I'm sayin' here, Bell? Bad guys and assholes, that's what it's all about." He came back to the bed, examined the IV tube, then sat down. "We can't seem to find your partner, Bell. Marty Blake, he's disappeared. That scares us. I mean the lawyer's up in his office bein' a good boy. You know—thinkin' up new ways to screw the system. But your buddy . . . it's like he dropped off the face of the Earth and what I gotta know is this: Is Marty Blake the same kind of asshole you are? Blink once for yes, twice for no."

Kosinski blinked twice, wondering if the lie would show on his face.

"And you don't know where he is, either?"

Kosinski blinked once, steeled himself against the pain, felt his head explode.

It took a long time. That was the most Bell Kosinski could say when it was finally over. He was aware of drifting into and out of consciousness, of blinking again and again, of maintaining the lie. He was standing up for Marty Blake, of course, but there was more to it than that. How could he live out his whole life only to cave in to a piece of shit like Tommy Brannigan at the very end? Nobody who knew him would buy it, not at any price.

"All right, Bell. I didn't think it would work, but I got bosses that don't know you." Brannigan rose, fished a syringe out of his jacket pocket, held it up for inspection. "Know what this is?"

Kosinski wanted to say, A pain shot, how thoughtful.

"It's potassium. Like comes in bananas. Only when you inject a lot of it at one time, it stops the heart in its tracks. Boom! Just like that." He uncapped the syringe. "It metabolizes so fast that it's hard to find even in the test tube, but the best part is that you can't tell anything from looking. You been there, Bell, so you know exactly what I'm talkin' about. The ME's gonna take out your heart, examine it and say, 'Kosinski's heart gave up the ghost due to trauma from multiple gun-shot wounds.' Or words to that effect. Me, I think it's too good for you. I told Crogan, 'This guy deserves to die hard. Let's give 'em . . .'"

A sharp knock at the door interrupted Brannigan's soliloquy. He re-capped the syringe, stuck it in his pocket, called out, "What the fuck do you want?"

The door opened slightly and a uniformed correction officer stuck his head into the room. "You got a phone call. The man says it's impor-tant, says I should interrupt. You can take it right here in the hall."

Kosinski didn't try to raise his head, didn't dare. But he could hear well enough.

First Brannigan said, "Brannigan," into the phone, then there was a long pause, then he said, "Sorry, Chief, it's too late. I was just leavin'." Then he hung up.

"Nothin' but headaches, right, Bell? The fuckin' silks never wanna give you room to operate." The door slammed shut as Brannigan strode back into the room. All business, he uncapped the syringe, jammed it into a port on the IV line, depressed the plunger.

The last thing Bela Kosinski felt was surprise. Surprise at how stu-pid he'd been not to have grasped the truth long before this. Because the truth—and he had to admit it—was that he'd loved it all along. Every day, every minute. He'd loved it and he couldn't get it back.

TWENTY-THREE

"A check?" Vinnie Cappolino's long, horsey face curled into a petulant frown. He looked, to Marty Blake, like a child denied a birthday wish. "It's Saturday. The banks don't open till Monday. What if the check's no good?"

"You think I'd bounce a check on you, Vinnie?"

"In a fuckin' heartbeat." Cappolino's fingers traced the long narrow scar on his forehead, then ran the length of his flattened nose. "Face it, Marty, for what you got in mind there's no tomorrow."

Blake nodded agreement, tried to laugh, failed. "What could I say? When you're right, you're right. I *would* lie, if that's what it took, but in this case I don't have to. The money's there." He paused, then smiled. "Vinnie, we both know you're gonna charge me five times what the job's worth. High risks go with high rewards. That's the way the game is played."

"You got a point, but . . . see, Marty, when Linda first came to work for us—before she and Walter got married—she sat us down and explained what bein' a mercenary is all about. After she finished, I knew what I was for the first time. I'm a whore, Marty. I don't spread my legs unless I get paid for it." He let his jaw drop onto his chest, pointed at the bald spot on the back of his head. "Plus I'm thirty-three years old and I gotta worry about my future. I'm not gettin' any younger."

The solution was simple, if painful. Blake had just over six thousand dollars in his checking account, most of it Steinberg's money. Vinnie, once he knew the balance, would take it all.

"How 'bout this," Blake said. "How 'bout we find an ATM and check the account balance. If I don't have enough to cover your fee, you can just walk away."

Cappolino's dark eyes glistened. Blake tried for a read, couldn't decide whether he saw mischief or satisfaction.

"What about the bank card?" Vinnie asked. "You could pull out five hundred bucks a day. That *could* leave me fifteen hundred short. Depending on how much you got in the account."

"I'll tear up the card."

Cappolino sat back in his swivel chair, rocked for a moment, then put his feet on the desk. "Yeah, that might be okay. Only, if ya don't mind, let's break it down into three smaller checks. In case someone beats me to the bank on Monday morning. Now, whatta ya say we get down to the details?"

Blake pulled the list out of his shirt pocket and passed it over. "I want federal tax returns for the first four, home addresses and phone numbers for the other two. If any of the returns show income from a privately held corporation, I want the corporate filings as well."

"I can get the addresses in a couple of minutes, but I can't do the tax returns here." He ran his finger down the list of names. "Gotta send it out. Gotta get social security numbers, too."

"Where you do it doesn't interest me. Fast is what I'm after. Like tonight."

"No problem. Anything else?"

"Yeah, a set of picks and some tools. Chisels, hammer, screwdrivers, volt meter, wire cutters—you know the routine."

Cappolino spread his hands. "That shit I got right here in the office. What else?"

"Firepower, Vinnie. Like I already said, I don't know how many people are gonna come after me, but it won't be one on one."

"You familiar with automatic weapons? Ever work an M40?"

"Hell, man, I don't even know what an M40 is."

"Marty, if computers shot lightning bolts, you'd be Dirty Harry." He chortled happily. "But I do have a little piece that fits your abilities one hundred percent. This is all gonna happen in a small space, right?"

"Right."

Cappolino got up, still grinning, and strolled into a back room. A moment later, he came back with a pistol-grip shotgun and two boxes of shells.

"It's a Benelli M3, semiautomatic, fires as fast as you can pull the trigger. Holds seven, 12-gauge rounds."

"Will it penetrate a vest?"

"Now, that's the beauty of it, Marty." He held up the ammo for Blake's inspection. "These bad boys are loaded with fléchettes. Picture them as little arrows, little flesh eaters. The only thing that'll stop these babies is bone. When they hit bone, they distort and ricochet. The rounds are packed twenty fléchettes to the shell. They came to me by way of a juicehead master sergeant at the Tobyhanna Army Depot."

Blake picked up the shotgun. He was surprised at the soft grip; he'd expected wood or a hardened plastic, but the pebbled surface molded beneath his fingers.

"Don't worry about sighting it," Cappolino explained. "In a small room, all you gotta do is pull the trigger and hold on. At ten yards, she'll throw a fifteen-inch pattern. You can't miss."

Blake worked the pump, nodded once. "How much, Vinnie? For the package."

"Well . . ."

"Why don't we save some time here? I've got a little over six thousand dollars in my checking account. And that's *all* I've got."

"Six grand?" Cappolino flashed his petulant frown again. "I was thinkin' more like fifteen."

"Six, Vinnie. And don't bullshit me because I know you're not putting out more than two, even if you paid full retail for the shotgun, which you didn't." When Cappolino hesitated, Blake shifted into his first outright lie of the conversation. "Look, the *only* reason I came to you is because I'm in a big hurry. But if I have to, I'll shift my plans, take my time, put it together on my own."

"Awright, awright." Cappolino dropped the frown. "Christ, you were always a prick, Marty. What you oughta do is grow up. Like I did."

Blake rolled down the Nissan's window as he drove along Northern Boulevard toward the Fifty-ninth-Street Bridge. He leaned his head into the cool rushing air, took a deep breath, decided that congratulations were in order. Congratulations for a decision he'd made years before. In the mid-Eighties, the S&Ls and the banks had mailed preapproved credit-card applications to virtually anyone who already owned a credit card. Blake had kept seven, had been sure to use each of them at least once a year. He'd seen them as an insurance policy, a quick fix for life's little emergencies. Now, he felt like a prophet. If it wasn't for the cards, he'd be dead in the water.

It took him the better part of an hour to negotiate the five miles to his destination, the Surveillance Shop, on First Avenue and Sixty-first

Street. Most of the lanes on the bridge were closed for construction, as they had been for nearly fifteen years. The traffic came as no surprise, but that didn't mean the delay wasn't torture for a man in a hurry. By the time Blake parked his car and walked into the store, he was ready to bite the head off a New York City rat.

"Charlie," he told the proprietor, Charles Baumann, "if you don't have what I want in stock, you've got three hours to get it."

"In three hours I'll be closed, Blake. It's Saturday and I got things to do." Baumann's sour expression never changed. His watery brown eyes were squeezed down into a permanent squint, a reaction perhaps to the cigarette smoke curling up from the corner of his mouth. Or to forty years in the sleaze business.

"You're lookin' at fifteen grand here. Easy." Blake noted the spark of interest, pressed on. "There's no tomorrow on this, Charlie. You can't do it today, I'll get the hardware from somebody else." It was the same threat he'd used on Vinnie Cappolino.

"What you want, it's legal?"

"Catalog material."

Baumann nodded, lit another cigarette. "How you gonna pay, Blake? Bein' as the only bulge on your body is comin' from the automatic you got tucked behind your belt."

"Plastic."

"*Your* plastic?"

Blake took out his wallet, dumped three credit cards on the glass counter top. "Look for yourself."

Baumann did exactly that, holding them, one at a time, under a small, powerful magnifying glass. When he was satisfied, he set the cards down, squinted at Blake for a moment.

"Okay," he finally said, "whatta ya need?"

Blake ticked off the items one at a time, watched Charlie Baumann write them down, watched him nod his head. Was he counting inventory or dollars? Blake couldn't make up his mind.

"I got everything you need out in the Jersey City store," Baumann said when the list was complete. "Take about an hour to get it here. But the video transmitter you want isn't gonna happen—long range is for cops only. I could supply you a system goes out about five hundred feet. More than that, you gotta go elsewhere."

"You couldn't make an exception? Being as I'm an old and valued customer." Blake tried on his sweetest smile.

"Forget about it." Baumann shook his head, folded the list, stuffed it into his shirt pocket. "Not for plastic, Marty. When you pay with plastic, you gotta go by the book. Plastic don't allow for denial."

Out on the street, Blake found a pay phone, called the *New York Post*, and asked for Herbert Coen, the reporter who's byline appeared above the "Whacked in Whitestone" story. He was put through to the city room where he repeated his request.

"Coen's on the toilet."

"I'll hold."

"Suit yourself, pal."

Five long minutes later, a sharp voice announced, "Coen."

"You the Coen who wrote the story on the two Whitestone cops?"

"The one and only."

"Well, you got it all wrong, buddy. The cops fed you a bullshit story about drugs and you wrote it down like you were taking dictation."

"What'd you say your name was?"

"I didn't."

Blake absorbed the ensuing silence, refused to break it. Coen was thinking it over, wondering if the story justified enduring Blake's attitude. That was just fine. Coen wouldn't take the bait unless he was hungry.

"Why don't you tell me what really happened?"

"Not over the phone."

"Gimme a break, pal. I got better things to do than jump through your hoops."

Time to throw the poor doggie a bone. Time to set the hook.

"It's about murder and blackmail, Coen. About documents and a tape recording. You remember the judge who committed suicide a few days ago?"

"John McGuire?"

"He's right in the middle."

Coen drew a deep breath. "Where do you want to meet?"

"There's a diner, the Pioneer, on the West Side Highway below the tunnel. Half an hour."

"Look, I'm in the middle of . . ."

Blake hung up, found his car, and headed downtown. He took the long way, tracing the eastern edge of Manhattan to the Battery, then curling back up what was left of the old West Side Highway. As he drove, he tried to concentrate on his successes—his deals with Cappolino and Baumann, his appointment with Coen—and not on the gamble he'd taken. If he had more time, he'd be going about it differently. He didn't and that was that.

Inside the Pioneer, Blake took a table and ordered coffee and a hamburger. He was on his second cup when Herbert Coen walked through the door. Short and wiry, the reporter's long, narrow face was saved from comparison with a rat's by the sharp intelligence in his eyes. Blake, as he waved Coen over, decided that he looked like a hungry weasel.

Coen slid into the booth opposite Blake. "You got a lotta balls here, pal," he announced. "This better be good." A waitress appeared with a menu. Coen ordered coffee and waved her away.

"It's better than your freakiest wet dream." Blake emptied the contents of a manila envelope—the one he'd planned to mail to his uncle—onto the table. He picked up the cover letter, handed it to Coen, waited until the reporter finished reading, then passed over the rest of the paperwork. "These are records of incorporation and dissolution for Landsman Properties. You'll note that Alan Green, father of Manhattan Borough President Edward Green, is Landsman's sole shareholder. The deeds show Landsman's purchase and resale of the Long Island City property to Johan Tillson, husband of Sondra Tillson. I don't have time to play the tape, but I guarantee that it's *not* ambiguous."

Blake sat back, took a bite of his hamburger, followed it with the dregs in the bottom of his coffee cup. He was enjoying his own confidence as well as the dramatics. Coen was drooling like a dog over a slice of roast beef, but that didn't mean his publisher would actually print the story—there was no way of knowing how far or how deep Harrah could reach. Still, it was as good as he was going to get. It was what he'd set out to do. "You wouldn't consider telling me your name?"

"Marty Blake."

"And your interest here?"

Blake sighed, took another bite of his hamburger. "Hope you don't mind," he mumbled. "I haven't eaten all day."

Coen nodded. "Okay, so it's none of my business."

"Plus, I don't have the time to get into it." Blake swallowed. "Sometime soon, probably within twenty-four hours, I'm gonna have a lot more paperwork. If you're interested."

"I'm interested."

"That's good, because eventually I'll be sending the package you're holding to other reporters. What you've got, Coen, is a head start. It wouldn't pay for you to sit on your lead."

"Any more advice?"

Blake shook his head. "I need a drop for the rest of the material. Not the *Post*."

Coen scribbled his address on the back of a business card. "I'll try to have somebody there for the next couple of days, but you can always leave a package with the doorman." He stared at Blake for a moment, then came to a decision. "Look, this story could mean a lot to me."

"Yeah, it's a definite career maker. There's a book in it, too."

"But the people you name here . . . face it, if I go in half-assed, I'll end up writing a gossip column in Chickenfart, Iowa. There's no way I can take the story to my editor until I document the facts."

Blake pictured Kosinski in his hospital bed, wondered if he could wait until Coen finished checking, decided that it didn't matter because it wasn't going to come to that. Coen, if he came through, would play the role of historian.

"The deeds, the corporate stuff—it's all public record. As for the tape . . . well, you might want to play it for the widow McGuire. See if she likes the sound of her own voice."

Blake took his time getting back uptown, working his way north on Hudson Street, then east on Houston to First Avenue, then back north again. His route took him directly past Bellevue Hospital and he stopped for a moment to stare at the grimy brick, the dirty windows. The life of the hospital was in full gear, people going in and coming out, nurses and the odd intern waiting patiently for the hot-dog vendor, relatives double-parked while other relatives visited. A short Latino woman tended a cart packed with small bouquets of white and pink carnations. There were no roses, no orchids, no birds of paradise. Bellevue was a municipal hospital; those who could afford the exotic took their business elsewhere.

"Awright, let's move it." A black security guard, looking thoroughly bored, made his way along the line of cars. "There's no parking here. Let's move it."

Nobody moved it, nobody turned to look at him. He had no

authority, not even the authority of a summons book, and he knew it. After a few minutes, he turned his back, tossed a belated "mother-fucker" over his shoulder and walked back down the ramp leading to the front doors.

Blake felt a sudden urge to follow, to find his way to the prison ward, to pull Kosinski out of the bed, carry him to safety. He saw the idea as childish, the wish of a toddler who still believes in magic, yet still went so far as to open the car door. He was halfway out when Tommy Brannigan stepped onto the sidewalk.

Blake's first impulse was to flee—not from Brannigan, but from all the nightmare possibilities suggested by his sudden appearance—and he might have done it if the cop hadn't spotted him. If the cop hadn't smiled.

"Hey, Blake, you come to visit your girlfriend?"

Despite the grin (and even from a distance), Brannigan's gaze was narrowed and calculating. Blake walked toward that look as if drawn by a magnet. He stopped three feet away from the cop, stood there without saying a word.

"Too bad about Kosinski. Guess it wasn't his day. He expired."

Brannigan's smirk widened as his hand edged toward the zipper on his windbreaker. Blake returned the smile, let him slide the zipper down, let his hand reach inside before slamming a fist into the cop's solar plexus. Brannigan grunted once and doubled over.

"Guess it's not your day, either."

Blake yanked the automatic out of his belt and slammed it into Brannigan's face. The sound of it the crunch of bone, the cry of pain—pleased him immensely, pleased him so much that he did it again and again and again.

TWENTY-FOUR

By the time Marty Blake arrived at the St. Albans home of Assistant District Attorney Marcus Fletcher, his thoughts were sliding back and forth like Max Steinberg's wig on a bad day in court. Attacking Brannigan made him subject to ordinary arrest for the first time. It transformed Harrah's pack of bent cops into that cop army he'd been fearing all along. Harrah had reached into a New York State prison for Billy Sowell, into a hospital prison ward for Bell Kosinski. There was no reason to believe a New York City jail—the Tombs or Rikers Island—would present him with any problems.

On the other hand, having Blake arrested for assaulting Tommy Brannigan would carry a serious potential for negative consequences. There'd be no way for Harrah to know which cop would do the arresting. Which of them would hear and record Blake's confession. Or that Blake, accompanied by a lawyer and a media representative, wouldn't stroll into the nearest precinct and surrender. If he demanded protection, claimed his life was in danger, he might succeed in putting himself entirely out of Samuel Harrah's reach.

But if he played that card, the correction officers would put him in protective custody which amounted to little more than solitary confinement. Blake had no trouble imagining himself alone in a six-by-eight prison cell, imagining a Samuel Harrah willing to do almost anything to prevent a trial, almost anything to get revenge. If Marty Blake was found hanging from the bars one morning, who'd step up to say it couldn't have been suicide? Max Steinberg? Joanna Bardo?

What he'd finally decided, somewhere between picking up the hardware at the Surveillance Shop, ditching the Nissan in favor of a Chevrolet Caprice in Long Island City, and returning to his motel room to pick up several copies of the material he'd given to Herbert Coen, was that if he couldn't control his thoughts, he'd have to work on his actual behavior. And the best way to do that (without second-guessing every move he made) was to stick with his original agenda.

Blake pulled the car to the curb, flipped the key, listened to the engine cough for a moment before shutting down. The tall black man pushing the lawn mower across the grass didn't look up. Maybe he couldn't hear the Chevy over the din of the lawn mower's engine. Or maybe he just liked to mind his own business. Either way, Blake didn't get a good look at the man's face until he reached the end of his property and turned around.

Blake's first impression was of unyielding strength. The widely spaced eyes, the short, broad nose, the full mouth, sharp jaw, and high, protruding cheekbones fairly screamed determination. But something in the set expression, as if at a specific point in the distant past the man had arranged his features and decided to hold them together by sheer force of will, put Blake off.

At that moment, as if reading Blake's thoughts, the man looked up at the Caprice. Their eyes locked for a moment, long enough for each to know they had business with the other. Then Blake, a manila envelope tucked beneath his arm, stepped out of the car and walked across the lawn.

"Are you Marcus Fletcher?" He stopped several feet away, kept his voice quiet, respectful, considerate.

"I am."

"My name is Marty Blake. I'm sorry to bother you at home on a Saturday, but it can't be helped." He paused, expecting a response, was rewarded with the same stony expression. "I have some information you need to see."

"Wait."

Fletcher continued to scrutinize Blake. He took his time about it, as though he had enough information to make an informed judgment. "If you don't mind, I'd like to bring this inside." He turned, started to walk, tossed a last comment over his shoulder. "I know who you are."

Blake started to follow, stopped abruptly. "Hold it." He waited for Fletcher to turn around. "You spoke to my uncle, that's obvious enough. Who else did you speak to? Who's in the house?"

"My wife is in the house, my wife and my two sons." Fletcher tried for a smile, failed, let his mouth drop back to its original set. "It's not a trap, Mister Blake. If you can prove your allegations, I believe you'll find me a valuable ally."

"Afraid not." Blake, his hand beneath his shirt, began to back up. "Your part in this farce is very minor. In fact, you don't even come into it until after the big climax. So, what I'm gonna do is leave you on the cutting-room floor. Have a nice day."

"Please." Fletcher's eyes widened and his lips dropped slightly apart. Blake recognized the fear immediately, but it took him a minute to see the greed pushing that fear.

"You want this?" Blake asked.

"Yes, I do. I want it badly."

"Why?"

Fletcher took a deep breath. "Are you a religious man?"

"Don't waste my time with bullshit." Blake continued to back up.

"Somebody has to stop Samuel Harrah."

"Guess who that's gonna be."

"Somebody has to hold him up to the light. Can you do that by yourself?"

"You still haven't answered my question."

"All right, Mr. Blake. I want the case for myself, for my career. Is that what you need to hear me say?"

Blake stopped by the door of the car. "Get in," he said. Fletcher, obviously relieved, climbed inside. He accepted the envelope from Blake, waited patiently while Blake started the engine, put the Caprice in gear, and pulled away. Then he opened the envelope, read Blake's cover letter, skimmed the documents.

"There are four voices on the tape," Blake said. "John McGuire's, Ann McGuire's, Bell Kosinski's, and Samuel Harrah's. Your problem is that two of those people are dead and the property transfer, by itself, doesn't prove anything. The good news is that the documents are a matter of public record and the tape was made with the full knowledge of one of the participants."

Fletcher nodded, then returned to the material, reading through it again, this time more carefully. Finished, he slid the documents and the tape back into the envelope.

"The husband, Tillson," he announced, "will turn first. His crimes—obstruction of justice and receiving a bribe—are relatively minor. We'll offer him immunity in return for his testimony, use his statement to reopen the investigation into his wife's murder."

"That takes care of Edward Green. What about Samuel Harrah?"

Fletcher dropped the envelope into his lap, folded his hands. "Harrah will take a little longer. Perhaps Ann McGuire, if she has direct knowledge, or Tillson, if Harrah acted as a go-between."

Blake pulled the Chevy to the curb. "You plan to take this to your boss?"

"I have no authority to launch an investigation on my own. But I assure you. Mr. Blake, the Manhattan District Attorney's office hasn't been subject to political influence for decades. You might . . ."

"I thought I asked you not to waste my time with bullshit." Blake reached across Fletcher's body to open the door. "Do us both a favor, don't take this material to *anybody*. You should have a lot more within a couple of days, enough to make your boss get his ass in gear whether he likes it or not. And by the way, everything you have and everything you will have goes to the press first. That's how much I trust the District Attorney." He smiled. "That's how much I trust *you*."

Everything about Marcus Fletcher (including his ambition) had seemed sincere to Marty Blake. Fletcher's eyes had flashed greed, not calculation; his manner had been direct, respectful, at times almost pleading. Nevertheless, Fletcher had seen the car; he might have memorized the plate number, might be dialing the phone, might already be speaking to Samuel Harrah.

Or so Blake reasoned as he drove out to Kennedy Airport in search of a replacement for the Caprice. He found what he was looking for at a small agency on the periphery of the airport. Set back on a dusty, Sutphin Boulevard lot, BottomLine Rentals' collection of older vehicles was a long way from the shiny sedans offered by the majors. A long way and a lot cheaper. Blake selected a 1991 Ford Aerostar van with a single, convex window on either side and bent louvers over the rear window. Thoroughly scratched and dented, it would be all but invisible on the street.

The radio was on when Blake started the van, tuned to WINS, an all-news station. He let it go as he made his way toward Barnett Avenue in Woodside, expecting a story on Bell Kosinski's death. Instead, a deep, resonant male voice announced the demise, by suspected drug overdose, of Manhattan Borough President Edward Green. Green's body had been discovered on the floor of his Centre Street office several hours after his wife called police to report him missing. According to detectives at the scene, who refused to dismiss the possibility of suicide, the medical examiner would perform an immediate autopsy, the results to be announced in the middle of the week.

So much for Joanna's big client, Blake thought. And so much for Johan Tillson who's gotta be next. If they don't get to me first.

Half an hour later, he was in Vinnie Cappolino's office, examining four sets of individual and two sets of corporate tax returns. Vinnie, resplendent in his newest AC/DC T-shirt and his oldest black leather vest, sat on the other side of the desk, complaining in tones that could only have been taught to him by Linda Francis, his partner's practical wife.

"Ya know them returns cost me a lot more than I expected. Maybe there's a shortage of corrupt tax examiners—I don't know—but I got squeezed so hard I'm gonna be walkin' bowlegged for a week. Tell ya the truth, Marty, I woulda held out for more money, if I thought ya had it."

Blake ignored this and similar conversational gambits, focusing his attention on the paperwork, taking his time about it. The overall scam was obvious at a glance (and as crude as he'd expected), but he continued to work at it until he had the figures clear in his mind. Samuel Harrah and his wife, Margaret, had filed separate returns in each of the four years Blake inspected. As head of household, Samuel Harrah's returns showed only his chief's salary and a bit of interest income from a small saving's account. Margaret Harrah, on the other hand, as sole shareholder of both corporations, South Queens Financial Consultants and Lefferts Office Supply, had paid a whopping tax on profits of more than one hundred and fifty thousand dollars a year, virtually all of which had come from the South Queens corporation. In addition, both Harrah children, George and Owen, as South Queens' sole employees, had drawn salaries of a thousand dollars per week. This was in addition to mid-six-figure incomes derived from senior partnerships at the Wall Street law firm of Wallach and Block.

"You look at this Vinnie?" Blake laid the papers on the desk, sat back in his chair, wondered what he would have done if the Harrahs had come up clean. If he would have gone home and simply waited. Or if he would have gone to Harrah's home and blown the mother-fucker's head off.

"Sure, I checked it out. But I don't know what good it did." He sat forward, laid his elbows on the desk. "Hey, you remember what Joanna said about me and corporate work? She said I didn't have the cachet for it. Ya believe that? The fuckin' cachet."

"C'mon, Vinnie, tell me what you think."

Cappolino shrugged, lit a long, fat cigar, blew a perfect smoke ring at the ceiling. "The financial company's a laundromat. They got nothin'—no accountant, no bookkeeper, not even a goddamned janitor. And what the fuck is it doin' out in the asshole of Queens? I mean you ain't seen fit to tell me where the money's comin' from, but I guarantee they ain't makin' it by handin' out stock tips."

"And Lefferts Office Supply? What's the point of owning a second company that barely breaks even?"

"Ya think I don't know?" He waved the cigar like a sword, flashed a lopsided, triumphant smile. "Look, outside of rent and utilities, there's only one thing an investment company has to buy and that's office supplies. Okay, they could've bought their supplies legit and tossed them in the dumpster, but that's the kinda thing attracts the neighbors' attention. This way, the paperwork is clean; they get invoices to put in the files in case the IRS shows up, but they don't actually take delivery on the material."

"Yeah," Blake admitted, "that's the way I figure it, too. It's pretty crude, really."

"I was surprised they didn't take their business offshore. Then, you woulda been screwed. You woulda had to pay me for nothin'."

Blake shook his head. "Harrah's not the Medellín cartel. And a hundred and fifty thousand dollars a year wouldn't be tip money to a Panamanian banker." He took a deep breath. It was time to put the last card into play. If he could slip it off the bottom of the deck without dropping it. "There's one other thing I need from you, Vinnie. Only . . ."

"Only you ain't got the money."

"Yeah, that's about right." Blake tried for a smile, managed a grimace. "I want you to sit surveillance for a couple of hours in a van I'm gonna set up with video receivers. All you have to do is copy the material and have it delivered to two people. It's a nothing kind of job."

"Unless I get caught." Cappolino waggled a finger in Blake's direction. His head was shaking like a metronome. "Then it's a five-to-ten years kind of job. In Attica. Or, maybe, the cops'll figure they gotta do to me what they already done to you."

"You'll be two blocks away. In a van. Look, Vinnie, there was a time—and it wasn't *that* long ago—when you would've taken the job for the adventure. I'm gonna drop some big players here and I just thought, being as you've always been a macho sort of guy, you'd like to get a piece for yourself. I mean it sounds to me like Linda's a guru instead of an accountant. Like she slaps you around if you get out of line."

"Forget it, Marty. It ain't gonna work. I'm a changed man."

"What you are is a prick, Vinnie."

Cappolino shrugged. "Then I guess I ain't changed as much as I thought."

"What I oughta *change* is your fuckin' face." Blake, though he tried, couldn't put any real conviction into his threat. Cappolino's face already carried enough scars to resemble a road map. "Forget it, Vinnie. Forget what I just said. How much do you want for the job?"

"Two, large."

"Two thousand dollars for a few hours? That's robbery."

"I don't think so. I think what it is is *business*. Face the facts, Marty. It ain't like you're gonna be a repeat customer."

Blake stood up. "I need a private phone. You mind if I use the one in your partner's office?"

"Who ya gonna call?"

"Joanna Bardo."

Cappolino's whooping laugh followed Blake into the next room. He closed the door, reminded himself that it wasn't the first time he'd eaten shit in order to get the job done. Then he dialed Joanna Bardo's home phone number.

"Hello."

"It's Marty Blake."

After a brief silence, Joanna, in her most imperious tones, announced, "You've ruined us."

"Does that mean 'us' heard about Edward Green?"

"Marty, you're digging your own grave."

"Seems to me I've already finished and I'm standing inside. Waiting for the dirt to fall. But, look, I didn't call to chat, Joanna. I need a favor. I need you to promise Vinnie Cappolino you'll pay him two thousand dollars to do a job for me."

"And why would I do that?"

"Because if you don't, I'm gonna tell the people who whacked Edward Green that you've been behind me all the way. I'm gonna tell 'em you set me up with the money, gave me access to the computer, that you've got everything I've got and you're not afraid to use it. I'm gonna tell 'em you're my insurance policy."

Another dead silence. Blake waited patiently, knowing Joanna would do anything to protect herself and her business. It was just a matter of time until she decided that paying off was her only serious option.

"Let me talk to Vinnie."

Blake set the phone down without replying. He opened the door and motioned Cappolino inside. "She wants to speak to you."

Cappolino, a smirk plastered to his face, returned five minutes later. He crossed the room to his desk and sat down. "Man, that bitch was hot. I never heard Joanna so pissed off."

"What did she say?"

"She started with the loyalty bit. Like I'm supposed to *owe* her somethin'. 'Forget the bullshit,' I said, 'an escaped slave don't owe his master.' Then she reminds me that I use her computers every day. That she could cut me off. I told her there's fifty companies offering computer info and whenever I need somethin' that ain't legit, she makes me go out on the street for it. I . . ."

"Do me a favor, Vinnie. Get to the point."

Cappolino opened the bottom drawer of his desk, took out a quart of Wild Turkey bourbon, drank directly from the bottle. "What ya doin' here, Marty, is rushin' a good story. Which is somethin' ya never woulda done a year ago. Looks to me like I ain't the only one that's changed." He capped the bottle and set it on the desk. "After Joanna seen that she couldn't psych me into refusin' the job, she switched to her heavy ammo."

"She offered you money."

"Yeah, four thousand dollars if I put one behind ya left ear and dump the body in the river."

"And what'd you say, Vinnie?"

"I told Joanna I made a deal with you and I got my honor, but if you come out of this in one piece, it wouldn't be real hard to arrange."

TWENTY-FIVE

Blake was in no hurry to reach the offices of South Queens Financial Consultants on Conduit Avenue, the service road for the Belt Parkway near Kennedy Airport. He felt good about his progress (not to mention rearranging Tommy Brannigan's face), good enough to stop in Rego Park for a slice of pizza that quickly became two, then three. Finding someone to retrieve the van and distribute the tapes and paperwork had been his last serious logistical problem. From here on the job became purely mechanical, a series of interlocking pieces to be carefully fitted together in order to . . . There were still too many variables for Blake to know what form the completed puzzle would take, but he was certain that Samuel Harrah and his cohorts would be taken down. Which, as far as he was concerned, was the whole (and, now that Bell Kosinski was dead, *only*) point.

It was nearly eleven o'clock when Blake left the tiny storefront pizza parlor. He stood on the sidewalk, watched the traffic on Woodhaven Boulevard, found himself wishing he'd packed a jacket. A patrol car passed and the two cops inside raked him with a glance as they slid by. Suddenly, the automatic in his belt seemed to weigh twenty pounds. He was sure the cops would see the bulge beneath his shirt, sure they'd come flying out of the patrol car, lean across the trunk and hood, demand that he assume the proverbial position. Instead, they turned left against the light and disappeared down Sixty-third Avenue.

Blake stared after them for a moment, then strode back toward the van. On the way, he passed an outdoor pay phone, hesitated for a moment, then continued on. He was going to have to make a phone call before his first and last meeting with Samuel Harrah; he was going to have to call his mother, and even though what he had in mind wasn't actually suicide, it carried enough risk to guarantee a grim conversation. Of course, he could always lie to her, tell her what she'd want to believe anyway, but then there'd be no point in making the call.

Who else? he thought as he pulled the van away from the curb. Who else do I have to call?

There wasn't anybody else and he knew it even as he asked the question. There weren't any friends in his life. The boys in the gym, his coworkers, even Rebecca Webber—they were acquaintances, one and all, objects to flesh out his existence, like his IBM, or his wardrobe. He couldn't imagine a conversation that wouldn't be embarrassing, a violation of some obscure set of rules that outlawed intimacy between mere acquaintances.

Christ, he thought, what I'm doing here is pure bullshit. It goes around and around in the same stupid circle. Chasing your tail is for puppies and kittens, not for men bent on murder.

Despite the bravado, Blake was seized by an emotion so strong it took him a moment to recognize it as loneliness. His mind drifted to Jeffrey Dahmer, the serial killer who couldn't bear to part with his victims, who kept severed heads in the refrigerator, bones in the night table beside his bed. Maybe Dahmer saw each victim as the cure. Maybe he thought he could fill the empty space where his life should have been, fill it to overflowing with dead memories and the souls of his victims. He'd already eaten their hearts.

Twenty minutes later, Blake drove past the offices of South Queens Financal Consultants. He didn't slow down, barely turned his head, circling the block four times until he was satisfied that Samuel Harrah hadn't anticipated this particular tactic and that there was no back entrance to the consulting firm. Then he pulled to the curb, shut off the lights, and settled down for a closer look.

North and South Conduit avenues, each five lanes wide, sandwiched the Belt Parkway east and west of Kennedy Airport. Their main function, besides acting as *de facto* service roads, was to carry trucks making the run from Kennedy to Long Island or Brooklyn. The Belt Parkway itself was off-limits to commercial traffic. Blake, sitting on the southern margin of the avenue, found himself looking out over sixteen lanes of traffic. Trucks and cars passed him at speeds above fifty miles an hour, which was all to his advantage. Drivers or passengers who saw him fumbling at a locked door would be here and gone before they had a chance to confirm any suspicions.

Pedestrians would be few and far between as well. The eastern half of the block was taken up by a long, two-story commercial building cut into individual stores and businesses. A fenced lot, filled with trucks and vans bearing the inscription Ozone Park Trucking, covered the western half. Samuel Harrah's company, South Queens Financial Consultants, occupied the upper floor at the corner of 128th Street. Below, its doors and windows covered with steel shutters, Airport Auto Supply stretched out to occupy the space beneath South Queens Financial and its second-floor neighbor, Paradise Travel, each of which had its own entrance.

Blake walked up to the metal-covered door leading to South Queens Financial, noted a sticker declaring, "Premises Protected by Allsafe Alarms, Inc." There was no window in the door, no way to reach the system, no way to disarm it except by climbing a utility pole and cutting the electric and phone lines. Even then, the alarms within the office might well have battery-operated backup systems, systems designed to trigger the alarm if the AC current was disrupted.

It was too much protection for a business that had nothing valuable to protect. A computer? A printer? A typewriter? Similar businesses would be satisfied with an insurance policy and a good lock, which, apparently, was how the owners of Paradise Travel had seen it. The only thing between the street and its upstairs offices was a pick-proof Medeco dead bolt. Blake examined the lock closely, then retreated to the van.

Inside, he checked the kit Vinnie Cappolino had put together for him, nodded with satisfaction at a cordless drill and a set of cobalt-tipped bits, slid a quarter-inch bit into the drill and tightened down the chuck. A familiar excitement rose through his body, a sensation he instantly recognized. He'd been at this point any number of times in the past, poised between the idea and the fact, between concept and execution. The way he saw it, he was supposed to be afraid, to remind himself that he was committing a felony, that a police cruiser might come by at any moment, that undercover anticrime units patrolled neighborhoods just like this one. He was supposed to remind himself that he could still back out.

Instead, he allowed himself to be overwhelmed for a moment, to blot out Billy Sowell and Bell Kosinski, Joanna Bardo and Max Steinberg, to enter a space where only he and Samuel Harrah existed. The rest of them, from Vinnie Cappolino and Marcus Fletcher to

Aloysius Grogan and Tommy Brannigan, were no more than weapons to be placed, to be moved, to be pointed. Triggers to be pulled at the appropriate time in the appropriate place.

Suddenly, Blake realized that he'd been waiting all his life for this confrontation. He recalled his father, still in uniform, coming home to drop his blue peaked hat on his son's head, to pin his badge on his son's chest. "We're the good guys," he'd proclaimed and Blake had believed it. He'd believed it and now he was going to act on it.

Blake left the van and walked at a normal pace to the recessed metal door blocking the way into Paradise Travel. Without hesitating, he placed Vinnie's kit on the ground, positioned the drill bit just above the lock retainer in the one-o'clock position and drilled downward at a forty-five-degree angle. The cobalt-tipped drill—sharp enough to pierce the hardened plate of a bank safe—cut through the metal outer surface into the door's hollow core like an ice pick jammed into a tub of butter. Blake kept pushing until he was through the dead-bolt retaining clip, until he contacted the door's inner surface. Then he withdrew the drill, laid it carefully on top of Vinnie's kit, thrust a blunt pick through the hole on top of the lock, and manually retracted the dead bolt.

Inside, with the door closed and locked behind him, Blake granted himself a smile. A minute and fifteen seconds to beat a Medeco without destroying the lock? It might not make the *Guinness Book of Records*, but it was good enough to seal Chief Samuel Harrah's fate. And, of course, his own fate, as well.

The windowless stairway ahead of him was pitch dark and he allowed himself the use of a small, narrow-beamed flashlight as he hustled up to the second-floor landing where he found a second door, this one secured by a push-button cylinder lock, the kind Hollywood detectives crack with an American Express gold card. Unfortunately, this particular door opened into the hallway, which rendered the credit-card ploy useful only if you were inside trying to get out. Blake took a linoleum knife, the tip of its blade angled sharply downward, pushed it between the door and the frame, then forced it down until he was behind the lock. He twisted the knife sharply into the frame, then snapped it back, retracting the bolt and opening the door.

The first thing Blake did, after his eyes adjusted to the streetlight coming through the unshaded windows, was look for a door connecting Paradise Travel to South Queens Financial. He understood it as a hundred-to-one shot and he wasn't disappointed to find himself on the wrong end of the odds. There was another way to get through the wall, a point of vulnerability usually overlooked by landlords and renters alike. But not, of course, by thieves. Or obsessed private investigators.

He packed his equipment over to Paradise Travel's large storage closet, found it unlocked, and stepped inside. He knew that South Queens Financial's closet would be directly alongside, that all he had to do was kick through the layer of Sheetrock between the two closets and he'd be inside Harrah's private kingdom. He braced himself, snapped the heel of his shoe against the partition, felt a shock run up his leg as he contacted something very, very solid.

Blake handled his first reaction—that he was dealing with a safe— by deciding that (given enough time and Vinnie's cobalt-tipped drills) he could get into anything. Then he began to hack out the area above the object with a pry bar, ripping at the paper holding the Sheetrock together, pounding through the plaster core until, his sweat-soaked hair flecked with grains of white plaster, he literally fell into the adjoining closet, landing in a heap on a large carton of Lasergraphic printer paper. He pulled himself to a sitting position, trained his flashlight on the object that had blocked his initial attempt to kick through the wall, breathed a sigh of relief when he found it to be three separate objects placed side by side. Samuel Harrah, when he'd set up his operation, had apparently been as afraid of fire as he was of burglary. A sticker on the middle drawer of each file cabinet guaranteed protection against an external temperature of twenty-five hundred degrees.

Blake jammed the pry bar between the top drawer and the frame of the middle cabinet and snapped off the lock. He chose a file at random, opened it, trained his flashlight on an eight-by-ten glossy. At first, he didn't recognize any of the four people—three men and a woman—in the photograph. Maybe that was because the woman's face was partially blocked by the enormous cock she was sucking. Or maybe it was because the meticulously styled hair that had become her trademark was plastered to the side of her sweaty head. Or maybe it was because Senator Margaret Frances Murray had been thirty years younger when she'd gone before the camera.

There was no real point to it, nothing to be learned from the individual lives contained within those folders, but Marty Blake spent the next half hour playing with the paperwork like a five-year-old with his birthday presents. Curiously, most of what he studied had nothing to do with sexual indiscretion. Kickbacks, outright bribery, embezzlement, arson, Medicaid fraud—New York, the city of scams and schemers, had lived up to its reputation and Samuel Harrah, one more hustler in a city of hustlers, had compiled the proof.

Inside South Queens' one-room office, Blake wanted to turn the computer on, wanted it so bad his fingers ached, but he couldn't risk a light, even with the windows covered. Using a flashlight inside a closed closet or on a windowless stairway might be safe enough, but if a passing cop saw a light behind the shades and decided to investigate, the game would be over. Especially if Blake made him for one of Harrah's minions. It was too much to risk.

Instead, he took an armful of folders from the unlocked file cabinet in the far corner, carried them into the closet and compared them with the blackmail files. He wasn't surprised when they matched up, name for name, file for file. South Queens' customers were, without exception, its victims. Blake felt the last piece of the puzzle click into place with the mechanical finality of slot machine: *chunk, chunk, chunk*—JACKPOT!

He returned to Harrah's office, sat on the edge of the desk, picked up the telephone. There'd be plenty of work to do when the sun came up, when he could see what he was doing, but, for tonight . . . He dialed the phone, took a deep breath, decided that heroes weren't supposed to have mothers.

"Hello?"

"Mom? Were you asleep?"

"No."

Blake ran his fingers through his hair, shook his head. She wasn't going to make it any easier. "I won't be calling back until it's over, so if you want to say anything, you're gonna have to do it now."

"Is that an ultimatum?" She didn't wait for an answer. "I want you to let it go, Marty. I want you to walk away."

"Weren't you the one who ordered me to do my duty?"

"It's a little late for the smart remarks."

Blake realized that she was right. And that they had no other way to communicate. "Basically, I called to say I'm still here and I'm still working." He hesitated for an instant, then rushed on. "Bell Kosinski's dead. I don't know if you heard. When they couldn't kill him on the street, they went after him in a hospital. What makes you think Harrah will let *me* walk away?"

It wasn't what he wanted to say. Not even close. But if there was some magic phrase that would span the chasm, close all the gaps, he didn't know what it was.

"You're digging your own grave."

"Wrong tense, Ma." He instantly regretted the sarcasm. "Look, when this started out, I had no idea where it was going. I was determined to get Billy Sowell off the hook by proving he was innocent. Kosinski tried to warn me, but I wouldn't listen. Just do the job and collect the money was what I told myself. Then, after my client was murdered in prison, I couldn't quit. Just like I can't quit now."

A long silence followed. Blake listened to his mother's breathing, waited patiently for her to get to the point.

"When I married your father, I had to give up my family." Dora Blake's voice was sharp and matter-of-fact, her story a recitation. "My own father actually sat *shiva* when I told him I agreed to raise my children Catholic. I thought I could live with that; I thought love conquered all, that I'd have another family, that my parents would come around. Instead, I've lost everything."

"For Christ's sake, I'm not dead." He could almost hear his mother shrug.

"An inspector named Grogan rang my bell a couple of hours ago," she continued. "He wanted to arrest you for assaulting a cop named Brannigan with a deadly weapon. I know what that means, what happens when they find you. What happens if you keep pushing."

"It's gonna happen whether I push or not. This way, I get to choose the field of battle." Blake added burglary to the assault charge, tried to imagine spending the next five years in a New York State prison. When he realized that five years was the best he could hope for, he shuddered. "Look, Mom, I've gotta go." It was time to bite the bullet, never mind the bitter taste. "It'll be over in twenty-four hours. You can figure I'll need a lawyer by then. Maybe you wanna work on that with Uncle Patrick." He hesitated again, hoping she'd respond, give him an out. No such luck. Finally, after waiting long enough to justify a bad attitude, he muttered, "I love you, Mom," and hung up.

Blake was tempted to unload the van immediately, but he knew it would take several trips and there was no good reason for a man in a Hawaiian shirt to be carrying boxes into a travel agency at two o'clock on a Sunday morning. The risk was not only unacceptable, it was easily avoided. On the other hand, the risk of someone stealing the van while he slept in Samuel Harrah's office was equally unacceptable and the only sure way to avoid it was to sleep on the Aerostar's backseat with his automatic for a pillow. From where Blake sat (Queens, New York, being the car theft capital of the United States), he didn't have any choice.

As it turned out, he fell asleep within minutes, waking several hours later to the glare of the sun. For the first few seconds he was disoriented. The rush of the occasional car reminded him of ocean surf, the sunlight streaming through the windshield of waking after a nap on the beach. Then he noticed the shotgun lying on the floor.

He sat up in the van, rubbed his eyes, tried to remember his dreams. They'd all been there—the good guys, the victims, the bad guys, the cowards—but he couldn't put them into context. He glanced into the rearview mirror and shuddered. His hair stood out at odd angles; his blue eyes were lost in dark circles, the stubble on his cheeks and jowls seemed to age him twenty years.

I'm not the same person, he decided as he climbed into the front seat and started the van. Not the jerk with eight suits in his closet and a low-end Rolex strapped to his wrist. And no matter what happens today, I can't go back to it. I've got to go forward. Of course, forward doesn't have a lot of meaning right now. A toilet has meaning. Coffee has meaning. But for right now, forward is a position on a hockey team.

He found a diner several blocks away, ignored the cashier's disgusted look, a look echoed in the faces of several waitresses, and made his way to the men's room. Ten minutes later, as groomed as he was going to get without benefit of shower and razor, he took a seat at the counter and ordered breakfast. The waitress, reassured, perhaps, by his thoroughly soaked, thoroughly flattened hair, clucked sympathetically as she filled his coffee cup.

"Been traveling all night, honey?" she asked.

Blake looked at her for the first time. Middle-aged and bony, her narrow mouth fattened with a layer of pink lipstick, she seemed perfectly at home, like the polished coffee urns or the sizzling grill.

"Working," he answered. "You got a newspaper back there?"

"*Daily News*. What section you want?"

"Section?"

"It's Sunday, remember? Newspapers come in sections on Sunday."

"Right. Let me have the main section. It's too early for the comics."

He found the story on page twenty-eight, took its position in the scheme of things to mean that "Whacked in Whitestone" was fast becoming yesterday's news. Still, Harrah hadn't placed any bets on a fickle public. According to the *Daily News*, Internal Affairs was reviewing Bell Kosinski's caseload for the three-year period prior to his retirement, looking for a "pattern of corruption." This after a "substantial quantity of cocaine" had been found in his apartment. There was no mention of Kosinski's death, but that, in itself, wasn't surprising. The first edition of the *News* went to print in the early evening, especially the Sunday edition.

Blake closed his eyes, tried to picture Bell Kosinski sucking on the business end of a crack pipe. The effort was wasted, but, then, Kosinski wasn't really the point. Unless Samuel Harrah was afraid of ghosts, the real target was Marty Blake. By discrediting Kosinski, Harrah also tarred Kosinski's still-living, still-dangerous partner. As a coke dealer's confederate, Blake would have less credibility than a New York politician. Which was less than none.

Though he hadn't bothered to check, Blake would have bet his computer that Harrah numbered journalists and cops among his victims, that he could plant either dope or propaganda whenever and wherever he wished. Information was his strength; it was also his weakness. Blake had no intention of copying Harrah's client files. He didn't have to because they were already in the computer's hard drive. All Blake had to do was remove the hard drive and have it delivered to Marcus Fletcher along with the blackmail files and a videotape of the games to come.

"Rise 'n shine, honey. Breakfast's ready."

Blake sat up, made room for a platter of bacon, eggs, home fries, and toast. He muttered a thank you, then picked up his fork and began to eat. After a few bites, he decided that all his food tasted the same. Or that it had no taste, just consistency. The bacon was chewy, the eggs soft, the home fries crunchy.

Nevertheless, Blake continued to eat—shoveling food into his mouth, chewing thoroughly, washing the mouthfuls down with coffee as he ran through his agenda, step by step. There were two basic elements to Blake's strategy: three pinhole video cameras, connected to transmitters by cable, broadcasting to receivers and recorders (and Vinnie Cappolino) in the van; two cartons of the blackmail files, the originals and a copy run on Harrah's Xerox, along with the computer's hard drive, also in the van. He'd set up the cameras first, one in a window overlooking the sidewalk, another at the top of the stairs, the third behind him in the office. Harrah would expect some kind of surveillance, but the cameras were no bigger than a pack of cigarettes and even if they were noticed, there wasn't very much Harrah could do about it. Not until after he dealt with Blake.

Once the cameras were positioned, the receivers and transmitters tested, the files copied, and the van moved to the other side of the highway, he'd have time to worry about himself. Because he was going to have to concede the first move to Samuel Harrah and he knew it. If he'd wanted to slaughter the man, he could have gone to his home and done it without spending fifteen big ones on electronics.

Of course, there was always a chance that Harrah would try to negotiate a deal, but it wasn't the kind of chance Blake intended to take. The far more likely possibility was that Samuel Harrah (or whoever he sent in his place) would simply gun Marty Blake down, then claim self-defense in the course of an arrest. Or dump what was left of him in the conveniently close Atlantic Ocean and pretend he never existed.

Blake had no desire to go for that final swim, but he understood that reducing his execution from a probability to a possibility was the best he could hope for. A kevlar vest would help, as would placing the desk against the far wall and using it as a shield. But the centerpiece of his survival strategy was a trio of strobe lights set between the desk and the door, then wired to a toggle switch. Harrah would get the first move; Marty Blake would get the second; Vinnie Cappolino would record the sequence. That was all there was to it.

"Anything else I can get you, honey?"

Blake shook his head, wondered if the woman ever completed a sentence without adding the word "honey." Maybe she used it to punctuate every thought, the way a heavy-footed rock drummer used a bass drum.

He paid the check, made his way to the van, glanced at his watch.

It was eight o'clock, time to go to work. He drove back to Paradise Travel, dragged the equipment upstairs, through the closet, into South Queens Financial. The labor soothed him, as it always had in the past; the tools, the equipment, the lights, and the cable grounded him in the solid world of cause and effect. Every action yielded measurable results: a hole was actually drilled, a screw actually set, a monitor revealed the actual street below.

Four hours later, he was in the back of the van wiring up the receivers, monitors, and VCRs. The van itself was parked between two cars on the other side of Conduit Avenue, approximately three hundred feet from South Queens Financial. If Harrah anticipated some kind of surveillance (as he was almost certain to do), he might choose to inspect any closed vehicle near the office. But he couldn't very well search every van or truck within a hundred yard radius of the building. Not if he wanted to stay within the time frame Blake intended to establish.

Blake flipped on the three receivers, watched the monitors light up, saw an empty stairwell, an empty office, a deserted sidewalk. He tested the VCRs, listened to the tape spin for a minute. The cadmium-nickel batteries would operate the system for six hours, more than enough time. After all, Harrah would be waiting (or, at least, *hoping*) for Blake to call, to re-establish contact. Even with Kosinski dead, it was a possibility that couldn't be ignored.

It was just after one o'clock when Blake left the van. He walked back to 150th Street, then across the parkway to a pay phone and dialed Vinnie Cappolino's home phone number.

"Yeah?"

"It's me, Vinnie. Blake."

"You ready for me?"

"Yeah."

"Where ya callin' from?"

"I'm not callin' from Harrah's office, if that what you're thinking."

"*Mrs.* Harrah's office. Don't be a sexist, Marty."

"Vinnie, when you're right, you're right. Tell me, do you think Harrah might have his wife hit? Eliminate the essential link?"

"For you, that ain't a problem. Bein' as Uncle Sam's gonna definitely eliminate *you* first."

"True enough. Look, the van's parked on North Conduit Avenue, directly across from South Queens Financial, and the key's behind the outside rear tire. I want you to stay sharp, Vinnie. You've gotta start recording as they're walking up to the building."

"Hey, Marty, I've done this before, remember? How long you figure it's gonna take?"

"A couple of hours, tops. You'll know when to leave."

"You want me to call an ambulance before I go, get somebody over there? Linda made Walter and me buy cellular phones, so it wouldn't be any trouble."

Blake smiled. "That might be nice. Look, you'll find two cartons in the back of the van when you get there. The one with the hard drive goes to Fletcher. The other package goes to the reporter, Coen. You wanna give me the number of that cellular phone?"

"No. You wanna give me Harrah's?"

"555-9844."

"Anything else?"

"Just stay alert. If you don't start those VCRs, I've got exactly nothing."

"Don't worry about my end, Marty. I wouldn't miss this for next week's lottery number. You have a good day."

Back in Harrah's office, Blake picked up the phone, dialed the chief's home number, listened to the phone ring several times before a woman answered.

"Hello?"

"Samuel Harrah, please. Tell him it's Marty Blake."

"Oh, Mr. Blake. Sam's been expecting you to call. He's at the office. Do you have the number?"

"Yeah." Blake started to hang up, felt his anger rise to the surface, his fingers tighten down on the receiver. "By the way, am I speaking to Margaret Harrah?"

"Yes, you are." Her voice was bright, cheery, every bit the helpful housewife.

"Do you know why I'm calling your husband?"

"I'm sorry, I don't."

Blake hesitated, told himself to let the suspense build, that timing is the key to good comedy. "You've been a bad girl, Maggie. A bad, *bad* girl."

"I don't know . . ."

"Yes, you do. Never kid a kidder, Maggie. By the way, do you have any idea what happens to an elderly white woman in a New York State prison? Well, your name wouldn't be Margaret any more. At Bedford Hills, your first, last, and only name would be Bitch. As in, 'Get over here, *Bitch*. Make my bunk, Bitch; wash my socks, Bitch; eat my pussy, Bitch.' Unless, of course, you've got somebody on the outside to send you money so you can pay off the baddest dyke in your cell block. But that's gonna be a problem, too, Maggie, cause the only way you're gonna be able to reach those two investment counselor kids of yours is to write 'em care of Sing-Sing."

"This is atrocious."

"So is blackmail. Not to mention premeditated murder. Look, get your husband on the phone, Maggie. Tell him I'll be calling in a few minutes and I don't wanna speak to his flunky. If he doesn't talk to me personally, we don't communicate at all."

Blake spun away from the desk. He walked over to the closest window, peeked around the shade at the street below. The Belt Parkway was jammed with New Yorkers making their way out to the beaches of Rockaway and Long Island. The cars gleamed in the afternoon sun, but the folks inside looked, to Blake, like they'd rather be somewhere else, anywhere else. They'd gotten up late, waited too long to get started. Now the day was ruined.

Five minutes later, he was on the phone with Sergeant Bennetti of NYPD Intelligence, asking to speak with Chief Samuel Harrah.

"Who wants him?"

"Marty Blake." Might as well get it on the record.

"You wanna tell me what it's about? The Chief's in the toilet."

As Blake searched for the perfect rejoinder, he suddenly realized that Bennetti was delaying for a reason. Naturally, Harrah would want the call traced. By this time, they'd have to know he wasn't coming back to his apartment.

"You don't wanna know what I want, Bennetti. Not unless you're Harrah's priest."

"Is that supposed to mean something?"

"It means your boss is an extortionist."

"That bad, eh? Let me be the first to admit that you floored me with the information. I'm lucky I didn't break my neck when I fell off the chair."

Blake looked down at his watch. A full minute, plenty of time for a trace. "Fifteen seconds, Sergeant" he said. "If I'm not speaking to your boss in fifteen seconds, I hang up."

"Oh, look, I see the Chief goin' into his office. Lucky for me, huh?"

Harrah's voice, when he came on a few seconds later, was oily smooth, as if he was trying to contain his heartiest chuckle. "You've got a devil of a nerve, Marty. Saying what you did to poor Margaret."

"In that case, we're even up, Sammy. If you remember, I told Grogan that I wanted my partner left alone, but you had him killed anyway. That was fairly cheeky."

Harrah cleared his throat. "Bela Kosinski is not dead. He's alive and well in Bellevue Hospital. I swear it."

"Really? Did Brannigan tell you to say that?"

"Look, Marty, I know about your confrontation with . . ."

"Forget the bullshit, Sammy."

"Brannigan was wrong. It's that simple. If your actions are in any way predicated . . ."

"*Predicated?*" Blake picked up the shotgun, tucked the stock under his arm, reminded himself to hold tight, to bring the barrel down to level after each shot. Then he flipped the toggle switch anchored to the top of the desk, watched the shadows at the far end of the room leap into focus under the glare of the strobes. "Predicated," he repeated. "I like the sound of that. I think it means you believe I'm squeezing your nuts because of something *you* did. Better reconsider the old game plan, Sammy. I'm squeezing your nuts because of something *I* did. And, by the way, if you want to prove Kosinski's still alive, you could always have him call me. You know where I am, right?"

"I do, but there's a problem. Your partner was severely wounded. He's on a respirator and he can't speak."

"I guess that's what comes of being a drug dealer." Blake glanced at his watch. "Listen up, Sammy. I want you out here in forty-five minutes. No excuses."

"Marty, please, I'm on the west side of Manhattan. I'll be lucky to get across the *river* in forty-five minutes."

"Drive fast. And don't forget to use the sirens. If you're not here in three-quarters of an hour, me and those files you had stashed in the closet are gonna be long gone."

Blake hung up, leaned back in the chair, allowed his thoughts to drift to Bell Kosinski. For the past twenty-four hours, he'd been deliberately keeping his partner at a psychological distance, fearing that grief (or rage) would make him careless. He'd come to love Bell Kosinski; the simple fact was undeniable, as solid as the floor under his feet. But that didn't mean Kosinski's voice would make him pack up and leave.

Kosinski had asked the essential question—*What's in it for you, Marty Blake?*—on more than one occasion. And, of course, he had failed to provide an accurate response, even to himself. Initially, he'd declared himself a professional; he'd pretended to be in it for the money. After Billy Sowell's death (after he'd done his job), he'd pretended to be outraged at Harrah's arrogance. Now he'd put himself in a no-win situation and the only explanation that made any sense was that he was just as crazy, just as suicidal, just as committed to a childish sense of right and wrong as his alcoholic partner.

The good professors at City College had trained Marty Blake to write computer programs, the ultimate exercise in logical thought. *This*, then *this*, then *this*, equals *that*. If it didn't, you'd know it the first time you tried to run the program. Blake had used that logic to force this particular resolution on Samuel Harrah; he'd given the man absolutely no choice in the matter, and he'd begun the process right after Billy Sowell's death, before any threat to Bell Kosinski existed.

This is what I wanted right from jump street, he finally decided. To be sitting in this room, looking at a shotgun loaded with Vinnie's bullshit ammo, waiting for the bad guys to show up for the showdown. I never left the bars, even though I stopped drinking; I never stopped crossing the line just to see what would happen. It didn't matter how many stitches I took. Or that the State of New York almost sent me to jail. And I don't have Kosinski's excuse, either. I'm not a drunk, or a psychotic. I'm not *legally* insane.

He picked up the shotgun again, ran his index finger along the barrel, over the grip, to the end of the metal stock, then suddenly realized that Vinnie Cappolino might be already in the van, that he might be watching and laughing. A glance at the office monitor revealed a broad-backed man with a mop of curly hair cradling a shotgun against his chest like he was about to nurse it.

Blake got up and went to the window. He could see the Aerostar, but there was no way to know if it was occupied or not. Vinnie Cappolino, street-smart enough to fully understand the consequences of being caught in the act, would be huddled down out of sight. When the time came, he'd do his job and get in the wind. No muss, no fuss.

On impulse, Blake went back to the files in the closet. He'd emptied and copied the first of the three cabinets, more than one hundred individual files. That had been enough to fill two large cartons, as much as he could reasonably expect Vinnie to handle. Now, he searched under S in the third file cabinet until he found the name he was looking for: Steinberg, Maxwell.

The folder contained a single sheet of paper, an affidavit from a man named Robert Merkurian, a juror in a robbery trial. Merkurian claimed that he'd been paid five thousand dollars by defense lawyer Max Steinberg to hang the jury. The affidavit had been given with full immunity from prosecution.

Blake went into the bathroom, tore the affidavit into small strips, dropped the pieces into the toilet. He saw his actions as another nail in Harrah's coffin. Steinberg had been humiliated, forced to eat Samuel Harrah's shit, to admit the act to Marty Blake. Unleashed, he'd sink his fangs into Harrah's throat and chew his way to the bone. If Harrah didn't survive, Steinberg would eat his reputation. Either way, it qualified as insurance.

He flushed the toilet, watched the bits of paper spin, the water swirl, Steinberg's criminal past disappear into a New York sewer. By the time the tank began to fill, he realized that his anger had followed the affidavit, as if he'd vomited it into the bowl. Steinberg, Joanna Bardo, his Uncle Patrick—they weren't to blame. They'd lived in New York long enough to regard justice as just another childhood fantasy. A fantasy to be surrendered upon maturity, like Santa Claus and the monster in the closet.

"Naive" was the word for it, he decided as he walked back into the office, the word Steinberg and the others would use to describe my condition. Naive and a shade pitiful, like a handsome priest locked into celibacy. Or a teenage girl with a birthmark on her forehead.

He sat behind the desk, checked the monitors, glanced at his watch. Thirty minutes gone. It was time to set himself, to drop anchor. He began to run through the expected scenario, got as far as Samuel Harrah's appearance in the hall monitor when the phone rang.

Blake stared at the plain, black instrument, listened to its insistent clamor echo in the closed room. He was certain Harrah would be on the other end, that he'd ask for more time.

"Yeah?"

"It's Vinnie. They're on their way up."

"Where? The monitor's empty."

"That's because they're huggin' the wall. Four of 'em. And their hot little hands are filled with .38-caliber revolvers. If I was you, Marty, I'd shoot first. Take 'em while they're comin' up the stairs."

"Or maybe you could do them from behind, Vinnie. That'd most likely surprise the crap out of them."

"Good luck, Marty. I'll see you in hell."

Blake looked down at the shotgun leaning against the desk drawers, then back at the monitors. He folded his hands and laid them across the switch on top of the desk. The tapes would prove that he'd faced Harrah with both hands in plain sight. That was the final nail.

He watched the door to the street open, saw Chief Samuel Harrah walk inside and shut off the alarm. Aloysius Grogan entered the hallway next, followed by two cops Blake didn't recognize. All four men were in uniform and all carried their weapons in their hands.

They came up the stairs very slowly, four silhouettes against the open doorway below. Clearly unaware of the camera less than a foot away, they huddled for a moment on the landing, then pushed the door open and stepped inside.

Grogan came through the door first, holding his Police Special against his right thigh. Blake checked a powerful urge to dive for the floor, watched Harrah follow, then a blond, baby-faced cop who looked to be two weeks out of the Academy, and a tall, fat, grizzled veteran.

"Congratulations, Chief," Blake said. "I was sure you'd forget the alarm."

"Marty Blake." Harrah drew himself up to his full height. "I'm placing you under arrest for the crime of assault on a police officer."

"You got a warrant?" Blake paused for a response, gave himself time to realize he'd never been happier than he was at that moment. "No? Well, I can see why you wouldn't want to put anything on paper. But, hey, despite what you may think about me, I'm a get-along kind of guy. If you want me to submit to an arrest, I'll be happy to oblige. As long as the arresting officer is my uncle, Captain Patrick Blake. He's at home if you wanna give him a call."

"This is not a fucking joke." Grogan was so enraged he could barely speak.

"Shut up, you moron." Harrah took a step forward. "Poor Aloysius," he said to Blake, "he should have retired years ago. As it is, he lacks resiliency. Every frustration goes right to his gut. By the way, you wouldn't be interested in speaking with your partner's physician?"

"You mean the one who works in the prison ward at Bellevue?"

Harrah smiled, nodded thoughtfully. "Point taken. But it does seem a shame." His eyes swept the room. "You know, all this could be yours."

"All?"

"Well, not *all*. Forgive the hyperbole. Are you interested?"

"Afraid not."

"Why doesn't that surprise me? Marty, may I assume you're recording this conversation?"

"No audio, Sammy. Cheap video was all I could afford."

"Curse of the amateur." Harrah chuckled sympathetically; his eyes were actually twinkling. He started to move forward again, stopped abruptly when Blake shook his head. "You're a hard-headed man, Marty. Like your father before you. It must run in the family."

"Does that mean your *father* was a blackmailing killer?"

"No more than it means that Matthew Blake was a rapist." Harrah paused, clearly expecting a response. When he got none, he turned to Grogan and smiled. "Hard-headed. There's no other way to describe him."

Blake looked down at his hands, reminded himself that he had to keep them in view, that he couldn't move first, couldn't appear to move first.

"Why don't we get to the point," he said. "If there *is* a point."

"The point is that we've compiled a good deal of information on Chantel McKendrick. The file runs to thirty pages. We interviewed her relatives, her friends, her criminal associates. Chantel, herself, is dead—of AIDS, naturally—but I believe we have enough to make a reasoned judgment as to your father's guilt or innocence. Would you like to see the file?"

"Maybe you could just tell me about it. I forgot my reading glasses."

"Nothing for nothing, Marty. You should know that." Harrah shifted his weight; his smile faded. "Make me an offer."

"How about twenty-five years in a state prison? Say, Attica."

"You're not giving me any options here."

"That's the whole point, Sammy. No options; no escape. We're all in this together."

Blake watched the four revolvers come up fast, much faster than he'd expected. He heard the first angry *crack* before he managed to jam his eyes shut. Then he flipped the switch between his fingers, grabbed the shotgun, and rolled off to the right.

He came up into a crouch a few feet away from the desk, jerked the shotgun into position, searched for Samuel Harrah's face. The four cops seemed to be firing at random, but they were still firing as fast as they could, the shots coming almost on top of each other. Then the shotgun began to roar, as if demanding the stage for itself, repeating its message at half-second intervals until it was empty, until the room gradually filled with the complementary odors of cordite and human blood.

Dropping the shotgun, Blake took a step forward, felt his left foot slide away from him. He looked down at his leg, noted the soaked trousers, the blood streaming over his shoe and onto the floor. Momentarily disappointed, he glanced at Samuel Harrah, saw an elderly man with his hands clutched to his belly writhing on the floor.

"It's not enough," Blake said to himself. "It's never enough."

He leaned against the wall, slowly dropped to a sitting position, found himself wishing for a single moment of life. Wishing for another sixty seconds to enjoy the cries of his fallen enemies.

TWENTY-SIX

As Bell Kosinski drove his '88 Toyota Corolla down 154th Street, he rehearsed the story again. He'd been doing it several times a day since leaving the hospital just before Thanksgiving. Rehearsing exactly how he'd tell the story to Father Tim. They'd be sitting in Cryders, of course, on bar stools, maybe in the early afternoon before the regulars showed their faces. Caught up in that first glow (when you could still taste it going down, when the vodka was sharp and clear, the relief immediate), he'd raise his glass, toast the good doctors at Bellevue Hospital, begin his tale.

"Never try to poison a guy tied to a heart monitor," he'd declare. "Not if there's an Alka-Seltzer in the house."

Father Tim would smile his tight, priest's smile. "Proceed, my son," he'd say. "And don't leave anything out. A full confession is, so I hear, good for the soul."

Ed, down at the end of the bar, would amble over, fill Kosinski's glass. "For me," he'd say, "Alka-Seltzer is life support. Between my head and my gut, I gotta buy it by the pound."

"In that case," Bell Kosinski would respond, taking a long pull at his drink, "you're in good shape. As long as you're tied to a heart monitor. See, Tommy Brannigan knew two things: first, that injected potassium will stop a human heart and, second, that potassium is metabolized very quickly, so it's hard to find at an autopsy. But here's what he didn't know. When the alarm on a heart monitor kicks off and they call a code, the first thing they do—doctors or nurses, I never could get it straight—is pump your heart to circulate blood. The next thing they do is put a needle in your arm, draw a little blood, then inject you with sodium bicarbonate, which is what they have in Alka-Seltzer. I'm not gonna try to tell you how, because I don't know, but sodium bicarbonate makes your cells take potassium out of the blood. When that happens, your heart, if it's not diseased, kicks off again, like starting up a motorcycle. Altogether, I was only out for three-and-a-half minutes."

"You're sayin' you were dead, right?" Ed, of course, would ask the practical question. Try to pin it down. "You're heart was stopped and you weren't breathing, right?"

"Dead? I don't know about dead. I mean I was unconscious, but it wasn't like I didn't know what was going on." There, let Ed take *that* and put it in his cash register. Let him enter it in his ledger. "Besides, I was on a respirator, so I was definitely breathing."

"Ah, wonderful." Father Tim, eyes glowing, jaw slightly agape, would ignore the last part. "Did you see Jesus? Did you see the light?"

"No, Father, nothing like that. It was like watching a TV set, like the camera was up above. Somebody was beating on my chest, somebody else was shuffling bags on the IV pole, somebody was working me over with a pair of shock paddles. The impression I got— and like it's only an impression because I didn't really care about the outcome, whether or not they'd make that limp thing on the bed come alive—was that they'd done it all before, lots of times. They worked really fast—their hands were flying—but they didn't get in each other's way. It was beautiful. That's what I thought at the time. I thought, 'This is really beautiful.'"

Father Tim and Ed would get into it, then. Father Tim insisting the story had spiritual significance; Ed denying it with a snarl: "It don't prove nothin'. So his heart stopped for three-and-a-half minutes? So what? He was breathin' all the time, right? And somebody was pumpin' his heart, right? Naw, I'm not buyin' dead here."

"Ed, please, Bell watched himself. From *above*. How could he do that if he wasn't dead?"

"How could he do that if he *was* dead?"

Eventually, Ed would prevail by sheer force of will, then turn back to Kosinski. "Brannigan's comin' up for trial soon. Next couple of weeks I heard."

"Yeah, ten days actually."

"He was your partner."

"That was a long time ago."

"And you're gonna testify against him."

"C'mon, Ed. He tried to kill me. Hell, his buddies killed my *real* partner. Whatta ya want me to do, let him walk?"

The problem was that he'd always imagined it as personal. He'd imagined it the way Blake had *done* it. Not sitting in a goddamned courtroom with twelve monkeys leaning out over the jury box. But maybe it wouldn't come to that. There was talk of a plea bargain going around, a rumor the cops could put Tommy Brannigan in that prison the day Billy Sowell was murdered, another rumor about DNA testing, that Brannigan was being offered a single count of second-degree murder and fifteen-to-life. That would keep Bell Kosinski out of a courtroom, but it wouldn't get him back into Cryders.

He lit a cigarette, sucked down the smoke, thought, No, no, no. Not Cryders. Not for a reformed drunk. For a reformed drunk, it's cigarettes and coffee and every night listening to other drunks recite their sad stories. For Bell Kosinski it's reciting his own sad story to a roomful of strangers.

In some ways, it was worse than being an alcoholic, worse than stumbling home after a night at Cryders. But it was the price—no question about that—and he couldn't forget Brannigan's face leaning over the bed, what he'd finally realized as Brannigan fed potassium into the IV tube. Bell Kosinski wanted to live. Alcoholics Anonymous was the price, the fat lady had sung her song.

That didn't mean he didn't want to tell the story. And it didn't change the fact that, aside from his Cryders' buddies, the only person he could tell it to was Marty Blake and Marty Blake was *really* dead. Not dead and brought back to life, but finished, gone, down-in-the-grave dead.

Which was exactly where Bell Kosinski was headed. Out to Marty Blake's grave at the request of Marty Blake's mother.

He took a left on Northern Boulevard, came to a stop at the traffic light on the next corner. He was driving very slowly, planting that appraising cop look on every civilian he saw. Not a glare, really, but offensive enough in a city where eye contact between strangers is grounds for an assault. It was how the veterans taught the rookies to drive a patrol car and it somehow kept the jitters at bay.

The pain had that effect, too. He'd been shot early in September and it was now the middle of January, but the pain never really went away. Usually, it hung in the background, like a toothache waiting for an ice cube, but now and again it screamed as if the metal plates holding his jaw together had been wired for electricity.

They'd given him pills, once he was able to swallow, and a prescription for Demerol when he left the hospital. He'd tossed the prescription away as soon as got home, reasoning that he liked the Demerol enough to want it even when he didn't hurt and if he had to be addicted to something, alcohol was a lot cheaper than dope. Now, he was used to the pain the way he was used to the slight tilt of his head caused by the pull of the scar tissue in his neck. He saw them, the pain and the tilt, as battle ribbons freeing him from the necessity for continued combat.

Kosinski took a right on 162nd Street and made his way south to Flushing Cemetery. He'd passed this particular cemetery any number of times in the course of his NYPD career, noted its carefully manicured grounds, actually stopped once or twice to have the obligatory coffee and donuts within sight of its blossoming cherry and apple trees. Even now, under the flat glare of a January sun, with its skeletal trees and barren flower beds seeming almost brazen, the grounds appeared to be torn from a Norman Rockwell painting of the perfect American graveyard.

A few minutes later, he found Dora Blake standing next to a polished black headstone. Marty Blake's name had already been carved into its surface, right next to the name of his father, Matthew.

"So what do you think, Bell? You think they're fighting it out down there? Marty and his father?" She went on without waiting for a reply, her breath misting the cold January air. "It was supposed to be my spot. Next to my husband, but I've decided to be buried in a Jewish cemetery." She paused again, let her eyes wander over the scars on Kosinski's neck and jaw. "I haven't heard from anyone on Matthew's side of the family in months. They've cut me off completely."

"They're blaming the victim, Dora. No surprise."

Dora Blake shook her head. "What they're doing is protecting their cop careers. Or trying to. You wanna hear something funny? Patrick, Matt's brother, once told me that his son was *meant* to become commissioner. Born to it, the way Joe Kennedy's sons—one and all—were meant to be presidents."

Kosinski shrugged his shoulders, blew onto his cold hands. He was here because . . . because she'd asked him and he figured he owed it to Marty, though he couldn't imagine why.

"Have you seen the videotape?" Dora Blake asked after a moment. "The Ozone Park Massacre tape?"

That drew a smile from Kosinski, a grudging smile. Vinnie Cappolino had sold the tape and files to "Hard Copy" a day after the shoot-out, had sold the originals for a rumored five hundred large. The cops had gotten copies.

"Yeah," he said, "I've seen the tape. Like everybody else in the country."

"Then tell me why."

"Why what?"

"Why Marty did it like *that*. He had the files. He could have put Samuel Harrah and rest of them behind bars without . . . without killing himself."

"Dora, look . . ." It was a good beginning, but that was as far as he got. There'd been no audio to go with the videotape; no one had survived to fill in the blanks. Had he, Kosinski, had something to do with it? Yeah, probably. But if Blake had wanted to protect his partner, why hadn't he used the incriminating material as a guarantee? Or did Blake think he was dead?

"Marty thought you were dead."

"Jesus." It was like she'd been reading his mind. "How do you know?"

"He called me from Harrah's office just before it happened. He told me you'd been killed."

Kosinski fished a pack of Kent Lights out of his coat pocket, lit one up, flipped the match into the wind. "I hadn't smoked one of these in fifteen years," he said, "before I got hit. What it is, Dora, is now that I'm off the booze, smokes and coffee are all I've got."

Dora Blake shrugged her shoulders, muttered, "It could be worse."

"Yeah, that's what I figure. The doc said my liver's not too bad, either. He said if I take care of myself, I should live to a ripe, old age." Kosinski stopped suddenly, realized he was rambling, that he wanted to say something to comfort her. Instead, he blurted, "I don't think Marty was out to avenge my death."

"Then tell me what he was out to do." She turned away from him, back to the headstone.

"It's not that easy." His mind wandered to his own story, the one he wanted to tell Father Tim. There was one part he never got to in his daydreams, the part where he tried to explain wanting to live when he thought he was going to die, but not giving a damn after he was dead. "See, when Marty heard that I'd been whacked, it freed him up. Just like Billy Sowell's murder freed him up. Do you understand?"

She turned toward him, mouth pursed. One gloved hand reached up to smooth the collar of her coat. "Maybe. Finish what you have to say."

"Marty had obligations. To me, to Billy Sowell, and to Max Steinberg. Sowell, the victim, went first; then Steinberg, the client; then his actual partner. After that, he was free to do what he wanted."

"And what about me?" Her voice was short and bitter. "Marty had no obligation to me?"

"Marty wasn't obliged to *protect* you." He took her arm, began to lead her away from the grave. "Look, you've seen that video as often as I have. Do you think Marty was out to commit suicide?"

"No," she admitted, "but the risk was unnecessary. He could have done it another way."

"Not when you consider what he wanted to accomplish." Kosinski opened the door of his Toyota and Dora Blake got inside without protesting. "I mean, face it, Dora, the only thing Marty Blake ever wanted to be was a hero."